# TENDER ASSAULT

Victorine was aghast at her rescuer's possessive attitude. "We live in the nineteenth century, not the Middle Ages. Has it escaped your attention that I am a citizen of the United States of America and protected by laws?"

"Some laws are more ancient than those of the United States of America," Cougar shot back.

"You know it's wrong, though." The blond beauty was starting to feel trapped instead of saved.

"Do I? Last night I bought you; I made a mountain marriage, recognized here by white men and red men alike. You're mine now, by the law of this land. And I'm looking forward to taking my refreshment of you—and giving you refreshment in return. That's as it should be . . . and how it shall be."

Refreshment? A faint pink blush appeared on her face.

Then as she opened her mouth in protest, Cougar pulled her into his embrace, covering her lips with his own.

First shock, then outrage consumed her. "Please don't," she managed to whisper as he moved his lips down to her neck.

But it was too late for Victorine. Cougar was in complete control; she had no choice but complete surrender . . .

# Mountain Mistress

## Nadine Crenshaw

**ZEBRA BOOKS**

**KENSINGTON PUBLISHING CORP.**

ZEBRA BOOKS

are published by

Kensington Publishing Corp.
475 Park Avenue South
New York, NY 10016

First printing: November 1987

Printed in the United States of America

*This book is dedicated with love to my husband, Robert Crenshaw*

# Chapter One

The pinto horses cantered in a rough side-by-side line, slack-reined to let them pick their own way. Victorine Wellesley's mouth was desert dry, and the ropes around her wrists hurt sorely. She was no longer certain how long she'd been on the back of this red-spotted horse, her arms tied around the waist of this sweaty Indian. As far as she could tell the sun was about two hours above the horizon — but was it rising or was it near to sunset of the same day . . . the same bloody day that . . .

She broke off that thread of recollection and turned her mind back to the fact that she had not remained completely conscious. After the attack, all her faculties had seemed to depart, one after the other, leaving only the dumb brute power to set her teeth and to persevere, and a blind belief that soon there would be rest and water. She scolded herself now for her lack of discipline, she really should have stayed alert.

The side of her face was pressed between her Indian captor's shoulder blades. She'd been forced to ride in such intimacy with this ruddy-skinned man that when she lifted her head now her cheek

7

left a red mark on his bare flesh. She sat up—or tried to. It wasn't easy, considering how she was bound to him and that she was numb with misery and fatigue.

And to her renewed horror she realized she was still naked, her bare breasts were flattened against his back. She was able to feel his cries of conquest and greeting as they vibrated through his very bones.

At the same instant, over the smell of man and horse sweat came the smell of wood smoke and grilling meat. Shaking her loose flaxen hair back from her eyes, she saw the village they were entering at such a boastful canter. She took in the buffalo-skin tepees, the cooking fires with their flags of smoke, the dark glossy heads of the women turning and lifting to stare and then to grin. A taut prickling sensation slithered down her spine.

Suddenly her hands were free and her captor was sliding away from her to the ground. She'd become so used to his slack-spined support that without it she sagged forward wearily, automatically folding her arms across her cooling breasts.

As soon as the Indian tethered his horse, he turned back to her, his eyes full of evil fun. She thought she recognized behind those eyes a personality bloody and treacherous, without honor or honesty as she knew it. His face paint—the grays and glaucous blues, the yellows and gaudy reds—were smeared. He was breathing quickly through his mouth. As his eyelids narrowed, his expression registered little that she found familiar. Her earlier feelings of mere shame at her nakedness were erased by something more vivid.

She tried to keep her own face free of expression. Already this day she'd looked death in the eyes many times. Yet, she vowed no trace of fear would mark

8

her, nor any hint of the gnawing anguish she felt inside. These people must never see it. They must never suspect.

The Indian pulled her from the horse's back and threw her face down on the grass. Immediately, a number of children surrounded her, all wearing moccasins but otherwise standing as naked as she was. They were obviously raging with curiosity.

She had a wild thought: Tobias had boomed with so much zeal for the salvation of these souls, talking about bringing them Christ and the Holy Book and calico to cover their heathen nakedness. (Yes, that was the ironic part—calico for the heathens so lost to darkness that they knew neither the gospel nor underdrawers.) And now, despite Tobias, or perhaps because of him, here lay his sister, sprawled as naked as any of them.

Several women were gathering with the children, guffawing crudely. Victorine lay there. She felt ill. Her stomach was full of slippery fear, clammy perspiration clung to her like cold treacle. When she started to sit up, she saw the woman nearest her was holding a tall staff with feathers dangling from it. She was poked with it, first her shoulder, then her side. Another woman leaned forward and pinched her calf. She didn't move under this horrible probing. *"Hi-ya,"* said the woman with the staff. And when Victorine turned to face her, hopelessness ran through her. The woman was making a sound she could only describe as cackling, something like the sound of scavenger birds, something like madness. Gradually, all the women and children began scolding her at once.

She barely got up onto her knees when two older girls, both dressed 'in leather dresses with angular beadwork designs, each grabbed a fistful of her hair

9

and hauled her to her bare feet. Pain shot through her scalp. She gasped. Only part of her was aware of the odd feeling of her exposed breasts changing shape as her arms lifted in self-defense.

The girls were shorter than she, forcing her to stoop as they dragged her toward the nearest tepee. The tent was throwing a long, lavender triangle on the ground away from the sunset. The girls pulled her into this shadow so viciously that she almost fell. She was so stiff she could hardly stumble along anyway, and when they yanked yet again, harder, she tripped. Her ankle twisted and she bruised her hand in breaking her fall, but the girls gave her no time to recover. They yanked her forward again. Pain in her scalp leapt up, lush, too thick to bear without gathering tears. It was on the tip of her tongue to plead with them, but what would be the good of that? She couldn't understand them anymore than they could understand her.

Before the tepee, the girls began to take turns pulling her about, this way, then that, and sometimes just jerking her hair with sheer glee. Victorine had been taught from birth never to allow herself too much concern for personal discomfort, but finally she'd had all she could stand.

She reached for the hand presently tangled in her hair, took hold of the wrist, and pulled the girl toward her. The girl gave a little yelp as she gave up her own grip. Victorine flung her pale mane out of her eyes, stood to her full height, and with her free hand slapped the smooth dusky face. It was a solid blow that left red finger marks. The girl clapped her free hand over her cheek and stared at Victorine in amazement. Victorine would have slapped her again, but the girl began tearing at her captured wrist, leaving Victorine's white knuckles bleeding as she was forced to let go.

Meanwhile, the second girl came from behind and snatched at her hair again, screaming. Victorine spun. This time her swing knocked the girl right onto her back.

A male voice shouted in her ear just before she felt a heavy blow to the base of her skull. She briefly felt her body go as loose as a sodden string. Then everything came to an abrupt halt, everything but the ground. The ground moved. It seemed to float up to meet her with a tenderness that was like a mother's goodnight kiss.

The Waiting Cougar's very quietness had the stamp of a man marking time, a man ready, biding his moment. He was well named, for he was cunning and crafty as a mountain lion.

"How have you fared these many moons since we have last seen you?" Rotten Gut asked him in the tongue of the Salish.

The Waiting Cougar's manner was respectful, grave. He had fared that well, thank you.

Though he dressed like the typical rough mountain man, he was not from the land the white faces called the United States, but from a place called Scotland, across a wide water. He had the airs of a man born into a powerful tribe, a man bred to greatness and splendor. He could be sharp and dismissive. He could ridicule. Or, if it suited him, he could put on the guise of command. His smiles were sometimes cold, a mere concession to gallantry; but more often his eyes looked out of a face kept as blank as a stone.

"Where do you come from?" Rotten Gut asked.

"My place."

Rotten Gut admired the way he spoke so easily of the black cliffs seamed with snow and topped with heavy white brows of rime where he spent his winters. Could there be a valley more desperately silent or hopelessly deserted than the Waiting Cougar's "place"? "What occasions your journey?" he asked.

The Waiting Cougar shrugged. "A man gets lonely. I thought to trade, to get me a new outfit, some utensils, knives, ammunition. The signs say 'twill be a mean winter."

Rotten Gut turned his eyes away. "Mean, yes. Much cold."

His fourteen-year-old daughter rounded the tepee just then, and the Cougar rose, a habit of his foreign upbringing which he had never shed, despite his seasons with the Salish. "Lone Goose," he said. And he took advantage of Rotten Gut's friendship to stoop quickly and kiss the girl's forehead. For once his smile was genuine.

Lone Goose tightened her blanket around her. Too shy to make much over their guest, she seemed nevertheless delighted and flattered by the Waiting Cougar's attention. She greeted him gently. "Please consider our lodge your home. Will you have something to eat?"

"Thank you," he answered in his rough burred manner of speech, "but your father has already filled me with some of your cooking." He'd eaten a great bowlful of bear meat flavored with wild onions. " 'Twas delicious."

When he sat down, she took a place between him and her father. She eyed him warily, sidelong. "My cousin Dark Sun will be sorry to learn he has missed your visit."

"He's no' with you here then?"

"He traveled here with us for the autumn hunt,

12

yes, but he is gone now with Two-Edged-Knife to seek the thieves who took many of our horses."

"There's been trouble then." He looked to Rotten Gut for more information, but the old man sat quietly. Only his eyes shifted.

Lone Goose said, "A little trouble, causing the people to lose heart. We needed all our horses for the buffalo hunt, but many were stolen. Dark Sun lost his favorite buffalo pony. My father lost three good pack-ponies. We do not expect Dark Sun back soon. He is very determined and painted black for war."

Rotten Gut couldn't keep silent any longer. "But for the stiffness of my joints and the blindness of my eyes—the sun blindness and the ice blindness—I would have put on my war paint and rode forth, too."

The sun set slowly, throwing a quiet light across the high plains of the upper Missouri River. Around the Salish village were the sounds of cooking and families gathered to eat. Their voices dwindled out across the prairie and melted into the twilight. When it was dark, deep dark, and the sky was crowded with stars, the Waiting Cougar received word that Rotten Gut wished to see him again.

Cougar found the old man inside his lodge. The interior of the conical tepee was spacious, but its arrangement was commonplace: a central hearth, the two sacred areas, and the place of honor between them. Here Rotten Gut sat.

Lone Goose had tanned the hides of the lodge-cover. She had scraped them to reduce their weight and to let in more light, then smoked the cover thoroughly to make it water repellent and to keep it

13

pliable. Knowing the labor that went into it, Cougar admired the beauty of the soft white skins painted with tracings of earth colors.

To one side of the entrance was a tidy stack of parfleches full of pemmican, the Indians' cold-weather survival food. There were several rawhide chests full of clothing and personal possessions further along the curving wall.

Lone Goose was sitting beyond these, on the women's side. She was painting intricate geometric patterns on a new parfleche. She hadn't looked up when Cougar came in.

He stood straight and tall beside the fire, his hands behind his back, until Rotten Gut said, "Sit down. I want to show you something."

In a fast, fluid movement, Cougar crossed his feet and lowered himself onto the buffalo-skin rug spread for him at the old man's side.

Rotten Gut filled his pipe. He lighted it and blew smoke to the sky and the earth and the four directions. Holding the bowl, he passed the stem to his guest.

Cougar felt strangely anxious. There was always something magical about sitting in a circle around a fire, but in this lodge the feeling was especially strong. Rotten Gut was a medicine chief, credited with powers to heal the desperately sick and repair the fatally wounded. His people believed he had other powers as well. They said he was a storyteller who listened to the wind, which brought him things — and sometimes that wind was like a hand that struck a man in the face. In the past Cougar himself had had occasion to wonder at the sometimes diabolical way the old shaman appraised people.

At this moment Rotten Gut was pulling out a

14

square of leather. He handed it to Cougar. It seemed just an old piece of leather, brown and wadded; Cougar couldn't see the significance of it. Though he didn't say as much, Rotten Gut must have sensed his confusion. "Wait, wait," said the old man, leaning against his willow back rest. His high old voice held all the inflection and turn of a Shakespearean actor's.

Cougar sat, wondering what the old shaman was up to. Outside sounds came muted into the lodge — the rumble of a dog, a snatch of conversation, the laugh of a woman.

Rotten Gut's eyes were half-closed, and he seemed to be meditating. Cougar was curious, in spite of this odd anxiety.

Finally Rotten Gut cleared his throat and spat, and then he spoke: "I was just remembering something I had forgotten." He waited for a full minute, then went on carefully, talking from his throat. His eyes were small and deep set, but a little flame shone in them. "It is from the future. That is why I forgot." He took back the folded leather and opened it. "Here it is, here." He was serious and solemn. "It is coming clear now." He spoke simply, he seemed sedate and sure. He was pointing at the leather with a tremulous, old, scarred forefinger.

Cougar still couldn't see anything. Then . . . he thought maybe there was something, an ill-defined something, a picture or a design . . . But when he leaned closer there was nothing but the grain of the leather after all.

"Yes, it is you, you and a woman." Rotten Gut paused again. His pauses were enough to kill a person with curiosity. "You must breathe the same breath and be one. She will say she does not want to breathe with you. She will fight you. She will not

15

like the Waiting Cougar and sometimes you will not like her. She will say that you have stolen her and that you are not trustworthy." Rotten Gut eyed him. "But you must insist. You must be a husband to her. You two seem to be different people. You have to settle with one another. That is what you must convince her of. Look—"

Cougar kept his eyes on the leather and on Rotten Gut's thick, chestnut-colored finger moving over it. Out the side of his vision he noticed that Lone Goose had stopped her work. She hadn't lifted her head, but she was listening intently. She sat stone still. What he could see of her dark eyes were brilliant beneath their black curling lashes.

Cougar still couldn't see anything except wrinkles and creases in the leather, yet Rotten Gut's voice seemed almost to create something there. The things he said were harsh and startling—and totally fantastical.

"That is what I remembered just now. I thought I had forgotten—"

He stopped abruptly, then went on: "In three days she will be with the Blackfeet. You must go among them. You must travel the trail that leads between the waters the Long Knife called the Teton and the Marias." He stopped again, as if to let the idea sink in. His nose pointed toward Cougar like a beak, and then back at the square of leather.

Cougar felt called upon to say something. "The Blackfeet are wolves that run through the mountains. They have that many medicine irons. And their faces are blacked against all strangers."

"You must go among them. Remind them that you are not their stranger, that they call you Buffalo Killer. They will not harm you. You will come face-to-face with the woman there. She is very handsome,

16

much woman. She . . . she has no name, at least no name that suits her. You must give her a name, one that touches the sky. It says so right here."

Cougar looked yet again at the square of leather. And again he didn't see anything.

The old man seemed exhausted. Cougar prepared to go. But before he left the tepee he stared down at Rotten Gut, straight down at the old face.

The pouched eyelids were half-shut, but he said insistently in his high, soft old voice, "You are two. Become one."

Cougar was getting ready to leave the hunting camp. Only half the sun was showing yet, flashing its still-tender light on the grass where the dew was liquid. There wasn't a cloud in the sky, not even a piece of one, and all the world was still and waiting. Rotten Gut had come to watch his preparations. The sun, burning so low, threw the silhouettes of the two men like pointed fingers to the west. One of Cougar's pack horses nickered; otherwise the camp was quiet. There was a lingering scent of burnt buffalo chips and dew-dampened rabbit brush.

Cougar wanted to ask the dozen or so questions that had cropped up in his mind during the night, but the Indian only rubbed the back of his brown wrist over his eyes and said, "You do not believe; your eyes are full of smoke, your ears brim with roaring waters. But you will see. It is true. It will *become* true."

This didn't particularly ease Cougar's mind. His life was never certain and that was the way he'd chosen to keep it here. He preferred it to be filled with danger, so that he had to whet himself daily, hourly, to a sharpness that would allow him to

17

survive. This prophecy of Rotten Gut's came as an uncomfortable hint that certain affairs were never of a man's own ordering.

He went to his horse's head. There was a steady, hard glare under his eyelids. He'd been waiting to say something, and he figured that now was the last chance he would have: "What would I be doing with a woman, Rotten Gut, the way I live?"

"Ah," said the old Indian pleasantly, "you will know what to do with her. When she first looks at you, you will know."

Cougar frowned, unconvinced and irritated. He owed Rotten Gut his life—and that was too big a debt to simply ignore. Still, his mind kept trying to think of a graceful way out of this thing. He felt like a mouse in a milk pail. At least he wasn't expected to commit himself. It was one of the Indians' own principles of politeness not to reply to any proposal right away. That would be holding it as a light matter. It showed respect to take one's time, to consider.

"Cougar," Rotten Gut said, as if reading his mind, "you think about it, but be quick."

"Why?" The mark of Rotten Gut's power over him was that he seemed to always be questioning the old man. But right now he was looking for clues, for answers, for some way of shrugging off this feeling that there were forces beyond his control at work. He wished he could simply dismiss this whole thing as a harmless old man's fancy, yet that he couldn't do. "What's the hurry?" he asked pettishly.

Rotten Gut shrugged. His chin closed, so that his lips were the thin lips of musing. "I have forgotten."

Lone Goose came up, black-eyed, black-haired, seemingly passionless. Her new womanly composure seemed much a surface thing yet, as if she was wary

18

of giving anything of herself away; thus, the careful pose of coolness. Cougar sensed that her body was maturing ahead of her emotions. The Indians' way of life forced their young people to grow up early. Just last year Lone Goose had had the slight body and the quick, impulsive ways of a child. She'd been thin yet, with narrow hips. But he could see as well as anyone that she was a woman now, entirely womanly. When he next saw her she could be wed, a mother even.

He went back to loading his packhorses with the bales of furs he'd intended to trade for supplies. Rotten Gut insisted he would need them to soften the hearts of the Blackfeet. Peltwise, he'd had a full season. Of first quality beaver pelts, called plews, he had three small packs; of good quality pelts he had two bales; and he had about forty otter skins. He hoped they would be enough to placate any Blackfeet he might run across.

Not that he'd definitely decided to look them up.

When he was ready, he mounted Irongray, the big thoroughbred horse he'd brought with him from Scotland. The leather of his English saddle was pliant beneath him. Looking down at Rotten Gut, he said formally, "The heart of the Waiting Cougar is full. I always listen to Rotten Gut with great respect. I've grown up as a child of the Salish. With what is yours you have caused me to grow, and now I hold Rotten Gut's hand as a child holds the hands of his father. I mean to reflect upon what you have told me, and hope to gain from it."

Rotten Gut nodded. He stood with his arms folding his blanket across his chest. "Safe journey."

"Safe journey," Lone Goose echoed, her voice grave and soft. "Remember—" she added impulsively, "Cats live violent lives and die bloody deaths.

19

You must be careful." Her youthful eyes were forbiddingly solemn.

Cougar turned his horse to the trail. Something about what Lone Goose had said bothered him. Was it fear for him that he'd sensed under that implacable reserve? Surely she believed her father's prophecies?

He shrugged off the idea that maybe Rotten Gut was getting too old to be the village shaman.

As he traveled, the prairie was still—but not too still. Things moved and made noises: a bronze thrush flitted in a thicket of buffaloberries, a coyote trotted along the edge of a creek, magpies cawed in some tangled cottonwoods. The sun got up higher, hot and shiny as steel. The air shimmered with heat.

*You must be a husband to her . . . a husband to her . . .* It echoed and echoed through his head like a bee bounding back and forth in a room full of windows. Who could this woman be? (That was saying that Rotten Gut had ever truly been capable of knowing such things.) Was she some fierce Blackfoot maiden likely to slit his throat while he was sleeping? He would rather face another mountain lion, or ten bitch wolves, than one Blackfoot squaw with a weapon in her hand.

He attempted a rueful laugh, then muttered an epithet under his breath. Was he really going to risk his scalp just to find out if Rotten Gut had the gift of prophecy?

Why not? There had been a restlessness in him for months, a restlessness that would not quiet. He'd felt as if he were moving in the wrong direction, no matter where he went. And at times his courage failed him when he remembered Scotland, when he listened in his memory to the chimes of the kirk at midnight. There had been times when he'd lain half

20

the night in his furs wondering how long these mountains would keep him enthralled. Why didn't he feel he could go home yet? Why did the scream of the cougar keep him tarrying here?

Considering how many questions he had, there didn't seem to be any reason not to see what the old shaman's vision led him to. Maybe he should go ahead and take himself a wife for a while. It wasn't as if these mountain marriages were binding forever. They were little more than temporary arrangements made for convenience, much like the old custom of handfasting still maintained by many highlanders. Of course, the logical part of him saw objections and knew that this was a foolhardy decision; but mountain men were foolhardy types. If he must spend another winter here, well, the winters could be that lonely. By the time of the hard, hungry moon of January a man's needs made him feel that restless.

Aye, that restless, indeed.

# Chapter Two

Victorine half awakened. A headache knifed across the back of her brain. Night had come. A fire burned somewhere nearby; it cast moving light on the hide wall she was facing. Everything seemed strange, as alien and as distorted as a nightmare. What am I doing here, she thought groggily. This isn't where I should be. How did I get here? It didn't look like anything she'd ever seen before.

Five minutes more of lethargic quiet passed. Gradually she realized again that she was naked. And that was odd—odd indeed. She seemed to be lying in a careless heap atop several folded furs and blankets, arms and legs akimbo, as if she'd simply been tossed there, her body thrown like a sack, out of the way.

At first, all she heard was the loud ringing in her ears. Her head ached, her tongue was swollen. But as her consciousness solidified she noticed other sounds, other sensations. Finally, she came fully awake to the sheer soul-splitting misery of her situation. She knew where she was then, and how she'd gotten here. The pain of recollection was a slicing flare of agony. Something had come to life—into

22

her life—something she'd never known about before.

When she dared, she rolled her aching head away from the wall of the tepee. The noises she'd been guessing at, the human movements and breathing, were borne out by the sight of an Indian woman cooking over a small fire. The fire was actually more coals than flame, and the small amount of smoke it put out was wafting up through the high smoke hole. The woman stopped her work to stare at her; one of her hands came up and clenched into a fist between her breasts. Her face gleamed red above the ruddy light. She was pretty, despite an unusual set of her eyes; she was stout and dark.

"May I have some water?" Victorine asked. She spoke in a precise way, her voice quiet, a little hoarse from thirst. The woman gave her a blank response. Victorine sat up, pulling one of the blankets out from under her to cover herself. In her desire for water, she hardly noticed the rope burns on her wrists, now darkly glazed. She made a drinking motion with her hand and looked at the woman with hope.

Suddenly the woman spoke—a brief barrage of unintelligible words—and she smiled in a way that sent shivers down Victorine's exposed back. The wild ferocity in that smile stunned her into momentary stillness.

The woman lunged to her feet (Victorine saw now that she was heavy with pregnacy) and came to loom over her charge. She reached out, hesitated, then stroked one chafed, laborious hand down Victorine's hair. She spoke again, but murmurously this time, and a little sorrowfully.

"Water?" Victorine tried again, her gaze direct.

The woman smiled as one recalled to herself. She nodded slowly and her hair, in twin braids, stirred darkly on her shoulders. Her odd eyes hardened again. She crossed the tepee, bent to pick up a skin bag, but halted when a tall, broad-shouldered warrior pushed through the willow-stiffened rawhide doorflap.

He stood just inside the opening, Teutonic, overbearingly haughty, blown with success. He was clad in short deerskin leggings, a mere dangle of cloth to cover his genitals, and a fierce war bonnet which Victorine recognized. She ought to, the feathers of it had tickled her nose halfway along the journey from the river where she was captured until, finally, mercifully, he'd taken it off because of the heat. At his waist hung a tomahawk. And once more he was resplendent in fresh war paint.

He didn't speak at all. He was having a long look at her, and his stare was pitiless. He seemed very tall, very authoritative, very menacing. She tried not to cringe.

At last he crossed to her, took hold of her shoulders and pulled her to her feet. Her eyes measured him uneasily. He ripped the blanket from her hands and began to inspect her, as a farmer would inspect a new cow — her flaxen hair, her sensitive fair skin. He pulled her about, poked and prodded, even pried her mouth open and pulled at her teeth one by one to see if they were all soundly attached. It was far beyond humiliating. She thought, a little crazily, that a lady should be able to stride away from such a scene.

Leaving the taste of his none-too-clean thumb and forefinger on her tongue, his inspection continued elsewhere. He felt her shoulders, rubbed his blunt fingers over her soft palms, put a bracing arm around her, and kneaded her abdomen and haunches. Grinning all over now, black eyed, his

24

cheeks streaked with that bizarre paint (made, by the smell of it from some kind of rancid animal fat), he began to squeeze each of her small, high-set breasts in turn.

She'd held still enough for him until this, but some intimacies she wasn't able to bear stoically — on top of which the stale sourness of his breath and war paint was making her feel ill. Stiff with outrage, she slapped at him.

He only laughed, caught her in a gust of passion, and rubbed himself against her pelvis so that she felt every inch of what was hidden by his breechcloth. His lusts were boiling, and for the first time in her life she felt the state of a man's arousal. A sound of disgust and terror welled up from the pit of her stomach.

He laughed again, and pushed her backwards. The ground went out from beneath her and the tepee revolved as she toppled onto the pile of bedding. All the fight was temporarily slammed out of her.

He remained standing over her another long moment, as if considering. He said something quietly; how she wished she could understand! He glanced furtively over his shoulder at the woman who stood watching with the water skin still grasped in her hands. The woman looked back with her impenetrable eyes. He gave Victorine another look that made her feel cold. Though she took care that not one flicker of feeling marred the smooth blandness of her face, he must have sensed her fear anyway, because he smiled.

Seeming to make up his mind, he spun on his heel and stooped out of the tepee.

The second the doorflap dropped behind him, Victorine scrambled to her feet. Her legs had changed to water, but she forced them to hold her up. She glanced at the woman. Her sensitivity heightened now, Victorine observed the look of hatred in those foreign eyes. Grabbing up a blanket with which to cover herself again, she made a dash for the opening, threw the flap back, and scrambled out.

As soon as she rose to a stand and tossed her hair back over her shoulders, she saw that the men of the tribe were gathered in a circle of self-satisfied faces around a large bonfire of fat pine. The fire blazed in the gentle August night. Its heavy, pungent smoke hovered in the air over the camp. In its red-tinted glow, she estimated two dozen or more faces. One man was talking fiercely with wild hand signs, while the others listened politely. Then one of them spotted her. The casual group suddenly galvanized its attention; fingers pointed.

She began to run with all her strength, to run for her very life through the camp, and running, she began to be frightened as she hadn't allowed herself to be frightened before. Near the edge of the camp, when she was close enough to freedom that the very shadows which could hide her seemed to peer at her from the spaces between the trees, an old woman, called to the flap of her tepee by the shouts of alarm, reached out a gnarled hand to trip her. Victorine lost her hold on her blanket as she fell heavily, face first, to the ground.

Several women had taken up a chase of her and now one of them struck her on the back with a heavy chunk of rough-chopped firewood. She felt the skin over her left shoulder blade fray with fierce, hot pain even as her breath left her. The side of her porcelain-complexioned face was ground hard into the dirt as the chunk of wood descended again in the same place. She thought her bones would surely

26

crack.

Shouts came from the campfire, outraged male voices. The women who had gathered to punish her backed off to form a silent, sullen ring.

Victorine was so stunned and bruised she could only lie there. When at last she managed to sit up, she shook her head, trying to shake off her pain. Just as she began to collect herself, one of the girls she'd bested earlier in the day rushed in and jabbed her thigh with a sharpened cooking stick. The slender point gouged deeply. In spite of herself, Victorine cried out. Instinctively, she covered the place with her hand.

She couldn't believe how savage these females were. Couldn't any of them empathize with her plight? Weren't any of them mothers? Did they know tenderness when cuddling their baby daughters? How could they reconcile that with this hellish treatment of her?

She looked down; blood was seeping up through her fingers. Suddenly enraged, she leapt up, reached for the nearest woman and pulled her to the ground. The one she chose was too much for her, though; the squaw wrapped bearlike arms around her and rolled so that Victorine was quickly flattened beneath her.

Still seething with rage, she struck out with all her might, landing two good blows to the woman's face. The others all shouted encouragement to their combatant and waved their arms and made punching motions with their hands, threatening and grim.

There came a shout like nothing Victorine had ever heard before. The women squealed and scuttled back. Even the one atop Victorine got hastily to her feet and backed off.

The big warrior chief entered the circle of women

27

and stood over Victorine. His face was a horrible congested color under the streaks of paint. There was some subdued, overwrought tittering among the younger women, then all laughter stopped. The warrior crossed his arms over his chest and glared down at Victorine. When he nudged her with his moccasined foot, she got to her knees warily. Her back was a throbbing hurt. Suddenly he bent, took a handful of her hair, and twisted it mercilessly. Tears ran from her eyes, and she cuffed out at him without thinking.

He lifted her by her hair and pulled her along that way, forcing her to seek her balance by grabbing for his hand, tangled so deeply at her scalp. She was dragged forward, stumbling and blinded by pain, until she felt the heat of the bonfire against her skin.

The pressure of his hold eased some. She blinked rapidly, trying to clear her eyes. Disgusted with such a weak exhibition (tears!), enraged by her momentary loss of control, she ordered herself to face the full shock of this new predicament at least with dignity.

She looked about her. Eyes glittered at her, and shadows thrown by the firelight fandangoed on the ground. The warriors sitting about the fire were all gaping at her, most of them with amusement, some with casual expressions, a few with avidity. She already had positive proof that any human being outside their tribe signified very little to them.

Their individual features were lighted in glimpses as the flames rose and fell, yet the smoke, flushed with the rosy light, obscured more than it revealed, blurred outlines, and hid much.

Her first impulse was to try to cover herself with her arms . . . but no, she squared her shoulders, straightened her spine, and let her hands fall to her

28

sides. A trickle of blood went unheeded down her leg, stopped at her knee, and began to dry. Her back, crushed and bleeding, went unattended. Seeing her in that moment, no one present could have guessed that she'd been raised in a cultured environment with all the niceties, all the puritanical modesties, of a Philadelphia theologist's home. She'd chosen a tree beyond the circle of men to stare at, her face rigidly composed to reveal nothing of what she felt.

Her stance did not just express her courage, it clarioned it.

In the very corner of her vision she spied a huge man coming to his feet with strikingly easy elegance. It took no direct glance to establish that here was someone notable, for the others fell silent. He was clothed in a voluminous hooded woolen capote against the night's chill, beneath which she saw only a pair of buckskin breeches and moccasins. She stood still, turning her weary eyes only toward his face. At first she saw just a flesh-colored blur . . .

She started visibly. He was fair—a white man! A tall, fair-skinned man with a mass of sand-colored hair and an elegant, almost feline quality to his movements. He was looking her over, mistrustfully it seemed, from under his tawny fur hat. In turn, she regarded him solemnly. She could have sworn he muttered something: " 'Tis you then." But surely she was mistaken. She felt awestruck by her own good fortune. This was like having a wish given before it had been made. A nugget of entreaty formed in her throat and she had to turn her face away again before it showed plainly in her eyes. Again she straightened her shoulders. The faint wind stirred the branches of the tree she chose to stare hard at and set the flames of the fire to fluttering; the shadows of the men danced grotesquely over the ground.

The white man began to sign, and sometimes to speak, in a deliberate, almost indifferent voice, to the warrior who still held her by the hair.

The Indian responded, giving Victorine's head a vicious shake, intent on inflicting pain. She stumbled and had to regain her carefully maintained stance. His words were spoken coarsely, and there was a sharpness in his tone that was unmistakable. In contrast, the white man's voice was pleasant and held a reassuring deep note.

The talk between the two went on. And on. The white man spoke in a reasoning vein, though sometimes with a certain frozen evenness; the warrior's tone grew more and more cunning. The tension between them grew . . . and burst.

The white man turned and left the fire. He moved with a long unhurried stride that covered the ground with catlike speed. Victorine's heart clenched to an ache. Outwardly she refused to let her expression change; inwardly, she trembled. She stared ahead in blank-faced fear.

He returned, carrying in his arms a bale of beaver skins. He caught her glance, but immediately turned his eyes back to the warrior holding her. He dropped the skins in the place where he'd been sitting before, then lifted his chin and waited.

His eyes eventually shifted back to her, however, as the Indian put his free hand sinuously on her shoulder. He drew her back against him, ran his hand slowly down over her breasts and belly, eventually roughing the blond hair at the join of her thighs. She pulled her stomach in with a quick gasp, shrinking at his touch. She knew a moment of panic; her eyes closed briefly. It was taking all her willpower to

30

keep her hands motionless at her sides. The coarse hand finally came back to her breasts, which the Indian began to press and pull possessively, making a comment that could only be lewd, for the others laughed.

The white man laughed, too. Victorine's pride shriveled to a kernel small enough to swallow. Her stomach heaved, and she tasted bile at the back of her mouth.

The white man's indifference seemed to make the warrior grow angry. His voice roughened. His hands let go of her as he began to gesticulate. She was free now, but she didn't dare move.

The talk seemed to enter a new phase. She sensed the conversation was precarious and incalculably delicate now. The trapper gave off no suggestion of intimidation, at least not by any change of his stonelike features. He had an autocratic high-bridged nose and a way of tilting his head back and staring awfully down it.

As the Indian continued to haggle, flushed with anger and exertion, the white man simply turned away, shaking his head. He was breaking off the bargaining with scorn and indignation; he seemed insulted.

Victorine made a small sound in her throat in spite of her resolve. Please don't leave me, she wanted to cry. Please, *oh please—help me!*

## Chapter Three

The man was leaving the fire again, carrying away his bale of furs, heading for his pack train and his cargo of peltry, which Victorine had previously made out among the trees. He reached the horses; they mouthed their bits and stamped restlessly.

But then, at the last moment, he returned to the fire with the bale, walked back, pulled a second bale of furs off one of the pack horses and heaved it back to the fire as well. He dropped it beside the first. He smiled broadly, his attitude had the appearance of foolish generosity. He looked about at the sweaty faces lit by the firelight and pending on his words, while he timed his final utterance with a preacher's instinct.

Whatever it was he said, a cheer went up among the gathering. The warrior stooped to sling Victorine into his arms. Careless of her injuries, he tossed her right over the licking tops of the high flames. The white man was almost taken by surprise, but in the final instant he raised his arms to catch her—with a sudden curse. Another cheer and more coarse-sounding comments went the round. She closed her ears to it.

She'd thrown out her arms to clasp the man's shoulders when she was tossed, and now she contin-

32

ued to grip him with the panicky clutch of a poor swimmer in deep water. Yet there was no real need. His chest was like a hard-surfaced wall, his arms beneath her back and legs were like wind-toughened oak branches. She knew unerringly that he could crush the life from her with one grim clench. He was looking down at her, and she blushed painfully and made a weak attempt to free herself, but he held her harder to him. A first flicker of panic darted through her. His gaze held hers. She hadn't looked directly into his face until that moment. He had intelligent eyes, alive and full of light. His lips parted to display clean, straight teeth. The wind tousled the hair that wasn't covered by his cap, hair that was thick and soft looking.

In turn, he seemed to study her intently—her appeal, her attraction. With the firelight behind her now her hair looked lighter than ever, like a living flame enveloping her.

Though his hold was painful on her sensitive back, she didn't struggle as he carried her to where his animals waited. Even with her weight, he walked straight and easy, with his head up. Fearless and unshaken, seemingly untouched by the least doubt or terror, he turned his back on the Indians.

When he slung her up sidesaddle fashion onto his horse, she gripped the huge animal's silky mane to balance herself. Her own mane fell in tresses over her breasts, partly concealing her. Though she was already so saddle sore from the day spent astride the back of the Indian pony, to sit sidesaddle before a fellow white person seemed infinitely preferable to the alternative of being left behind.

The horse was a fine iron-gray color. She knew very little about horses, but she guessed that this one was a thoroughbred of some sort. It felt warm and powerful beneath her as it shook its head and pawed the ground. A gun sheath was tied behind the saddle; the carved wooden butt of a rifle protruded, ornamented and tied with hawk feathers.

The man untethered his pack train. When he came back to the horse and stepped up into the saddle, the gray snorted and pulled nervously at its reins. The man lifted Victorine to find his seat, then settled her onto his hard, buckskin-clad thighs. He opened his voluminous capote, pulled her against his chest, then closed the garment around the two of them, leaving it for her to position herself so that her injuries were not made more painful than necessary. He slipped one hand outside of the cloak to take up the reins; his free arm surrounded her waist beneath the capote. Thus they started away, pulling the pack animals along behind.

They rode for a mile or so before she let herself believe that the Indians were actually going to allow them to go. Until then she didn't dare speak. He hadn't spoken either. He was looking ahead with a vaguely uneasy frown on his face. He smelled of smoke and rawhide and horses. She wondered if he was Canadian. French Canadians were known for their success at getting along with Indians.

She was feeling embarrassed by the silence, and by this unacknowledged physical proximity (she was filled with distaste for being this close to him, handsome and interesting though he was), and decided the time had come to open a conversation. "Do you speak English?" she asked in a voice that came out a bit timid. She glanced up at him.

She thought she felt an imperceptible tightening of his embrace. She could feel every movement of his powerful chest muscles against the side of her naked breast. He answered at last, evidently amused:

"Aye, I speak English—the King's English, that is; no' your colonial dialect."

She was surprised at his strong accent. There was a blustering burr . . . "You're a Scot—that's the accent."

He said with a twisted smile, "I have an accent?"

What did she know about Scots, about Scotland? She plumbed her mind for things she'd read . . . and came up with precious little: images of rocky coasts, great headlands and bare heathery hills, mountains sliding steeply down to the water, grand winds, bitter cold, and rain; and tea; and tales of big monsters in the lakes, which were called *lochs,* she believed . . .

All this furious thought was a foil for her gladness, which had to be held in tight. She could have sobbed with relief at that moment, if she'd let herself. Not only white, but English speaking! It wasn't her way, however, to show her feelings, so in the end, though she was biting her lower lip with delight, she said simply, "I want to thank you for what you did." She said this with a shyness that was utterly unaffected, and thus doubly tender. "I owe you my life. I had no hope of being rescued, none at all." She was looking at him with naive adoration.

He didn't answer for a long while. He shifted in the saddle; she felt his thighs move beneath her, too intimately. She tilted her head to look up at him. Once again his arm muscles tightened about her.

They picked their way down into a ravine, through the dry, waist-high grass at its bottom, and climbed back out of it. At the top of the rise he said, "You know that I bought you?"

"Yes, and I'm so grateful. I think those women would have killed me." She moved a little, trying to ease the continuing throb in her back.

"No' likely *killed* you," came his considered reply,

"though they might soon have made you wish you were dead. Savage Goat was going to make you his wife, as I have the understanding of it." His quiet voice gained depth. "That anxious he was for it, too. Aye, you cost me four times what I'd usually have to pay for a slave squaw. Two bales of beaver—six hundred and forty pelts—would be worth nigh two thousand American dollars in St. Louis goods this year. Of course, Savage Goat could see just how much I had on my horses. That drove his price up considerably—that and the fact that he wanted your pretty pink lips for himself."

She shivered involuntarily. He pressed her closer against him with his circling arm. "Cold, lassie?"

Now her breasts were actually resting on his forearm and bare wrist. She was hard-put not to protest in some way; yet, at the moment she felt inclined to be tolerant toward his intentions, considering that he'd dealt so charitably with her difficulty. Perhaps he hadn't noticed the intimacy. She swallowed and looked up at him. "Not cold, just grateful to you." A worry line appeared between her eyes. "Again I thank you, Mr. . . . I don't know your name."

"I'm called the Waiting Cougar— or just Cougar."

"Isn't a cougar a wild animal?"

"A wild cat, aye, a mountain lion. They're furtive creatures, usually solitary. They stalk and rush, or wait to pounce from trees or overhangs. They kill by ripping their prey open, or by biting its throat— though neck bites of a tamer sort occur during mating." His voice was bland and totally unreadable."

"Don't you have a real name?"

"In the mountains that is my real name. Out here you earn your name; it has significance. A man's life proceeds from his name, the way a river proceeds from its source. I earned mine by killing a cougar with naught but a knife and my bare hands. 'Tis said the cougar's spirit entered me then."

She thought this over, her senses newly alert to the strong hand snug around her ribcage. "Well, my name is —"

"You do no' have a name yet, my heart. 'Tis one of my tasks to name you."

"One of your tasks? But —"

"That's enough talk for now," he said with a kind of rueful severity. " 'Twould be best for you to try to rest some."

She ignored that. "Where are you taking me?"

He didn't answer.

Suddenly it seemed very important that she know where they were going. She couldn't force down a rising alarm. Her heart began to run, and her teeth clenched together against all the day's suppressed fear, which wanted to leap loose. "Please! Where are you taking me!"

"Do no' sound so frightened. You've no reason to be."

Her breath escaped her in a long sough, for he'd bent his head to speak tenderly and the look he gave her lacked any hint of evil intent. Indeed, there was something amazingly tender and vigilant about him now.

"I'm only taking you to my camp. 'Tis an hour or so along. Now lay against me and try to sleep."

She looked up sideways, still somewhat apprehensive, at the face so close to her own, yet so impossible to judge in the dark.

"A little longer, just a little longer," he whispered reassuringly down to her. "Lie against me, rest. 'Tis no' so far we have to go." His voice was almost crooning.

Gradually her whole self relaxed. She couldn't even have said when it was exactly that she laid her cheek against his shoulder. The beat of his pulse in her ear seemed natural, soothing. Her aching body lolled bonelessly, held to his by the easy strength of his arm.

But then she was alert again. And for the first time her voice had some of its old businesslike practicality: "Two thousand dollars! I don't know how I'll ever pay you back. We never had much money, and Tobias spent all of what little our father left us on this journey—"

"I do no' want money."

"That's very generous of you, but still, I feel I must find some way of repaying you. It's only right. You must have spent months trapping for those skins."

"Aye, most of a year, but you do no' owe me anything . . . extra. I bought a woman, paid for her, and now I have her. 'Tis done."

She sat up abruptly, wincing at the pain it cost her. She looked up at him, scanned his face in the darkness, her own white-ringed eyes stunned and doubting her own ears. His hand was around on her ribcage, so that she knew he could feel her heart galloping in her chest. Seconds passed. It seemed he was waiting for some realization to sink into her—or could it merely be that in her disturbed condition she was hallucinating? "I'm sorry, Mr. . . . Cougar, but obviously you can't mean what you just said. Perhaps if you could be a little more specific . . . I mean," she said with a little laugh, "it sounded almost as if you feel you've bought me, body and soul."

"Nae, no' your soul, that's yours to keep." He eyed her, his rugged face mere inches from hers.

38

" 'Tis the nature of things here. A man wants a woman, he steals one, or uses someone else's 'til the urge passes him — or, if he can no' get what he wants any other way, he buys one."

That was certainly specific. More seconds trickled by. At last she said, "I don't believe this."

" 'Tis hard for me, too. I did no' ken I wanted a wife particularly, 'til I saw Savage Goat running his hands all over you. Rotten Gut was right, I'm thinking. And cleaned up, bonny as ever, I believe you'll suit me fine. I like the feel of you against me already, and your voice rings fair and sweet after so many years of mostly baritones."

What could he mean? Who was Rotten Gut? She didn't understand any of this. She was briefly conscious of being a part of some fateful riddle. Something was happening to her, something she had to think over.

And yet she did understand, dimly, that part about her suiting him. "Cougar . . ." She searched for a way to express her revulsion, and when it eluded her, she could only finish despairingly, "How can you feel right about a thing like that? I — " she whispered, "I'm a human being." She did feel cold now, chilled to the marrow, frozen brittle.

"Ah," he answered more gently than he'd spoken before, " 'tis coming clear to you now. And you thought I was your great white paladin." His smile was kindly. "Mayhap I should have kept silent 'til the morrow, but I always believe 'tis best to start as you mean to go on. But now you're frightened all over again. You need no' be. I'm a human being, too, no' a big beastie. We'll work it out — settle it." His voice rang with the slow, quiet certainty of a man who spoke out of conviction, and who knew that time alone was needed to bring her to his viewpoint.

"Leave the way of it to me."

For the second time in as long as she could remember, tears welled up in her eyes; her nose threatened to run. She turned her face away from him quickly and blinked hard. As she did, she felt his rough jaw along her temple.

His whispered breath was warm. "You tremble as if I would take a bite right out of you. Nae, indeed, I mean to see that no one harms you anymore. I'll be like a wall behind which you're sheltered from the wind. I'll build walls within walls to lock harm out. 'Tis a promise." His wrist moved on her, slid up ever so slightly, as if to test the weight of her breast against the back of his hand. She stiffened in protest. Unnoticing, he went on: "I'll no' mistreat you— be at ease on that account; but make no mistake, you're mine to keep, and fortunate you are that I'm having you."

He frowned and seemed to be considering what more he should say. "Once you're healed and your grieving time is over—you have crying to do and I know 'twill take some time—but once 'tis done I'll teach you and take you tenderly. You'll be as dear to me as a wife should be, and I'll give you all the pleasure a husband can—'till your mind whirls and your blood rings. You'll be my bonny lady. Once your crying time has ended."

Crying time. She found herself quite unable to think of that now. She could pit herself against only one ordeal at a time, and her first, without a doubt, was simply surviving.

"I seldom cry," she answered evenly. Her mouth had set determinedly against her grief. (Yet she could feel it just below the surface, held in. So much sorrow restrained in so small a spot!) She turned back to him. (He mustn't see it. She mustn't cry in

40

front of him.) She forced her facial muscles into severe discipline. "Tears are for the weak and the very young, and I'm neither of those. Does that mean I get no time to reason with you?"

"I see you're a wee bit temperish. 'Tis understandable."

"Do I?" she insisted.

"Must you ask all these questions now? Why no' leave things as they are for the time being. I would no' like to see you distressed further this night."

"I want to know!" She could feel the scream in the back of her throat. Her muscles strained to escape him.

"Keep up your heart and stop talking foolishly!" He tightened his hold on her. "I promise you there'll be naught more trouble for you to face this night than what you ride with right now."

They traveled on for another mile in silence. For Victorine it passed as a single moment; she felt strung to the highest pitch. Yet, slowly she fell into a sort of trance, perhaps mesmerized by the very danger she felt crowding all about her. It was his voice that brought her back to awareness, thrust her back into a perception of time.

"Here we are, a place to rest for a time."

She looked about at the grove of big trees. The moon had set and this wood was dark with deep midnight. "Your camp?" she asked muzzily. She felt him lift her off his thighs. Except that her battered shoulder and gouged leg pained her, she slid easily to the ground, clutching his forearms to break her descent. His hands at her waist were surprisingly warm and strong.

Then the chill air hit her and made her feel her nakedness again, especially after the heat of his body and the protection of his woolen capote. There

41

was the cool moistness of dew under her bare feet, and the feel of the night wind, just a breath of it, on her back. He came down beside her, and under his gaze the blood came hotly to her cheeks.

"Much woman," he murmured. His implacable gaze moved slowly, consideringly, over her. A dart of the purest apprehension struck into her. Her sense of peril was now allied clearly to her understanding of his leashed strength. He'd said he would give her time, but he might well be treacherous. She felt no trust in him now, she felt that she'd already been too malleable, too easily confused and manipulated.

There was only the two of them. They were miles — months! — from the borders of civilization. She was utterly at his mercy. She turned abruptly, holding one forearm across her small breasts to hide them, and the other hand flat upon the join of her thighs. The night wind fanned her bare bottom, which remained exposed.

He swept the hooded capote about her. Ankle length on him, it dragged the ground on her, and was heavy. "Thank you," she mumbled, swaying, at the limit of her endurance now.

"I'll be seeing to the stock," he said, smiling crookedly and touching his forehead with good-natured deference as he left her. He seemed in no hurry. His horse gave a quick whinny and pricked its ears as he led it away.

Without his cloak, even in the dark, she could see that he was a man built on the extra-large side, big boned and tall, easily carrying off two hundred pounds. His shoulders were as wide and square as the crosstree of a gallows. He was muscular and clearly toughened by exposure to the life he led.

He handled the pack horses with easy familiarity. They cocked their ears back to capture his voice, deep and soft, as he spoke to them.

Then he was talking louder, to her again. "I've hides for a shelter, but 'tis too stuffy to sleep indoors this time of year. Besides," he finished from where he was staking the horses, "I like to watch the summer stars wheel overhead."

Her eyes picked out the details of his small encampment in the dark. There was a fire ring containing a thin bed of fluffy white ashes, a few bundles, a roll of bedding. Weariness sat as heavily on her shoulders as the heavy cloak. She couldn't bring herself to move but stood rooted, hurting in every joint and muscle now, and especially her back and leg. She half heard him finish with the animals, saw his shadowy form move back into the camp area. He dropped deliberately upon one knee to unroll a buffalo hide and a blanket beneath a tree with silver leaves. "Over here." He was gently signaling her with an open hand. Come to me, it said.

When in doubt, don't—that was the policy her father had always preached. The late Reverend Robert Wellesley had been nothing if not a man of hardheadedness and good sense. "No," she said to Cougar. Would it begin now? Would he drag her to bed, handle her and hurt her? Her face became acutely fine drawn.

"Come, lassie," he said, again, "you're looking that white and wobbly." His eyes were like a cat's, drilling two holes through the night.

A horse stirred behind her.

Suddenly all thoughts of opposition went spinning away. In her exhaustion she surrendered her fears, her anxieties, her buffeted emotions to this strange man's irresistible confidence. And she moved toward his promise of rest automatically, past thinking for herself any longer. She walked as straight and stead-

43

ily as her body would allow, trying not to waver, her bare feet padding silently. Almost as if under the magic of the Pied Piper she went to him, step by step. She knelt on the blanket and brushed off the leaf mold that had stuck to the bottoms of her feet. He squatted opposite her, waiting. The Waiting Cougar.

"In the morning, when I can see, I'll look to your wounds."

She nodded her head dully. "But I'm so very thirsty. They wouldn't give me anything to drink." Childish pity for herself sprang up and it was a struggle to keep her voice even. As it was, her next breath came in two loud, heaving sobs. "May I have some water?"

He'd been easing her down with a hand on her arm, but now stopped with a polysyllabic exclamation (she thought it must be Gaelic) ending with, "Aye, and that you can!"

He was gone . . . and then he was back, holding a sturdy blue-rimmed tin basin in one hand. In the other was a silver flask, beautifully tooled and set with carnelians. The liquid in the basin caught and reflected fugitive flashes of starlight as he helped her guide it to her lips. The water tasted odd, but she drank it anyway, greedily gulping, trying to drink half the basin in one swallow. She coughed.

"Easy, lassie, easy." He was smiling.

She drank again, more slowly, then lowered the rim of the basin thoughtfully. "Thank you. You've been very kind." She said it as if to herself, still with that strange, under-a-spell look.

He said nothing for a good ten seconds, while all the amusement died in his eyes. They grew undefinable. "I can be kind," he answered at last, as if conceding a point. "And you can be that brave."

44

Here his voice fell, with the faintest yet most eloquent shadow of sorrowful regret. "You'll have to be, I'm afraid, mortgaged as you are to a wild cat."

She looked at him white faced. His words had reminded her that this was no dream. Heaven help her, none of this was a dream. This was happening. This was a continuation of the events that had begun at the river at noon. She said nothing, but suddenly her vision went blank with horror.

"What makes your eyes that big now? Drink, drink the rest of this. I put a capful or two of whiskey in it. 'Twill help you sleep."

She did as she was told. The dry musty taste of the diluted liquor was less offensive this time. She finished it all, panting from the effort. And already she could feel her senses growing dizzy (She'd never even tasted alcohol before).

He urged her down on the robe, tucking the blanket around her. Her aches and pains had faded to one low throb that seemed almost comforting. His face, leaning over her, filled the sky. He took a lock of her extraordinary hair and twisted it around his fingers. "God, how you shamed them! Standing there like a queen, no' even deigning to look at them, as if they were unworthy. Where did you come from with your pale hair that falls in such ferny strands and your sky eyes and these white-as-candle hands? Who would bring a woman such as you out here—and why?"

"Tobias," she murmured sleepily. Slowly and ethereally, a glow was coming upon her, beginning deep down inside and spreading out to the very tips of her toes. "Tobias brought us. Jewel and me."

He was quiet. He possessed an element of gentleness that sat peculiarly upon a man so large. "Two women, two window flowers." His voice had a touch of incredulity. " 'Tis a man's country out here, and no' a place for women like you—or for tall boys who call themselves men. Your Tobias must have been a fool."

"Yes," she agreed, almost humbly, "poor foolish Tobias . . . poor—" Her eyes grew wide and frightened again. They reflected minutely the little stars above her. In her mind and heart was a blinding turmoil of pain, disbelief, and sorrow.

His voice cut into it like lightning. "Hush now. Sleep calls."

Her eyelids slipped down, closed, then opened again, slowly, once more beating exhaustion off . . . at least a little way.

His mouth twitched a little at her stubbornness. He watched her until her breath came deep and even. And then, with an expression of unsmiling satisfaction, he said softly, "A little window flower, blond as morning birds, aye, and much woman."

She hardly heard him. His voice had become a seductive lullaby, the voice of promised comfort and a dreamy sort of domination. She knew only that he was being kind to her—for now. She was in too emotional a state to analyze how genuine his words were or what they pointed toward. She was simply living a minute at a time, second by second, and wondering how she could still be alive after such a test. She wanted to believe that the test was over now. It must be over, she felt such hollowness—no anger or sorrow, no ache, no reality even. She simply felt hollow, blank.

At some point she slept, without ever being aware that she had slipped over the edge.

# Chapter Four

Victorine passed a dark night. When she half awakened, trembling, near the middle of the night, arms soothed her. Someone whispered in her ear that she was safe, and she slept again, but not peacefully. She was trapped in unpleasant fancy, toiling to escape, yet barely reaching consciousness before she descended back into dream. Her sleeping mind struggled with the trip out from Philadelphia, the crossing of the great prairies, and then the abrupt end of everything she'd known before.

In dreams, again the prairie sizzled under the hot August sun, the mirage of bluish-green sage fused with the blue western horizon. The tall grass beside the upper Missouri River brushed the hem of her green skirts, which floated behind her in the wind. Again, the first war cry shattered her musings. As she turned, in the slow motion of dreams, she saw the Indian ponies in full gallop coming over the dry blown grass, heading straight for the vulnerable little river party. The sounds the warriors made started her heart running. She became sensitively alive to the minutest details: those inhuman wails, so mind-chilling, skirling again and again, closer and closer;

47

the beat of the horses' hooves vibrating like drums. She stood somewhat above it all on a knoll, her skirts ballooning in the innocent wind. In her dream she shouted a warning to Tobias. A futile warning.

He'd already seen the danger, of course, and though he must have known that running for the boat was useless, that was what he tried to do. He took his wife Jewel by the hand and she struggled to follow his lead. Victorine saw rather than heard him shout something up to her. She saw his eyes search her out on the knoll, saw his mouth moving, but the sound never reached her. He was too far away and there were those battle cries, and the rumble of hooves, and the ever present, muffling wind. The grass continued to sway and the Indians came on, riding their galloping horses.

None of the whites had any weapons except Mr. Clayton, the captain of the boat hired to take the missionaries as far as the Great Falls. He kept a hunting rifle near him at all times when he was ashore. Victorine now looked to him with the hope that he would somehow ward off the attackers with it. She saw him turn with it in his hands, he turned and faced the rushing Indians, turned and . . . stood absolutely motionless. He stood frozen in fear, his control completely lost. Another member of the boat's crew grabbed the gun from his hands and managed to get a shot off before the horses came thundering down on him, horses carrying red men swinging tomahawks above their heads. Then all was a violence of horses and men and screams for long jolting minutes. The missionaries' Flathead guide, Little Rattlesnake, ran, but when he tripped to his knees on a mat of briars, he was pierced through the back with a lance. He looked down at the lance point sticking out of his belly before falling face forward.

The rest of the boat's crew began to fall, one by one, splashed with blood.

Belatedly, Victorine thought of herself and started to run, petticoats flying. If she could find a place to hide . . . She ran with terror slowing her legs and strangling her breath. She ran with her heart taking an uneven rhythm from her racing feet and her lungs blowing in disordered panic. She'd been seen, however, and her retreat was soon side-tracked by three warriors. She shouted again to Tobias, a sharper edge in her voice this time, as her flight was directed away from the river and the boat. Her scream was lost in the thud of horse hooves and the sough of wind.

Her hat, its bow shaken loose, fell off her head; her hair blew free of its pins. The warriors stopped her flight. She stood immobile, surrounded by them, her fingers over her mouth, staring with bright, wild eyes. They were in a gully on the far side of the knoll where she'd been standing before, separated from the main attack. In the sudden cessation of noise here, the grass continued to move with the wind, waist-high grass, soft, the color of ripe grain. Now the only other sound came from the Indians' horses which were blowing hard. Their bodies were mottled dark with sweat. Their riders slowly slid off their backs.

Three of them. Each with his hair in two long braids, wrapped and decorated with beads and feathers. They were nearly naked except for woven loin cloths, ankle-high moccasins, and ropes of beads that hung on their smooth chests from throat to navel. They had high-cheekboned faces, sharp, narrow-bridged noses, flat-lidded eyes, and fox-grins, full of teeth and no humor. They had her

49

cornered.

She gathered up her skirts and tried to escape, knowing it was hopeless. They toyed with her, let her run from one opening between them to another, closing it at the last moment. Their eyes twinkled at her from every direction. She thought, Oh my God, this can't be it. That was when she first understood that her life could end this quickly, without her ever having found how she wanted to live it.

With that cold knowledge, her panic dissolved. She felt surprisingly calm and even managed to look as if she'd regained her air of spirited arrogance. She discovered that she was the sort of person who, in extremity, became more self-contained than ever. Something resolved itself in her: it was a determination to handle whatever came.

The Indians moved in close. One came at her from the side. She didn't try to dodge him and when his hands were on her, the others moved in.

They took slow delight in tearing her clothes off her, piece by piece: her leather half boots, the small white muslin apron she wore to preserve her dress front, her close-fitting bodice with its high-fluted collar, her green calico skirt, the little wool-padded bustle she wore across her upper hips, and her chemise. Eventually she was down to nothing but her straight-legged cotton pantaloons. For a moment they let her keep those, but there were more indignities coming.

One man grabbed her around the waist from behind again, while the others yanked the underwear down her legs. There was a sharp ripping of material. Then the man holding her said something in a low voice. The others stood back while he released her. She was made to stand alone in the midst of them, completely naked now, her hair blown forward, surrounded by three menacing Blackfoot Indians with tomahawks and knives.

Her fragile beauty, foreign to them, seemed to give them a momentary sense of wonder — her white skin, her long, straw-yellow hair, her pale blue eyes. There was some jabbering now, while her fate was ruled.

The next instant they slammed her down into the grass and the scene dissolved with ghastly speed into a new kind of violence. In their black eyes was a clear picture of what they wanted to do with her now.

Yet this misery was hardly begun when a fourth person joined the group. The three who had been trying to spread her paused. Every eye was fixed on the newcomer; even Victorine waited breathlessly. She struggled to sit up against the hands on her, but fell back defeated.

The new Indian had on fresh paint; nothing about him seemed human, not even his eyes. There was no trace of the human in them, nor of the civilized; they were the hard glittering eyes of a predator looking at his prey. She thought a falcon must look like that when it moved to plunge and strike.

Savage Goat sat there on his red-spotted horse. The animal's high head was swinging; the chief's tall feather headdress fluttered in the wind. He studied Victorine, studied the gleam of light on her belly as soft as silk, then he gave a command that was obeyed on the spot. She was lifted and slung up behind him on his horse, and her wrists were tied around his waist.

The spotted horse's head tossed as he loosened the reins in his hands. When he hit the horse with his heels, it jumped forward. It set out at a gallop; chunks of earth were heaved high by its pounding

51

hooves. Savage Goat let out a high-pitched formless scream, an inhuman sound. Victorine smothered a cry.

He took her to the scene nearer the river. There was Jewel, struggling in the arms of a grinning young brave. She was as naked as Victorine and crying hysterically.

The red-spotted horse spun. And there was Tobias, wounded and bleeding on the ground. Victorine couldn't tell if he was dead or merely unconscious. The warrior straddling him was preparing to take his scalp. He made an ululation over his kill. The sound seemed to startle Jewel. Somehow she broke free of the brave holding her and made a dash for her husband. The scalping warrior saw her coming and defensively brought up his blade. Jewel had no time to stop her mad rush. The Indian *ki-yied* as he skewered her; then, unfeeling, he threw her limp body off his knife.

The young brave who had lost his hold on her tried to regain his honor now by striking her three times with his tomahawk. She died quickly as the other Indians screamed and milled about her. Meanwhile the warrior kneeling over Tobias bent back to his task.

Victorine cried out to the great empty wind of the plains against the horror, all the horror, the unbelievable horror . . .

"Wake up!" a rough voice called to her. "Wake up now!"

It wasn't Savage Goat's voice—the words were English—but when she opened her eyes a new bolt of terror struck her. She whimpered and pulled away from the vague head and large, bare shoulders looming over her in the dark. Her stomach turned giddily within her and she was afraid, desperately, unreasonably afraid.

"Nae, you're out of harm's way. I'm holding you, I am. 'Tis all right, lassie." Cougar took her to his chest, trying to quiet her with the strength of his arms and the security of his body, yet her grappling continued. He pinned her to him completely. " 'Tis all *right*."

"No! Don't! My God, don't . . . *don't!*" It was all confused, Tobias lying there, the brave hacking at Jewel's fallen body . . . and she could do nothing but sit by and see it happening.

"Nae, calm down!" Cougar was scowling now, with both his face and his voice. " 'Tis over! No more!" He added more softly, whispering, "Courage, my heart." And he kissed her cheek.

She began to cry, hard, dry sobs, for crying was an art in which she was unpracticed. "They killed them! They *murdered* them! Tobias . . . Jewel . . . *why?*"

Immensely strong arms held her, gently, and she unthinkingly crept even closer into their hard warm embrace, seeking the solace and safety that was offered there. Her body curved into his as utter misery blunted the edge of her awareness.

She hadn't known tears were so scalding. She could recall no moment in all the years since she'd crossed into womanhood when she had cried before. She lay trying to think what she should do to stop this.

However, when Cougar's lips grazed her forehead and her temple, the tears stopped abruptly. Panic beat up inside her once more. She realized that she was still naked. Even the heavy capote she'd worn wrapped about her to bed was mysteriously gone. And worse, the man who held her beneath this woolen blanket was naked as well. She forced her terror down until it was merely a sickening sensation in her stomach, for she had more immediate problems to deal with.

It was still mostly dark, though the night was loosening its hold. Her hair tumbled over her shoulders to cover her breasts, but that was all that separated her from Cougar. Their bodies were stretched full length together on the buffalo robe, her breasts flattened by his powerful chest. One of her knees was tangled between his hard-muscled thighs. His arms around her were steely, though his hands were being careful not to press her wounded shoulder. He was being gentle, he was soft spoken, yet he emanated a certain inner tension: he seemed both the safest man on earth and the most dangerous.

She drew the deep breath of the sleeper at last awake, saying, "Please let me go."

"Aye then, and you may go where you will." But he did no more than loosen his arms and leave it for her to extricate herself from the interweaving of their limbs. As she did, he smiled at her, unabashed.

She eased onto her sore back.

"Are you comfortable?"

"Yes, thank you," she replied, her cheeks faintly hot. She couldn't leave the bed altogether, for there was no hiding her nudity without the blanket (and no hiding his if she were to take it for herself).

She rubbed a lingering tear out of her eyes and looked up hard at the tops of the trees just visible in the dim pre-dawn haze. In a dreary little voice she asked, "Haven't you another blanket?"

He chuckled, his eyes gleaming with mischief before he also rolled to his back. His wide shoulder grazed hers, but she had no choice but to bear it.

"Nae, we sleep wing to wing and feather to

feather." His head rolled to look at her; his eyes were fixed on her bare shoulders and his expression was satyric. "And 'tis no' so easy on me as you think. I'm only a man, after all."

"Please don't." She covered her face with her hands as an unwanted vision of Jewel's body, bent over the Indian's blade, flashed before her eyes again. She saw the Indians swarming around, heard echoes of their wolflike howling. Her memories were tormenting her, confronting her with violence which a day ago had been totally beyond her experience, tearing her mind apart with glimpse upon glimpse into the hell she'd so narrowly survived.

"Forgive me," Cougar said, the words grinding like glass with self-disgust. He came up onto his elbow and put a tentative hand on her waist. "You have ghosts to grieve and I lay teasing you like a devil. You must tell me how it happened."

"No. It was hideous. They *mutilated* them." Even those words had to be forced out against great inner resistance.

His hand squeezed her side. "Let it out, lassie. 'Tis no good keeping such burdens on the mind."

She lowered her hands, clenched them into fists over her breasts, and said in a flinty little voice, "No, I've just got to get hold of myself. I must staunch it. I can't —" A sob checked her words. "Oh . . . I — I'm sorry, I don't usually carry on like this. I think I've g — got a bit of sunstroke."

"You've naught to be sorry for," he said with a touch of amazement. " 'Tis the most natural thing in the world to cry when you're heart's been split open. 'Tis necessary, like a clearing rain. Now you'll tell me about it — you'll feel better when you do."

The authority in his tone was all that was needed. And perhaps he was right. So, with her voice kept to a monotone, she told him all of it, beginning with how Tobias had lacked permission to cross into Indian Territory so that their small river party had avoided the widely spread military forts meant to prevent just such unauthorized whites from entering. She told him how the journey west had taken three months. No unnecessary details were included. In her flat, unemotional voice, the lengthy pilgrimage was made to sound commonplace.

Cougar eventually cut in. "You crossed half the breadth of North America, maid . . . why? No' many men even dare it. Why did you?"

"You must understand . . . Tobias was forty-three, nineteen years older than me. He left home when I was still a child. I hardly knew him at all until our father died last year. Even when I went to live with him, he was a hard man to know. I was trying to like him, to make him like me, I suppose. That's why I agreed to come with him."

And then, at his further urging, she described the attack: the war cries; the frieze of horses, their heads going like hammers and the dust lifting pale and thin behind them, moving like a string of dark beads toward the riverbank where the missionary party had paused for their noon meal.

"Why didn't they kill me, too?" She sounded unutterably weary. "Why was I the only one to live?" It seemed that she had failed Tobias somehow.

"Jewel would probably be alive, too, if she'd no' escaped the brave holding her. Mostly women are taken for slaves."

"But how can one human do things like that to another?"

He didn't seem to have any consoling answers. " 'Tis too bad you had to learn so much truth all in a day—that life is no' a fairytale, that the world is a

56

wicked place." He sighed hugely. "You be only a young woman. You should never have been exposed to such knowledge. What was your brother thinking of, bringing you out here? Did he no' ken that this country is full of Blackfeet and that their hearts are bad? All this is their hunting grounds, to the north and east. And they've bent their wills to the extermination of all whitefaces who dare to trespasss on it. They're a vengeful and dangerous people.

"Even other tribes have to evade them in order to hunt buffalo. Smaller tribes such as the Salish are being gradually prevented from entering the prairies at all, forced more and more to stay in the wooded valleys west of the Continental Divide where they can hunt only the glacier mountains for deer and mountain sheep, and harvest berries and camas roots. Even mountain men venture cautiously into this district, and most of them simply travel south of the river. Did no one tell your Tobias any of this?"

"Yes, Little Rattler tried. But Tobias was a brave man. He felt he had a mission—"

"He was mad."

For a moment her eyes were blank. For anyone to call the Reverend Tobias Wellesley mad! For her admired relative to be disposed of in words so terse and pungent! But then another tear straggled out of her eyes and trailed into the hair at her temple. "Yes, I think now that maybe he was. He thought . . . he believed a cloud moving ahead of us was God's personal message to him; he believed the country and the Indians could do no harm to him since 'Providence' went before him. I was afraid, and I think sometimes Jewel was, too, but Tobias . . . he believed he was chosen, and he was a hard man to reason with.

"Still, he was all I had—and now he's gone. They

57

butchered him."

Cougar lifted his hand to her face, sliding his knuckles across one high cheekbone, which was sunburned and windburned and sensitive. Then he threw the blanket off himself and rose. He moved out into the darkness, seemingly unconscious of his shocking nudity. When he came back, he said, "Sit up long enough to drink this."

She took the tin basin docilely and began to sip, staring at the blue brim, careful not to look at him as he got back under the blanket with her.

"Drink it all. 'Tis mostly water again. There's barely enough whiskey in it to warm you. Better now?" He took it back and set it aside.

She felt a need to keep talking as she lay back beside him. "Tobias wanted to bring Christianity to the Indians; that was his dream. I wouldn't have come—I didn't really want to come—but he could bully me, just like Father always could."

"I begin to see. Aye, that I do. He was one of those immoderately twittered faithfuls, following the lead of those Methodists who established a mission three years ago among the Salish—you would probably know them as the Flatheads, though their heads are as round as yours and mine."

"That was where we were headed, yes, to find the Flatheads." Her eyelids were growing heavy again. "I . . . . I'm so tired. Strange how whiskey makes one feel . . . rosy. I never knew."

Warm, comfortable, drowsy, and numb, she lay at the edge of a shallow pool of sleep, half hearing the sounds of the woods, half floating in surrender to blessed languor. She only vaguely recalled struggle, suffering, and death. It had all been farce really— and as in all tragedy, as history writes it, the lives of the humans involved were expendable.

The numbing effect of the whiskey had worn off. Victorine's mind began to circle, to seek a reason for the profound sense of danger with which she was waking. And memory, flying back, told her why.

She woke fully to the mingled scents of wood-smoke and dew, and she opened her eyes to find spatters of late morning sunlight coming down over her. She tried to sit up among them, but her mouth made a *moue* at the stabs of pain through her back, leg, and head. She lay still again for a short moment, steeling herself against the resistance that had settled in each muscle of her body. Then she sat up quickly, stiffly, catching the red woolen blanket against her breasts. With a movement of her hand she combed back her long hair, though it slid forward again almost immediately to frame her face. She felt too weak to bother with it, however, feeling no stronger than a single strand of that ripe-wheat-colored hair.

Cougar's camp was better revealed to her in the light. They were in an aspen grove beside a grassy meadow with a stream in it. The steep cliff face of a buffalo plateau came close to the opposite bank of the water. Cougar's iron-gray horse grazed out in the open meadow between the creek and the trees. The smaller pack horses stood four square in their hobbles, like carvings, absorbing the sun.

Cougar himself, dressed in his buckskins, was squatted with his back to Victorine beyond the small fire ring. His tomahawk hung from a limb not far away, above where his rifle leaned, and his knife was ready at his belt. He was rummaging in a parfleche. He extracted a large handful of dried meat strips. His mocassins were muddy, and Victorine deduced that he'd been walking along the stream already.

"Breakfast is coming," he said, though he hadn't looked directly at her. By some intuition, or a keenly tuned sense of hearing, he'd known that she was awake. "I've no' had a chance to hunt for a day or two, but we've plenty of jerky for now." He rose, brought two tin plates, and placed one in her lap before sitting cross-legged on the end of the buffalo robe with the other.

She realized that she was very hungry, shaking with hunger, in fact. Not ready to face him, she looked down at the food he'd given her instead. Along with the dried meat there was a mound of fresh blackberries. She tried one, found it tart but juicy and marvelous, and abandoned herself to eating. Even the dry meat tasted wonderful to her.

When she felt less jittery, she said, "I was a little overwrought last night. I apologize for making a scene."

The comfortable crackle of the small blazing fire was her only answer. Cougar got up, crossed the carpet of golden leaves to dig another handful of meat out of the parfleche. He put it on her plate. He also scraped what was left of the purple berries on his own plate into hers—with a slightly overstated courtesy that made her blush.

"Eat," he said.

She astonished herself as she went at these second helpings ravenously. A basin of steaming sage tea appeared beside her. It too tasted exquisite. She ate and drank with single-minded concentration until she at last felt strong enough to actually look at him.

"You've rested; your eyes are clear now," he said.

He'd put his own plate aside and was sewing something out of soft-looking doeskin. She'd never

60

seen a man sew before; it made him seem less intimidating, although there was nothing dainty or artistic to his sewing. He punched holes in the leather with a bone awl, thrust his needle through it and pulled the leather through one hole after another.

She asked, "Are we safe here? I mean, we can't be very far from the Blackfoot camp."

"They'll have gone by now. They spotted a party of Crows yesterday riding hell-bent across what the Blackfeet consider their territory and were planning a chase."

"They're very bloodthirsty. Why is it they didn't kill you?"

"I once did a favor for them. 'Twas a piece of luck really. I was watching them hunt—hiding out and hoping no' to be seen—and saw one of their lads fall off his horse. A bull buffalo charged him, and—'twas something I did without thinking first, you know—I shot the old bull. Turned out the laddie was a chief's son. Now they call me Buffalo Killer and let me pass through their territory, though I do no' test the privilege any more often than necessary."

She considered this. Then, because he seemed an honorable man—heroic even—and because her courage was bolstered by a full stomach now, she said, "You didn't really mean what you said last night, did you? About keeping me?"

# Chapter Five

Victorine gave Cougar a brave little smile. He kept working his needle, but his cloudy-green eyes skipped up to hers. "You do no' understand yet." He reached for his belt-knife to cut the strip of buffalo sinew he was using for thread, knotted it, and put his project aside. He replaced the awl in its sheath of carved wood.

She felt overcome with nervousness again. "Well, I realize you paid a lot to rescue me, and I'm sorry if you're disillusioned about what you got. And of course," she appended hastily, minding her manners, "I'm grateful for your high estimation of me and honored by your proposal—but I'm not the kind of woman who—that is, I never thought I'd make a very good—" Her composure entirely gone, she was quivering like a steam engine again. "What I'm trying to say is—" With a terrible wrenching effort, she brought it out: "Some women were never meant for marriage. I don't think I was. No, I shouldn't be a bit successful at it. I would end up making any man I married very unhappy. I'm just an old maid, you see. I've come to terms with my life; it might seem meager to others, but it's got its rewards, its dignity, and—" When she saw the slight movement of his eyelids, she simply gave up.

His face was shuttered, his eyes half shut, hiding his expression. "Whatever you've been before, you're my wife now."

He filled her basin with more tea. She sipped it in silence for several minutes, her musings in a turmoil. It seemed he was giving her time to consider. He seemed very practiced in gallantry for a backwoodsman.

At length, smoothing her hair with fingers that still trembled, she met his eyes again. He'd been waiting, she saw, and now he said, softly, "Pleasing a man is the ancient habit of woman. Listen to the womanliness inside yourself."

A flicker of fear crossed her eyes and then was hidden. She was determined to remain unperturbed, to keep her imagination from rioting away with her common sense. Nothing could be gained if she gave way to fear. She gathered the blanket tighter to herself. "Look, Mr. —"

"Cougar." This was said patiently, as from instructor to pupil.

"Very well, Cougar." She was abrupt now, unconciliatory. She was determined to show him just how strongly she resented his position. "I have no intention of 'pleasing' you, or any other man."

"You're that sure?" There was a quality of silence about him, a silence like the warning of an ambush.

She swallowed heavily, clearing her voice, fighting for coherent thought. She was resolved that he shouldn't see her dismay. "I don't believe you would force me. You don't seem the sort . . . you couldn't—" To her distress her voice was unsteady.

She noticed too late that he had a mouth that could tense in a second to express unrelenting resolu-

63

tion. It tensed thusly now, and his face reassembled itself into something more callous than it had been. "Let me do what I can to clarify the situation. If I'd no' bought you, you would already be Savage Goat's squaw — several times over, no doubt — and no' fed on blackberries and patient words, your virtue safely intact."

He hadn't moved at all, yet he'd grown threatening in her eyes, looked larger than before.

"Now I'll tell you what you are and what you'll be to me — so you can weigh what you're up against. I'll explain it to you this time as I would to a bairn — or a saint unwitting of the world — how mountain law permits me to join with you; and, if you insist, I can demonstrate rather less delicately how that joining can be accomplished should you set yourself against me."

He paused, then began again more pleasantly, "If I freed you today you would be lost. You're that dependent upon me. I say this no' to gloat, but to state the facts. To begin with, you would go hungry." His eyes flicked to her plate, twice emptied. She felt herself flush. "Poor little morning flower, I wish I could make this interview less painfully honest."

"Not at all," she said quickly. "I realize perfectly that I must rely upon your experience . . . for a while. And I'm grateful, really, for all you've done so far."

She was. He'd come as a shelter in a time of storm. Savage Goat . . . she rubbed a hand across her eyes to wipe out the visions of that intolerable alternative, visions of the Indian's bronze face smeared with red ocher.

When she looked at Cougar again, she found him studying her with cool interest. "You're grateful, aye, yet you believe I should act the gentleman and protect you, feed you, and clothe you, all without even thinking of placing you under any obligation to me in return."

"Well, it is rather churlish of you, under the circumstances."

His eyebrows shot up, accordion-pleating his brow, and he said, a bit craftily, "Ah, the circumstances, but that's where your argument fails, lassie.

"Out here, life is pared down to basic necessities: powder and lead, traps, horses, a shirt and a pair of breeks, a blanket, a knife, flints and steel. Luxuries are few and no' to be squandered: coffee, sugar, when a man can get it, an hour with a woman—any woman.

"Do you begin to see? Here we be, at the very base of the Shining Mountains, and you seem to have no man but me to protect you. I've already held you close against me in my bed . . . You're mine, 'twould appear."

"But I have my rights, surely! We live in the nineteenth century, not the Middle Ages. Has it escaped your attention that I'm a citizen of the United States of America and protected by laws—not at the mercy of every passing rapist?"

"Some laws are more ancient than those of the United States of America. This place that belongs to the Indians and a few mountain men, 'tis an enormity. Too enormous for any authority to guarantee a lone woman's rights. Even your young and chivalrous colonial government can hardly be expected to send a company of dragoons all the way from St. Louis—with a pack train, arms, and foodstuffs such as journeys like that take—all in pursuit of a man who has acquired himself a wife."

"You know it's wrong, though!"

"Do I? Last night I bought you; I made a mountain marriage, recognized here by white men and red men alike. You're mine now, by the law of this land. And I'm looking forward to taking my refreshment of you and giving you refreshment in return. That's as it should be . . . and how it shall be."

"Refreshment?" A faint pink blush appeared on her face. "But you say nothing of love."

"To a person like myself love might prove an inconvenience. And I should warn you, too, before you damn me for a rogue and defy me to my face, that I can divorce myself of you as readily as I married you. Should you no' give me the delight I expect you will, I can tell you to leave my camp — and you'll have to go. If I feel a little at fault for the situation, or pity you some, I might provide you with a small bundle of supplies to help you on your way — or I might no', depending on how charitable I'm feeling."

She drew herself up. "I think you're making the mistake of equating me with an Indian woman. I'm not a squaw."

"Aye, and more's the pity, because the husband of a squaw is a lucky man. Besides getting a comfortable and interesting bedmate, he gets a helpmate with an unrivaled education in the art of marital partnership. If you were a squaw you would eagerly dress my furs, make my robes, moccasins and breeks, raise and strike my shelter and keep the inside of it clean and orderly, supervise my equipment, administer my horses, skin the meat I bring in, and carry my wood and water."

He was gazing at her with the totally uninterested look one bestows on servants. It aroused sudden sharp antagonism in her which perhaps showed in her face as she gave him a look that would have frozen the sun at high noon. "I think I could learn to dislike you."

"If that's what you want, I think I could teach you," he countered, his smile bland. "Shall I try?" His eyes had lost their previous disinterest and had become startlingly observant.

Her own glance faltered and fell.

"Nae," he pressed, "mayhap we should test ourselves right now, your will against mine." There was an expression on his face—a dreadful resolution.

All in an instant, with the swiftness of the cougar for which he was named, he was poised over her, forcing her to shrink back so that the sun dappled her face again. "You do recognize my will, do you no'?" He took the plate from her lap and tossed it away, lying down close to her at the same time, so that the whole length of his body was pressing hers. She could smell the clean tang of wood resin on him.

"You're no' under the impression that this is a game I'm playing with you, are you?" His arm went under her neck, catching her head in the crook made by his elbow, while his free hand pushed down the blanket to seize the curve of her waist. Now she writhed to get free. Yet he was strong! Stronger than she'd ever believed or known a man could be. His chest was rigid against her defending hands. She was forced to look up into two very honest gray eyes, which didn't waver upon meeting hers. There she lay, half-naked, half-beneath him, her elegant breasts shuddering.

Slowly, those gray eyes holding hers mercilessly, he lowered his mouth, drawing out the approach as if to prove his total control of the situation. His lips touched hers lightly, briefly, then touched them again. She was more than surprised by this first touch of a man's mouth—surprised by the gentleness of it. Still, she tried to dodge her head away, but his arm, unlike his tender mouth, was a metal brace.

"I could take you here and now, as Savage Goat would have done already—painfully, without a thought to your injuries, and certainly no' to your sensibilities. I want you at least as badly as he did, and probably much more, given the fact that in the end he was persuaded to part with you, while I paid an outrageous price. I'm only holding myself back for the time being, but 'twill no' always be so."

She felt his muscles harden about her and his kiss was repeated again and again. "Please don't!" she whispered between times, helpless in the clamped steel of his embrace.

"I'm no' going to force you. But I could. Think on it." His eyes remained on her mouth and again he bent his head. Again his lips came down on hers, this time lingering, insisting. With a shock, she felt his tongue slide over her lips. This was strangeness passing the unknown! She opened her mouth a little to protest, and that was all he needed. She whimpered as he introduced the soft flame of his tongue between her teeth.

His previous tender kisses hadn't prepared her for this. She felt herself grow weak. Fleetingly she considered biting down, but didn't dare. Or was it that she didn't want to, since what he was doing was so novel and, yes, slightly pleasant?

Where was the physical outrage she should be feeling? Something was happening to her. To her mind. Her capacity for forming rational thought. Her hands on his chest floundered as her fear was blunted by this new thing, this thing that relied more on the reasoning of nerve endings than on the reasoning of the mind.

68

He seemed to sense the change in her, and his exploration of her mouth became bolder. His lips moved on hers, and she felt something flower in her, something warm and voluptuous. Her fear was shading into quite a different emotion. She began to notice how he tasted of blackberries. She inadvertently moved her own mouth in an echoing response. Strangely, she felt in league with him now, not set against him. The hand on her waist slid upward beneath her breast, moved up to cup it. His thumb brushed over the top of the silken globe, hardening it instantly to a nub.

But then, abruptly, he finished the kiss; his head lifted an inch. He inhaled once, twice, as if he'd been running and needed to catch his breath. He had a look on his face, an odd blurred look. She'd never had a man look at her quite that way before. His hand was still on her breast, but she didn't push it away. She was too riveted by that look.

She understood in some instinctual way just what it meant; he was showing her that he was in earnest. He wanted her beneath him. He was resisting a tremendous need to triumph over her, to penetrate her and exhaust himself within her deepest depths until he lay drained and gasping over her. Yes, he wanted her, and was exercising the sternest self-control to keep himself from taking her this very minute.

She lay quietly, beyond fear and on the far side of humiliation. "Let me go. You've proved your point," she breathed. "I concede that you're the stronger."

"Strength was no' the question." His eyelids flickered. "Though, as you see, it does admit its own prerogatives here."

"I'm from another world and we live by different rules." She tried to sound merely tired and irritable.

69

"Be no' deceived by my patience and sympathy. As of this day you live by my rules—and I will hear you agree to that 'afore we're finished." He watched her face as his fingers moved again on her breast, encircling it now with gentle pressure.

She closed her eyes against the blatant challenge. He was daring her to try to stop him. What kind of man could he be? How should she proceed in regards to him? He was so hard to place as a recognizable human type. Was he a villain or merely an ordinary man who sincerely believed he was her husband because he'd paid for her, or . . . was he human at all? Her stockpile of adjectives failed to pin him down. Well, he seemed to be in charge for the moment.

His hand continued to take liberties with her, awakening dreadful desires in her. She was soon shivering all over. Drawing in a ragged breath, she said, "All right, I concede that you may impose your rules upon me—for the time being; however, I recall a promise that you would give me some time."

The movement of his hand stopped. His arm lowered her back to the buffalo robe and pillowed her head there. His hand came up to play with her hair, which lay over the robe like pale, spread straw of sunlight. He was no longer constraining her actively, yet she sensed it would still not be wise to attempt an escape.

"I do no' want to use force. This was a demonstration only; I assure you that I would rather be tender, given the opportunity."

"I see; you would rather I *let* you violate me."

"It need no' be a violation. I noticed you began to like it when I kissed you."

"I was momentarily stunned. I'm not used to being invaded so."

70

He didn't quite manage to hide his smile. "Then I must stun you often. Aye, mayhap that's the way." His tone was mischievous. Then he added more seriously, "You did like my kissing; do no' deny you did."

Her lips compressed; her proud spirit rallied. "This is all very interesting, but if you don't mind, my back is uncomfortable; I'd like to sit up." In truth, her shoulder was throbbing like a rotten tooth.

He lifted himself lazily. "Aye, 'tis time I took a look at you anyway—but feel free to reopen this discussion any time you're belabored with doubts about just what I intend."

As she sat, he shifted to kneel behind her. His hands gathered her hair, swinging it over her right shoulder to expose the left. He made a disapproving sound. "You put up with that all night? Sweet Jesus! I've bought me a braw one. I beg your pardon for causing you to lie on this even for a moment. You must forgive me for it, my mind was momentarily full of anticipation, excluding all else."

"It's nothing," she said, shivering and wincing involuntarily at his feathery examining touches.

His voice was clipped. "Naught to a dumb animal, mayhap, unable to feel pain."

"It's only bruised and scratched some, I imagine."

"Aye, bruised, and scratched some—but they did no' shatter your shoulder blade—no' quite." He sat back on his heels, his hands still holding her upper arms in a painlessly firm grip. " 'Twill have to be cleaned thoroughly—scrubbed right open." His tone was edged with hardness.

"Surely not."

He sighed, and moved to face her, resting on one knee with his forearm propped against his other thigh. "You must ken that ever since your departure from St. Louis your life has been suspended by a filament over the abyss; the slightest misadventure could prove lethal. Your brother and sister-in-law have already fallen. You somehow survived their fate. But should you develop a fever now, there's no doctor to come to let your blood or soothe your delirium with laudanum. Here we must encourage wounds to bleed on their own, thereby cleansing themselves."

What he said made absolute sense, yet she swallowed. "Very well. How shall I do it?"

"I'll do it — in yon burn." He nodded toward the creek. "The gouge in your thigh, too. I've no' forgotten it and fully intend to treat it as well, so 'twill do you no good to try to hide it from me."

Which meant he wouldn't stand for any prim attempts to preserve her modesty. What he'd bought he would take proper care of, regardless.

He relaxed at her side, saying, "Think of it this way: I honestly regard you as my good wife, someone requiring all my concern and protection. And if you can no' call me husband yet, then at least admit that I'm the only person on earth you can look to to keep you alive."

She understood this proposition and the logic that lay beneath it. And the truth was, she was in ghastly difficulty. He could save her life. He was a mountain man; he could cope with this wilderness. She really had no choice.

"Trust me," he prompted.

"Yes, I must, I suppose, to a degree."

He smiled. It was an illuminating smile. She was briefly dazzled by it and suffused by a curious sense of safety. His hair was rather long, and a velvety gust of wind blew it across his forehead in a thick

72

fringe. She remembered his story of how he'd gotten the name Cougar. He'd killed a vicious wild animal with little else but his bare hands. To argue with such a man was to no purpose.

"Aye, I'll settle for trust — to a degree. The rest will fall into place naturally, I think. Things are all as they best may be. You must no' worry about it. I'll look after you."

"I'm deeply moved," she said briskly, sitting straighter, trying to regain her former feelings of mutiny, "but I'm not an infant, all tears and troubles, to be 'looked after.' "

He laughed then. "Lassie, has no one ever told you 'tis best for the innocent never to spar with the desperately wicked?"

His gray-green eyes were shining so oddly; her mouth went dry. Her throat contracted painfully. "Why me?" she whispered. She felt disquieted, unsure again. "You must have been content without a wife before."

He merely smiled again, absently. "But even in contentment I often felt the need. I was half hunting, seeking the wildest beauty in the mountain world. When I was sent to the Blackfeet, I did no' believe I would find her; but then I saw the very one. Two soft jewels fixed in her face, her hair pouring around her without a sound, her courage as stubborn as the flame of a single small candle in the darkest, draftiest kirk . . . aye, 'twas you." His voice was serious now and peculiarly gentle, while his deep eyes were more searching than ever. "I knew you at once. And I had to have you."

Her stomach froze tight. "And it makes no difference to you that I'm to be sullied beyond redemption by this squalid experience?" Her neck felt rigid with the effort of self-control.

He only laughed again, lifting his hand to touch the tip of her nose with one finger.

Scraping the barrel of her unsophisticated word stock, she thought of him as a boor, a blackguard, a rip, a rake, a person without gentlemanly instincts. But all the while she was marking him down in this fashion she was fully aware that inches from her was a man more worldly than her, stronger, and ablaze with virility.

She looked at him, face disciplined, expressionless, eyes clear and empty. Will we live in the open then, like this?"

"Nae, I'll be taking you to my lodge. Wintertime nighs."

"And how long do you plan to keep me there?"

"Why, forever."

Absurd! He couldn't keep her like a stray puppy. Was he insane? Keep her forever? Nonsense! He was just swaggering. He couldn't get away with this abduction forever. He couldn't. She would find a way back to civilization — though civilization seemed irretrievably lost to her already, too dim and distant to be regained.

She fought to keep her face from breaking up with anguish. "Have you no sense of honor at all? Your own countrymen wouldn't condone what you're doing."

"But they would. Our marriage was performed in accordance with age-old Scots law — declared before witnesses. 'Tis a custom still used on occasion, and considered perfectly legal."

"You classify those Indians as witnesses?"

"Aye, I told them I wanted you for a wife. I deem the union binding in all ways, lassie." He was still smiling. "You're too stubborn to agree to it yet, but

-74

I'll change your mind." He bent and kissed her mouth tenderly. "So independent and brave," he mused.

His lips left hers moist and tingling. "Please let me go," she whispered. "I can't live intimately with a man I don't even know—let alone love!"

Amusement flickered over his chiseled features. "I suggest then that you fall in love with me, and 'afore too long."

"I can't love to order. And besides, you said you would give me time," she said, and hated the pleading in her voice.

"Aye, and I will. You do no' have to keep reminding me. I've said so, haven't I? There's your bereavement to be gotten through, and your hurts to be healed—and your bashfulness to be downed. You're still too nervous, too shy of me—bonny, oh aye!—but like a doe, all ears and eyes and fright." There was warm indulgence in his tone. "Time, aye, and time can crumble all."

He was going to indulge her—for a while—but she was in his power nonetheless. In the power of a perfect stranger who wanted to know her intimately. Her good sense told her there wouldn't be any immediate escape from him.

As if he could read her mind, could sense her tallying-up of the facts, his smile was rich with satisfaction.

The sun had crossed its zenith and was moving toward the western part of the sky. Now the day danced with heat. At the edge of the wide, shallow stream, Victorine paused. She almost stepped on a sleepy, blinking toad. It flopped away through the reeds. The water was crystal clear; she could see the golden, rainbowed sides of the fish that lived in it. Hugging Cougar's capote about her, stalling for time, she said, "If you would just leave me alone, I'm sure I could lie in the water and soak the wounds clean."

"It might work — if you stayed in there long enough," Cougar said. "Meanwhile, I guarantee you would die of the chill you would catch. This is snowmelt."

"Even so, I'm sure I can manage on my own." And if she did catch a bit of a chill, wouldn't he have to give her just that much more time? She felt like a captive virgin of long ago, searching out a way of escape . . . or stalling for a more gallant rescuer.

He put his rifle down (she was already learning that he never for a moment put his rifle more than a few feet from his grasp) and reached for the lacings of the capote, saying, "Get in the burn, lassie." She took a quick step backwards. He followed with a sigh. "There's no sense in prolonging the inevitable."

Still, she clutched the garment about her.

"Remember how you stood at that pow-wow last night? You had courage then."

She recalled the circumstances well enough. "It's not that I'm afraid . . . oh, very well! Let's get it done with."

"A wise decision."

Still she waited. She couldn't help flushing a little, with his gaze on her.

"Will you undress yourself," he asked, "or will I?"

She glared at him as if wishing him dead, but threw the capote off her shoulders nonetheless. Immediately she moved to the stream's reedy edge and waded out to the middle, affording him as brief a view of her bare legs and buttocks as she could. Ignoring the cold, she sat down and wriggled her

76

toes into the pebbly sand.

She felt a fish brush past her, a mere slither of silk that made her shudder. The water was barely deep enough to cover her, and was so crystaline it hardly concealed anything. Her breasts were as white as the flesh of apples, while her nipples already had gone dark, almost red, in the icy cold.

She heard Cougar wading in behind her, felt him lower himself, saw his legs stretch out on either side of hers. She had a momentary hysterical urge to laugh. She'd never seen a grown man's bare knees and feet before. His lower thighs were thickly muscled, the calves bunched. He seemed more human suddenly, less impersonal. Yet that realization didn't reassure her at all.

Water ran off her arms as she lifted them to sweep her hair aside for him. "Do it quickly."

## *Chapter Six*

Cougar gripped Victorine's shoulders and pulled her toward him, dunking her to the chin before pushing her upright again. " 'Twill hurt some."

"I'm prepared for that."

Yet she waited on for him to begin. "Well? I won't whimper and squeal, if that's what's holding you back. Please just get it over with."

And so he began. She held to her promise and made not a sound, and though her face reflected what she felt, she turned it into the hair over her right shoulder so he couldn't see.

At long last he pulled her backwards again, and cradled her there, careful not to disturb what he'd accomplished. She stared up at the blue sky so far above. The numbing stream gradually washed away much of the pain, yet an involuntary tremor ran through her. He must have felt it, for his grip tightened. He tipped her back further, until her hair floated in the sunlit water, so he could see her face. "Forgive me," he said.

"I'm all right." She even managed a small smile.

"You'll have to stand so I can clean your leg."

She did so, but stumbled and naturally reached to

78

balance herself with her hands on his shoulders. She felt his muscles brace to take her weight. She felt his skin, the texture of it, the cool wet slipperiness of it, beneath her fingertips. She shuddered with surprise as the impact of pleasure ran through her. He looked up, his eyes soft and thoughtful. It wasn't the first time she'd seen compassion in them.

When the brown crust over the smaller but deeper wound in her thigh was gone, and the raw place was bleeding freely, he placed his hands on her hips to draw her back down into the stream with him. Her own hands relaxed on his shoulders which she realized now that she'd been gripping hard, for there were red finger marks in his golden-brown skin.

"We can let you heal now."

She was moved by the relief in his face. "Thank you." She almost said more, but a sensible reserve intervened and held her back. This was a situation which called for care, for calculation, for calm. If she'd yearned to be a heroine awaiting some wild lover to carry her off and make her his pagan princess, this might possibly seem an attractive and romantic farce, but quite definitely that was one role she'd never wished to play.

She was hunched down, as much to try to conceal herself as to give her back a good rinse. The water was up to her neck when he scooped his arms under her knees and lower back. Water ran off them both in shimmering torrents as he rose.

"Put me down!"

"When we reach the bank."

"You're making me dizzy!"

"Hold on to me then. Put your arms round my neck—tighter than that!" His laugh rang out arrogantly.

She wished, as she felt the cool, hard nape of his

neck, that he would just put her down. Instead, he carried her out of the stream, placing his feet carefully along the soft bottom, and set her down on the spread capote. "Do no' be covering yourself all up now. Let the sun dry you."

The sun did feel good after the aching cold of the stream. There had been a few puffy clouds above the tree tops earlier, but high, unfelt winds had herded them to some other part of the sky. The tall reed beds shut out any breeze, and the white sand threw the sun's heat back at her. She gave herself up to its heady warmth and to the sound of the birds making their honey calls.

Cougar reentered the stream and, as unself-consciously as a wild animal, bathed himself. He used sand to scour his skin, and employed a good deal of dunking and splashing.

Victorine was fascinated. She wished she could believe he was as harmless as he was attractive—a huge, brainless, compliant man. But honesty wouldn't permit such a string of lies. He was huge, yes, and most definitely a man, but he gave no indication of being either brainless or compliant. In fact his speech and reasoning had already convinced her that he was extremely well educated. And he had the manners of a European courtier. As far as compliant, well, he was rather likable, and seemed to have extraordinary gifts, but, she thought, he was also pretty unscrupulous. He played all his cards—if not more.

Her mind wandered, she fell to musing: so this is how a man bathes, this is what his armpits look like, and his bare back. Yet she doubted if most men's backs looked like Cougar's. Tobias, for instance, had been a much slimmer man. Cougar's back was definitely muscled, so wide and boned at the shoulders. His neck, she believed, was also thicker than most men's. Had she ever seen a man's neck so thick? She couldn't recall, but then she'd seldom, if ever, considered men's necks before. Or their arms. Or the narrowness of their hips. And certainly not their male parts. Funny, those, looking so innocuous when—

*Victorine!*

Caught unawares by this maiden examination of purely masculine beauty, she swung her eyes upstream. But not soon enough, evidently, for she heard Cougar chuckle as he splashed his way toward her.

He flung himself face down on the grassy ground. She turned sideways, primly. She could hardly complain of his indecency when she herself sat there as naked as a newborn, yet this situation was as unseemly as any she could imagine.

The cold water was dripping off her shoulders onto her breasts, making little goosepimples there, forming drops that clung to the tips of the nipples. She became conscious of him watching this process, and turned completely around, giving him the view of her raw back.

"Savage Goat was that pleased with himself last night. Aye, he brought you over to the fire to show you off. 'Hair paler than the hair of the yellow cougar,' he said."

Revulsion swept over her. For a long breath or two she said nothing, then, "If the way I was treated was an indication of his pleasure, I would hate to see him annoyed. He very nearly pulled my hair out by its roots."

Cougar reached to run a fingertip along her lower spine, catching a trickle of water and carrying it to his tongue. She shivered and scooted further away.

"Please keep your hands to yourself."

After a moment he said, "You're a hard lass, and no mistake."

She heard him moving, and glanced over her shoulder to see him roll onto his side, resting his head on his hand. And the glance confirmed as well that he was taut with sexual desire. She turned her head away again quickly.

He murmured after a long drowsy pause, "I feel that pleased myself, right now."

"I don't know why," she answered archly. "By your own account I'm nothing but a liability to you. I've cost you who knows how many months work trapping those beaver skins; I'm uneducated in the work of a squaw, and—as you pointed out so graphically—I can't even feed or clothe myself. It seems to me you would want to be rid of me as soon as possible, even if it meant a detour to a fort."

"Still hoping for a fairytale ending?"

"I was never told any fairytales, so I wouldn't know about that. I'm just saying that if I were you, I would have headed straight for the nearest fort last evening."

He chuckled. "And if I were you I would foresee a fine future for myself in the law courts."

His voice behind her was twinkling with amusement. When she glanced back, his eyes seemed unnaturally transparent; she found it impossible to look away this time.

She became aware of the ridges down his abdomen and stomach. They were long and leathery. The whole right ride of his belly was wealed with old lacerations. The sun had gilded them, but they were there, mute reminders of endured suffering.

"You see how hard to best I am?" he said softly. "Even the cougar failed. Come along with me as a good wife should. 'Tis the only way for you. To be trying anything more desperate would no' be worth the risk to your own hide."

A good wife. *His* good wife. Could she bear it?

Of course she could. She wasn't a sissyish type of female.

But she didn't want to.

Partly it was simple defiance. She'd resisted marriage over the years by resisting any closeness with men. There had been several who had shown more than passing interest in her looks, but she'd discouraged them. She'd grown up having her father invade her thoughts and actions until it seemed there was nothing left to her. And she'd been indifferent about trading that paternal control for a husband's control. At least under her father she had a bedroom to go to where she could be alone — a place to think through a few clandestine thoughts, have a few fantasies, dream a few dreams, a place belonging exclusively to her.

And partly it was simple cowardice. She realized that she simply didn't feel grown up enough to face an alliance with a man. She had to suppress a fastidious shudder at the very idea. It was as though she'd masqueraded all these years in a grown woman's skirts, play-acted.

Cougar was regarding her musefully, and it seemed almost as if he'd been listening to her thoughts. " 'Tis a pity I can no' court you with Sunday carriage rides and little presents of lace and pearls. I ken these past two days have been nightmarish for you, but you must try to accept this as something you can no' reverse. You're my bride; soon you'll be my mate, my woman, my partner on the trail and through the glens and up to the highest peaks —"

83

"Where exactly is this place we're going to?" she interrupted in despair.

He smiled. "In the mountains."

"*Where* in the mountains?"

High up."

He pushed himself onto his knees. He seemed to move like some easy, mythical creature, unbound by the rules of the civilized world. Like a Greek god, he seemed able to give comfort or torment while feeling neither. She sat enthralled, watching him. But then she faced away again. Her voice, when she found it, was a bit tart. "Must you be so brazen?"

"You find me ugly?"

For some reason this maddened her beyond tolerance. She might have screamed were it not for all her hard-learned breeding. "That's not the point!"

"Then what is the point? I thought you would feel less shy if I sat naked, too."

She prayed for forbearance. It was so awful sometimes to be female and have so little control of one's existence. "I don't believe that for a minute. You're simply trying to seduce me."

"Is it working?"

She didn't answer.

"Mayhap you would like to touch me. 'Twould allay some of your misconceived fear, I think."

She wanted to speak, but her throat closed and no sound came. The man had a peculiar and uncomfortable ability to put a finger gently wherever the sore place was.

He didn't wait for an answer, but sat beside her, facing her, his naked chest and belly full in the light, his legs sprawled out so that he was boldly exhibited. He was smiling at her in a way that made her breathless and frightened. He had very much the look of a man who had every right to display himself openly before her, and to look at her openly as well.

"I'm not frightened."

"Nae? Prudish then. And a married woman should no' be too steeped in prudery."

*Too steeped in prudery!*

"Married or not, it is detestable and improper to allow another to look at one naked!"

"If the sight I show you here were so detestable to you, you would no' have kept glancing back at it under your eyelashes. Admit the truth now, you're fascinated with what you see. Go ahead, touch me as you will."

She couldn't even look at him now.

"Come, you want to touch me." He paused, waiting to see if she would, then shook his head. "You amaze me by being at least four-and-a-half different people rolled into one. The way you keep them together in that bonny tight skin—without them quarreling anymore than they seem to—is remarkable."

He reached for her hand, brought it to his mouth with another one of his brilliant, sparkling smiles, and touched his lips to the inside of her wrist. He cupped her open palm to his jaw. His message was clear: He was utterly at her disposal. "Touch me, lassie. Start with my face. I know you're curious; I saw you watching me. Be brave. I will; I promise I'll no' flinch from it."

There was no ill will in his eyes. He seemed perfectly serious. Her palm drifted down his jaw, down his neck. Her fingertips grazed his hard collarbones. With a tentative timid forefinger she tested the foremost muscle of his powerful left arm. She hadn't known there were such men, with such bodies . . .

She snatched her hand back. "No!"

His lips gave a quirk. "Your mind's like a tough spring. I'm afraid 'twill have to be mightily stretched, and even then, every instant 'tis left to itself, 'twill no doubt fly right back to its tight coil." He sighed. "Well, all right then, if you do no' appreciate my offer, I might as well get dressed."

She heard him behind her, pulling his breeches and shirt on.

She still felt stunned with what she'd done. How could she have let him mesmerize her like that, even for a moment? She'd barely withdrawn her hand in time.

Suddenly she turned to face him. "Who are you?"

He laughed and knelt on one knee behind her, inspecting her back again. "I told you last night. I'm the Waiting Cougar."

She stared at the moving water, screwed up her eyes against the glare, and tried to recall last night; but at this moment she could only see the sun in the water and could only remember waking to find his warmth around her when she was frightened.

"Come here," he said softly.

"What are you doing now? I can walk!" She knew she was helpless to stop him from taking her into his arms again, but she felt safer in struggling and arguing.

Lifting her, he said, "You can grab the capote, and you can stop trembling. Do you mind me now? 'Tis no' an ogre who has you!"

She went still and small as he packed her back to the grove of big aspens and placed her on the buffalo robe.

There was a breeze to be felt on this higher ground, and the trees lifted their soft limbs into it, moving like the arms of dancers. From the pot hanging over the fire came a rich, meaty-smelling steam. The place was beginning to feel like home.

"Now for some medicine." He went to rummage among his possibles bags until he found a vial made from the tip of an antelope horn.

"What's that?" she asked suspiciously. Even from a distance it smelled potent, wild, and foul.

He looked at the uncapped contents a little suspiciously himself. "Beaver's oil and castoreum." In the cathedral hush under the trees his words carried clearly. " 'Tis what I bait my traps with."

"I thought you said it was medicine."

"Aye. 'Tis what they plastered me with after my wrestling match with the cougar, and it seemed to help."

He was already begining to apply a coat of the greasy red-brown stuff to her back. She'd been holding the capote over her breasts for decency's sake, but when he moved to her leg he unceremoniously flipped the covering aside and pulled her thigh toward him.

"Ouch!" she said bitterly. "Must you be so liberal with that?" She was fast losing interest in his brand of surgery.

"Sorry." His tone was heartless. "It stings some, does it no'?'

"A fact you failed to mention before smearing it all over my open flesh."

He grinned, one hand lingering on her knee, stroking softly. His face was very near hers and there was a restless light in his eye. The sun lit the edges of his hair to a coppery glow. She felt the steady heat of his fingers moving at will up and down her leg — and she thought it best to distract him quickly. "Who are 'they'?" She nodded toward the antelope horn vial, then looked up at him through her eyelashes. "When you were injured—who tended you?"

With a smile half-mocking, half-admiring, he watched her a moment longer, then reached for the wooden plug he used to cap the horn. "The Salish — the Flatheads, some call them."

Climbing on this topic with excessive eagerness, she said, "The tribe Tobias was going to teach."

He smiled. " 'Tis debatable how much he could have taught them. They're a proud people. I stayed with them my first year here, after the cougar ripped into me. They taught me how to live in the mountains." He rose.

"Why did you come here, so far from your home?" she pressed carefully.

"I was a young lad looking for adventure."

The answer came too easily, too quickly, it sounded too well rehearsed.

"Did you leave family back in Scotland?"

He smiled down at her. "You have to know all you can, do you? Aye, I have a mother living. I must tell you the story of my life someday when you've beheld a little more of the world. For now, suffice it to say a man does no' have much time to think about family here, or who he once was back in Scotland. That was a whole different person, with little connection to me now." His voice was firm, as if he were talking to an unreasonable child. "Here I'm the Waiting Cougar. And now you are to play opposite me as my heroine. Good or bad, it seems I've been chosen to lead you into a minor epic—or at least through a first class penny novel."

She watched him put the ointment away. As he straightened, she said, "I could just take the first opportunity that came and simply walk away. I really don't have to stay with you."

"Oh, aye, but you do. And 'twould no' serve for

88

you to even suppose otherwise. Think you there's no worse fate than to rest in my arms? You be wrong. Try to escape me and you would no' live a week. You would be wolf's meat. I would no' like that. Nae, there are some things that are no' pretty for a man to see. They're too hard for him to forget. But all this is if you *could* escape me, which is no' likely."

Victorine had another nightmare. She woke suddenly, sat up under the night sky, her eyes wide and her whole body rigid with horror. Beyond the foot of the red blanket the coals of the evening's fire still shone with a faint rosy glow. All else was darkness.

She'd hardly made a sound, so it must have been the brush of her hair across Cougar's chest that woke him. "What is it, lassie?"

She realized she was weeping. She was shocked at herself again. She didn't approve of tears; tears weren't necessary to a woman if she was strong-minded enough.

Yet, these tears were far removed from any histrionic display of feminine emotion. They brimmed her eyes and trickled down her cheeks silently. Knowing that Cougar was watching her, she turned her head to hide her despair.

"Ah, sky-eyes . . ." He sat up and pressed her cheek into the hollow beneath his collarbone. She accepted it for what it was, a spontaneous gesture of sympathy.

"Why do you make this effort to smother it?" he went on. When sorrow attacks 'tis the natural thing to weep—long and frequently. But you seem afraid of your own self. You sit here like a woman at the edge of the tunnel, holding off entering, though you know you can only come to peace by passing through the shadows. Cry, cry the memories away."

She shook her head. "They'll never go away."

"Everything passes, even the most outrageous pain."

"I didn't know I could hurt like this. It hits me . . . over and over it hits me and it hurts so . . . much. There isn't any rest from it, even while I'm asleep. When I sleep I dream it, time and time again . . . I see that Indian singing to his knife and I scream—I scream—but he doesn't stop! He—"

*"Shh."*

Resting against his chest, tears streamed down her face. She'd held back so long, she couldn't anymore. At last she really began to cry, with hard, shaking sobs. She wept for the very obstinacy of death, its imperviousness to argument, or to a woman's grief. She wept over its cruel presumption. She wept as she hadn't known she could weep, shuddering, torn apart until gradually she was exhausted. She allowed him to lean her back in his arms then, and for a time rested there. She knew she'd made the necessary first step toward finding an uneasy peace.

It was just growing light when she felt Cougar's cool hand on her shoulder once more. "Wake up, my morning glory."

He was squatted beside the pallet, fully dressed. She blinked up at him sleepily to find him regarding her tousled appearance with secret amusement.

"I'll be gone for the day. I leave you food enough." His eyes rested on the fine skin of her half-displayed breasts. Automatically she pulled the blanket higher. He smiled wryly. "Aye, and you'll be safe enough, as long as you do no' wander."

She sat up, slowly, and then, luminous eyed, fully alert at last, she asked, "Were are you going?"

"I'll try to be back 'afore dark." He put his hands on her shoulders as if he meant to kiss her. She shrugged away with a quick, hard gesture. He didn't insist but stood and started for his horse which she saw was already saddled. Iron-gray looked toward her with bland interest.

"I'll be taking the pack horses with me. They'll slow me down, but I can no' put it past you to try out some foolish invention of your mind if I leave them."

Panic and disbelief mingled in her, clouding her ability to make sense of what he was up to. Before she could stop herself, she cried out, "You're not going to leave me alone?"

He swung into his saddle and sat looking at her. "You'll be fine. 'Twould no' hurt if you soaked in the burn again a while this afternoon. There's a pair of moccasins for you." He gestured to a pair lying on the blanket near her feet. "I would've given them to you yesterday, but I'd forgot I had them."

She stared at him, open eyed and speechless. As he gazed back, it seemed he regretted having to do this — at least his look gave her that feeling. And yet he was going to do it! He nudged the horse with his heels and set the packtrain in motion.

"Wait! Can't I go with you?"

"Nae. I'll be back by dark. I promise you. Do no' be afraid. I would never leave you if 'twere no' safe. 'Screw your courage to the sticking place,' lassie."

By these last remarks she realized she'd given herself away; he knew she was terrified. She felt a certain pique at being seen through so readily and fought to calm herself. In a cooler tone she said, "I guess I'll just have to manage on my own then."

"Aye, I guess so." He grinned and touched his finger to his brow in salute.

When she lost sight of him among the trees, she tried to take stock. He'd left her a small parfleche of dried meat, enough for one day and no more—another safeguard against 'foolish inventions' of her mind, obviously. Water was as nearby as the stream where there were also berries for the picking. She had his word that she was safe here, but what about scouting Indians? Hungry animals? Could he have anticipated them? Suddenly the place seemed to seethe with unfamiliar sounds, with jerking branches, mysterious scuttlings, breathings, and humming winds. She realized she had no way to defend herself except to remain here in the area of the camp where there was a low, smokeless fire burning and a feeling of familiarity.

He'd left her alone. He'd actually left her here *alone!*

## Chapter Seven

The sun rose and sent its first light shooting like a
flaming bird into the blue expanse of the sky. Another day of crystal weather. Victorine felt braver
then, and braver still as the morning advanced without incident.

Afternoon found her in the middle of the rushing
stream, her outstretched legs and long yellow hair
afloat, the tips of her breasts breaking the water. On
either side of her the reeds swayed with the current
like barley bending in a field. A red-winged black-
bird hopped about in the creekside willows.

The stream was so cold she couldn't force herself
to remain in it for long. She waded to the bank
where Cougar's capote and her new moccasins
waited. As she sat with her back to the full-pouring
sunlight, her knees drawn up in the circle of her bare
arms, she considered those moccasins.

They were elaborately quilted and beaded, clearly
meant for a woman, perhaps a sort of special-
occasion shoe. She wondered why Cougar would
have them. The obvious answer made her uncomfortable: These were the sort of moccasins a man might
use as a gift. An Indian girl would probably be

pleased to get them. Probably grateful. Probably willing.

She wished she could stop thinking about him! If just for a few minutes. She tried . . .

. . . and there he was anyway, invading her mind, big, hard limbed, taking over her life, and all the time smiling that gentle smile and exuding that deadly attraction.

Enough! No more idle fancies! He was a ghastly male monster who said that for her own good she should do what he told her unquestioningly, even though what he told her was immoral and wrong. His most memorable characteristic was his pronounced self-conceit. He was so secure in it that he feared very little in this world, if anything. He felt he could be nice when he wanted, rude when he chose, or even viciously cruel if that should please him. And to think that she was dependent on his kindness! What, after all, could anyone do if he decided to abuse her?

No, she sighed, no, if she wasn't going to be fanciful, then she had to admit that there was nothing monstrous about him. There was no sign of viciousness or cruelty. In fact, he'd been mostly warm, honest, and generous.

The day became long. An unseen dove lamented from somewhere. Otherwise the aspen woods were dry and quiet. In fact, being on her own was so safe seeming as to be monotonously dull. A dozen times she convinced herself that she should simply start walking in an easterly direction . . . and a dozen times faced the truth that nothing, not even remaining with Cougar, could be more dangerous. She wasn't terribly sure of her geography, but she guessed there must be at least one thousand five hundred miles of hostile Indian territory between her and St. Louis.

Still, her father would have expected her to risk the trek. He'd always preached that life is noble only if it is held cheap beside honor and virtue. That had been easy enough to agree with when she lived safely in Philadelphia. It was easy enough to preach to a woman when you were a man.

If *she* were a man—oh, if only she were! A mountain man, with shameless will and immense strength—then she would know how to hunt and fish and travel without getting lost, how to avoid risk, or best it!

She wasn't a man, let alone a mountain man, but as the sky turned amber she resolved that she would soon know what a mountain man knew. This was at least a plan of sorts. If she had to submit to being Cougar's unsanctified wife . . .

Yes, she admitted that that seemed inevitable. Being a reasonable person, able to foresee events to their logical conclusion, she knew full well that sooner or later his insistence would lead to a certain scene in which she would be a reluctant participant. There was no escaping it.

But if she did have to submit to him, in return she would somehow coax him into teaching her everything he knew about survival, until one day soon she would know enough to survive without him.

It was deep dusk before he returned, a slow appreciative smile on his face at the sight of her. Her own reception was mute and chilly. She'd been waiting tensely by a rather over-large fire (for the first star, sharp as steel, had pricked her daylight courage).

He staked out his animals and joined her on the fallen log she was using as a settee. For a long while they just sat there, watching the flames resist the pull of the nightwind. She didn't want to ask him where he'd been, and he gave away nothing, neither the purpose of his absence nor its gain. It was as if he'd put the matter out of his mind.

He ate a little, then led her to the buffalo robe. He reached to untie his capote and slip from her. It fell open to reveal her shoulders and the division of her breasts, but there she held it closed stubbornly. Her eyes stared at him with accusation. "The least you can do is tell me why you found it necessary to leave me here—without so much as a knife to defend myself—the whole day long."

His smile was tired. "As long as you have that hagborn tongue, you're hardly without some defense. I would be willing to wager you could hold a small grizzly off with it."

She flung the cloak into his hands, at the same time kicking off her moccasins, and she slipped down to pull the red blanket over her.

He went about his own undressing in a more leisurely manner. When he joined her, his body seemed to relax pleasurably. They lay barely touching, both preoccupied. At last he said, without warning, "It took me some time to find the place, but . . . I buried your brother and his wife."

A little gasp caught her. She turned to face him so quickly that she forgot to protect her sore shoulder, and yet she didn't notice the discomfort.

"I could no' bear to see your eyes looking like such blue-bleak embers. I felt it might ease you to know your people had been set to rest properly, on a hilltop, with a stone cairn to mark their places."

Her eyes were wide and dim as she looked back for a moment; then she closed them and shook her mind free of the scene she'd briefly re-envisioned. When she gazed at him again through the firelit darkness, it was with profound thankfulness. "You can't know what it means to—" Her voice broke and she was reduced to making a tiny gesture with her hand to emphasize her feelings. For the moment, she'd thrown all her shields away. For once she wasn't even trying to be reasonable and objective. "You can't know," she whispered, tears almost drowning her voice.

And she noted a surprising sensation: she wanted to cling to the man and feel his arms go around her as they occasionally had done. When he rolled onto his side and brought her head to pillow on his shoulder, laying his free hand on her cheek, she accepted the comfort gratefully.

"Sleep now, and dream of pleasanter things this night. All is past amend, unchangable." He pushed her hair back over her shoulder and kissed her neck beneath her ear, inhaling the natural perfume of her body. "Sleep."

After two more days spent in the aspen grove, Victorine's back and leg were nearly healed—except perhaps for a slight bruised feeling, and even that was fading. Her spirit was recovering as well. She was beginning to wake each morning with more of her old feelings excitement, the excitement she'd always experienced with the start of a new day. Tobias's memory was with her, it always would be, but now those sickening visions of his last moments were eased. There was a marker on earth to show that he had passed this way. It was the most any mortal could ever hope for.

Meanwhile there was her own life to be ciphered, her own troubles to be dealt with. Foremost among these was Cougar. She found herself watching him, trying to learn to read his face. Though he mostly maintained a remoteness, at moments she sensed that she was an almost unbearable temptation for him.

Then again sometimes she found him watching her, his eyes screwed up above his high Scottish cheekbones, as if against the dazzle of the sun. Then her breath would catch, for she could suddenly guess what storming desires burned in his heart. Sometimes he stopped what he was doing—whether sharpening his knife on the half-pound chunk of obsidian he used for a whet stone, or stretching a hide over a smoky fire—and reached to cup her cheek or stroke her hair. She felt in his strong hands more sheer masculinity than she'd ever imagined before. With them he could already have taken her by force.

It was uncanny, but the fact that he had the strength to take her, yet didn't, seemed to stir something in her. She began to imagine his hands moving on her. What would it be like? And she wondered guiltily if he guessed this, even if perhaps he intended it to be so. Doubtless he could be very tricky. She yearned for a bit of guile herself. She felt she was going to need it. Common sense told her it was only a matter of days before this situation was resolved. Meanwhile, he was being a tower of strength, winning her liking and respect and giving her friendly, sympathetic attention. But all the while they both knew he was simply biding his time.

She'd asked him how she might avail herself of something to wear and his answer was, "When your back is healed enough to wear anything snugger than that capote, I'll see to it that you're clothed."

It was this sort of comment that set her teeth to grinding. So arrogant, so full of master-slave connotations, so humiliating for her. Remembering it as she sat curled on the red blanket this morning, she seethed all over again. She was so tired of wearing next to nothing, of being careful, of having to move slowly lest the capote fall open and reveal her.

Cougar shattered the smooth water of her irritated thoughts with, "Stand up for me." She looked up to find him looming over her. He was wearing a shirt of yellow flannel that he occasionally alternated with his usual leather. "Up." He gestured imperiously.

She considered refusing, but that would be like trying to set between them a door with no lock to bolt. Not that she was afraid of him, not that she thought he would hurt her, but then he hardly had to beat her to get his way, did he?

"Woman," he said as she continued to hesitate, "I sometimes find it difficult to be ever patient with you."

Wrapping the capote about her, she rose. And she was surprised when he knelt at her feet. Now she saw what he had in his hands and understood what he was up to: he wanted to measure her foot on the piece of elkskin he'd been smoking over the fire for the past two days. Still a bit grumpy, she said, "I already have footwear; what I really need is a gown."

"A gown is it?" He paused to look up at her. "Aye, remind me to order the carriage. We'll go 'round to the dressmaker's this very morn, 'afore we make our calls."

He went back to his work, asking her to stand down on first one foot and then the other. "Meanwhile, since you've already got slippers for the dress ball, my lady is more in need of good stout walking boots."

She glanced at the beaded moccasins she'd been wearing and said off-handedly, "I wondered why you happened to have a pair of moccasins like those. Were they meant to be a gift for someone?"

"Mmm," was his answer.

"Someone special?"

"Aye, that special." He was preoccupied when he got off his knees, and didn't volunteer any further information.

She watched as he deftly set about manufacturing a pair of moccasins with attached, knee-length leggings. "These might well be the worst you'll ever wear. I do no' usually make women's footgear. And they may no' be smoked enough. My own were sewn from an old lodge skin that was half-smoke already. Mocs that are no' smoked enough soon pinch. You'll have to make do for a while, though, 'til we can buy you half a dozen or so pairs from a squaw somewhere."

"These fit well enough," she said as she pulled on the finished products and walked around the fire ring. "The leggings are to protect against thistles, I guess?"

"Thistles, aye. And rattlesnakes. I've seen a rattler strike a woman in the leg, but they rarely penetrate a good pair of leggings, at least no' the first time. Which reminds me, I must teach you how to use a tomahawk one of these days."

"Yes, I think maybe you should," she said, shaken. She'd seen a few big western rattlesnakes sunning themselves beside the river during the journey with Tobias. They were very different from their eastern relatives.

Now Cougar took a deep breath, as if gearing himself for something difficult. His face went taut, his tone brusque. "Now come here to me. I want to stand here and let go of that capote."

"Why?" She was suddenly aware again of her

vulnerability.

With his face stern, he said, "My lady does want a better traveling costume?"

"Yes, but—"

"Myself, I do no' care," he went on, now with a suddenly bright, oblique glance. "We'll be doing some riding in a day or two and I would just as soon carry you on my saddle naked as the night I bought you. Riding can get that dull, and the feel of your soft—"

"All right!" She hesitated only a moment more, then flung down the capote and stood before him, forcing her eyes to look off into the middle distance where some birds moved from tree to tree in bits of flight. A spark of defiance prompted her to say, "You'd better be quick, though."

He fit two pieces of velvet-soft deerhide up to her, front and back, stretching them across her breasts, her hips, pulling her arms out to measure their length. "Hold still, squirrel; we'll have to begin all over again if you keep squirming away."

The truth was, though she hardly admitted it, she'd become less squeamish about her body over the past few days. It was difficult to sleep naked in a man's arms every night and retain any sort of reserve about him seeing you naked during the day. So she really didn't have to struggle with herself too much in order to bear this as stoically as a seamstress's mannequin—until, kneeling before her, his hand smoothed up her leg and grazed her inner thigh. She stepped back quickly. "Unless you're making me a pair of breeches, I don't think that's necessary."

His expression was full of fun. "Breeks for a woman? When a dress is so much more practical? Nae."

She reached for the capote, swung it around her

shoulders, and from within its safety said, "I've always believed dresses to be highly impractical. Women are so unreasonably restrained by skirts."

"I was speaking of a different sort of practicality—from a man's viewpoint. Skirts being so easily lifted, you see."

"That's disgusting."

"Indelicately put, mayhap, but never disgusting."

The tunic-style dress he made her was merely a smaller variation of the style of his own shirts, only longer, ending mid-calf, just below the tops of her new leggings. There was a line of fringe across her breasts, and a collarless yoke that laced up the front. The neckline was a shallow scoop, emphasizing the transparency of her skin and the fine bones of her shoulders.

He stood back, eyeing it critically. "Well, a squaw could do better, but 'twill suit you for a time."

Dressed decently again! It brought a sense of freedom that was unbelievable. She stroked the garment almost lovingly; it felt as soft as rabbit skin. She strode across the camp and back, saying, "Thank you, Cougar. You know, you've really been very good to me and it's time I started earning my keep. There must be something useful I can do."

"Aye and there is."

That stopped her dead for a moment. "Besides that," she answered flatly. "Maybe I could pick some berries, or . . . you know, I would really like to learn to shoot. I'm sure I could even learn to hunt."

"I'm sure you could learn to do just about anything. The question is, what should I be teaching you first? Since I bought you more for bedmate than for helpmate—"

She grabbed a rawhide bag. "I'll look for berries."

He caught her wrist. "Aye, I would like some

102

berries, I have a taste for berries, I have an urge to gather me wet snowberries from the tips of your breasts." His face was stark with desire. "Come into my arms, lassie."

"Not yet, please, not yet, not now!"

He pulled her nearer, slowly, leisurely. Her resistance was as useless as placing her feet on the slippery rocks beside a waterfall. "I begin to despair of you," he said quietly. "You're all childish resentment and rebellion. Come, we're both worn out with the preamble to this situation, and here's the time to stop talking."

Pitted against him in earnest for the first time, she felt weak. Her mind had glided adroitly around the problem of how she would stand up under his demands when they became immediate. She'd remained acutely aware that there would eventually be such a problem, but had classified it always as a bridge to be crossed later.

But later, to her total terror, had arrived now.

He pulled her to him and turned her into his arms and kissed her deeply, forcing her mouth open with his urgent lips. "There's only so much enticing a man can withstand," he said a long moment later. He was leaning over her, arching her back in his arms, moving his mouth on hers to speak ever so softly. "You're like a china sculpture," he went on murmuring, moving his lips over her face, from her cheek to her eyelids to her temples. "Aye, the pleasure of clothing you is the pleasure of undressing you again, slowly, 'til I'm down to the porcelain of your skin once more."

This display of ardor was all too sudden, too impetuous, for her to deal with. "Cougar, I'm not ready," she pleaded breathlessly, her hands on his chest.

"I am." He was kissing her throat now.

"You can't want me if I don't want you."

"Can I no'?"

"You couldn't enjoy it," she flung at him desperately.

"Could I no'?"

"I'll do everything I can to resist you!"

"We shall see what that amounts to then."

"You're bullying me—it's wicked of you!"

He reared his head back—then lost his temper. She saw it plainly in his eyes. And it was a great shock to her, for until then he'd been so kind and patient that she hadn't realized that he had a temper to lose. She instinctively recoiled from the menace of it.

Extraordinarily, that violent stranger vanished as suddenly as he'd appeared. Yet the instant's fright he'd given her left her so weak she swayed in his arms. He wrapped them around her waist firmly. "I was hoping you would find the courage and wisdom to accept the way things are, since you can no' change them. I expected your intelligence to overrule this foolish fear." With unnoticing ease, he lifted her off her feet and carried her to the buffalo robe, where he knelt and pressed her down onto her back with the weight of half his body over her. He started kissing her again.

"Cougar!" she broke away for breath.

"Nae, so far I've indulged this taste for argument you have, but that's finished. You'll do as I want now. I'm sworn to have you—and I will." He kissed her again.

She wrenched her mouth from his long enough to cry, "Wait! Not like this!"

His mouth only took hers again. And in spite of her dismay, a luscious longing sensation was flooding her; she felt she was spinning like a rifle ball, and it was a long moment before she had the chance—or remembered—to make her plea again. "Cougar . . . if you'll wait—*please!*" She caught his hand at the lacings of her new dress. "I-I'll let you! I won't struggle!" She had his attention at last, and added quietly, "But you must give me just a little more time."

"I've given you time."

"I need a little more—a few hours. Is that too much to ask?"

His eyes were hooded. "What difference can a few hours make?"

"I didn't realize until now what it would really mean, or even that you were truly serious, but—"

"What bad manners, lassie, to doubt my word." His mouth descended to her throat. His hand, making free with her, pulled the hem of her dress up, uncovering her hip and caressing it. "Let this be a lesson to you to always believe what I say in the future. . . . What exquisite skin you have, flawless, silk-soft—"

"Stop!"

"Pull yourself together and face the facts, woman! We're married. 'Tis my right to have you—"

"No!"

"Never you tell me no! I know perfectly your inclination to be strong willed and independent, but I intend to be your husband."

"All I ask is a few hours! It would make all the difference to me! Please, Cougar!" Despite his hand grasping her bare hip, and though she could tell his mind was still strongly set, he seemed to consider. She felt a burning heat in her face, yet knew she must press ahead with her point now, or lose it.

"You say you want me for a wife, yet you're

treating me like—like some creature you only bought to *use*. I'm not a woman of the town—I've never been with a man. Please, if you mean what you say—that you think of me as your wife—then give me the consideration every bride deserves—time to . . . to bathe, to make myself pretty, to settle my thoughts. Let me get used to the idea that its going to happen now."

He began to ease off her. "God blast your eyes," he muttered. His tanned, handsome face conceded no sign of the fury she sensed in him. He walked to the pole that supported one end of a rack of drying berries and leaned against it. Taking a handful of the fruit, he chewed thoughtfully, watching her.

At last he said, "Virginity strikes me as overrated. I feel I've had enough bashfulness to last me for the rest of my days. 'Tis high time we conquer your prudishness. Past time. You show unmistakable signs of sensuality . . ."

He straightened. "Aye, I'll grant you a few hours then. But when I come back I'll expect you to tender me all I ask. No' even your being as pure as starlight will deflect me again. Do you harken, love? I shall take whatever steps I deem necessary. I'm going to have you—tonight. I'm going to start at the beginning as I mean to go on."

He grabbed his rifle, buckled his tomahawk around his waist, and started out of camp afoot. He turned back to look at her once. "I'll no' be that far off, so do no' even think of taking a horse. If I have to go chasing after you, my heart, you'll be that sorry."

He disappeared into a dark green furrow of the hills.

Victorine sat motionless on the buffalo robe for a long time. She sat so still that a butterfly landed

106

right on her knee, its large wings heaving as if with the efforts of flight.

This man, she decided, was inexhaustible in his standpoints. To see him was like trying to see the woods from within: one must gaze, and move, and gaze again. A lifetime wouldn't be enough to feel sure of him.

She hardly dared believe that she'd won this reprieve from him—that she'd whittled down the desire she'd felt in him until it was a reasonable thing. Even so, the victory was at best only temporary. Now she must reconcile herself to what she must yield. She told herself that she wasn't afraid so much as simply wary. She was fairly certain he wouldn't hurt her; what she didn't know was what it would be like to give herself to a man, a man she didn't love— a man she hardly knew! . . . to let him lay her open, to yield to him her most vulnerable secrets . . .

Women married all the time, of course, and, as far as she could see, they survived their conjugal duties, but . . . was there really no alternative? She must be dispassionate now; she must demand the truth of the situation . . .

And the truth was that Cougar was going to consummate what he believed to be their marriage. If she resisted him again, especially after giving him her word that she wouldn't, her existence might be unendurable before very long. It had been so spine-chilling, that evidence of temper in his eyes!

She let herself absorb this very unpalatable verdict. There was no surprise in it. In fact, she was furious with herself now for not foreseeing the strength of his determination all along.

Well, sitting here thinking about it, trying to imagine something she'd never experienced, wasn't doing her any good, so she got up to go down within the sound of the water. She'd made him a promise and she would have to keep it, for all her reasoning boiled down to two choices: prepare herself for his love-making, or prepare herself for his rage. Either way, he was going to possess her within a few hours. It would be useless to beg him for more time to get used to him. She was simply going to have to make the best of it.

# Chapter Eight

Victorine was waiting for Cougar right where he'd left her, on the buffalo robe, with nothing but the red blanket covering her. She'd bathed, washed and dried her hair, and combed it to silk with the wooden comb he'd carved for her a few days ago, and now she felt as ready as she thought she ever would.

Evening had begun to enthrall the steep face of the cliff opposite the creek, mollifying it, leveling it down. The dusky-rose and purple sky started to numb her senses. One yawn engendered another, and she was seriously considering a nap when Cougar came striding out of the wood with a grassy tread.

She greeted him with a tight smile that didn't reach her eyes. Suddenly she was wide awake again. She held the red blanket tighter to her breasts and huddled herself further under it, like a cornered spider.

He acknowledged her silently, placing his rifle by the side of the buffalo robe before sitting on it. He pulled off his cougar-skin cap and ran his hand through his tawny hair. It was damp and disheveled; he'd been swimming upstream. He sat there in dark silhouette against the evening sky.

"I see you're a woman who keeps her word." He seemed hesitant. "I apologize for frightening you this afternoon. 'Twas no' how I meant to be with you. I meant to entice you, seduce you, so you would hardly realize . . . Well 'tis too late for that now. But if you'll let me, I can ease this crossing you must make, this last crossing from your world to mine. I do no' think you'll have cause to complain. In truth, I'm sure you can learn to relish our arrangement. But you must no' set yourself against me." His expression was patient, his words practical. He was doing his best to calm her worries, using his glossiest manners.

She sat heavy, paralyzed by the meaning of what he was saying. Nervously she tucked her hair back behind her ears, revealing the rapid pulse in her temples. If this wasn't the situation of quick possession she'd most feared, it still was one of the most uncomfortable moments she'd ever lived through.

He smiled. His hands came up, reached out, took her shoulders.

"Cougar —"

With steady strength he drew her into his arms, smothering her words with his mouth.

Her control slipped; she felt alarm crawl along her skin again. The urge to scramble up and run was overwhelming. Suddenly she recognized the wide chasm between working everything out calmly and sensibly, and being on this robe, waiting to be taken by this man.

"Cougar!"

"Nae, we'll go slow. 'Twill be good." He laid her back on the robe while he pulled his shirt over his head. She refused to watch him undress, to be spellbound by the arrant beauty of his masculinity. As he pulled his breeches off he spoke one of his pet names for her—flower, or flame, or something—laughing softly at her apparent primness. Then he was bending over her, causing her to lie back. "Kiss me," he said.

Now she had to look into his face.

"Kiss me," he repeated.

She hadn't expected him to require anything of her beyond submission. She'd thought merely to accept him, like a bloodless and rigid stone. She faltered, then reached warily to place one hand behind his neck, bringing his head down while she lifted hers. Inexperienced, she merely touched his lips briefly, and then, because she knew he must consider that insufficient, she repeated it—and repeated it again. Peculiar little nibbling kisses.

Meanwhile, his hands were uncovering the warmth of her flesh. He tugged the edge of the blanket loose from her other hand and sighed as he cupped a soft breast with one big palm. He murmured between feather kisses on her nose, "You've been arousing me constantly . . . each time you brightened your eyes at me, . . . each time I looked at your face, your shoulders, your legs . . . I was pushed further along toward simply taking you . . . In truth, my kept yellow bird, 'tis no' a wonder so much that I nearly forced you this afternoon, but that I stopped myself from forcing you yesterday or the day before."

He kissed her lips swiftly and firmly. Then his hand left her breast to fling the blanket off her altogether.

"Don't hurt me!" she said involuntarily, voicing her deepest fear without meaning to.

"Why would I hurt you? You're my bonny lass. I would never hurt you. Nae, I only want to see you, to lay bare your beauties which you've been guarding so well."

What choice did she have except to believe him, to trust a vagrant instinct . . . and that hypnotic and steady brilliance that was his gaze?

He half reclined beside her to admire the pale glow of her naked thighs. He bent to kiss them gently, high up, then kissed her warm belly, and fathomed her navel with the tip of his tongue, making her shiver. His left hand slipped under her waist; it felt cool against her bare back. He used it to lift her, arch her, and she gasped when his hot mouth closed over her breast.

There was no mood of hurry in him. The movements of his right hand were long and slow along her legs, coaxing them to relax, and fondling and kneading the breast he wasn't suckling. Her breathing became a little ragged. She felt herself dissolving. "You're tormenting me; you shouldn't."

Even as she spoke, he moved to take her head between his hands, to pull her mouth up to his. "I've barely begun to torment you," and he kissed her deeply and repeatedly, both his arms around her, his weight pressing against her.

She made not the least effort to stop him, even when his hand lowered along her back to stroke the cheeks of her bottom. He seemed only to want to kiss and caress her endlessly—her breasts, her soft belly and legs—she didn't guess that he was investigating how far she would let him go before protesting.

She recognized that she enjoyed being handled this way; yet, she never quite became drowned in sheer sensation — for with his jutting manhood pressing against her she could never lose sight of the invasion to come.

Now he was stroking tenderly up her thighs, until he touched the delicate moss where they met. Her legs were closed. He claimed her mouth at the same moment his fingers began to insistently delve into her secret place. Though her body tensed, his whole hand was soon lodged between her legs. It was all she could do to keep herself from reaching down to restrain him.

"Please—"

But the objection she meant to voice ceased as he dipped a fingertip tenderly into her. Instead she gasped — and then began to protest actively, wriggling away and pushing at his chest.

He withdrew his hand. "Nae . . . now listen to me, heart." He was laying down again beside her. She recoiled, but his left arm around her pulled her close to his chest. He held her there with rigid strength. Never had she been so close to him before. When she tried to speak, he pressed his fingers against her lips. "Be still. I want you to be still, so still you can almost hear the blood in your veins."

She tried to struggle, but he held her whole body in check.

"Harken," he whispered, his lips moving against her ear, his teeth nipping the lobe. A start of sensation went through her. She hardly noticed that his hand was back at the join of her legs, until it started delving again.

His arm beneath her tightened to cords of iron, holding her where she was, forcing her to endure this first gentle trespass. His fingers explored . . .

113

and waves of erotic sensation lapped over her. He was holding her so tightly that her breasts were almost painfully flattened against the flexed muscles of his chest, yet suddenly there was a need building within her which she didn't understand, a desire to have his body even nearer, nearer still. She found herself wanting something in her powerlessness, as if she'd been wanting it for years. There was a throbbing in her mouth and tongue, and in all the flesh between her thighs, and in her belly. She found herself arching up against him.

"Aye, you begin to see," he whispered, his cheek still imprisoning her head against his shoulders. " 'Tis time . . . time to provide me vent for this wild passion you've aroused." His fingers went on moving, on her, inside her. He lowered his head to lick her breasts. Her bare thighs gripped his wrist at the fork of her legs. Those persistent fingers went on firing her blood, until it seemed that only fire itself could put out the burning.

Her own hands fluttered helplessly — and one encountered his eager male part. The accidental caress seemed to galvanize him. His knee parted her thighs as he abruptly pulled her beneath him.

At first she only knew that his fingers weren't there anymore, and she could have cried out in frustration. Then, in sudden panic, she realized that he meant to go on now, and she recoiled again, curving her body away. "No, wait!"

"Easy, lassie, easy," he breathed softly. "Yield to me. I'll no' harm you. Come to me now."

Using just enough of his weight to keep her down, she was aware now as she hadn't been before that he could have overcome her much sooner if he'd wished. The knowledge was humbling, triggering a dismay so profound it sent her senses tumbling.

114

He guided himself into position. Now she felt the warm hardness of his body entering her, and she faced the urgency of his claim at last.

A sudden thrust sank him deep within her. Her breath caught in her throat as he pinned her. She stiffened, her jaw clenched.

"Relax with it, my love; breathe deeply." His arms made a cradle to comfort her now. "The worst is done. Forgive me, but I thought it best to be quick. 'Twill be easier after this."

She lay unmoving. She felt as if she'd been skewered by an oaken stake, which remained within her yet. The pain lulled, but the stiff wooden peg stayed, lodged profoundly, filling and stretching her.

With effort she said, "If you've finished, please remove yourself."

After a breath, he said, "Mayhap 'twould be better for you no' to use that tone with a man who's in the position I'm in."

At first the words froze her, but then she realized he was laughing at her! Yes, looking up at him, she saw the gleam of laughter in his eyes.

How could he? At a time like this!

"How long is this likely to go on, then?"

"No' long enough. Kiss me, lassie."

He lowered his mouth so she could touch it with her lips. Her thighs, spread by his hips, moved, seeking a more comfortable posture. She drew her knees up and too late found that this only set him more firmly in place. The stretching and distension were almost too much.

"Gently, my love." He withdrew himself a little, relieving her. "You must be more cautious; 'tis a dangerous game." He returned his mouth hot and hard to her lips, devouring. "My window flower, my morning glory, my heart, I fear I can no' pause

115

much longer."

Incredibly, passion rose in her in response to his kisses. She could feel heat glutting her flesh where he was embedded. The tissues throbbed with hot blood. He lifted his head to gaze down at her, his eyes blazing. Then his hands and lips were on her, rousing her slowly to sensations she'd barely imagined, until she felt she would burst with feeling, with desire, with this longing for closeness, more closeness with his hard-muscled body.

He commenced to move, slowly and with care. He pushed deeper, deeper than she'd thought possible, until her deepest depths he occupied. Holding himself on his elbows, he enclosed each of her small breasts in his palms. His staunch part withdrew from her, then pressed inward again.

"Do I hurt you?"

Her head nodded negatively against the buffalo robe. No, it wasn't painful. It was a more a sort of sensational shock. In fact, rather than hurting, what he was doing was reigniting those flames she'd felt before.

His movements gradually quickened; a few more strokes and she seemed to be trembling and gasping in a climb to some unknown apex. Pressed beneath him, she felt herself mounting the cliff of some inexplicable madness. Her body seemed to know better what to do than her mind did. Her arms wound themselves around his neck, her hips lunged upwards to meet his. His thrusting was awakening feelings in her which she knew she shouldn't want to experience; yet, having broken into her, he seemed to have broken open some wellspring at the same time, and the delight was flowing in.

She felt she would die if he kept on, and he kept on, and she didn't die. Her mouth widened, pressed up to find his. She wanted his tongue. She used her hands to pull his head down to hers. She revelled in the tight corral of his arms. She strained up against his chest and could feel his sinews and bones, the very contour of his ribs. She knew his structure, his body, it was the scaffolding to which she must cling . . .

All at once she cried out, flooded suddenly with pleasure beyond bearing in silence, and at the same instant he tensed and fountained within her. His arms scooped her to his chest and held her there, so hard it was hurtful, yet she loved it. This was what she had wanted, had wanted forever, had so wanted and hadn't known she wanted, this, which he'd given to her.

His hold loosened by degrees, his breathing slowed. He let her move from beneath him, though his arm flung over her waist was enough to keep her from going too far. His palm polished her hipbone; he pressed soft kisses onto her bare shoulder; he said with a laugh, "I feel like a man who took his ax and went alone to cut down a whole nest of dragons." Contentment softened his features and seemed to have left him playful.

For her part, Victorine was completely dazed, almost too dazed to speak.

He kissed her lips. "What sweetness . . . mmm . . . I want you again this minute."

Startled, she tried to shift unnoticeably out of his gentle grasp. "You mustn't."

For the second time she felt his body shake with humor. He placed another sound kiss on her mouth; then kissed it again tenderly, and slipped his hand beneath her long flaxen hair to fondle the nape of her neck. "Nae, lay you down and stop your wriggling. I'll let you sleep the rest of this night undisturbed — though I mean to have a little more of you in the morning."

In a small voice she said, "Surely you've had enough of me for a long while."

"Enough, yet no' enough, like a bullet that has passed right through, high in the breast — enough to wound, but no' to kill." He collapsed as if in a lethargy of enjoyment beside her. His arms pulled her near. "Ah . . . that a woman should have the power to make me feel something is right with the world."

She could feel the last trembling traces of her own pleasure like a flush between her thighs. And because of it she avoided looking at him. She was so ashamed of herself. And so afraid. "Cougar . . ."

"Aye, my heart?"

"Nothing . . . nothing. I — I'm going to sleep now."

"Aye, and sleep sweet, my good wife."


"Flame."

The sun was slanting through the trees nearly horizontally. It seemed to be lingering on its way to its zenith, making the morning breathless and gloriously warm, but also speaking a soft warning, too, saying its arc would lie lower and lower on the sky each day now, for the summer was all but over.

Cougar had Victorine's hand as they walked, but he didn't seem to notice the slight flush of anger on her face.

As reasonably as possible she asked, "Why Flame?"

"It suits you — for many reasons, one being the way your face holds the light like a candle."

"How very poetic. But I'm afraid I find it some-

118

what unseemly. Don't I have anything to say about this? Because I think my real name suits me fine—Henrietta Victorine Elfreda Wellesley." She got it out before he could stop her again. It struck her as incredible that he didn't even know her name, considering all that had transpired between them. "Most people call me Victorine."

He stopped walking, looked down at her in amazement, then threw his head back and laughed.

He was still chuckling a moment later when he tugged at her hand and started walking again. "Henrietta Victorine El—" He looked down at her for help.

"—Elfreda Wellesley."

"Elfreda!" Another shout of laughter.

"I don't know what could be less amusing." Her eyes burned with the wrath of the Old Testament.

"Nor I. What a burden to place on a frail girl-child's person."

"I was never frail, and my father saw to it that I had a name as strong as I was."

"And your mother?"

"She died a few months after I was born. I was raised by my father. And he hated feminine weakness of any kind."

"Aye, mysteries begin to clear themselves up."

"What is that supposed to mean?"

"I've wondered at your insistence upon reason over feeling. I suspected an authoritarian hand somewhere in your upbringing. It sounds as if your father wanted another boy-child, and set out purposely to make you masculine." He lifted her hand to his lips in a courtly gesture. "I admire your ability to be as objective as a man in your thinking, but I'm that glad he failed so utterly otherwise. You're a sensitive and tender woman—when you're yourself, that is."

What extraordinary charm the man had! That wide infectious grin! And how it worked for him! She would do well to maintain her distance.

If it wasn't too late for that. She'd already given herself to him twice, and so . . . so disgracefully, so unreservedly.

He stopped again, put his arms around her suddenly, and pulled her so close and held her so hard that she could scarcely breathe. He kissed her, and when he raised his head a long while later, he explained, "I could no' help doing that. Unlike you, reason often fails me." His hand slid from her back to her waist and finally came to rest on one globe of her breast.

She didn't try to stop him. There seemed no point in acting out a charade of unflawed chastity now. She turned her face into his chest in shame. Though he'd kept his word not to molest her in the night, she'd half awakened twice to find his mouth on hers and his hand lightly moving on her breasts, just as it was now. And she'd kissed him back eagerly, almost begged him aloud to do more.

A single night out of all the nights of her life, and yet she felt wholly changed, wholly alive to her body, as she'd never been before. Her cheeks burned as she remembered his mouth and hands, his satin-muscled skin under her fingertips, and the weight of him on her. Even now it made her feel strangely languorous. It seemed incredible that yesterday he'd been a stranger.

Shame for all of this flushed her body as she remembered what she'd given, how thoroughly and easily she'd succumbed to his skill, his experience. Oh, he'd been clever. He'd understood from the beginning exactly how to handle her.

This morning, for instance, he'd been kind agin,

concerned that he might have misused her the night before, but then he'd loved her again, and again she'd responded — reluctantly, but deeply. What else could she have done? He was superbly adept. He seemed already to know every inch of her, and how to rouse each inch to passion, to ardent, ecstatic fulfillment.

She looked up at him now, solemnly, her eyes in search of his purpose. He stood there, tall, powerful, clearly the master of the situation. Instead of speaking to her mute appeal, he kissed her again, then inhaled the fragrance of her hair. She began to tremble. She could feel his power spiraling around her again. Her eyes grew heavy under the magic of his eroticism and her body started to glow and grow restless. The very smell of him warmed every vein.

His hand came up to caress her neck, to untie the lacing at her throat and slowly work the leather yoke open so that his fingers could delve for her breasts unimpeded. They were already sensitive from his previous use of them, and the nipples hardened at his first grazing touch.

She felt something like the flame of a candle warming the pit of her stomach. For several moments she leaned almost motionless in his arms, one hand resting on his waist, the other on his chest, then suddenly she roused herself enough to say, "Aren't we going to walk?"

He didn't stop her from leaving the circle of his arms. She began to retie her lacings, but as they moved on, he put his arm around her once more, and it wasn't long before he slowed his steps to turn her to him. He lifted her chin with his knuckles and gently, warmly, kissed first her lower lip and then her upper lip.

"I wish I'd put off making this thing a bit longer."

He gave the fringe of her dress a tug. "I would give another bale of pelts to have you naked again right now — you're so bonny that way."

He pulled her down with him into the fallen foliage beneath a spreading tree. She only half resisted before sinking into the deep bed of leaves beneath him. He gave her his arm for a pillow as he kissed her long and hard. Her lips surrendered to him . . . until abruptly she disengaged herself and sat up.

She looked everywhere but at him. "What are you doing to me? What do you want? Last night, and again this morning, and . . . it's only been a few hours!"

Sitting up beside her, he took her hand to place it on his chest. She felt his heart beating hard and steady. His sandy hair was fallen forward over his forehead, giving him a boyish appeal. "Is it possible you really know naught of men at all? I assure you I'm dealing with you no differently than any man deals with a bonny new wife." His hand left hers to slip under her dress, sliding up above her knee.

"But . . . I know I promised not to — to *impede* you, but —" She could feel her face tensing to hide her true feelings; she was too proud to admit to the anxiety she felt at her own strong responses, so she showed him anger instead. "But I think you're taking advantage of me!"

"Sweet Flame, you like what I do." He looked her straight in the eye as he slowly unlaced her dress again.

A spasm crossed her face. She trembled as the dreaded voluptuousness grew in her.

"Sky-eyes," he murmured in encouragement, "loveling, my brave Flame. You must no' be afraid. You're mine, and I shall treasure you."

She found herself lifting her arms to allow him to pull the dress over her head. And when her hair fell down her back, she shook it off her shoulders and lay back in his arms, awaiting his will.

"Aye, you're mine, you see, my woman, my wife, my heart."

## Chapter Nine

They prepared to ride out the next day. Flame (as it seemed Victorine was now to be known, whether she felt it suited her or not) protested that she would rather walk than ride enthroned before Cougar. "I've traveled many a mile without a horse to carry me."

He laughed. "Aye, but I've heard it rumored that too much walking makes the feet unshapely — and yours are too perfect to risk." With that he lifted her high onto Irongray's back.

Before climbing into the saddle himself, he drew his rifle, checked its load, and shoved it back into its scabbard. Mounted, he nudged the gray beast into motion, and saw that the pack animals were following along behind.

"We'll be heading up to my winter place soon," he told her, "but we'll be doing some hunting on the way. We need meat enough to last us through the deep snows."

She shook her head, both to flick off a biting fly and to banish her trepidation. "Where is your place?"

"West and a little north," was all he said. And she let it go, knowing she was being a credulous, cowardly thing.

As they splashed through the stream where he'd cleansed her wounds, she fought to maintain her regal posture, and at the same time to control the sting of tears that came to her eyes.

"Mayhap I should have named you Rainwater Eyes."

Her voice was stifled with shame. "I can't think what's wrong with me." She did know, though. She had the sinking feeling that, no matter what she planned or tried in the future, today she was leaving her last small hopes of returning to the life she knew.

"Regrets?" Cougar asked quietly.

"I . . . I wish I'd never let Tobias talk me into coming here." There was pain in her voice.

" 'Twould have been best, no doubt, but, like most wisdom, it's come too late to be of much use."

She rubbed her eyes fiercely, and when they were dry she felt there would be no more tears. She felt as if she'd recently suffered some great emotion, but that it had burned itself out.

Cougar took both reins in one hand and with the other hand burrowed beneath her hair to stroke the nape of her neck. She felt that awful tingle of vulnerability.

"I'm that glad you did no' decide to walk," he teased. " 'Twould be a shame to spoil such perfect feet. I do no' recall that I've ever met a woman who had such perfect feet — who was as nigh to perfect everywhere. You even have a bonny neck; it gives your head the carriage and freedom swans have, and African savages, and mayhap Cleopatra — ah!" he made a sound of disgust. "You're trembling again! You would think you were in the hands of a toothpuller."

She refused to comment. She *was* trembling, and she despised herself for it. What was this strange bewilderment that overtook her everytime he touched her? Until she'd met him, she'd considered love-making much as she supposed most women considered it: in marriage it was a wife's duty to receive her husband, outside of marriage it need never be a topic of thought to a lady at all. And since she'd never planned to marry she'd never given it deeper consideration than that. But now . . .

She felt his body, hard and athletic, against hers. With his hand around her back he was holding her folded close. Under her cheek she could feel his heart beating, and an emotion clutched her. Her senses flooded. Shutting her eyes, she wondered what it would be like if he truly was her husband and they were on their wedding trip. Her throat tightened with sudden torment.

He must have sensed it. With a hand on her throat, he raised her head. She closed her eyes, waiting for his mouth. At the touch of his lips a shiver of response went through her. His kiss hardened — and she was kissing him back.

When he lifted his head, she realized that the horse had stopped moving. She blushed deeply, trying to recall herself, but Cougar only smiled, holding her.

Eventually they moved on, along a trail cut by elk, moose and bear.

What was happening to her? He'd made love to her altogether five times since the night before last. And each time he'd given her pleasure such as she'd never imagined. Surely it was wrong. Surely she shouldn't like what he did to her so much.

*What was happening to her?*

126

Her fingers nervously entwined her blond hair where it fell into her lap.

Perhaps it was the novelty. Things would be different now that they were on the move. No doubt he would be less rested, less engrossed with her, less demanding. But if he wasn't . . .

If he wasn't, he simply couldn't find her willing every time the whim to have her struck him. No! She must get herself back in control.

More important, she must get away from him — no matter what risks she had to face. Before he took her much farther into the wilderness. And before winter, if possible. She'd tried her hand at packing a horse this morning. Of course, he'd had to redo almost all of her work, but she would try it again and again, until she acquired the skill. She was determined to learn enough from him to leave him. She couldn't long endure this ambiguous attachment.

She glanced up and found his eyes on her. And the expression there told her more forcefully than words that he too was determined.

She turned away guiltily. A pair of eagles stretched on the wind ahead; mysterious hills shimmered in the distance; the wilderness extended all around them. He was taking her deeper into this land which seemed to seethe with hidden dangers, yet which seemed to shimmer as well, to beckon treacherously. It lay like a place out of the imagination, where queer things could happen, incongruous as dreams. Wasn't she already lost to it? Wasn't she only fooling herself to think she could escape? Would she really be allowed to leave it? Ever?

She knew Cougar was still regarding her with that pale gaze of his, which saw far too far and much too much. "What are you scheming?" he said at last.

She blinked innocently. "You have a suspicious mind."

"That I have, lassie. And I do no' like it when you're silent like this, with prickles in your great blue eyes. I would far rather you be breathing fire on me, or making a nuisance of yourself."

"I don't seem to be able to please you no matter what I do."

A great stillness descended over him, yet his emotion was apparently strong, for his words came out rasping with unquiet. "Oh aye, you please me. And that's what worries me most of all."

She was to be called Flame. It made her sound like another person, someone quite unconventional. And this person, this woman called Flame, was living as the bride of a man called the Waiting Cougar, a man who didn't seem quite like other men. He seemed a little less — or a little more — than an ordinary man. He was a little leaner and harder, with a certain grace that put one much in mind of a muscular cat.

On the move, as Flame had forecast, his mind was preoccupied. Though he kept her always in sight, and always comfortably fed, warm, and safe, she knew that with every breath he took he was also gauging the countryside, mapping their route through this rolling hill land that was covered with scrawny pine and cedar. Riding, or walking beside Irongray, he moved with that muscular cat's loose swift ease, his back as straight as the long barrel of his rifle, his gray-green eyes distant. He would look east, then north, and sometimes his eyes stopped and sighted on something, as if he spied game, or Indians, then after a while they went on, only to stop once more. She tried to see what he saw, but there was only a stream winding ahead, or the cant of the hills, or maybe a gully with a few trees where some birds chirped. She stared until her eyes ached, yet she could see only sage and shriveled flowers.

Still, she sensed that he saw more, and that he was continuously feeding information into his mind and checking it with what he knew and what he expected. There, no doubt, were economies of time, effort, trouble, and horseflesh on which their success or even their survival depended. She guessed that he must be taking into account things about the season, the water supply, the weather, what equipment they had at hand, their meat supply, the condition of the grass . . .

Yes, this and much more must be perpetually present on the margin of his mind. Yet, though he was apparently absorbed by these problems, as a mountain man he seemed to have mastered them. He had skill, craft. He was huntsman, wrangler, furrier, freighter, tanner, smith, gunmaker, dowser, merchant . . . She'd seen nothing so far at which he wasn't adept. But above all, he saw, he smelled, and he heard.

If he'd been more talkative she would have picked his brain shamelessly, but he wasn't talkative now. He was too intent upon their passage.

They made fifteen miles that first day, and when they camped near the ford of a small stream, her back and legs ached from the hours spent on horseback. That night they ate jerked meat, boiled and pounded with prairie turnips. The fire burned warm in its circle of rocks until Cougar allowed it to die;

129

then they sat and looked at the night, looked out at the distant hills that stood like piles of darker night. She fell asleep with his arm around her, with the roughness of his chin on the sensitive skin of her temple.

After an early start the following morning, he stopped about two miles out. He showed her a spot where an Indian had silently watched their camp and as silently slipped away.

"Will he attack us?"

Cougar didn't seem to hear her.

"Are we in danger?" She let her full impatience show in her voice: "For heaven's sake, answer me! Who would watch us, and why?"

He shrugged, and let the words out quietly: "The Blackfeet. Evidently they have it in mind to escort us out of their hunting grounds." His discerning eyes swung to her. " 'Twould be a witless thing for you to try to flee. I ken you've had it in your mind. But do no' try it, lassie, for your own sake."

They put another fifteen miles behind them before the night, and twenty more the next day. Flame had seldom been so exhausted. Or so dispirited. When Cougar told her they would set up a temporary camp beside a shallow, muddy creek trickling at the foot of a bare and windswept hill, her gaze went to him, and traveled from his face out to the night wavering over the land.

" 'Tis sufficiently safe. Even our escort knows we must take meat to live."

About dawn the following day he pointed out a wolf near their camp and told her that buffalo couldn't be far away. A few minutes later she stood beside him on the hilltop. There she sighted the immense herd.

Cougar lifted his gun that was always in his hand now and refreshed the priming, then he went up onto Irongray's back without touching the stirrups. "We'll have steaks for dinner." He looked down at her with an especially sunny smile. The horse slung its head, dancing in a tight ring, but he dragged it around and drove it toward the bison.

The outlying animals began to move as soon as they sighted him, but there was no great stampede, no great sign of alarm. He used Irongray to cut out a huge bull. The horse routed the buffalo's trot off at an angle from the rest of the herd. Cougar shot once from the saddle of his horse. Flame saw the buffalo stumble with the shock of the ball entering his shoulder, but otherwise the animal hardly faltered. Meanwhile Cougar reined Irongray and jumped from his saddle, all the while priming and loading his rifle for a second shot.

Wounded and angry now, the buffalo reeled to face his attacker. He spied Cougar on the ground and started toward him, moving faster, faster, rising on the very edges of his hooves, his ears rigid with anticipation, his tail fixed straight out behind him. His head dropped and his muscles bunched; his horns were like dark-colored pitchfork tines, his eyes were lit like looking glasses. His power built up smoothly, stubbornly, with a precision perfected in his breed by centuries of ancestral battles. He ran with amazing agility for such a boulder of a beast. Ever closer to Cougar, he lowered his head even more for the charge.

The pitchfork horns were aiming straight for Cougar, who calmly knelt on one knee, took aim, and fired. It was done with such practice, with such casual disregard of the danger, that Flame stood dazed on the hilltop, watching as he walked to the animal and nonchalantly commenced to butcher it.

He brought back to camp only the choicest parts—the fleeces from each side of the backbone, weighing perhaps one hundred pounds each. They included the hump, where he said the very best cuts were found. Flame discovered buffalo tongue that noon, and she learned to value the marrow bones, both because the marrow was delicious and because Cougar pointed out that the whopping bones could be strapped onto the pack horses and carried for traveling fare.

He tied what they did not immediately eat to a tree branch, out of reach of the hungry gray-and-white wolves that apparently were always to be found slinking on the heels of a buffalo herd. "Meat's improved by a brief period of hanging—the way a woman's improved by letting her rest when she's spent."

That put her on her guard. The times he'd made love to her in the aspen grove had come to seem remote, in time as well as distance. And of course it had all been horrible. Horrible and yet . . .

He's winning, my girl, she told herself warily. Be careful or he'll have you corrupted beyond redemption.

Yet, he didn't try to seduce her that evening, or the next. He merely lay listening to the night sounds, running his hand caressingly over her until she fell asleep.

She foolishly relaxed her watch.

He killed two more buffalo over those next two days. She learned to pierce the slices of meat he butchered out, and to string them on lines for drying in the smoke of the fire. They worked companionably, almost like a real married couple.

When he held her in both his arms on the third night and let her lie undisturbed for a time, she was already half-asleep when he began to massage her breasts with a leisurely circular motion, his palms grazing the peaks. Almost without her realizing it her relaxed breathing became tighter and more pronounced. Still, it seemed he was only dallying. Not until her nipples were so sensitive that his touch was almost painful did his hand slide down below her ribcage. She thought then that she should try to stop him, she really should . . .

His hand continued downwards, his fingers stroked her pelvis. He rolled her onto her back by slow degrees. But when he pressed her legs open to give his hands deeper access, she suddenly stiffened.

"Nae, lie still . . . lie still." There was a soft silver light in his eyes, mesmerizing.

His fingertips stroked firmly along the soft flesh of her inner thighs, from her knees to the fleece between her legs. This, a dozen times repeated, created a building of antipation. She didn't even care that she was making herself totally and immodestly open to him now. The desire he was igniting overcame all her scruples.

But then his fingers were delicately parting her, sliding inside, the pad of his thumb softly caressing without. She felt herself becoming fluid under this handling, felt a melting sort of ecstasy growing within her. Her heart and soul and senses began to move as with music, her blood was lava, her pulse was ablaze.

"No." She struggled up weakly. "No, don't — " But she was too late at any effort to save herself. Those deft fingers were already bringing her to the final

133

moment, to a climax which had barely ended when he got to his knees and wrapped his brawny arms about each of her legs and pulled the lower half of her body up onto his thighs. A few pushes and she was impaled. The sensation immediately brought on another rush of seething spasms, stronger this time. She moaned and boiled over. It was as if a river of feeling was drowning her banks; the flood was in control of her. She felt herself clenching around him. He felt it, too, and inhaled with a gasp and thrust deeper into her.

As she struggled to catch her breath again, he began to caress her once more. His fingers trailed over her tingling breasts, the flat of her stomach, and down her thighs. She was still exquisitely sensitive everywhere, and his light touches brought her breath back to a shuddering response. She was spread to him; he was kneeling between her opened legs, impaling her, she felt exposed—yet it was delicious.

"I can no' believe I have you like this," he whispered. "You're that bonny. Kiss me and give me your tongue." He leaned over her, holding himself on his arms on either side of her.

The movement thrust him even deeper into her. She moaned softly as she ran the tip of her tongue over his lower lip. He put a hand under head, lifting her mouth to him, and with the other hand he gently stroked her hair back from her face. She gingerly explored his mouth with her tongue. His teeth were smooth, the insides of his cheeks incredibly delicate; his lower lip was full, like ripe grapes. When she nipped it between her teeth, the effect on him was electric. Shifting his position fractionally, he withdrew, then pushed his manhood deeper, yet

134

deeper into her. A shiver passed through her; her eyes opened wide with anxious expectancy.

His hands were on her waist. He pulled her against him and sank himself into her at the same time. She gave a start, though her eyes continued to gaze into his. He thrust again and again. Soon all she knew was this insistent friction, these sharp, deep pangs of pleasure. He kept it up until he reached his climax. She felt him in her innermost recesses, throbbing. She heard him grunt as though he'd been hit, felt his body convulse. Her arms reached for him, he came into them and laid his head on her breasts.

At last he pulled away and carefully lowered her hips to the robe again. He kissed her face, forehead, eyes, mouth. "You're like fruit, secretly filled with such sweet juice." His lips found one of her nipples and drew it to his tongue pleasantly.

It was a moment before she was free of the torpid spell cast over her. She realized then that he'd waited for this. He'd waited; waited for her guard to be lowered, waited for her will to be weak, waited for her resistance to be indecisive. He'd waited, as he was always going to be waiting.

"Another triumph for you," she muttered bitterly. "Why don't you just take me, why must you make it such a defeat for me?"

"Why no' just beat you, tame you once and for all?"

"I don't know—why not?"

He made a sound of impatience. "Do I seem the sort to want a spiritless woman? I was born a Scot. I like a bit of a storm now and again, a bit of a battle, a bit of pith. I was born a Scot, my heart. I do no' submit to anyone, nor do I look for tame submission from my wife.

"Still and all, though I do no' want to break you, I'll no' let you foil me, or keep parts of yourself back from me. I shall have you, all of you—even your pleasure. I oft' think I'll never quite fathom you, but I desire you, and as long as I do I mean to make your pleasure my pleasure."

"Cougar, let me go!" she pleaded suddenly.

"Go where, lassie?" His voice was gentle. "Back to the Blackfeet? To the wolves? Where will you go?"

"I loathe you," she murmured wretchedly, glaring at the stintless stars. "I absolutely loathe you."

"Oh aye, I can tell."

The next day they filled several parfleches with the smoke-dried strips of buffalo meat. On the surface their relationship was all very ordinary seeming again. Yet she was finding life with him like riding a strong current, like being swept along without her assent.

Strangely, though she wished she could escape his passion, it gave her a rueful satisfaction to know that he wanted—*needed*—her for something, even if only as an outlet for his sensualism, for she was learning more fully each day how desperate was her reliance on him. With each meal he provided it became more apparent to her how she needed him for her very survival. He was a wall to place her back to; he was her only shield against death.

As they packed to travel again, he said casually, "As soon as we're over the Divide we'll be visiting a village of the Salish—the people you call the Flatheads."

She was helping to load the horses (and doing a better job of it by this time). "Will it be safe?" She was careful to keep her voice as casual as his, but

136

the truth was she felt tight as a bowstring, at the mere mention of coming in close contact with Indians. She flashed him a quick glance, and found him watching her with an almost paternal expression.

He went back to getting the last of their outfit together—his flints, a stray possible sack, some gun powder. "You'll be safe as long as you stay with me."

She didn't know if she was reassured or not.

That morning, for the first time, there was frost on the ground; it crunched as they started out, and a raw chill was in the breeze. They left the muddy creek and struck north, then turned west again. They climbed into foothills, and the Rocky Mountain forest began to appear. Up into stands of lofty timber they climbed, into woods so deep the light was green and tarnished.

The horses moved with the light crackle of pine needles under their hooves now. The leaves of the hardwoods were scarlet and gold, already burned by frost here.

The sun sank and shadows stretched out across their path. They camped that night near the summit of a pass with mountains poised on either side of them. The wind was particularly bitter. It lashed her full in the face, a stream of arctic air with fangs and talons of ice.

Cougar had pressed their pace all afternoon, and now even the pack horses were tired. As if sulking at being worked so hard, they turned their tails to the wind and cropped at what dry grass there was to be found in the area of their picketline.

Flame gathered a pile of dead cedar limbs. With his flint and steel, Cougar built a fire for her beneath a stone outcrop, and she huddled near it to brew some sage tea. He soon left to do some hunting.

The snow-cold wind blustered off the peaks to lift plumes of sparks off the fire and whip up the smoke and steal most of the heat away. Cougar had left her his capote (he didn't seem to feel the cold), but even with it wrapped about her she couldn't stop shivering.

It was full dark by the time he came back with a liver and hams of an elk. He took a place beside her under to stone outcrop, to the windward, obviously offering his big body as further protection from the wind. Recalling last night, however, she was resolved to keep her distance from him. Without exciting his notice (she thought) she moved away from him, even though it meant placing herself more directly in the wind.

He set about slicing some meat for their supper, which they roasted on sticks over the fire.

Afterwards, he dug in his pack for a clean cotton cloth to wipe his weapons. He seemed never to tire. There were times when it was wearying to keep up with his quiet invincible energy.

He fed the fire again, until it popped with fat wood, then looked at her, his mouth forming a small smile. "Are you no' feeling a wee bit cold over there?"

"I'm fine."

He blew out his breath, watching the steam it made. The tawny fur of his cap gleamed in the firelight as the wind ruffled through it. "I thought I saw you shiver just then."

The breeze curled around her. lapping at her with its tongues of rime. "N—no."

"Come, lassie, do no' be so foolish. Come back over here and let me warm you."

She stayed where she was.

He unrolled the buffalo robe and the red blanket, then paused to look at her. "You can no' spend the night huddling there."

With a heaving breath of resignation, she stood and went to him. But as she took the capote off, he said, "Best to leave your dress on tonight." He pulled her down and curved her back into his belly. He spread the capote over them as an extra blanket.

"Goodnight, lassie."

Neither of them budged again through all of the long, cold night.

# Chapter Ten

Though everything was frozen in the morning and they had to await their start on the thawing of the pack covers in the heat of the fire, they were on the move once more before sun-up. "The Salish live in yon strath," Cougar said, pointing down from the high summit to a wide-open river valley.

As they picked their way down, the valley was filled with early morning mist, which turned to gold as the low sun touched it.

It didn't take Cougar long to find the village. Flame girded her courage to the occasion. Deep inside her stomach was a small hard spot. She hated this whole idea so badly she wanted to jump and run.

As they came in sight, a young brave shouted, and Cougar raised his hand in greeting before wiping the dust off his face with the sleeve of his shirt.

Women wearing blankets, their black hair dressed in chignons, stopped in the act of digging roots to stare at Flame. The brave, their guard, evidently, spoke to Cougar in the Salish tongue. They were waved on into the village.

They halted outside the outermost ring of tepees,

and as he lowered her from Irongray to the thick and slippery carpet of pinestraw, he said, "I want you to stay with the animals 'til I come for you. You're to behave yourself, now—harken." Then, all too quickly, the smoky-fawn leather of his shirt and breeches disappeared around the nearest tepee.

A tide of irritation rose in her. Behave herself, indeed!

Meanwhile, their arrival was being loudly announced by three Indian dogs that looked like skinny wolves. (They were just skeletons, really, with their spines humped up). Soon Flame found herself surrounded by villagers, all wrapped in blankets, their black eyes alight with curiosity. Men's, women's, children's faces were looking at her, each containing wonder. No one raised a hand against her, no matter how hard they studied her. They only grinned, and gently moved their heads up and down. Ready to flee nonetheless, she hesitated in opposition to all her instincts.

A warrior pushed through the crowd. His overbright eyes fastened on her with what seemed wariness. As he came closer, she automatically backed away. He appeared to her a hardened, cold, brutal young man. She looked around frantically; Cougar was still nowhere to be seen.

The young warrior stood staring at her. The sun was on her hair. He'd probably never seen anyone as light complected and fair haired as she was; yet, he examined her without a sign of admiration, without giving her a hint of friendliness. His eyes were so sharp that she felt like a butterfly on a pin.

Finally he reached to finger a few strands of her hair. The gesture was too fraught with memories of the Blackfeet for her to bear stoically. She jerked away, and turned to push through the crowd of

141

solemn, wide-eyed faces. The people became murmurous, but they made way for her.

She broke through the last of them, bent on finding some place to run to. But she was caught from behind and lifted by a pair of strong arms. Her hair swung wildly, momentarily blinding her, and her feet pawed the air for purchase as she plucked at the arms holding her.

"Whoa, lassie!"

"Cougar!" She twisted in his hold and he set her down. Behind him the dark-haired Indians had begun to disperse. Their exaggerated show of indifference made her feel ashamed. One woman went back to the deerskin staked out by her tepee; she took up again the tedious job of scraping it. Others went back to building brush windscreens around their homes, preparing them against winter. Suddenly they all seemed perfectly harmless.

"I guess I was a little nervous."

"Aye," Cougar agreed softly.

"They . . . there were a lot of them, though. They made a big circle around me and . . . I wasn't sure . . ."

" 'Twas only because you're a stranger to them at present." There was a half-amused and half-incredulous look on his face, a kind of what-will-she-be-doing-next! expression.

"Well, they're strange to me, too," she said defensively.

"Mostly they only wanted to see this." He gave her hair an affectionate tug. Then, in his most courtly way, he offered her his arm.

He led her to a large tepee in the very center of the village. Outside it sat an old man, pitch-dry with age. Behind him was a tripod with a medicine bundle hanging from it. Cougar sat across the small outside fire from him, indicating that Flame should also take a seat on the spread buffalo-skin rug. He began to speak to the old man, gesturing to her often. The Indian nodded and grunted, scowling.

He wore his gray hair in two long plaits. His face was broad and brown, the skin wrinkled and soft. He was wearing a long vest sewn with gray rabbit furs. It was old, and there were small hairless patches where the bare rabbit skin showed through. He was small, shaken, elderly, but he had a dazzling, shifting glance.

His eyes kept going to Flame's hair. She understood by now that any Indian was going to have an urge to examine it. For a moment she sat paralyzed; she'd already been touched on an old sore—her ordeal with the Blackfeet would deluge her mind with memories if she let it—but she defied her terror and stood. A few steps took her around the fire ring to the Indian's side. She knelt, somehow looking him straight in the eye. She was solemn, while the old man's expression changed to something even more implacable than before.

"Easy, love," Cougar said softly. "Rotten Gut's counted more coup than there are hairs on your pretty head."

"Give me your knife," she replied, not taking her eyes from the chief.

Surprisingly, Cougar didn't hesitate. He leaned across the low fire and placed the handle of his belt knife in the palm of her hand. She in turn offered it to the Indian. She then separated a hank of hair from underneath and turned her head, holding it out—bending and baring her tender neck at the same time.

Without a word, Rotten Gut sliced the hair off. Holding it up in his left hand, a silken strand nearly

143

a yard long, he grunted. He didn't actually smile, but his face was lightly transformed. He wrapped the strand around his fingers, then turned and slipped the coil of it into his medicine bundle.

After a considering pause, he handed the knife back to her. And now he grinned. The dazzle in his eyes was stronger than ever. He surveyed her with a bright bird-like glance, as if she were the only specimen in captivity of a breed beyond the reach of his old mind.

At last he began to chatter in his soft slurred language, his voice rusty with a age. Unable to understand, she smiled as she eased away. Cougar took his knife back and sheathed it as she sat beside him once more.

The men's conversation continued, though she couldn't help knowing their talk was still about her. Rotten Gut often twinkled at her obliquely. And after a long monologue by Cougar, the old Indian chuckled, then began to laugh.

His laughter caught in his chest; he coughed and couldn't stop. A woman from a nearby tepee rushed to bring him water. He took it, and soon started to speak again, but still laughingly.

"What's he saying?" Flame murmured, unable to bear being left out any longer.

Cougar's eyes crinkled as he looked down at her. He scratched the side of his nose and shifted awkwardly. His voice, when he answered, was elaborately offhanded. "He says you're well formed — 'much woman' — with languishing eyes and a flexuous mouth. He sees that you're brave, too, and . . . he questions how I managed to deflower you. He supposes I had to make noises like a grizzly to terrify you into yielding."

Her face turned icy hot. "I suppose I must abide

144

this kind of vulgar ridicule."

He laughed uneasily, half with wry amusement, half with seemingly honest regret.

Rotten Gut called out over his shoulder, and after a moment a young woman reluctantly ducked out of the big tepee. Flame's immediate impression was of black hair, narrow bones, and hungry eyes. Cougar rose, as a gentleman would do when a lady entered a room. Rotten Gut spoke to the girl briefly, and she in turn looked at Flame with a peculiar strained expression on her face and mouth.

"This is Lone Goose, Rotten Gut's daughter," Cougar said.

The girl had a smile for him. She even came to sit on the other side of him. She seemed to know him well. As she spoke to him her fingertips touched his knee.

He looked from her to Flame. He said something in Salish, evidently for the girl's consideration, his sandy brows lifting in question. Lone Goose's answer seemed distrustful.

Flame blushed to the roots of her hair. She'd had enough being discussed as if she were an object. With as much grace as she could muster, she rose. "Excuse me," she said stiffly.

"Do no' leave the village," Cougar warned.

She didn't look back at him. On her way around Rotten Gut's big tepee, however, she found her path blocked by the same hard-looking warrior who had frightened her earlier. He barely glanced at her now; instead he was watching Cougar, sitting so cozily with Lone Goose. His eyes were hooded, but not enough to hide the anger in them.

Flame found a place to sit with her back against a tree near Cougar's animals, and there she waited to see what might come next.

145

Nothing came, at least nothing of note. Now and then children passed near her while chasing doves into the afternoon. When they stopped to giggle and shyly peep at her around the tree trunks, she couldn't resist smiling back. Otherwise, except for a lazy green lizard, in whose territory she seemed to be trespassing, she was left alone.

Flies buzzed and settled and buzzed some more. A leaf left its bough in the canopy overhead and spiraled to the ground. About the village venison steamed over fires, and grandmothers sat close by, bent under blankets. Smoke lay low, blue, over the tops of the tepees. A group of men eventually came in on ponies, dragging newly cut and trimmed lodge poles.

As evening came on, the younger men of the village joined together outside the perimeter of the tepees for some sort of arrow and hoop contest. As the married women visited together, comparing their babies, the younger girls slipped away to watch and cheer the boys' games.

Flame tried to take in everything she saw. These were the people who had taught Cougar their forest secrets—their cures, their ways of hunting game, their omens and talismans. Had he also learned from them how to cast a spell over a woman? How much of him was the adopted son of the Salish, called the Waiting Cougar, how much the Scot whose name he wouldn't tell her? He seemed to have a dual temperament, a man by turns crude and courtly, cautious and reckless, a man as skilled in ornate speech as he was in mystic silences.

The tethered horses stamped the flies off; Iron-gray's harness jingled. He turned his hindquarters into the setting sun and drooped to rest on one foreleg. Flame heard a man chanting from some-

146

where: "Hey-ya-ah-no-ah . . ." It was growing dark. It seemed a long time since she'd last seen Cougar.

She was brought food. It was Lone Goose. Up close the girl looked perhaps fifteen. She didn't smile, not even in a stiff way, and didn't seem at all friendly. Since there was no way for Flame to converse with her, she was just as glad with the suspicious-seeming girl soon slipped off again.

She ate alone then. Her supper was a mixture of dried corn and beans cooked with buffalo marrow. By and by, loneliness crept up on her. Pictures of homely rooms and attractive gowns and friendly, familiar faces invaded her unguarded mind. She stared ahead, unseeing, lapped by unexpected misery. Oh, to be *home* again!

She reminded herself that in fact she had no home. Tobias had sold the house their father had left them to fund his foolish expedition. She had no other relatives close enough to go to without feeling she was imposing. Nevertheless, she would never be satisfied until she'd regained her own homeland and left these mountainous wildernesses far behind.

She'd been asleep, deep in a humming hive of dreams, and awakened with a start when Cougar lifted her from the ground. It was late. The sky above was dark navy, nearly black. He was carrying her with long strides to Irongray. Groggily she thought, He's carrying me off again.

He was laughing quietly. "Rotten Gut's got the notion you're a spirit woman."

A tart response edged to the tip of her tongue, but looking into his eyes, she swallowed it back. Let the old chief believe what he would.

As Cougar hoisted her onto Irongray, she asked,

"Are we leaving here tonight?"

"We'll go a ways off to make our own camp."

"Won't they be insulted or something?"

"They know me; I've always liked my privacy. There'll be no hard feelings."

Once more seated across his saddle, supported by his solid chest, she asked, "Why do you like your privacy so, Cougar?" She'd had several hours to think while he was occupied, and as usual she'd found herself thinking mostly of him. Why was a man of his obvious ilk wasting his life in a wilderness?

Her question was met with silence, but she wasn't willing to let it be passed off so simply. She looked up at him. "So far I know that you're from Scotland; you are—or *were*—a gentleman, for you show some knowledge of the behavior of a gentleman; and you mentioned once that you were a student in Edinburgh. Sometimes you speak very poetically, so I assume a onetime interest in letters and the arts. What brought you out here, a man of education, breeding and—"

"Mayhap I'll tell you my tale one day, explain how 'twas, though the fable will no' enlighten you a bit into the philosophy of life. Meanwhile, I prefer to research more closely this flesh that looks like ivory." His head had lowered, his lips trailed along her cheekbone. "Aye, 'tis ivory smooth." With a gentle effort he reclined her backwards on his arm and slid his free hand under the hem of her dress. His breath brushed her mouth as he murmured, "I think we'd best put up a shelter this night. Indians can be nosey when their interest is piqued. They'll all be wondering how I handle the braw spirit-woman who battled the Blackfeet and survived."

His hand was sending thrills of excitement crackling through all her veins. "You're making me dizzy," she protested, a dazed look on her face.

A smile. A grin—incongruously full of sunshine at this hour of the night. Then a chuckle. And finally semi-acquiescence laced with that charm that made her want to forgive him anything. He kept his hand where it was buried between her thighs, but said, "Suit yourself, lassie—until we get a shelter up anyway. You'll no' deny me then, will you?"

He was still smiling; she felt that that smile was one of the most unnerving temptations she'd ever had to struggle against. She didn't want to struggle at all for the moment; she only wanted to watch it, enthralled.

"Will you?" his great silky voice demanded.

He was so very much a man, and his eyes told her that she was very much a woman, and that they were alone together, and that he knew she would respond to him.

His hand under her dress moved again, delicately, unequivocally.

What a rogue he was!


Cougar poked his head into the buffalo-hide shelter he had erected the night before. "Good morning to you." He was grinning wickedly. "I hope I did no' wear you out last night. Will you be able to get up anytime this day? I wanted to see you in this."

He tossed something onto Flame's feet. She looked up at him with a face still vacant from sleep. For a moment she didn't know where she was, then the framework of willow wands and the walls of the dome-shaped shelter came into perspective. She could tell by the quality of light on the skin walls that it was late for her to still be abed. He'd probably been up for hours.

She sat up and, holding the red blanket over her breasts, reached for the parfleche lying across her feet. She opened the rawhide envelope slowly, shaking out the new garment inside, but waiting for him to leave before she slipped it over her head. The skin was tanned nearly white and was soft as velvet. A design of beads had been sewn across the front yoke. The inner fur made it warm. There were new moccasins with rabbit-skin leggings as well.

She crawled out of the low shelter and took a deep breath of the cool, mountain-clean air as she stood. She smelled evergreens and woodsmoke and the damp musty freshness of fallen leaves.

They were camped next to a tiny lake amidst a golden aspen wood. In the morning sunshine, drifts of yellow leaves were falling about the trees' mossy roots. The flames of Cougar's campfire were pale in the light.

She paused to smooth the wrinkles from her new dress. Its hem fell a little farther down her calves than the one Cougar had made for her, but had slits up each side to above knee-height. A few weeks ago she would have given anything for a proper gown, even one of the drab ones her father and Tobias had preferred (they liked to keep her dressed as plainly as the Pilgrim mothers), but she was learning to be happy with leggings and these freedom-inducing Indian dresses.

She was in fact very pleased with this new gift, but before Cougar she pretended indifference.

He said, "Aye, that's nice." Sitting cross-legged on a buffalo skin by the fire, he seemed to consider her disheveled dryad loveliness. "Fancier than my handiwork — and made a little bigger, I think. I notice you fill out the other pretty well."

"I haven't put on any weight." She glared at him, though perhaps it was true. He would know. Never had she enjoyed such an appetite, and he was a good campfire cook.

"Take no offense. I like a woman with flesh on her." There was laughter down deep in his voice. "As I recall, you were a mite thin when I first took you on my horse." He squinted at her, musing. "But if you'd seen yourself then, that young and humbled, too lovely to be bought so cheap . . .

"Still and all, a few more ounces in the right places make you the more womanly to my mind—and to my hands. I never had a taste for half-formed adolescent girls. Nae, 'tis a woman I want in my bed, full-bodied, desirable, warm, with a ripe mouth that trembles against mine—"

She interrupted with, "Aren't I the lucky one then, to be so close to just what always you wanted?"

He scratched his shaven chin. His tone was grave, though his mouth twitched. "Oh aye, I think you are."

She made a face at him, coming closer to the fire for its warmth. He abruptly grabbed her wrist and pulled her down across his lap, bottom up.

"Tsk, give you a fluff of plumage and you take on like an Amazon queen." He was holding her across his thighs, one hand busy on her bottom. "Nae, a few more ounces here can only be to the good, I'm thinking."

"Let me go!" His impetuousness had taken her by surprise. She wriggled in his lap, endeavoring to escape.

His giant yet gentle hands went on pressing her down and caressing her at the same time. "Stop making such a fuss, lassie. I'm only checking my investment."

151

Appalled, she managed to twist around, and she upset his balance at the same time. He rolled backwards, carrying her with him.

"Look at this! Getting so braw you can knock me right over and hold me down. You are becoming an Amazon. I'll feel lucky to be keeping my skin — that is if I'm to be let up from here. Next thing you'll be taking advantage of *me*. I'll be naught but your love-slave, chained wrist and ankle, living in God-forsaken brute despair."

She laughed outright, her eyes flicking his impossibly big shoulders and the knowledge in his look.

It was a huge joke, of course. The truth was that he was holding her clasped on top of him; yet his face was such an exaggeration of fear that she couldn't help but laugh again. It was a light ripply laugh; and a pair of dimples that she'd never showed him before appeared fleetingly in her cheeks.

His face softened and he laughed, too. It gave her an odd twinge to realize she was behaving as carefree as a girl. Early in her childhood she'd learned sobriety and made it her habit. Yet, here she was, laughing in happy confusion at the banter of a man who called himself after a vicious wild animal.

She was oddly reluctant to give the moment up. Her embarrassment had fled away and she wished simply to prolong this "contest". But give it up she must, for their play had been sufficient to bring him pulsatingly erect. She flushed to realize it. "Let me go; I find you uncomfortable."

" 'Tis a pity. What can I do to make myself more comfortable to you?"

She felt a tension growing inside her. "Let me go," she said, incapable of analyzing the unsettling feelings rushing through her body. Her wriggling movements now caused a luscious rubbing against him, and she had a sudden and shockingly vivid picture of him above her, her own knees drawn high . . .

*. . .her head thrown back, her eyes closed . . . she was making a mewing sound . . .*

His smile gentled, as did his hold on her, and she was able to rise to her feet again. She was trying futilely to shut out that picture . . .

*. . . she was in wild excitement, her fingertips pleading at the small of his back, her own back arched with spasms of delight . . .*

Sitting up, he said, "Flame, when was your last moon?"

She gave him a blank look, then her expression faded into understanding—and self-conscious offense. Her chin jerked up. "I'm hardly going to discuss such things with you."

"And why no'? I'm your husband, else I would no' be venturing into this no-man's land. Do you think I'll no' notice when—"

"Please!" She turned away toward the lake. "I don't want to discuss it."

"Aye, but we're going to. Sit down." It was an order, though not harshly put. Only when she gave every indication of ignoring it did his voice take on a note of warning. "I can make you sit down, heart; would you be wanting me to do that?"

She halted, yet stayed where she was, her back to him. The lake lay before her. He had baited a hook sometime before, and thrown it in. The line lay languid. The water barely lapped. Tiny bits of light, like gold flecks, jumped about the surface.

"I advise you, lassie, that sometimes 'tis far wiser to go with the will of the wind."

She felt a tingle along her forearms.

The little gold lights jumped on the lake.

What point would there be in putting his threat to

153

the test? Her hands were clasped tightly before her, cutting off the circulation to her fingertips. She turned her upper body, looked at him hesitantly around her hair, then did as he wanted: returned to kneel at the edge of the buffalo skin, sitting back on her heels, but with her spine straight enough to make it clear she was prepared to listen only against her will.

"My little light, my own little trembling Flame, I like your modesty, and respect it — I'm with the old Scotsman who wanted less chastity and more delicacy — but as your husband —"

"I've never recognized that title you give yourself, nor the use you make of it."

His head lowered, but his eyes held their steady gaze from beneath his sandy brows. "You wound me, love. Still and all, since I am making use of it, I'll also make myself accountable for it. I realize you were brought up an innocent, but surely you're aware of certain conditions in which married women periodically find themselves. To be perfectly frank — I admit I would prefer to be frank for the moment — I'm talking about the possibility of bairns."

She inhaled sharply. He held a hand up to stay her. "I assume you ken how women get bairns, and I assume you're bright enough to be aware that you're now susceptible."

She felt her face turn chalk white. "Can it happen so quickly?"

His smile was rueful. "Aye, I'm afraid so. With caution, however, we may avoid the problem. Which brings me back to my original question — left unanswered by all this matter of fact about my husbandry."

Her mind was whirling, and it took her a moment to recall his first question. When she did recall it,

154

she didn't know how to answer it. "I . . . my diary was lost with the boat. I don't remember . . . I don't know how much time . . ."

Through her distraction she heard him murmur, "Come here, lassie." There was understanding in his voice, and without consciously moving, she found herself kneeling before him. He took both her hands in his and held them to his heart. "We'll start marking your days next time then."

"What do you mean, 'marking my days'?" Her voice was threaded with panic. Her puritanical upbringing and lack of experience had not prepared her in the least for avoiding the usual consequences of regular love-making.

"Never mind; I'll take care of it."

"Oh, Cougar, I don't want to have a baby! Not here! Who would help me? I wouldn't know what to do. I don't know anything about having babies!"

And how could she ever go home again? How would she explain an illegitimate child? She would be the subject of unkind gossip and conjecture for the rest of her life.

He frowned quickly and pulled her into his arms to cradle her. "Do you think I'll let it happen if I can help it? I've no desire to change your name to Mother Eve a summer hence."

155

## Chapter Eleven

Cougar's frown became a scowl. "Nae, this is no place for a woman like you to give birth—even if Rotten Gut does claim he sees signs of a family of hunters and dream-weavers . . . Nae!"

He took both Flame's hands in his own and went on softly, "My heart, I'm sure that if we'd been married by a preacher in a kirk there would have been some woman to tell you these things—and much better than I have. As it stands, 'tis my duty to accomplish your education."

"But you can keep it from happening?"

His hand caressed her slender neck. " 'Tis no' a fool-proof method, but—"

She pushed away from him. "But chastity is, isn't it? I wouldn't be at risk at all if it weren't for you."

Very softly he said, "Those are dangerous, self-arousing words you sow. If 'twere no' for me you might be carrying the seed of Savage Goat's bairn right now. Or, if he chose no' to keep you as wife, you would be prey to any brave, from stripling to old man, who had the strength to pull you to the ground. You would be the tribe whore, and your bairns would be born slaves."

She swallowed hard; her eyes had gone dull and splintery, like uncut jewels. "No . . . no, you're making that up to scare me." She wiped her knuckles across her lips.

"I'm no' making anything up. I bought you, paid two bales of pelts for you—I would have given everything if he'd only known it!—because I would no' be able to live with myself knowing how you would be degraded and abused. I would always see you in my mind's eye, raped and broken."

She flinched and turned away.

"Flame, forgive me, I'm being that brutish, I ken I am, yet I've got to make you see—"

"—that I would die," she finished for him simply. "That without you I would die." It was the lesson he'd been trying to teach her from the beginning. And she felt at last the stark truth of it. There could be no escape from him. It would take her years to learn enough. He'd bought her—and she was incredibly lucky that he had.

Neither of them spoke for some time. A flock of glossy white swans arrowed overhead, their whistles as faint as ripples over rocks.

In the end it was she who broke the brittle silence: "I . . . I'm grateful to you for . . . for your protection and provision. In return, since I can't repay you what it cost you to . . . buy me, I can only try to make myself useful. I know how to work—I'm not at all unaccustomed to work—I believe I can easily bear a more equal burden of the labor necessary for our well-being. You've pampered me, I know, and you mustn't do that anymore. Assign me whatever tasks are within my abilities, and I'll do my best to obey you in those matters. In other matters I make no such promise."

She was no longer trembling, but felt leaden with

the misery of discovering her secret hopes had been nothing more than fantasies all along.

"You claim to be my husband, but I can never consider that claim to be valid, and I can never willingly grant you a husband's prerogatives. What you want from me in that way you must always take—using such strength and guile as you have.

"As a realist," she hurried on before he could interrupt, "I concede that you are strong and full of guile and that my defenses are yet feeble. Facing this—" she faltered, then looked at him candidly, "—facing this, I would be comforted to know that you're at least taking precautions to see that we . . . that I . . . that there's no child."

Her eyes had fallen away from his, but now they rose with pride again. "Nevertheless, don't think that I feel so grateful to you that I won't always be on the lookout for some means to escape you. The first opportunity I see, I'll take. Remember that, Cougar—you can't keep me forever."

There was something in his eyes, something dreadfully like an urge to do her some injury. He turned his head and considered her sidelong.

"I'll make you a bargain," he said suddenly. "Stay with me the winter—promise me you'll no' do anything stupid while the snow lies—and in turn I'll promise to see you safely down the Missouri when the grass is green again."

Hope flicked back to life in her breast. Now it was her turn to consider him. "How do I know I can trust you?"

"You can only accept my word on it." He added gruffly, "I'll probably have had my fill of your mulishness by the spring anyway. Well, is it a bargain?"

Very slowly she nodded.

"Aye, but 'til then you be aware that I consider our marriage fully legitimate. In Scotland a woman who accepts such an arrangement is called *handfasted*. Here she's called a winter squaw. I'll call you wife, and treat you as a wife—whether or no' you accept my husband's claim on you."

She rose wordlessly. She felt a little light-headed, felt she needed to bathe her face, needed an hour alone to compose herself. He didn't try to stop her as she left camp.

When she found the mouth of the creek that fed the lake, she knelt to scoop up a handful of water. It tasted cold and sweet. Sunlight glanced off the stones and vegetation and was absorbed by the water's dark, gently rippling surface. She knelt a long time there on the sandy bank, under the dappling shadows of the aspens, water trickling off her chin. After a while she realized that the faint rushing noise she was hearing must be the sound of a waterfall. Has there ever lived a woman or man who could resist falling water? Slowly she gathered herself together and stood.

She headed upstream. Dense undergrowth grew along the banks, but there was a path. It ran close up to the foot of a sheer cliff. The fleecy falls came over this cliff's high lip to drop a good one hundred feet, casting up rainbows and rags of mist at the bottom.

The path detoured around the cliff-face, but climbed steeply, and came out at last above the falls. Here Flame found Lone Goose, naked, standing ankle deep in the broad shallow pool behind the fall's edge. Her hands were on her long brown thighs, her black hair was loose and wet, and water was dripping off her small blunt face. She was looking down at her reflection in the glassy water.

Flame hardly wished to intrude upon what was clearly a private moment. She turned to go.

But something stopped her: a bush down the path that shuddered, just barely; a dead leaf that rustled. Someone was coming stealthily up the trail. Her fear of Indians returned instantly, and she followed what she knew was a cowardly impulse, and shrank down among the spindly leaves of some tall bear grass.

She glanced over her shoulder to see Lone Goose straightening casually, her brown eyes looking for her clothes on the shore. She didn't seem to be aware of Flame, or of the other person who was coming. Flame now felt awkwardly caught — if she stood up to warn the girl, Lone Goose would think she'd been spying on her. She decided her best course was to remain hunched, stone still. With luck, once the Indian coming up the path passed by her hiding place she could slip away without anyone being the wiser of her presence.

Meanwhile, Lone Goose was wading ashore. Her movements were leisurely — until she, too, became aware of someone on the path. Evidently she was not expecting anyone, and especially not the man who appeared, for her hands came up in an attempt to conceal her breasts and her other secrets as the warrior emerged onto the shore and stood there boldly. She paused in the water, staring back at him, before she began to edge toward her clothes again. As she touched dry land, he stepped forward and caught her arm.

Flame recognized him as the young man who had frightened her yesterday. She saw his fingers dig into Lone Goose's flesh so hard that the girl winced. Still, she made no sound, which Flame thought odd.

Instead, she struck out with her hand. The warrior ducked back, loosening his grip enough so that she was able to twist away from him. Since he had her cut off from her clothes, and the path blocked with his body, she started around the front of the pond, searching for a break in the undergrowth. Flame stood up now, ready to make some effort to help her, though the big Indian warrior frightened her.

He was following Lone Goose around the pond's edge, and his temper was visibly climbing. The outer corners of his eyebrows were up-tilted, his mouth was drawn back tight, showing his teeth.

The chase went half-way around the pond, dangerously close to where the water fell off the cliff-edge, then came back, and ended with the warrior, sweating slightly now, herding the girl into a corner made by fallen logs and treacle-thick mud.

He had her now. Flame felt she should do something—but what? Sound an alarm? In English? Call Cougar? But their camp was too far for him to hear her.

That left only one possibility. She began to frantically search the ground for a chunk of wood sturdy enough to serve as a weapon.

In the meantime, Lone Goose had turned to face her adversary. It was obvious that she was about to be captured, and she seemed to give up. She stood as if waiting for him to grab her. And he appeared to be satisfied with her waiting attitude. He crowded closer, but slower now. And in that instant, while he moved in so lazily, Flame's mind raced.

She intensely felt the girl's comparative weakness against a man nearly as big as Cougar. And she admired Lone Goose's courage when, seeing there was only one last outlet available to her, the girl took it.

Three light steps through the mud, a bound, and

the girl dove flat onto the surface of the shallow water. She came up, however, to find the warrior wading in after her, moccasins, breeches and all. She twisted and plunged her head under the water, so that only the twin rounds of her bottom broke the surface.

But brisk tiny creature that she was, it seemed she wasn't much of a swimmer. The warrior caught one of her fluttering feet easily. Fierce-eyed, tense with purpose, he pulled her toward him—ankle, knee, thigh, waist—he lifted her up, and before she could dodge away again, caught her in a bearlike embrace.

Now he rubbed his hands up and down her bare back and pressed back her naked breasts against his chest. She was very slim, with a waist he could almost span with his two hands. He obviously liked the feel of her water-cooled skin, slippery with wetness. She struggled weakly, but still she made no sound. Flame was confused by this. Should she interfere or not? Was there something going on here that she didn't understand? She decided to wait another instant, wood chunk in hand, before she made a move in the girl's defense.

Both Lone Goose and the warrior were panting from their chase. The warrior began to speak, forcing Lone Goose to listen to him. His voice came to Flame softly, though his grip on the girl seemed hard. Flame watched his back, shiny with sweat and drops of water, each individual muscle standing out in relief, swelling and shrinking as he moved to counter Lone Goose's little attempts to get away from him. His wolfish eyes were hooded by their slumbrous lids.

Lone Goose couldn't be trying very hard to escape. Could it be that this child of fifteen was secretly delighting in the friction of a man's body against her own? Could she own any experience of such things at her tender age?

After several long moments of speaking quietly, in an almost coaxing tone — but occasionally giving her a shake to reinforce his words (and occasionally running a hand over her spiky little breasts, her tight round belly, the glossy skin of her thighs) — he simply let her go. Regally, he waded ashore. He barely paused when he saw Flame standing there, a branch of dead wood gripped in her hands. He moved right past her, soft footed, and disappeared down the path.

Lone Goose waded ashore more slowly. Only her eyes started when she saw Flame. She knelt down stiffly by her clothing, her back to Flame and her hands pressed tight to her knees. Her eyes were brimming, but she held up her head with a tiny flicker of pride. Everything about her proclaimed, Go away!

She was merely a child, Flame reflected, a girl who didn't know how to handle a man who wanted her — wanted her fiercely. Her impulse was to try to comfort the poor thing, but common sense told her to simply leave the girl alone.

Common sense won, and after another moment she quietly slipped away.

Because she avoided the path on her way back (she was afraid Lone Goose's warrior might still be lurking) she got a little lost, and it was a while before she found the camp by the lake again. Cougar, when he heard her coming, turned from where he'd been standing and let go in a boom, "Hell's teeth! And I was wondering where you'd got to. Aye and I was, just!"

She didn't need to be told he was angry. His face was pale and for once his voice matched the size of

163

his chest. Yet with everything she'd been through already today, she was infuriated by this greeting. There was a point beyond which life couldn't intimidate her, couldn't beat her down. She had some self-respect left, after all. Almost past speech, her eyes dared him. She tucked her hair behind her ears and snapped, "Wonder away then! I go where I please."

He made an exasperated noise, strode across to her, and pulled her roughly into his arms. "You're overbold. You do no' ken when 'tis best to flinch," he said, giving her a little shake. "No wonder Rotten Gut insisted you have a keeper."

"Don't be so extravagant—and let me go!"

"You'll be let go when I'm ready," he said tautly. He pulled her closer into his arms, his mouth came down urgent and ungentle against hers. The whole scene seemed very like what she'd just witnessed at the top of the falls, with different players in the parts. She managed to wrench her mouth from his, but before she could say anything she saw Lone Goose standing at the edge of their camp. She looked just as Flame must have looked to her from the pond: confused, embarrassed, unsure.

But then her eyes flashed with (yes, Flame would have sworn it!) icy delight to see Cougar so angry with his strange yellow-haired woman.

When Cougar became aware of a third person's presence, he turned. She spoke to him in Salish. He quickly responded, but with a frown.

"Rotten Gut has called a council," he said in a clipped voice, putting Flame away from him. "You'd better come along with me. I see I can no' trust you on your own for a minute." He moved to find his fur hat and clamp it on his head.

"I would rather stay here," she said.

"Come, little greenhorn; do no' make me cuff

164

your ears."

If Lone Goose hadn't been standing there watching with such an expression of satisfaction, Flame might have taken a stand, but she had no desire to have to defend herself against an "earcuffing" before an audience.

So as Cougar strode toward the main village, she fell in behind him and bristled when he kept looking back to make certain she was still there. Lone Goose walked next to him, trying to keep up with his long stride. After a while he slowed his pace for her, then he was smiling again, his head back, the sun on his fur hat. He even paused to joke with some children.

Little greenhorn! Cuff her ears! Indeed!

Flame felt drained from the strains of this day; and she saw no reason why she had to be dragged along to this council. She wouldn't even understand what was being said.

The gathering was before Rotten Gut's big central tepee. Cougar sat down among the warriors. The old men of the tribe sat in the first ranks, the warriors next, and the women and children hindmost.

The first business was to smoke. The pipe Rotten Gut brought out from his hanging medicine bundle had a thick squat bowl and a long wooden stem festooned with multi-colored braided cloths and dyed feathers. He lit it and drew the smoke deep — and coughed an old man's rasping cough. As the pipe traveled around the circle, Cougar seemed to be at ease with the ceremony of it. He took his turn and passed on to the next man — who was, Flame realized with a start, the same warrior who had accosted Lone Goose.

Eyeing him sidelong from where she knelt behind Cougar, she saw there was something daring her in his expression; but his lids were dropped so that she couldn't see his eyes. She couldn't help noticing again the breadth of his shoulders and the way his stomach muscles stood out in static ripples. He was taller and heavier than any Indian she'd seen so far; she thought he must stand an inch or two above six feet and weigh more than one hundred ninety pounds.

The talk went on and on. One man after another rose to speak, while the rest kept a profoundly polite silence. Cougar occasionally summarized parts of it for her in quiet asides. It seemed a hunter had been mauled that morning by a huge grizzly bear, "what the Blackfeet call Real Bear." A medicine woman was even now busy putting poultices on the man's injuries.

As Cougar translated, she listened more and more skeptically. None of the Indian women ever spoke, she noticed. Evidently a woman's role here was one of merely listening. She found that increasingly dissatisfying, especially as the talk went on and on.

And so it came out — the question she'd wanted to ask forever — it came out involuntarily, without conscious choice, indeed, with immediate contrition for her rashness, for all talk around the circle halted, and all eyes flew to her face, most of them filled with infinite disapproval.

Cougar was looking at her, too. His eyes were unrevealing, but he couldn't quite repress his mouth. Rotten Gut spoke from the head of the circle. Elaborately Cougar turned to the old man and translated what she'd said. Now there was a quick scornful murmur among the men.

What she'd asked was, "Why on earth don't they stop all this useless chatter and just go out and kill the bear?"

166

Only the warrior beside Cougar seemed to nod in agreement with her. He didn't look at her, but she got the definite feeling she'd just come up a notch in his estimation. Meanwhile, Rotten Gut's heavy-lidded eyes were scrutinizing her strangely, as if he were seeing her but seeing something more as well. His people fell into an expectant silence. If Flame had known him better, she'd have recognized his far-away expression as a sign of one of his moments of foresight.

His answer, when it was spoken and translated, was, "A spirit woman who could survive capture and torture by the Blackfeet could perhaps kill such a grizzly bear. But we are only mortals. Sometimes we can slay a grizzly; more often grizzlies slay us."

Cougar briefly explained that a grizzly hunt was as dangerous as going to war. "For up to a thousand yards a grizzly, big as he is, can run as fast as a horse. With Dark Sun still out after horse thieves and the best hunters out after game, there's no' enough experience here to face a Real Bear."

She wasn't overawed. In fact, she was thoroughly bored by the time the council broke up with nothing decided.

Cougar visited throughout the village for the rest of the afternoon. Flame refused to follow him about, and he refused to let her return to their camp alone, so she remained instead near Rotten Gut's tepee.

Cougar, she saw, was very popular with the children. They hung on him and leaped about him with noisy abandon, and he seemed to enjoy them equally. He was frequently asked to lift his forearms with a child hanging from each one—his strength seemed to astonish the young Salish.

Flame noticed, too, that each opportunity Lone

167

Goose got she spoke to him and looked up at him with an appeal of some sort in those flashing eyes. She would glance at Flame and then murmur to him and shake her head. He listened to her with patience and seeming regard.

It came to Flame that those beaded moccasins she'd first worn, the ones meant for someone "that special", had been for this girl. Flame tried to be quite stern with herself, saying in her mind, It's nothing to me. But for some reason the idea made her burn inside.

The warrior who had harried Lone Goose earlier was not much pleased by the girl's attentions to Cougar, either. More than once Flame saw his black eyes shoot thunderbolts at the pair of them.

Observing him with more sympathy now, Flame decided that he was handsome—in a way. His features were strong, and he carried himself absolutely straight. But he didn't seem an easy man; not once did his cloak of majesty slip.

Meanwhile, Cougar seemed altogether too tolerant of the Lone Goose's girlishness.

*It doesn't matter,* Flame's mind answered with shrill fury born of frustration with herself. *Will you get it into your head: it just doesn't matter!*

But it did. How he felt about the girl did matter. The taste of her own possessiveness was sour in her mouth and as dry as sawdust as she tried repeatedly to swallow it down.

The afternoon waned; the clouds dispersed across the sky began to swarm together, gathering into rounded, somber-edged masses and rearing into lofty thunderheads. Though it didn't actually rain, Flame felt drenched with pessimism.

At last Cougar came to her and bowed deeply, courtly, in the purple dusk. There were secret

168

shadows in the green of his eyes. (He didn't always have to smile with his mouth, she was discovering.) She realized anew how very attractive she found him. When he held out his hand to her, her own opened and extended slowly and engaged his. Lost in a wilderness she couldn't survive alone, his hands were the only home she could rely upon.

He led her toward their woodland sanctuary. When they passed by Lone Goose on their way, the girl's expression was set, but Flame sensed that she was worried.

"Your little friend looks at me as if she suspects you're in some sort of danger from me."

Cougar answered casually, "Aye, she's sure you mean to kill me somehow."

Flame felt righteously impatient. Of the two of them, it certainly wasn't Cougar who was in danger.

Then she was only aware of a quickening, aware that in a moment she would be alone with him again—and aware of the fact that she was glad.

To cover any clue he might have as to her shameful feelings, she searched for something prosaic to say to him. "Who was that warrior sitting to your left at the council?"

He thought back. " 'Twas Two-Edged Knife I believe . . . aye, Two-Edged Knife. Caught your eye, did he? He's a braw man."

Her features were set into a look of casual calm. "Is he anyone special?"

"A minor war chief. When a brave has counted enough coup, he can lead a war party on his own, call himself a war chief and wear the scarlet robe and carry a tribal medicine pipe. Two-Edged Knife's young for the title, but as fine and brave as they come. He would have gone after that grizzly with you today, but couldn't get permission from Rotten

Gut and the others. He's needed to protect the village, they say, with Dark Sun gone."

She considered telling him what she'd seen between Two-Edged Knife and Lone Goose, but thought peevishly that he'd had his head filled with the girl's presence enough for one day. Instead, she asked, "Was that a tribal medicine pipe you smoked, with all those funny bits and pieces in the bundle with it?"

Hugely amused, he said, "Those bits and pieces, woman, are holy objects: snake rattles, cougar skulls, weasel claws, bird skins and sacred herbs . . . and a skein of yellow hair from a spirit woman. And that was no mere bundle, but a quilt made of patches of bear skin and wapiti hide and one or two eagle skins—all of which defend the pipe and must be unfolded to the sound of prayers and ritual chants. And the pipe itself is hung with symbolic objects, all of great liturgical significance."

"You sound as if you half believe in all their mumbo jumbo." She was surprised, for he had struck her as a man of very little religious feeling.

"Aye and I do . . . *half* believe . . . everything." The old gleam was in his eyes. "Even these cool lips that tell me they do no' want me to kiss them. Sometimes I half believe they mean it."

He smiled, and it went clear through her.

She let him embrace her. She let him kiss her breathless. It was strange, she thought, how a person could resent a kiss and yet like it so much at the same time.

"Well done, lassie," he murmured. "I do believe I'm managing to melt a particle of your wintriness." He released her only to pull her on toward their camp. " 'Tis long I've waited to be alone with you this night. Aye, you're that smooth and sweet, that

170

fine and bonny and lovesome, that you haunt a man."

He was soon urging her into the low shelter. The flap fell shut behind them and they were at once in total darkness. Flame sat on the soft heap made by the folded buffalo hide and red blanket, allowing her eyes to adjust.

She knew he was going to make love to her, and she felt afraid. She thought she was always going to feel afraid, for his lovemaking was so humbling: it left her completely visible; nothing could be hidden from him.

He found her, and began taking tentative kisses in the dark and drawing her trembling body to his by his arm around her waist. Now his lips took more time with hers, he kissed her again and again, until a subtle, unabated desire came alive, flamelike, within her.

He worked at the yoke of her dress and got hold of one round breast, which throbbed under his gentle grasp. From his warm palm a glow started. Its slow radiance suffused her body with warmth, flowed downward like fluid lava, down, down through her stomach, down the insides of her legs.

Again his mouth took hers in a long kiss, until he lifted his head to whisper, "I want to taste your sweet breasts."

She could refuse him nothing. She was all aflame from head to foot, uncontrollably pulled and mastered by needs so intense they defied her most righteous conventions, her deepest resistances. She let him pull her dress over her head.

Now he was holding her in one arm, suckling her breasts and running his free hand over her thighs. She leaned against him and opened to him. His fingers moved, so slowly, so willfully, to take intimate possession of her.

She moved restlessly under the double onslaught of his hand between her thighs and his mouth on her breast. Her face found the cave of his throat where it nestled for concealment. Then, seemingly of their own accord, her lips moved up, softly grasping the lobe of his ear, her tongue gently licked the tender skin. His hand left her, for a moment only, to unfasten his breeches. Then it was back, his fingers re-opening and entering her. She shuddered.

"Kiss me," he murmured.

As she did, he continued caressing her, until she felt she would faint away.

At last he inclined her backwards. The folded bedding formed a soft pillow beneath her hips so that she was lifted to him. It was too dark to see him, but she felt his face close above her hair, his cheek against her ear. Wordlessly he spread her and went into her, without arousing any resistance.

At his first thrust, she felt light travel from his body through hers, a small piece of dawn, a beam of pure, pearl light. Then they began a rhythmic intimate waltz. Her breasts lay soft and naked; her nipples were rolled beneath his velvety buckskin shirt as his chest rocked forward and back over her.

It was different this time. But then each time it was different, unique and unrepeatable. His breathing was slow, rhythmic, easy; he was taking her slowly, rhythmically, easily. They were so quiet together she could have heard the sound of the nightbirds in the trees. But she was listening to the sound of his breath, and to her breath: now they were in counterpoint, now in unison.

Each time he withdrew, she felt a brief darkness, an emptiness, a longing; then he reentered her, and that pearl-pure light illuminated her senses again.

172

Cougar, the Waiting Cougar, stirring over her pantherlike, yet surprisingly gentle, withholding his full strength and taking her instead with soft persuasion.

The pleasure built. A thought came to her like a dream: *I lived without knowing anything about this, so that when it came to me it was without warning, and now it is wrenching me from who I am — or who I thought I was.* She felt she was floating like a phantom between who she had been and who she was becoming. And when he penetrated her and occupied her as he did now, she didn't know whether she was Victorine or Flame anymore, and couldn't be sure if he was forcing her to be his wife or if being his wife was what she had really been meant for all along.

Then even her thoughts dissolved; she felt she was all fluid — no skeleton, no muscle, no resistance — simply a liquid casing for his exquisite movement and nothing else.

"Cougar . . ." And they clung to one another with tender urgency as the promise brightened; they stood together at the pinnacle of light, over which they both fell utterly.

They prepared to leave the Salish village the following day. Though spent by the previous night of hot blood and shame, Flame was glad to pack up; she'd quickly grown tired of watching Lone Goose follow Cougar's every footstep like a guarding shadow. That the girl thought Flame was out to do him harm seemed nauseatingly unfair.

"Lone Goose is really very silly about you," she couldn't resist saying. "I wonder that she isn't here, all packed to go along with us — to protect you from me."

173

He laughed lazily. "Aye, she'll make a good loyal wife, that one. She'll no' always be trying to scramble out of her husband's arms like some I know."

Flame thought it best to ignore that jibe. She fastened the last strap on the last pack horse and stood back to check her work. The stiff damp breeze molded one side of her dress against her body. "This one's ready," she said, turning only when no answer was forthcoming.

Her eyes met the cold fire ring, the skeleton of bent willow wands where the buffalo-hide shelter had been pitched. She called, "Cougar?" But he was gone, all in a moment, without saying anything to her.

The silence of windy woods and murmuring lake shore closed around her, and an eerie feeling crept down her spine. Moments passed; a clatter of thoughts fell into her mind, ridiculous thoughts, such as: He's decided that Lone Goose is right, that he should abandon me.

So ridiculous!

No, be realistic, she told herself; he would never go far without his horse, would he? She eyed Irongray. The great animal tossed his mane and his muscles rippled beneath the gray satin of his coat.

Sit down and wait, she told herself. He's just gone off to the village to say a last goodby.

She found a log to sit on, and cleared a space in the fallen leaves so that, with a stick, she could draw designs in the dirt. *FLAME,* she wrote. It still looked like a stranger's name. She scratched it out and wrote again: *VICTORINE.* But sitting there in moccasins and leggings, in a deerskin dress, with her loose hair hanging forward over her shoulders, that too seemed like someone else's name.

"You're working hard, I see."

He'd come back, making not even so much noise as the sound of rain against rock. She faced him slowly, flooded with relief. "I finished." She gestured vaguely toward the horses.

Her eyes, however, were on the animal he was leading.

## Chapter Twelve

Flame stood and stepped over the log on which she'd been sitting.

"Is this no' the prettiest pony you've ever seen?" Cougar asked her.

She stroked her hand down the spotted brown-and-white nose. A sudden light broke over her. "Is it for me?"

He laughed. "Now that's what I call avaricious." She flushed as he looked at her so knowingly over the pony's rump. Yet his grin was reassuring. "No need to stand there looking like a bonny beet root. Aye and she's yours, and how did you guess?"

"You know I really can't accept her. But I'll be glad to use her as long as I'm with you."

He shook his head in mock exasperation. "Most mountain men would no' put up with you. They would've beat you black and blue by now."

"Yes, I'm surprised it hasn't come to that."

The smile slid off his mouth. He came around the pony's smooth neck. "Yet. It has no' come to that *yet*. But I'm glad you're aware of the possibility. You begin to understand me, I think."

"I've always understood you well enough to know

that I would be foolish to put anything past you," she said sourly.

"What's got you into such a rough mood?"

"On, some roughness is bound to be gained with one's ruin, I expect."

"Ruin! A man brings a gift for his good wife — barters some furs for a tough, fleet mare and a buckskin bridle to offer as a token of his appreciation for her favors — and she cuts him in two with her tongue."

"Oh come now, you bought the pony so you wouldn't have to lug me around on your lap anymore."

He threw up his hands and turned away, all offended innocence. "Have it your way, woman." Walking to his own horse he complained to the universe in general, "I talk to it as if the creature were born with the sense to use its mind."

"I would I *could* have it my own way," Flame murmured into the pony's ear. The mare had its slender neck bent over the grass, and when Flame rested her cheek against its silky coat, it turned its eyes and gave her a look of feminine sympathy.

"May I name her?" she called to Cougar.

"She's yours," he said disgustedly, adding a few awful-sounding Gaelic words. "Do what you like with her."

Flame smiled at the round-eyed animal, and said sweetly, "Thank you. I rather like Spot — if it doesn't sound too silly."

"It sounds daft. 'Tis a name for a dog." Mounted, he was already leading the pack horses out of camp. "As you can see, she's unshod. She'll soon wear those hooves down to the quick on the rocks we'll be traveling over, so you'd better make your Spot some

177

hide shoes in the next day or two."

She positioned the pony by the log and crawled onto the animal's back.

And there she was, her hair blowing in the damp wind. "Go," she said, nudging the pony with her heels. "Giddy—up . . . go!"

Cougar's triumphant laugh rang out from between the trees. "Need some help, lassie?" He waited to see if she would answer.

Her face burned with irritation when he finally turned Irongray back and dismounted to tie Spot's lead behind the gray. So she was to travel with the pack horses now! Well, at least she wouldn't be nuzzled and stroked by *him* half the day.

"All set?" he said. He'd remounted and had Irongray's reins in his strong fingers again. When he shifted his weight in the saddle to look back at her, the leather creaked.

She lifted her chin in brief and haughty assent.

He continued to gaze back at her. " 'Tis lucky for you that there's no' enough meanness in me really to hit a woman, because one of these days you're going to make me that mad."

She didn't answer and he turned to set a sedate pace, holding tight on his reins.

Not the least bit frightened by his bluster, Flame called ahead, "Where are we going—and don't say 'north,' or 'to my place.' Tell me *where*."

After a moment, he asked, "Have you got a head for heights? You're going to need it, because we're going up where the trees stand short and the mosses tall, up where the eagles fly . . . up there." He pointed to the mountains rising among somber clouds to the northwest of the long broad Flathead River Valley. "Into the Bitterroots."

The peaks he pointed out were high, steep, and sharply wrinkled. She recalled his statement of a previous night: I like my privacy. No doubt he found a lot of privacy in those rugged and inaccessible mountains. And no doubt she would find escape from them impossible. He was tightening the last knots of their "marriage." Soon she would be bound by snow and terrain as well as the ever-closing circle of his arms.

After several hours on the trail they came out of some thick timber into a grassy clearing. Irongray sidestepped, as if shying at a bad scent. Then he calmed. But next he raised his head and gave a scared snort. Something was spooking him. Cougar stopped shortly beside a creek where they could rest and drink. Flame thought to slip away behind some brambles, to make a call on nature, but Cougar said, "Go no' further than yon trees. We're getting deep into bear country. 'Twas probably a grizzly that made Irongray nervous back there."

She made a face that signalled her impatience with all this bear furor. No doubt the Indians found them hard to kill with lances, arrows, and knives, but Cougar's custom-made, European rifle was surely protection enough against anything alive. She was surprised that the Indian's fears and frenzies had infected him so. They certainly hadn't infected her. She eyed the berry brambles. They were tall enough to conceal her; the nearer trees were more public.

"You think 'tis a joke?" he said, studying her face. She saw a flash of purpose in his eyes. "Look here then, 'afore you go breasting off like a horse in skirts."

Along the creek bank were pawprints larger than

179

any she'd ever seen. They measured just under a foot long and over half a foot across.

From then on the tracks cropped up constantly, though the bears never exposed themselves. "They must be fanatically shy," Flame said, and valorously added, "I'm anxious to see one of these Real Bears."

Cougar's lips shut in a thin line.

It pleased her to know that she could worry him and irritate him this way.

"How much farther is it to this place of yours where the eagles fly?"

"We'll go up through a pass, fifty or sixty miles though the mountains, mayhap another week's travel. I'll let you know when we get there."

The journey continued up a boulder-strewn mountain. At the end of the day's advance was the search for firewood and for stakes to tie the horses. Clouds stood triple towered in the sky, laced with peacock blue, bright gold, and purple. Flame, her arms full of deadwood, stood at the upper slope of their camp, entranced by the eldritch light.

Where was Cougar taking her really? She studied the surrounding snowy summits blanketed with white, wondering how far up those peaks they would climb.

He was setting up their night's shelter, looking as if he were the overlord of all these braced mountains, with his pure animal poise and his disciplined eyes and that exquisite effortlessness that pervaded everything he did. She put down her collection of wood and strolled past him, and flung out her imagination beyond the clouds, hoping for some tangible good in all this unknown. Her face in the storm light was pensive.

Cougar lit the fire, then came down the slope to

stand beside her. His light touch on her arm seemed to say, I'll be with you; fear not. But she wasn't in the mood for accepting comfort from the very man who brought her this distress, and she moved away.

"The toe of the moccasin, does it pinch?" A touch of sarcasm threaded his voice.

She didn't catch his meaning for a second, and then realized he was alluding to her agreement to stay with him the winter. She tossed her long yellow hair off her shoulders. "I'll survive."

A strain of amusement glinted in his face. "How cold, how hard. The things you say hardly match the softness of your skin and the pools of your eyes. I warn you I intend to hold you close." His gaze traveled over her, taking in her wind-blown hair. "Aye, but you'll survive. There's witchery in you."

She moved a step further away from him.

"You're that nervous of me this night."

"Would it matter to you if I were?" She heard a little note of despondence in her voice.

He stared at her, and lightning flitted between them. "I've oft' admired your courage," he said. His eyes seemed to hold paired lights as he continued to gaze at her. "Come here, Flame. Come here to me."

She obeyed as if she had no will of her own left. When she stood before him, his lantern eyes blinked lazily. She felt his hands smooth back her hair from her face. His own hair was ruffled by the wind, his chin was faintly gold with the day's growth of his beard. He had a forceful chin, and well-molded lips, and cheekbones holding hollows beneath them.

"You've been goading me all the day. We'll no' argue about it now. But I'll get my own back . . . when I have you safe in my glen. We'll see how brave you are then."

For a moment longer she stood gazing up at him as if sculptured; she barely seemed to breathe, only her hair blew back in the wind. This wasn't the first time his eyes had drawn her to him, fascinated her against her will, and as he bent to her, she gave a little shiver. His strong arms encircled her. His fingers felt a little cruel as they took her around the waist to pull her to him. She gasped as he lifted her right off the ground. And there he kissed her. It was the most heathenish thing she'd ever known. It startled and thrilled her. Her arms twined around his neck; she clung to him, and her lips returned the pressure of his. He made her feel boneless in his hold.

"There," he murmured, still holding her as if she were weightless. "For the first time you kissed me as a woman should."

Sudden wrath shook her head to foot. She stiffened and struggled to be set down. "Why are you dragging me into your life?" she demanded.

She twisted out of his hold and turned to run, anywhere, she didn't care. She heard the sound of his pursuing footfalls behind her, and there was a sob of panic in her throat as he caught up with her and took hold of her again.

Though he wasn't hurting her, she shrank away from his hands. "Oh, why don't you leave me alone? Do you know, Cougar, what you're doing to me? Do you care?"

His eyes were lost in shadows. At last he said, "You'll survive."

The mountain lake was disturbed only by little circles from the rising fish. Beside it was their sixth camp since leaving the Salish. The sun was nearly gone, and dark was creeping up the wooded slopes around the water. The sky had gone clear and luminous, and the lake lay bright within its edges. And from somewhere, or everywhere, came a fine, high singing. Only when Flame was quiet could she hear it; but then . . . there it was, thin and getting louder, dwindling, then getting louder again. It was the mountains talking, and the pines, and time itself, humming, remote and old.

Cougar had led her past many small alpine lakes, each liquid jewel seeming bluer than the one before, reflecting the ever-nearer sky.

He was squatted at the water's edge now, bathing his face and upper body. Fascinated, even shivering a bit, she watched the muscles flexing along his broad bare back.

For the hundredth time she told herself he was only a man. Possessed of formidable skill perhaps. Possessed, too, of arrogance and effrontery hardly to be comprehended. But only a man, nonetheless.

Besides their daily travel, he'd been busy with fishing and hunting. And keeping her busy too with drying the meat on racks above smoky fires. Yesterday he'd brought in an elk, and two days before that an antelope. Of an evening he took fish from the streams and lakes. Their parfleches were beginning to bulge.

Tonight their shelter was pitched between the blue water's edge and the timberline. Proud Irongray and little Spot stood with the pack horses. They were full of autumn grass and sound asleep over their picket pins, their legs drawn under them, their tails to the slight wind. Spot now wore "moccasins", which Flame had made of circles of green buffalo hide.

183

The protective shoes were saving the pony's hooves very well. She was getting more efficient at the chores of mountain travel and camp keeping.

The firelight played over Cougar's face as he came to sit with his back to the water. His rifle was at his side, his tomahawk and knife at his waist, and he was facing the only direction from which an enemy could approach—the woods. But it was Flame he was watching over the top of the fire she'd built.

"You look more pagan and more bonny to me each day." He allowed his gray gaze to drift over the curves of her breasts. She felt herself blush. A crooked smile flitted across his features before he turned his attention to the stringer of cleaned fish that hung forgotten in his hand. He started to pierce them with sticks for cooking.

"I probably am looking like a pagan," she said. Her hip-length hair was bleached by the sun until no two strands seemed exactly the same color. And at her wits end with trying to keep it tidy, she'd finally taken to plaiting it Blackfoot-style, bound at the ends with strips of rawhide. Thus it fell over her shoulders to her waist in two thick flaxen ropes. Because she had no hat or brass hairpins to keep the shorter wisps out of her eyes, she'd been reduced to tying a wider rawhide band around her forehead. On top of all this, she was turning as brown as an acorn. Her skin was already a shade darker than her hair. She was afraid her complexion would soon look as tough as old leather. That Cougar could study her so thoroughly and manage to say she was looking "bonny" almost softened her heart toward him.

As they ate the sweet flakey fish, the twilight failed. The wind whispered—just a fretwork on the

184

water, a breath on the fire—and as Flame took her first sip of hot tea, the wild yips of a lone wolf sang out. Before the echoes of his wail could dwindle away, a full pack of his brothers and sisters answered from the opposite ridgetop. Flame gazed up and saw what they were calling to: Pegasus, Cassiopeia, the Dippers, and sprayed behind, the filmy Milky Way. There were stars sparking against stars, stars behind stars, stars seeded so densely that the patterns were quite ungraspable.

Cougar was still watching her, making her nervous again. As usual on the move, he hadn't made love to her. But now she caught the faint sheen of his teeth as he gave her one of his unshadowed, unearthly smiles. She wished he would look at something else—the fire or the lake or the stars.

Some evenings he told her to pick a star, and then he told her which constellation it was a part of and the myth behind its naming. Occasionally, he told a tale obviously made up on the spot, to point out some moral he thought she needed to hear.

One such he called "The Daft Maiden." This was all about a young woman rescued from certain death by a manly warrior. "She was bonny, aye, with hair like gold threads—like the threads in tapestries. And her voice was like music in October. Still and all, she was slow to show her gratitude, and her warrior, though reluctant (she was that lovely, you understand) was nevertheless forced to drown her in a mountain lake." Here he sighed heavily. "Aye, 'tis true . . . But the night sky had fallen in love with her and took up her floating corpse and vowed to preserve her cold form forever. You can see her up there now, a lesson to all ungrateful rescued maidens, sparkling but cold . . . cold."

She smiled to recall his forlorn look. He seemed not to be in the mood for telling stories tonight, though.

"Where are we?" she asked. It was her constant question, asked as much out of peevishness as curiosity.

"You would no' have any idea even if I told you."

He was right. All she knew for certain was that they were winding endlessly in and out among these huge peaks. She wondered that he seemed to know where he was. He carried maps in his mind, and evidently very explicit ones, too. When, for immediate purposes, he drew one of them for her in the sand with a twig, he was quick to erase all traces as soon as the information was communicated. It was a rule with him not to leave tracks of any kind behind.

He threw some more wood on the fire. "The evenings grow frosty this high. But 'tis a fair country, is it no'? Wild. Wild and lovely, like a virgin woman. Whatever a man does he knows he's the first to do it."

Her lashes fluttered. "Does this lake have a name?"

"It does now — Loch of Flame."

She smiled. "I'd prefer Lake Victorine."

He squashed that with, "Aye, and why no' Loch Henrietta-Elfreda? That ought to scare the fish away forever." Then, "Nae, Loch of Flame. It fits; 'tis blue in the sun, yet shines with a cold fire in the moonlight — like your eyes when you're being loved."

In answer she looked out at the water. "Can you really do that? Name it for me, I mean?"

He shrugged. "I suppose and if I passed it along to enough men, it just might stick." His voice was gentle, his phrases considered.

After a comfortable pause, she said, "We haven't seen any other men, though."

"They're around. A few of your noble and vicious Blackfeet, and fewer of the perpetually thievish Crows."

She let this worry her, then let it sink beyond consciousness, then let her mind fall open to those thoughts that were always waiting on the threshold, thoughts of getting home again. Cougar was taking her further and further into the mountains, and soon winter would be upon them. Would he really set her free come spring?

A sound came from behind her and she turned quickly, her eyes prying into the darkness. The shapes of three men on sure-footed horses moved cautiously under the trees at the edge of the woods. They had rifles across their saddles.

Cougar's rifle was in his hands in an instant, and he moved to place himself between her and the intruders. She came to her feet as well, but prudently stayed behind him.

The rifle was ready at his shoulder. Seeing him there in that gleam of time, his weapon aimed, she felt alarmed anew at being at the mercy of such a man. Her future was in his fist, yet he was an incongruous element, misplaced in her picture of herself and her life. She'd seen the gentler side of him, and now she was seeing another side, a side that could level a weapon at another human being — and use it, she suddenly had no doubt. It was a revealing instant, quick but profound.

A voice called out, "Friend! We 'ud be mighty glad to set by your fire a spell." The man speaking was stepping out of the woods on a white-and-black spotted buffalo pony. His size was indeterminate

187

since he was clothed in a huge cloak. He climbed down from his pony very slowly, sheathed his rifle, and walked toward the edge of the camp. "Name's Reade. Hosea Reade. And this here's my brother Radford, and the kid there, that's Jack Goodspeed."

Flame looked at "the kid" and was surprised at how young he was. His beard was downy with youth, and he had the wide homesick eyes of a boy.

Cougar lowered his rifle slowly. The man took this as permission to come forward into the moving firelight. When even Flame could see plainly that none of them was pointing his weapon, Cougar said in a belatedly magnanimous manner, "My fire is always open to men who come in peace."

Yet, his eyes squinted ominously at the three who were hobbling their horses with rawhide and turning them loose to graze. The spokesman came back first, nodding his head in solid satisfaction. He threw down his cloak to use as a rug beside the fire. He was rough, pockmarked, short but broad-shouldered and heavy, with strong hands and stubby fingers. There was a vague grossness in his appearance. His grin flashed in his beard as he spoke in a rumbling, croupy voice. "Sure we come in peace, don't we, boys? We ain't aimin' at nothin' but keepin' our hair on and our bellies full — and maybe havin' a time. We're nothin' but a party of mountain men who've spent their beaver."

The two others followed behind him. There was a sincere shaking of hands with a liberal scattering of "hells" and "damns," like farmers strewing rye. Radford looked like his brother — squat. He didn't seem as flagrantly hardy as Hosea, however, and one of his hands was deformed to the shape of a claw.

They all seemed in a larking mood at this unex-

188

pected meeting, and they didn't appear to notice that Cougar remained somewhat distant and formal — and that he kept his rifle in his hands.

Hosea laughed. The thick roll of his belly moved. He was still panting from the exertion of getting off his horse, and he smelled rancid, maybe because Cougar scared him. He hadn't quite looked at Flame yet, except with the tail of his gaze. But when he did look, his eyes traveled from her moccasins and leggings to the dress she had on and the band she wore around her forehead.

"Say, what you got there in your shadow, Cougar? Is that an albino squaw or what?" He leaned forward and pinned her with his eyes.

The other two stepped nearer to have a closer look as well, Jack, penny-eyed, Radford opening his mouth like a starved baby bird.

Embarrassed, she edged nearer to Cougar. He murmured to her, "Sit down." She felt his hand on her upper arm, the touch without weight, yet reassuring.

Hosea took a seat on his cloak, cross-legged, directly across the fire from her. His face was screwed up in puzzlement. "She ain't pink-eyed. No, boys, I think that this here's a white woman!"

His brother said, "I'll be damned," and the boy, Jack, said wonderingly, "A white squaw."

"What in hell's a white woman doing up here?" Hosea said to Cougar. "She your squaw for real?"

Cougar's eyes riveted on Flame now, as a man might rivet a ship's glass on a distant object. She felt he was trying to communicate something to her. At last he made the courtly answer: "This is my wife."

"That's not quite true," she said quickly, primly.

His mouth hardened.

189

"Not quite, huh?" Hosea winked lewdly at Cougar, one man to another, then looked back at her. "Which part of you ain't quite?"

"She talks like a schoolmarm," Radford said, giggling.

"What's your name, missy?"

She was growing uneasy under their limelight scrutiny. This didn't seem to be the time to alienate Cougar. So, glancing at the men—who were all staring back at her so bright-eyed and loose-lipped— she said, "My name is . . . Flame."

## Chapter Thirteen

Hosea Reade threw his head back and laughed. *"Flame!* Be damned she *is* a white squaw!"

From the corner of Flame's eyes she glimpsed Cougar's face. She saw approval there, and felt relieved.

"How'd you get yourself such a prize, boy?"

"I bought her from the Blackfeet." Tersely, he explained.

When he was finished, Hosea sent Radford back to their horses for a jug. "This here's only molasses and alcohol, but she's good. Concocted her myself," Hosea boasted.

The jug began a slow passage around the campfire.

Jack asked Flame, "What was it like back home? What was happening? What did you have to eat?" He seemed eager to know everything, sick with longing. "Have you got a picture of your mother?"

The jug had now reached Cougar. He tipped his head beneath the heavy bottle, his body tilted back to compensate for the weight of it, and his throat jerked as he swallowed. Lowering it, he clenched his teeth and shook his head. "That's as braw as any whiskey at the rendezvous trading booths."

He leaned to hand it back to its owner, but Hosea said, "How about the girly. Ain't she thirsty?"

Cougar gave her a doubtful look. All the men's eyes were on her again. Indeed, they had hardly left her from the first. Cougar sat with the jug on his knee, his forefinger hooked through the handle and an almost forbidding look on his face. "A drink, lassie?" Clearly he wanted her to say no.

"Drink up, Miss Flame!" Jack cried.

"Get a little of that in you. Warm you up," Hosea urged.

"Nae, she's no' used to it," Cougar said, again leaning to return the jug to Hosea.

Defiantly she reached to intercept him. She took the jug, wiped its mouth with her palm, then struggled to lift it to her lips. At last, with a mighty heave, she tilted the base briefly to the sky.

It was fuller then she'd expected and whereas she'd meant to take a small token sip, her mouth was flooded. The sweet liquor was potent and fiery, like sparks on her tongue, like a fire in her throat, like glowing coals in her stomach. When Cougar took the jug back, her eyes were brimming with hot tears. One side of his mouth crooked, as much as to say: "I told you so."

The men laughed and called her a good sport. "Have some more," Hosea urged, but she said, her voice oddly breathy, "No thank you."

"I'll have another little swallow," Radford said,

motioning for the jug. When he got it, he grunted, lifted it with his good hand, and took a mighty swig. It then began another circle amongst them. They became more and more jovial. Radford sang a French song, his voice husky. But after a few more rounds, he suddenly toppled backwards. Hosea pulled him back to a sitting position and propped him against his own shoulder. Radford mumbled, "She sure is pretty."

It was then that Jack (who seemed none the worse, though he'd certainly swilled his share) said to Cougar, "How much you want for her?" His face was sad and youthful. Flame was touched. He wanted to buy her freedom.

"She's no' for sale."

"That good, huh?" said Hosea.

"How 'bout the use of her then?" young Jack came back quickly.

Flame stared at his pale, black-browed face, stunned.

"I'll give you twenty dollars gold for an hour with her in that there shelter you've got fixed up."

"You got twenty dollars gold?" Radford slobbered, struggling up from his brother's shoulder.

Hosea, like Jack, said nothing. They were both too intent on Cougar's face.

Cougar didn't seem to have heard. He was looking into the fire with his eyes slitted. Flame sat rigid beside him. Jack's eyes veered to her; he gave her a look that seemed to decrease her to a single function. She saw a desperate, cold appetite in his eyes, which she must have missed — or misread — before.

Hosea got out a twist of tobacco, broke a largish piece off, and stuffed it in his cheek to let it soak. In the end it was he who broke the tension. He reached around Radford to slap Jack on the back. "Hell! He don't want to share. He's so firmly set on the nest we'ud have to pry him off with a crowbar." He chuckled lewdly. "Wouldn't you be, if you had a pretty squaw like that? There ain't room in her puddle but for one big frog." He spit, and sucked in his lower lip afterward to get the driblet off.

"You got to excuse Jack here, miss. He's sassy as a hunter pup, pointin' anything that quivers its tail. He was a young hot-blood with a stern pa back in St. Louis. Put his money down on too many cards and horses, too much engaged hisself with the pleasures — if you know what I mean — and so his daddy sent him for a wholesome change out here with us."

Cougar's lips tightened. He said, pointedly, " 'Tis the rumor Jim Bridger is planning to make a return engagement up this way. Have you seen anything of him?"

Latching onto this, Hosea said, "Well now, if he's coming, all he's like to get is Blackfeet. There's scarcity enough of beaver with the Company takin' 'em all. We won't be seein' no twelve-dollar plews anymore. Damn Company's got us by the short hairs now, since Fitzpatrick and Bridger throwed in with 'em. Ain't no one to bid ag'in 'em. And them Londoners makin' silk hats, if what I hear is right." He spat into the fire. "Beaver's dropping lower than a snake's belly."

His eyes were jumpy. Suddenly, as if he couldn't stop them, they veered back to Flame and, lowering his voice cozily, he said, "Where you from, missy?"

"Philadelphia."

He hunched his shoulders. "Sad thing, losing your brother like that. And you being a lady, anyone can tell. Jack Goodspeed!" He glared at his young charge. "Can't you see this here's a lady?" He glanced at Cougar, then back to her. "Your Scotchie

194

treating you right?"

"She's doing that fine," Cougar answered for her. Flame could tell he was exercising an enormous patience.

"Oh, fine for you, I can see you're happy. Can't you see he's happy, Jack? He thinks to be a mighty big nabob with such a pretty gal to bed." He laughed roughly. "But what about the lady here? Looks to me like you're planning to keep her up here in the high country for the winter. Now missy, we're heading south." He let that hang suggestively.

She sat up straighter and leaned slightly forward, ignoring all her instinctive caution concerning him. "Are you going to any of the forts?"

"We could go as far as Laramie."

"But Hosea—" Radford interrupted.

"Shut up," mumbled Jack, nudging the drunken man with his elbow.

Radford's jaw sagged like a censured boy's. "But Jack—"

Jack began to curse him in a low-toned voice, venomously. Radford hiccuped suddenly and drew himself up.

Hosea said, "Rad, I'm only telling her we could go that far—to help her out. I think what we got here is a lady being kept ag'in her will. I'm wondering if she don't scratch a little when Cougar here lays hold of her."

"She's staying with me the winter," Cougar said blandly.

"That's what you say, but what's Miss Flame say?" He grinned at her invitingly.

She could see the alcohol in his eyes. They were eyes that had seen a lot of alcohol. "I—"

Over nothing Radford said, "Oh, damn!" and laughed.

Hosea looked at him and then explained to Flame, "He just talks to listen to hisself sometimes, like a boy shootin' a rifle at nothin'. He's a little bit simple. Now . . . what do you say?"

"She has naught to say," Cougar interrupted again, his burr increased with anger. His jaw muscles were rigid. "I speak for her."

Radford had fixed his vacant eyes on Flame's tense face. Jack leaned forward. "You want to go to Fort Laramie, miss?"

She studied his face. He was so young, perhaps not even eighteen, yet now she saw that his eyes seemed immemorially aged. She swallowed hard. "No, I—I think not."

"Aye, and now we can consider that subject closed." Cougar's voice had an ominous softness.

Hosea nodded. "All right, all right. So! Seen any Injuns lately? We got ourselves scared by some day or two back. Almost caught us clean by surprise, but somehow they passed us without rubbing us out." He shuddered. "Lord, how I hate redskins. It's my ambition to scalp a hun'erd of 'em — and not take just their topknots either, but the whole thing, clear to the ears and halfway to the eyebrows."

Jack said in his eager young voice, "I killed me a Flathead looking like he was going to steal my possibles."

Hosea's shoulders moved with laughter until Radford threatened to topple. Hosea shored him up once more, rubbed his own eyes with a dirty sleeve, and gasped, "Yessir, that was the funniest thing I ever heard. We come in one night and the boy has this story. I says, 'He was into your possibles, huh?' and the boy says, 'No, but he looked like he was going to get into them, so I made wolf's meat of him!' Looked like he was *going* to! Ha! Ain't that enough to split your gut?"

"Skulking Indians," Jack muttered.

Cougar didn't smile. In fact, he'd turned pale with supressed fury. Flame could see that unless the men left soon, there was going to be violence.

Sensing it, the strangers gradually prepared to leave. Cougar rose to see them off. As soon as Radford was in this saddle, sleep overpowered him. He slumped and began to snore. Hosea's parting words were, "Your Scotchie there, he's somebody now. He's true beaver. But we're heading south, miss. You change your mind, you catch us up. We'll take you to a fort. Hell! we'll take you all the way to Taos if that's where you want to go." He spit over the neck of his horse. It trotted sideways and he muttered soft obscenities to control it.

After a few more minutes of confusion and growled oaths, they were gone, leaving only the vibration of hoofbeats on the air. Then a great silence filled the camp. The little fire strutted importantly.

Flame was standing now, her face so white and still it might have been cut with a chisel. At last she said, "How dare you treat me like that in front of them." And she added, almost defensively, "I could have gone with them. You couldn't have stopped me."

Cougar opened his mouth to blast her, then checked himself. "Go with those three?" He spoke so softly and with such a hint of meaning that she was terrorized.

"Maybe not with them," she glanced nervously toward the woods, "but if they're going south there must be others who are, too."

"Aye. We passed another party the day before yesterday."

197

"I didn't see them!"

"I meant for you no' to. Nor for them to see you."

"You deliberately—"

"I deliberately got you away without being spotted, aye." He considered her. "Come, you're no' stupid. Men like those would do things to you."

"No more than what you've done!"

He laughed bitterly. "You're remarkably thick witted, love. What I've done, aye, only three times over, and without my tender mercy. Still and all, you're right, the two brothers might no' be too hard on you. As long as you were cooperative, mayhap they would offer you the rudimentary decencies in return. Hosea would be the kind to attempt a bearish playfulness as he embedded himself in your delicate parts. Imagine it . . . And Radford, dullwitted as he is, would certainly be quick—but then the quicker a man is, the more likely he is to be insatiable.

"And then there's the lad, poor little homesick Jackie. That one would hurt you more in an hour, and enjoy the hurting—" He shook himself. "And he would no' quit 'till you were exhausted, 'til you'd yielded your will to him, 'til you were his creature, to be abused in any manner he chose."

Her mind flinched from thinking about it. "I just want to go home," she said.

"I've told you I'll see you home after the winter. And you agreed to it. You agreed to do naught foolish."

"If I get a chance . . . surely you don't expect me to stay a moment longer than I have to in this atrocious farce of a marriage?"

" 'Tis the problem with the world, mistress, all this haste." Less kindly he added, "I can no' have you running off after them, or anyone else, lassie. Do no' make me do something ugly. You've got to promise me again that you'll no' go off like an opium eater, in love with your crazy delusions."

Perhaps it was the whiskey she'd swallowed, perhaps the humiliation she'd just suffered. Whatever, she felt childishly rebellious. "I don't have to promise you anything."

"You already have. Do you mean to say you would break your word?" His eyes narrowed. There was silence again, holding for a long time. At last he said, "I see I've taken too much for granted. I'll have to watch you closer." He was looking at her in an odd way. There was a glow in his eyes that made every nerve in her body tingle. "Renew your promise to me, woman." The green glow in his eyes struck chill.

She shut her face against him. Suddenly she felt despairing. Pain squeezed her heart mercilessly and she turned to look out at the starlit lake.

"Do no' think I need a promise from you. You'll be staying with me whether you agree to or no'. You'll no' be getting away from me. A fawn would have a better chance against a grizzly. What's really in question here is how close a guard I have to keep on you. If you ever even tried to make off, I would be forced to treat you that badly. You would no' like it, your hands tied, hobbled out with the horses on the picket line whenever I have to leave camp."

"You wouldn't!"

His eyes were glinting like silver-green points of steel in the firelight. Abruptly he stepped forward and pulled her into his arms. His hold was tight, uncomfortably tight. She twisted and squirmed, did everything in her power to break free of him, but it was impossible. When her first angry flush died away, she lifted her head and said, "You're the cruelest man I've ever met."

"Aye, I can be cruel. But I've no' been cruel to you, no' yet. Is it cruelty you want? Toothmarks on your breasts and bruises on your thighs? I could give you them. Aye, I could do that. 'Twould be easy." His hands pressed her hips against him intimately. "Nae then? Well, what we've experienced has been preferable. We've shared moments of ecstasy, you and I. And 'tis time you faced the lightning truth of what we are: husband and wife . . . and lovers. Aye, and you've become more important to me than any woman I've ever known. You make me feel selfish and jealous and possessive. And you should be grateful to know it, for 'tis what will protect you from predators the likes of those you met tonight."

He let her go then, and she stumbled back out of his reach. Turning, she went toward their shelter. At the entrance she paused. "Perhaps they are predators, but so are you."

"I am that," he agreed.

"We're not husband and wife—or lovers. You've taken advantage of my misfortunes and used me . . . but you won't touch me again."

"You're mistaken," he answered quietly. "If 'tis my desire to touch you, I'll do it. If 'tis my pleasure to take you, I'll see it satisfied."

"Then you'll do it by force!"

"Like that, is it? Have a caution. Do no' forget I bested a cougar with these hands, and you, in comparison, are naught but a tabby kitten with white paws and bib."

Cougar was following an ancient Indian track through the mountains. The path was narrow, winding like hairpins, so that at every turn Flame's pony

200

seemed sure to plunge into a void. Underfoot the dark soil was damp, making it slippery and yielding. And the land seemed to lean always more sharply. A mist was blowing, and this too added to the feeling of unreality and danger, to the feeling Flame had that she was riding at the edge of nowhere, to a place that could never be real.

Ahead of her, Cougar's profile was outlined by the stormy light. He hadn't tested her challenge last night, for he'd remained awake and on guard against the return of their visitors. Yet she had the definite feeling he hadn't forgotten it either, not for a minute.

All day he'd been terse and curt with her. She told herself she didn't mind, so long as he left her alone. Still, she found she missed his camaraderie, his smiles and warming glances. Without them she felt as though a part of her had gone numb, and that she was dragging that part along with her like a cold, dead weight. It drained strength from her.

Cougar glanced back at her now, and for the first time he seemed to consider the weary slump of her spine. For once he spoke to her kindly. "Another hour or so, lassie, and you'll have a glimpse of my glen." His face seemed pensive. "It hides behind yon fine peaks. 'Tis a deep and lonely place, but a place of great beauty."

The secret valley appeared suddenly as they topped a particularly high saddle covered with aspens. From this height she looked down into the cup of a small but very sheltered vale, shining with several winding creeks, lying unspoiled and quiet between sheer ridges. It was half-meadow and half-trees. There were thickets of dwarf mountain maples and groves of evergreens that would shelter game. The place had all the serenity and dignity of a tiny hidden kingdom, withdrawn from time itself.

"I call it Skyhaven," Cougar said.

They camped on the summit that night. The winds blew the clouds apart and the starlight came through. The following morning, while the sunrise touched the distant peaks with an almost uncanny beauty, they broke camp and plunged down into the valley.

It was warmer off the summits. The sun shone sporadically from a sky dotted with small white clouds; it touched Flame's hands gently and refreshed her like rain does a wilted lettuce.

Cougar led the way across one corner of the valley, into a hollow that deepened and narrowed. A log and mud cabin stood up under the trees of a grassy crease, with steepening land on either side and behind it.

They dismounted and tied their horses beneath one of the pines. As he went toward the cabin door, Flame remained with Spot. The wind gusted, whipping her hair and clothes. She stood staring at the surrounding mountains, azure veiled and gold spangled. The almost mythical beauty of the scene somehow increased her low mood. Such a prison should not be sunlit, she thought, it should be dark. Afterall, this was the hideaway of the brigand who held her captive.

"Flame." Cougar's face still held a brooding look that his voice echoed. "Come inside where 'tis warmer." His eyes were fixed on her, very gray and without a smile in them, bleakly taking in her face, her eyes, her straw-pale hair whiffed from travel. The wind played with the worn fringes of his buckskins as he began to regard her in a way that suggested swift and cogent thought. She reminded herself to be careful. His was a completely unorthodox character. Almost perverse.

In the end, his face hardened, he came back for her. In his eyes was a lethal calm. It was in the very set of his head, in his shoulders, in the firmness of his stride. She retreated a step, but his hands caught and held her.

"In case you did no' hear me, madam," he said, staring stonily down at her. There was a little gleam of hunger in his eyes as his arms went around her, lifting her bodily.

She struggled. "Don't!"

He growled deep in his throat, " 'Tis the custom for a bride to be carried over the threshold of her new home."

With a few long strides he packed her into the cabin. He stood just inside, holding her close to his hard chest, his lips inches from hers. "You glare at me as if you'd married the devil himself."

She mistrusted the set purposes of his face. "Cougar . . . I'm tired . . . and you are deviling me. Surely I made my feelings about this sort of thing perfectly clear to you last night." The fast beating of her heart made her voice shake slightly. She half closed her eyes, for she felt faint under the slumbrous resolution that was stealing into his expression.

"Aye, perfectly clear."

He put her down and went to the fireplace. There were logs laid ready. With the fire blazing, casting a trembling light, the austere, masculine cabin was bathed in a warmer and more pleasant glow. Even its tight-shut odor faded.

Unfortunately, the light also showed how thick the dust lay. And the cobwebs in the corners, which could only have been made by fat black spiders.

Cougar's personal belongs, however, were neatly

stored in leather bags hung from posts. A bed, raised about three feet from the ground, was made from great buffalo hides which had tightened on their frame as they dried. It stood in a corner nearest the fireplace. Over it was thrown some luxuriously soft-looking wolfskins. A blue enameled basin sat on a rough counter at the other side of the fire, an oil lamp stood on a crude wooden table in the center of the room, and there were two roughly fashioned chairs pushed beneath it.

One wall was hung with the horns of a white-furred mountain goat; skins of a black bear and a spotted gray lynx made rugs on the unplanked floor; the mantel was strewn with a medicine pipe, a ceremonial headdress, and a pair of intricately beaded headbands; a bow and leather quiver of arrows stood in the corner nearest the door. Flame felt the power of this assortment of mementos, collected by a man who was living life in great bold strokes; their effect was to make her feel more minimized than ever.

Cougar, still squatting by the fire, said, "Did you think I would be keeping you in a flimsy hide shelter while the winter winds blew?"

"I had no idea. I thought perhaps a bark hut, or even a tepee."

"I told you I had a lodge for you."

"But I suspect you're a superb liar." Though she saw the battle light blaze up behind his eyes, she went on recklessly. "I wouldn't be surprised to learn you're capable of any degrading or shameful vice. I've no doubt you came to this God-forsaken place out of necessity. Probably you're an escaped criminal who had to quit Scotland secretly or else find yourself swinging from a crossroads gallows."

He made a strong and masculine answer; then, in

a tone that held a warning, added, "Your attitude has been that troublesome these past few days. And I've been too forgiving. I let you off too easily, which I'm afraid has the effect of encouraging you." As he spoke his voice grew brisker, and she had an idea that he was developing a plan, was about to move on it.

"The problem is, I do no' act when my blood's warm, for fear of injuring you. I even hold my tongue for fear of bruising your delicate ear."

He'd risen from the hearth and was crossing the room. His fists were opening and closing. His moccasined footfalls were silent, yet might have been as loud as the thunder of stamping bulls.

She turned for the door, directly behind her, but he overtook her in time to lean his hand against it. She forced herself to face him squarely, ashamed now for her momentary urge to flee. "Please don't treat me like a child," she said, pretending to be uncaring of the strength in his leashed body, and putting all the chill she could into her voice.

He reached to smooth away some tendrils of fire-lit hair from her cheeks. "I've never treated you like a child, always like the woman you are, and that's how I'll treat you now. Let your punishment fit your crimes."

"Cougar . . ." She was unbearably aware of him as a man there in the glancing light, tall and arrogantly at home. She looked down at the lynxskin beneath her feet in order to avoid his face.

"Afraid? Aye, but you might have thought of the consequences sooner."

"I'm not afraid! Not at all! Why should I have the least concern over you and your intentions? It's just that you unnerve me, towering above me like—like this." Fingers seemed to clutch at her throat; but the very fact that she was apprehensive—and that he knew it—made her feel just that much more defiant.

He took her wrist and led her nearer the fire's warmth. There he straightened to his full height. His expression had a dangerous glint of admonition. "Now you'll apologize."

## Chapter Fourteen

"Apologize! I won't do anything of the kind!"

Cougar stood blocking her way to the door, holding both her hands now; he looked grim in the fireshot light, his eyes blistered with displeasure. "Let me caution you to be reasonable, lassie. You richly deserve to have some of that pride cut down, but I'm willing to settle for a simple apology."

"I can't believe this! Are you drunk? What am I supposed to apologize for?" she asked a little wildly. "Because I dislike the way you treat me, for wishing to be free of you, for—"

"For goading me, for being sarcastic beyond endurance, for being ungrateful—to name only a few of your faults."

She closed her eyes and nodded her head. "All right, I'm sorry for ever doubting that you had a gilt castle awaiting me in—"

"And for insolence!" There was anger in the hands

that seized her shoulders.

Now, when it was too late, she regretted the childishness of her remarks, but she would not apologize for them. Never. "Well, you can hardly call this luxurious, can you?" She looked around meaningfully at the rude room he was going to force her to live in. "Are you sure the roof won't come down on us with the first snow? And who is going to sweep out all this filth?"

"How can I impress upon you . . . ?"

"Please take your hands off me." She tried to back away.

"Nae," he warned, that gleam in his eyes. He pulled her to him with hands that weren't gentle. "Here!" He kissed her, quick and hard. "Mayhap another demonstration will do you some good—aye, struggle all you want, but there's more to come. You say I must touch and take by force? Well, aye, I can employ force, more force and harshness than you've experienced this far."

As he held her with one muscled arm and kissed her again, he used his free hand to unlace the capote she was wearing. It fell from her shoulders, and he stooped to slide both his hands under the hem of her dress, lifting it as he caressed her bare thighs.

"Oh! Stop that!"

"This frightens you, doesn't it? As well it might. 'Twas rape I saved you from when I bought you— but 'tis rape you seem to wish for." His hands were savoring her buttocks.

She tried to push away from him, but he moved with her, easing her backwards until she came up against the wall, where she stood trapped with her thighs parted by his knee. He pressed against her, arched his hips even nearer. Her moan mixed with his breath. She squirmed against his large, steely body pinning her to the wall, and felt his hardness taunt her in response.

"Woman, I do no' think you really want to fight me. Come, let us enjoy each other." His right hand moved to fondle between her thighs, but her objections increased the moment he pressed a fingertip tenderly into her.

Nevertheless, he leaned his weight against her and teased her to wetness. She felt her treacherous body responding to his coarse strategy. "Aye, you see you can no' prevent me from subjecting you to pleasure. Accept the sensations, welcome them, relish them, for you're bound to feel them whether you will or no'."

She moaned again, faintly, shudders were running along her spine. He observed her with knowing and with entreaty, as he continued.

When she gave no sign of surrender, she felt his free hand loosening and opening his breeches, then he was forcing her legs further apart, bending his knees, pressing slowly upwards, steering himself into her clinging depths.

It had been a while. Her corridor was narrow and snug, while his arousal was at its height. The resistance in her mind was great, yet her eyes were glazed and she was shuddering continuously. He had her by the hipbones now, to steady her as he nudged his way deeper within.

"No!" She started to hit at him, suddenly fevered by fear—fear of her own unwilling passion—but his hands held her firmly in place as he came to dock in the haven she had so cavalierly forbidden him.

"I'm inside you. Feel me there; yield."

"Never!"

"You want me—you do!—yet you'll no' admit it. You're too stubborn by far. Very well, then."

He started his slow movements. He was so strong! "Oh, not like this!" she cried, making every effort to stop him even as pleasure permeated her.

"And how then?" he murmured in her ear. "How would you have it, my heart?"

The very quietness with which he spoke was like the tip of a whip flicking over her skin. "You have no right to treat me like this!"

"But 'tis how you said I must treat you."

"For pity's sake . . ." she gasped, and again she tried to push him away. In answer, his hands left her hips to grasp her wrists and force them wide apart to the wall on either side of her shoulders. She moaned softly.

Then she heard him sigh. "Am I cruel, Flame? Or am I being too kind to you again just now?"

"You . . . are . . . cruel."

"You resent me because I take you, but then you begin to enjoy what I do despite yourself, and that makes you resent me even more. See how 'tis with you? You're a woman with strong instincts and natural responses—and you can no' deny them for long."

She was trembling like a leaf as the tide of desire climbed in her. What shreds of self-control she had left were quickly disappearing. His movements were neither slow nor fast, but calculated. He was staring hard down at her face, watching the play of emotion there. Yet his own expression was one of secret commiseration. He was holding her on the brink, tantalizing her, taunting, while his weight kept her from any reciprocating motion. She opposed him to the crumbling point, but at last she cried, "Cougar!"

"Aye?"

Still he restrained her, just short of the edge over which her body strove to leap. Her breathing came

210

and went in long sobs. "Finish it!" She begged desperately, the words torn reluctantly from her tongue.

"Nae, 'twas force you asked for, and I'm afraid you must endure it for as long as it pleases me."

"Oh God!" she wailed, her entire body churning furiously.

"What a plight your headstrong ways have landed you in this time."

"Cougar . . . *please* . . ."

"Aye now," he said with a deep burr of relief in his tone, "for 'please' mayhap I can do better."

His next thrusts came harder and rocked her body against the wall. His mouth took hers. His kiss, his tongue, his firm lunges brought her to new heights of sensation. She was responding totally to his rough methods now and didn't care if he knew it.

Suddenly she gasped, her crisis overtook her and she writhed ecstatically between him and the log wall. This was like coming home. It was like doing awake what was left from a dream. It was like doing what she'd done before.

Her little cry was lost in his own muted cry of final triumph. He lunged hard and delivered himself within her. Passion seemed to well up in him so impetuously that words for it were impossible. He withdrew, then plunged into her to the hilt again as a second savage spasm seized him.

Breathless, but still holding her where she was, he murmured, "The victory is mine again. Nor is this the end of the matter. However difficult you want to make it. I intend to be your husband."

When he stepped back from her, her legs gave way. He caught her, carried her to the bed, and laid down with her on the silver wolfskins. She searched his face. She knew he could feel the hammering of her heart, for he said, " 'Tis all right." He stroked the wisps of hair off her forehead. "I'm no' angry anymore."

Humiliated, she turned her face away, giving him a profile that she hoped was cool and distant. Her lips didn't tremble now; an icy control had descended upon her. She didn't want to speak or be spoken to. She didn't want him to know that she was utterly confused, thoroughly miserable, nearly beside herself with the urge to cry.

He murmured, " 'Tis all right, my heart. I'm getting to know you better as time passes, and to understand you. The winter's going to be sweet, aye, that sweet, my lady."

Flame woke early the next day. For a short time she simply sat there on the wolfskins clutching the red blanket to her breasts, looking about for Cougar. When she saw that he was already gone, she dressed quickly, not pausing to do more than smooth the tangles out of her hair with her carved wooden comb. Then she went out.

She paused outside the door, still searching for Cougar, and when she didn't see him, she headed for the back of the cabin. She walked past the shed where her pony and the other horses were installed, and started up a faint path that she'd seen yesterday. It cut up through the trees in the direction of the top of the mountain behind the cabin.

She climbed until her calves ached, until at last she came out of the trees to find herself close to the rim of the valley. Mountain sheep roamed against the skyline to her left, curiously grave and lonely looking. Below her all she could see of the cabin beneath the trees was a long finger of smoke.

This was what she wanted, some distance, some privacy, an hour to herself in which she might absorb the shocking truths that she'd been forced to face yesterday.

The path led on to a narrow passage between two crags and finally brought her out of the valley altogether. She suddenly found herself standing on a ledge in the sky with nothing around her but the wind. Below were mountains upon mountains, and summits and towers and steep valleys — all the savage sunlit grace of the Rocky Mountains. Bright clouds hung far, far away on the horizon, caught on the purple teeth of yet more mountains. The forests fell away and away into the land's deepest recesses.

The view was enlightening. She was well and truly lost in these timbered mountains black and splendid with health, among these pinnacles and sheer ravines; Victorine Wellesley had faded into the embrace of the forests, had faded and vanished. Now there existed amongst them a woman named Flame, who must survive as best she could.

She'd never felt so slight and remote as she did there at the verge of that cliff, the wind blowing her loose hair. She'd never felt so much a captive bride as she did this morning, after Cougar's mastery of her. She'd never felt so cut off from all the well-known platitudes of her former life.

She wasn't sure how long she'd been standing there when her nerves notified her of Cougar's approach. Even before he strode out onto the stone sill behind her the very air seemed to quicken with his presence.

"It's no' taken you long to find my aerie," he said pleasantly. "I call this the Drummond's Seat. I've named the mountains 'round the glen as well: Culblean Hill, Morven, Camelong, Ben Nevis—"

"What, no mystic Indian names?"

He didn't answer.

"How did you find me?"

" 'Twas no' hard. You left a trail a bairn could read."

She felt his hands on her arms, turning her. How gentle those strong hands could be! How handsome and caring he could seem! After seizing her the way he had yesterday, after seizing her and ravishing her and forcing her to feel . . .

. . . to feel rapture . . .

She glanced up fearfully as he drew her against him. His lips touched hers softly, but then he allowed her to pull away.

She turned her back to him again. "I get rather tired of you grabbing me and pushing me one way and then another."

He didn't respond to that, but remained behind her, as if he were waiting, like a confident mountain lion just waiting for his moment.

After a while he said, " 'Tis a powerful feeling to look down on the world from here. 'Tis a bonny view, is it no'?"

She stood in a protective attitude, the sun and wind in her hair, moving it. "You've asked enough of me—you can't ask me to praise my prison as well."

" 'Twill seem like a prison if you're going to mutiny against what is."

He had a sort of friendless look on his face that surprised her as he stepped around her, out onto the very edge of the stone. A half-dozen cliff swallows darted out of their nests below his feet and milled wildly in the void.

"This is a world only for the bold and the strong, both male and female," he called without looking

214

back. The swallows began to race through figure eights before him.

It frightened her to see him so close to that drop that went down forever into the valleys below. She realized now that in his presence there was always that trace of fear in her, always the knowledge that he was truly as reckless as he seemed.

In the next shout of wind she called, "Must you stand so far out?"

He half turned and gave her a ruthless smile. "Does it worry you?"

"I just wouldn't want them to start calling this place the Cougar's Leap." In the face of that continuing smile she reminded herself that she must be careful, must manage by her wits what she couldn't handle by mere mental resolution. She said, "I'm cold; I'm going back."

His hands were warm on her as he caught her and turned her again to look at him. He gazed down at her for a long silent moment, his eyes lit by a shimmer of disturbing passion. "You *are* a spirit, Flame. Elusive and quaintly lovely. A flaxen flower in the winds of time. I would like to have you painted as you look right now."

She reacted with profound amazement. "Painted! And where would you hang it? On your log wall next to the sheep horns?"

His arms tightened around her as he replied, "I know of a place, where sunlight falls and sparkles through mullioned glass."

"Where?"

His arms were hard about her, and there was no escape from him; she even admitted to herself that she didn't want to escape him this very moment, yet a spreading creeper of silence separated them, even as he kissed her.

Back in the valley there was much work to be done before the snow set in. The weather was chill all that day, with a persistent hint of icy wind, even through the midday sunlight. Cougar spent his time locating trees he had fallen the previous year for firewood. He used the pack horses to drag them to cabin.

That night the dew froze on every scarlet maple leaf, every golden bough of the black birches, every bending blade of grass. When the silvered morning dawned, Cougar started cutting and cording his trees. His ax biting into wood was the only noise in the world all that week, except for a late bird now and then. The air in the hollow was heavy with the smell of split pines.

Flame helped gather what he cut. Her arms became sore and her back creaked with weariness at each day's end, yet she couldn't give into such minor discomforts when she had only to look up to see his bare back straining to the sinews as he wielded his ax.

She found herself looking at that magnificently muscled back far too often; it got to be a habit with her, and when on occasion he caught her at it, and smiled, her heart plunged straight to her moccasins.

His next project was the cabin. With an old shovel he banked dirt all the way around it, to the top of the first log. He carried creek mud, and showed her how to use it as mortar to fill the cracks. Then, with wood stacked about the outer walls to the depth of three feet and fear of death by freezing defrayed, they went to work on the shed. This was nearly as big as the cabin itself, though not so weather tight, being open at one end. It was used as a shelter for

216

the animals, as a place to cache Cougar's winter harvest of furs, and for general-purpose storage. It warranted a thorough shoveling-out after standing unoccupied all summer, and one corner of the roof needed shoring up with a post.

The first snow came at the end of ten days. Cougar pulled her, still half-asleep and completely naked, from their bed to the door. Irritated, she opened her eyes to an alien, white-frozen place. It was just dawn. The snow was falling lightly and the air was brittle cold — cold, gloomy, and unfriendly. Cougar, nonetheless, seemed full of self-congratulation. She asked him, "Are you really so glad to see it snow?"

"Snow has its own kind of beauty." There was a dazzle of lightning in his eyes which told her immediately that much of his pleasure had to do with a sense of relief. Now she was his indeed. The snow had come to guarantee her presence; it was the last bar of the cage put in place, the door swung shut, the key turned.

She'd feared that now he would be idle and restless, with only her to busy himself with, but she was only partly correct. With the back of the good weather finally broken, it seemed he must set out his traps. He took her with him, though he wouldn't let her handle the traps. "I only want you to see how and where I'm likely to set them, so you'll no' stumble across one and lose your foot to it."

She shuddered to imagine those vicious metal teeth snapping shut on her ankle bones.

More snow fell, and during those days of reflection, indoor tasks kept them both occupied. They had winter garments to make. Cougar claimed he had no talent with a needle and thread. "My hands are too big and clumsy for it." But though his

217

needlework left something to be desired, she knew he had a musician's mastery of those large hands. If his sewing was less than perfect, it was only because that particular task didn't interest him much.

After sleeping in the open for so long, the cabin gave a feeling of immutability to their "marriage." In a mood of grudging acceptance, she cleaned the place from top to bottom the day he went hunting.

Her cleaning chores by necessity required her to organize their stores, and reassured her of their ability to survive the winter. She found that Cougar had a thousand rounds of ammunition; that there were parfleches of wild pumpkin seeds, nuts, and serviceberries; and since they both had sound bodies and mountain appetites, she felt that they should be able to manage.

As twilight deepened over the forest behind the cabin, Cougar brought an elk home, slung across Irongray's rump in limp death.

"He must have been beautiful," she said sadly.

"Aye and he was, and he'll make good eating, too." He gave her a sidelong glance. His gray eyes seemed to brim with knowledge of her. "I thought you were no' the sentimental type of woman."

She blinked hard, remembering herself and tearing her gaze from the limpid eyes of the dead animal. "I'm not talking sentiment; I know it's necessary to kill things for our own survival. But sometimes it does seem too bad."

He cocked his head and smiled sadly, and for an instant she believed he understood, perhaps even shared her regret. He said softly, more to himself than to her, "It seems to be the way of things, though, this slaughtering to survive." She sensed a deep current of thought underneath his words.

It was moments like these that left her confused

about him. What kind of man was he? He wasn't exactly a villain, even if he indulged in villainous acts — and even then his motives could be explained if one were willing to follow his process of reasoning. And though she could hardly endure him sometimes, he was of a constant, quite generous, possibly even noble nature. She dared to think that, given the right circumstances — and the right sort of woman — he might prove a most dear husband.

"Aye," he cut into her musings, "man is ever a hunter and must ever seek his quarry. And when he finds it, he takes it."

He laughed then, as though knowing he'd just foiled her yet again. She seethed as they began skinning and quartering the elk.

It was cold enough now to keep meat without jerking it. He brought in another elk and a deer, the choicest portions of which they hung loosely shrouded in buckskin wraps from branches of the pines by the side of the cabin. And every night they feasted on juicy dripping steaks.

The red blanket had been warm, but it was nothing compared to the great beaverskin robe that now covered their bed. Now she learned what it was to lay naked between furs like a libertine. (Libertine had been one of her father's words; she often had little stabs of thought for him and what he might have to say about how she was living now.)

After Cougar's victory over her the day of their arrival, she'd tried another ruse — to refuse to sleep in his bed at night. This ploy was short lived and long regretted, for now he merely swooped her up, carried her to the furs, and tossed her down on them each time he required her presence there.

This evening, while she was clearing the table of their meal, he sat on the black bearskin before the fire. He had his forearms around his knees as he watched her. She could never get used to him watching her, though he did it much of the time.

"You've plunged happily into housekeeping," he said. "I remember once you told me you did no' think you had the talent for making a home, or for making a man comfortable." When she didn't answer, he went on. "Seeing you bustle about like a thrifty Scot's wife makes me remember my mother. She makes much the same show of toughness as you, and beneath it has the same warm and generous heart."

She gave him a slight smile. "What is her name?"

"Inary."

"What is your name?"

He shook his head gently. "My Flame, you never give up, do you? I've told you who I am."

"Have you . . . that is, do you have a wife . . . a *real* wife . . . back in Scotland?" She moved around him to the fire, pushing more wood into it, but keeping the edge of her vision on him, waiting.

He laughed, and she felt teased. "Do you no' like to think of me with someone else?"

The question struck her as infinitely callous and she stiffened, but before she could reply, he said, "Nae, I have only one wife. And I find being her husband that pleasant."

He suddenly stood, swept her up into his arms and covered her mouth with his. As he crossed the floor with her, for a change she didn't protest.

"What's this?" he said, bending to place her on the furs. "Have you learned at last that 'twill do you no good to tussle with me night after night?"

She reached her arms around his neck, pulling his head down and kissing him deeply, as he'd taught her. She felt his body ripple with surprise, then he melted over her. "Ah, lassie, you have a mouth like a flower bud. How I love to feel it open to me."

"Undress me, Cougar," she whispered.

He fumbled with her lacing, then drew the hem of her dress up. She lifted herself as he pulled it over her head. He went on to remove her moccasins and leggings, his hands drifting freely to her thighs.

When he would have gathered her again into his arms, she said, "My hair." She knew by now how much he admired her hair; after making love to her he often toyed with it, spreading it across his chest, arranging it over her breasts, or fanning it like a sunburst over the furs—all the while warning her not to move lest she destroy his artwork. So now she waited with fluttering patience as he unplaited her Indian-style braids and combed the hair out into flaxen waves with his fingers.

She waited, too, as he quickly undressed himself, shedding his shirt first, then kicking off his moccasins and breeches, all the time watching her, his eyes burning with wary satisfaction at her show of willingness.

Then he was beside her on the wolfskins. His body smelled musky and vital. He seemed to want to enjoy his good fortune, for rather than take her quickly, he forbore to even touch her except to place one hand on the shallow of her stomach while his mouth took in the rose-tipped peak of one breast.

She shivered; her breath caught in her throat. She thought it best to make her move now. "Cougar," she said in a small voice, "are you truly a man of your word?"

He lifted his head slightly, enough to look at her from beneath his brows.

"I know you've been keeping a record of my days . . ."

He tensed and raised higher on his elbow. His face had gone suddenly hard. In a lithe movement he got up and padded to the mantel. There he kept the stick on which he'd faithfully whittled a notch for each day since her last "moon." Quickly the flat of his thumb moved down the marks. The side of his face was like a carving on a bronze coin. But then she saw him turn white with rage. Holding the stick in his right hand, he whipped the palm of his left with it, once, twice, then turned slowly and came back to the bed. "I ought to use this on your back."

Downing the flare of fear she felt, she sat up and leaned forward, offering her back to him. She lifted the curtain of hair away from the side of her face to look at him. "But you said it wasn't in you to hit a woman. And you said—you gave me your word—that I wouldn't conceive a child."

His temper steadied, yet his eyes were narrow, his mouth a thin line. "So you thought to tease me, did you? To taunt me a little? You're a bold woman."

Casting a look at his face, at his dark frown, she felt not bold—and not the jeering victory she'd hoped for—but a nervous anxiety. And an emptiness. She realized she felt ashamed for what she'd just done.

He sat down on the edge of the bed, blowing out his cheeks as if after a great exertion. He touched a fingertip to the now hardened tip of the breast he'd wetted with his tongue earlier. For a long moment the only sounds were the faint crack of the fire, the soft, ghostly sighing sound of more snow falling on the roof, the gentle breathings of the two of them.

He suddenly laughed, a mixed, sweet-bitter chuckle. He laid the stick aside to wind strands of her hair about her slim throat. "I could choke you with your own loveliness. Still and all, I'll no' break

222

my word." She was almost ready to draw a sigh of relief when he added, "But I'm that sorry to have to tell you, lassie, that I need no' worry you with a poor bairn in order to enjoy you thoroughly." His expression was diabolical. "The question now is: Are you a woman of *your* word?"

# Chapter Fifteen

"Your actions just now promised me much," Cougar said. "Do you deny it, Flame? You encouraged me to desire you, to believe you would receive me without opposition for once."

"I—I was testing you."

"Aye, and now I'm testing you. Did you or did you no' imply your willingness—even a certain eagerness?"

"Well, perhaps I did imply . . ." Her voice fell away.

He quirked an eyebrow.

Careful, she told herself; he can talk a black man white, and vice versa.

Aloud, she said, "But that doesn't change the fact of *your* promise." She fell back onto the bed and started to cover herself with the beaverskin robe.

He stopped her by spreading his open hands over her breasts. He moved closer to her, one hand drifting down her abdomen. "There are things you ken naught about yet." He bent, his lips following the trail of his fingers until his goal was clear. She reached to restrain him with her hands in his hair. He paused. "You're no' going to do the honorable thing then?"

She put her fingers to her temples and gave a little gasp of anguish. "I—I'm trying to do right thing, the *moral* thing."

"A moral person insists she's doing what she thinks is right under the circumstances, even if 'tis no' exactly what she said she would do. An *honorable* person keeps her word. A man can at least ken what to expect from her; he can reckon on it. Which be you?"

"I . . . you're confusing me."

His tongue delved into her navel. He laughed when she shivered because of it. "Just relax, lassie. 'Twill no' be a painful lesson."

"What are you going to do?" For this moment she was terrified.

He bent over her. She battled not to cover herself, not to turn from him. He stroked her thighs. He kissed them, pushing his fingers between her legs and spread her. He kissed her belly, then lower. Then, with his fingers, he reached into her silky dampness and handled the tender little lips and lay her open.

With his head descended, she gave a terrible shudder. She covered her mouth with her hand and beneath it cried out softly.

He was nibbling and playing his tongue on her. She let out another little cry before she could stop herself. She felt on the verge of weeping, struggling to keep still. A third cry was muffled by her hand over her mouth.

Cougar had found the tiny nodule between her tender flesh; he worked it back and forth until her legs began to move restlessly. She raised her satiny hips, arching her spine in spite of herself. Her expression was the picture of distress. She was twisting her head from side to side, her hands now drawing up the soft furs into knots. The nipples of her breasts were drawn up as firm as tiny pebbles.

All her senses magnified and crystallized. She felt as if a dark liquid force were curling and rushing over her. She felt both a panting struggle for breath and a mumbling helplessness, as if she were being tumbled by the boil and bubble of that dark wave. Her hands grasped his head, tugged at his hair, but on went his tongue—until for a long instant her thighs stiffened, quivered.

She shuddered violently with unwilling pleasure. Time stopped. There were no more minutes, no seconds. She was suspended at that point of great feeling. It seemed both a moment and an eternity.

"That's it, that's it, heart."

At last she relaxed, though his mouth still lingered, playing gently now, stroking, kissing her, giving her the fullest pleasure and seeing that she lost none of it. The fire threw its warm, rosy radiance over her. Her hair lay on either side of her head. Cougar, raising on his elbow at last, looked up at her with his little smile.

She lay still, moist, rosy, with her eyes closed, breathing deeply. He said, "That was lovely, my heart."

She had her eyes still half-closed. "Oh," she said, and laid an arm over her forehead. He leaned beside her and looked down at her. His hair was tousled over his eyes, which were strangely animated. He bent to bite at one still-tightened nipple, playfully, not hurting her. He bit the other, and licked them both with his tongue.

She watched him from beneath her arm, then scrambled quickly out of his reach, off the bed, searching for her clothes in belated shame. He'd removed her dress, however, and knew where to find it first. He closed his hand over it heartlessly. She looked away from him. Oh, how was she going to come through this? "I must get away from you!" she said in a release of fear that seemed to explode from her. "What will you think of next? What will I be when spring finally comes, after a full winter with you?"

"I wonder," he said without the slightest sign of remorse. He was gazing at her with horrid gentle enjoyment, knowing all about her, it seemed. "Shall I tell you what I hope?"

"Oh don't!" she cried with even more heat. "Cougar—you must let me go! Now! Before—"

"Nae, let's no' talk of that anymore. I'll deny you naught within reason. Ask me for that which I can give you."

She buried her head in her hands. "If only someone would come to help me!"

"Come back to bed now, Flame."

"No! Never again!"

His expression rendered words almost unnecessary. He tossed the dress aside and moved to corner her, and when he had her in his arms, he lifted her and carried her again to the furs. With a sigh, he tossed her down. "Correct me if I'm wrong—I'm afraid I'm all topsy-turvy by now—but it seems we're back to where we started." He grinned evilly and fell on her with studied ease.


The snowstorm left the sky a thin and stippled gray for days. Enclosed in the cabin, Flame suffered. Cougar could overwhelm her careful defenses any time he liked. He stalked her with the sure control of a hunting cat. His style was subdued but deliberate,

227

a methodical destruction of her inhibitions. Gradually he was wrenching her away from what she'd been taught was proper, replacing all her learned restraints with yearnings for pure sensation. More and more easily she was lured, sometimes by a mere softening of his eyes, or by a single touch, or even a whispered, "Come to me." Lured into the labyrinth of desire, into the Waiting Cougar's muscled arms.

When the snow storm finally cleared, and a morning dawned when all the world was a blaze of sky, she was relieved to watch him tramp out to check his trap lines.

He came back at noon, however, carrying nothing but his rifle across his saddle. Flame, on her way back from the shed, was stepping carefully over the snow that had drifted in some places deeper than the tops of her leggings. She met him uneasily at the cabin door. Their breathing formed a single mist of steam that floated up and wafted away.

"All our traps were empty, lassie," he said.

He followed her inside and sat to take off his frozen moccasins and slip on dry ones.

"Well, it's been cold," she offered inanely.

He nodded.

It *had* been cold. She had no idea just how cold, but tall trees had cracked now and then like rifle shots, and flakes of ice still blew in the wind.

When the traps were empty again the next day, he said, "Something's raiding them."

On the third morning he said, " 'Tis a bear. A grizzly."

"What will you do?"

"If I find it, I'll have to kill it—unless it finds me and kills me first." She gave him a scornful, disbelieving look, and he frowned. "Few encounters with grizzlies are planned. Nae, they're sudden and lively.

'Tis no' wise to be so blind in so hard a place as this, Flame. Life's none so long as to be risked unnecessarily."

The weather was clear and warm all that week. The layers of early snow melted away out on the open valley floor, leaving lingering patches under the trees. Flame was restless and wanted to get outdoors while she still could. As Cougar prepared to go hunting again, she asked him if she might go with him. He said carefully, "I would feel better if you stayed here. There's a grizzly out there somewhere."

"I would stay close to you."

Suddenly showing the tough side of his personality, he said, "Sorry, no' this time." He took a chunk of jerked buffalo and a handful of dried serviceberries, and went out the door. He was fully armed with his rifle in his hand and his tomahawk and knife on his belt.

Fuming, Flame spent some time beading a pair of fur-lined moccasins for herself, and a lot of time thinking about him. She knew there was no use in her carrying on so. However, something drove her to do just that all day long. She started out for a walk across the valley once, on her own and against his orders. She still doubted all those wild Indian tales of the grizzly bear's ferocity; it seemed a comparatively timid beast to her, unwilling even to show itself. As for Cougar's notions, she didn't care a snap for any of them.

Yet, soon she found herself hollow-hearted, out alone, knowing that there was an animal generally considered dangerous in the vicinity.

It would have been a nice chance for a walk, but she turned back after going only a little way. She sighed. Canadian geese and lines of swans drifted overhead. The stone-shouldered Rockies stood up all around her, their white peaks sparkling with sun. What on earth was she doing here? This was a place for giants, for gods, a place where myths entered the heart. It was not a place for a bookish young woman from Philadelphia.

What, for that matter, was she doing living as the wife of a mountain man called the Waiting Cougar? Was it all the fault of some aberrant collision of stars? He *had* come like a comet across her life. Now that was as silly and oversubtle a thought as she'd ever had.

But how else to explain it?

She still felt irritable when he returned in the fading gleam of the afternoon, whole and healthy and handsome as ever. She heard him coming, but perversely decided to treat him to a dose of silence.

When he opened the door, a taper of slanting sunlight entered with him. Flame made no sound of welcome, so that he was all the way inside before his eyes found her in the gloom. "There you are," was all he said.

He was preoccupied with something and seemed not to notice her refusal to speak. She put her sewing away and placed before him some stewed venison in a wooden bowl. "Well, did you find your big bad bear?"

"The only new tracks I could find were at the lower end of the valley," he said, eating his dinner and supper at once, with appetite, but no particular sign of relish. She might have placed a bowl of worms before him for all the attention he spared it.

He was so unnoticing of everything, including her mood, that she felt she really had to get out of the cabin. It wouldn't do to let her feelings show right now. It would only set them more at odds, when already they were like two clocks ticking in counterpoint. The last thing she wanted was another quarrel.

"I'm going out for a minute," she said, swinging the buffalo-hide cloak she'd made for herself around her shoulders.

He nodded, assuming, as she meant for him to, that she was making a call on nature. "Have the wit to no' wonder too far," he warned at the last minute before she pulled the cabin door shut behind her.

She shoved aside the high brush on the narrow path leading upwards behind the cabin. His casual tone of voice had only made her furious. *Do no' do this, do no' do that, lie still now, close your eyes . . .* She was tired of being ordered about!

She climbed uphill briskly, until she was out of breath and had to lean against a tall spruce to rest a minute. The sun was going down in a thin strata of colored cloud high at the horizon's edge, and the forest shadows were depressingly long. There was snow in the shade of the trees and big rocks, but the path was open here, and relatively dry. She could smell the melting snow, the dripping stones, the ice oozing down into little streamlets. A last beam of sunlight glanced against her face in going, yet it held no warmth. Her breath was steamy in the cold air.

She stepped out from under the tree's drooping branches, ready to go on, determined to go all the way to the Drummond's Seat, just to spite Cougar, but then she stopped and listened. Though she was unable to explain it, the silence cloaking the slope seemed somehow different to her. She told herself that it was only that everything looked spooky in this first blue of the twilight. But then she heard faint rustlings in the brush fifty yards or so away, stealthy sorts of sounds—a furtive crackle of pine needles, the dry pop of a twig, a rattle of under-

231

brush. Whatever it was, she knew it wasn't the ordinary and harmless patter of squirrels' feet.

She started to back away, on the lookout now for anything that moved, testing each step for noise before she shifted her weight, alert for more sounds.

She made it to the next tree down the path. A deep and eerie silence ensconced her. Glancing down, she saw some tracks in the spongy soil, each one longer than and triple the width of her own foot.

Now she stood stone still, all her senses poring over the evidence. A spine-tingling sensation swept her, a feeling that whatever had been in the dense brush was surely now watching her. She could see the roof of the cabin through the trees below her, so far away, all the way down at the edge of the forest.

She stood still a moment longer, still aquiver, still alive in every fiber, listening for a repetition of those rustling sounds.

Suddenly a noise came like a crack of lightning to her strained and oversensitive ears; the underbrush splintered. She could barely turn her fear-stiffened neck in the direction of the noise—but as she did she heard another splintering, this time much closer.

Just forty yards away the bushes began to move. Her breath stopped in her throat; she could only pant shallowly as the leaves split apart like a green stage curtain, revealing three brown yearling bear cubs. They didn't see her at first, but then one of them stood up on his small hind legs and sniffed the air. His snout moved in a half-circle, and then his eyes struck Flame's eyes. There was an instant's pause before he charged right for her, as if flung into movement. The other two followed as though pulled along by strings.

She'd been so scornful, but faced with three bears

232

at once—even though they were only cubs and hardly bigger than large dogs—she found she was petrified.

Half grunting, half growling, the rushing, chocolate-colored beasts closed the distance between themselves and her. The first barreled a mere half-length in front of the others. Flame cried, "Stop! Go away! Shoo!" but they kept coming, their small brown snouts glistening in the twilight, the rolling fur on their backs undulating like prairie grass in the wind. When their jaws opened, revealing razor-sharp baby teeth (startlingly visible even at thirty yards), her body at last reacted. She jerked her arms up, trying to ward them away.

They neither wavered nor slowed. She realized at last that, though they were small, they were monsters at the kill.

She whirled and started to run. A glance over her shoulder confirmed that the glaring little bears were still coming. She was half-prepared when the blow came: The fastest bear had lunged. His staggering slam against her hips knocked her forward so that she fell pell-mell among the forest's eager claws. Dirt jammed her mouth. Her forehead smacked against a patch moss. The bear had her pinned down; he was making thick, gutteral, animal noises and breathing spasmodically. A voice within her screamed.

Another of the cubs roared to a stop near her head. His piglike eyes glared down at her as he stood up on his two, short hind legs, weaving his head back and forth.

The third bear rushed up, huffing. He squealed, then pounced with ferocity, joining his twin on her back. Things seemed to go dark for a moment, the scene teetered in Flame's mind. Part of her detached and began to lecture: *Call out for Cougar.*

233

*I can't!* the other part of her claimed. *I can't get a breath!*

*Don't be sissyish. You can if you try.*

Meanwhile the cubs were biting and scratching at her buffalo-hide cloak. She felt the nip of teeth on her back right through the thick fur layers of both the cloak and her dress. "Cougar . . . help me . . ."

The bears, as if startled by her small sounds, scrambled off her. Immediately she got to her feet and began to run again. She pushed the tall undergrowth aside, stumbling now, screaming, *"Cougar!"*

He couldn't have heard her earlier pitiful whimpers, yet somehow he'd known. (His sixth sense, that something that was uncanny about him.) She saw him already cutting into the woods in her direction, his rifle in his hands. As she made for him, he stopped dead. She saw his mouth move: Damn!

He brought the rifle to his shoulder, then lowered it hastily because her necessarily zig-zagging course through the trees kept bringing her across his line of aim. He started running toward her, but when she met him, he passed her by. She skidded to a halt, heaving in gulps of air. Turning, at first she saw only that the cubs weren't on her heels as she'd believed. But she'd heard something behind her, chasing her . . .

That was when the mother bear reared up, a nine-foot-tall beast, not more than fifteen yards from Cougar. The bear's small eyes scanned the scene briefly. Her powerful curved claws hung at the ends of her arms before her. The ring of pale fur circling her chest and muscle-humped shoulders heaved.

Cougar fired. The animal's body barely reacted to the impact of the ball. Sinking soundlessly to all four feet, she moved forward again in an unpleasant, rolling gait of fat and fur, quickly building up speed. Her silver-edged coat shimmered and changed colors, almost as if arcs of power were surging off her.

All Flame's instincts drew up in her: Real Bear! Everything Cougar had told her—which she had scoffed at (she was a fool of uncommon magnitude!)—came back to her in a rush: "Even experienced men have had close escapes—or died . . ." "It takes six to ten braves to kill a single bear . . ." "I must confess, lassie, I would sooner fight two churlish Indians than one grizzly . . ."

Cougar had been busy reloading his rifle. Shouldering it again, he said tersely, "Flame, get inside."

But the silver bear was so close now! He stood exposed to it. It was sweeping forward in a rush, powerful, determined, larger than life, its growl like something coming down out of the clouds. It was nearly on him, coming like a landslide on four legs, ears pinned back, tongue out, mouth and throat forming an O-OOAGH!

How, Flame wondered, can something so huge move so fast?

Cougar was trying to take his second aim, every tendon taut, but the she-bear lunged forward before he could get his shot off. She slapped the gun's barrel aside—a walloping blow delivered with the speed of a shiver. The rifle flew out of his hands.

Now plainly visible within the drooling jaws were the repugnant yellow spikes of her teeth. Time seemed to halt as Flame watched the blunt claws descending.

Cougar was smashed to the ground as if his own strength was nothing. Yet when the bear had him under her, he started to curse her and punch her head. Such futile efforts seemed bizarrely humorous.

235

However, his fisted assaults seemed an affront that permeated the big creature with a mountainous rage. Astonished, burning with anger, the she-beast's chest exploded with a succession of wild woofing roars; she loomed up on her hind legs with Cougar between her feet.

Up came one of the cubs just then, walking on two legs. This additional distraction seemed to make her so mad that she took the time to box the babe's ears, all the while making horrible bear talk.

Cougar was given just enough time to get out his knife. In the same instant he shouted his previous order to Flame, this time with great violence: "Get inside, woman!"

Immediately the bear turned her attention back to him. But as she lowered over him again, he lunged up and stabbed her in the neck behind her ear. As if she felt nothing, she beat the knife out of his hand the same way she had the rifle—and came close to ripping off one of his fingers as well.

Cougar was bleeding now and the bear had him under her, but then another cub ran in. The youngsters seemed to be obeying a desire that dwelt deep in their instincts—the desire to take part in the kill. Again the mother bear took the time to cuff her own offspring. The little one, declining further combat, ran off. Meanwhile Cougar had pulled his hatchet from his belt. He sank the blade into her chest.

The pain seemed to madden her. She clamped her fangs on his forearm, sending those sharp teeth deep into his muscles as she hulked over him. She lifted her head, his arm in her mouth; her immense paws were on his chest, levering against it, as if she meant to rip his arm from his body. He struggled to reach up with his free hand, to take hold of the hatchet still gripped in his fang-clasped right hand. The bear

236

kept yanking his arm about, yet somehow he managed to get hold of the handle, then he was drawing his left arm back to smite the prow of the beast's nose, a bruising blow landed with the blunt head of the tomahawk. His arm fell back again and he hit her again; this time the blow struck her nostrils. Now he turned the weapon in his hand and plunged the blade deeply into her chest.

The beast jumped back in hysteria. She went up on her hind legs, her arms out before her, indomitable, bellowing. She was hacked through the chest and shoulder, stabbed in the neck, even shot, but she merely spouted blood in all directions and showed her resentment and readied herself to attack again.

Flame knew her next pounce might crack Cougar's ribs, might crush his big heart, might kill him. She saw his rifle lying between her and the battle. It was taller than she was, and so heavy that as she raced forward and tried to snatch it up, she found she could hardly straighten her back. He'd already primed the piece and rammed down the ball. At least she prayed that it was ready to fire as she struggled to bring up the barrel. The grizzly turned to face her.

The pine needles on the slope were slippery underfoot, the gun was heavy. " 'Tis too heavy for a woman to lift," Cougar had told her when once she'd asked him to teach her to shoot. She was afraid now that he was right. It came up slowly and stubbornly, but somehow she got the butt to her shoulder. The end of the barrel rose but wobbled so violently in her hands that she couldn't direct it, close as the target swayed.

"Flame! Nae!"

She braced the butt deeper into her shoulder, took a firmer grip, yet still she couldn't control it enough to put its sight on the target. The bear took a step toward her. Her face had a white-pinched feel. She felt very sick and very afraid. Finally, without aiming at all, she simply yanked back on the trigger.

The air around her exploded. The gun knocked her backwards, right off her feet. The crack of the shot reverberated across the valley and back. Her ears hummed, her nostrils burned with the scent of black powder.

Otherwise there was silence. Dead silence. She found herself staring up at the blue-sheeted sky.

As soon as she got her wits gathered, she rolled onto her side. The great grizzled animal lay quiet, its head near Cougar's leg. She crawled across to where the two lay sprawled. A scratch on Cougar's cheek dripped doggedly. The right sleeve of his shirt was warm and gluey with blood.

All was deep, intense silence. The bear's blood leaked silently into the damp dirt. Flame remembered the cubs, and swung her eyes around briefly for them, but apparently they had slunk away.

"Cougar? Are you dead?" His head lolled when she touched his face tentatively.

He moaned. "No' yet." Slowly he moved his left hand across his chest to clutch his right forearm. Red blood seeped through his fingers. His eyes opened. "You should no' have tried to fire that gun. You should've gone inside—and smartly—like you were told."

"That's right, don't bother to thank me for saving your life."

His smile was only a little forced as he lumbered to sit up. "Oh heart, for that I do thank you; aye, for that I just do." He was looking at the bear's head, where the bullet had entered its open mouth and pierced its brain, then he looked back at Flame, with wonder and admiration.

"Try standing," she said. "See if you can walk."

There was nothing wrong with his legs, yet he teased, "I feel a little helpless, a wee bit beset. I'm afraid I'll have to lean on you." He put his left arm around her shoulders, bracing his injured right arm against his chest. She winced as he pressed her close. The recoil of the rifle had left her shoulder aching and throbbing. "What makes you look that white? You're no' hurt, too?"

"It's only a bruise." Her face felt oddly waxen now, and she started to shiver as the wintry hand of shock closed about her.

"You'll soon be well, with my lips to soothe you."

Knowing her will was faltering, she spoke sharply to shore it up. "You would be better to save your soothings for yourself—because *I* get to do the wound cleaning this time."

# Chapter Sixteen

Cougar took a seat at the table when they reached the cabin. He didn't behave as if he were hurt seriously, though Flame had seen the bear bite him and knew the punctures in his arm must be so deep as to pierce his very bones. His thumb was badly gashed as well. All the wounds would contain dirt and hair and bear saliva. She forced her voice to a flatness, trying to keep her mind on surface matters. "You'll have to take your shirt off."

"Flame, you'll make me blush. I'm a gentleman, you know."

"You're a gentleman only as it pleases you, and now it pleases you to annoy me."

But he complied, with her help, revealing where the grizzly had left the marks of its terrible claws and teeth. Working swiftly, she cleaned the wounds, applied his foul-scented beaver bait, and used the remains of an old flannel shirt for a bandage. She made a sling from strips of hide and looped it around his neck.

"What a shot!" he said, testing the weight of his arm in the cradle of the sling. "Straight through the beast's mouth and into her brain. You did no' tell me you were a marksman."

"I didn't know," she mumbled. Her voice was a tired trace. As her protecting irritation with his mockery wore off, she began to tremble. Physically, it was as if an unhurrying fist caught her hard in the midriff. The foul scent of the beaver-bait "medicine" suddenly became more than she could tolerate. Looking down, she saw on the tabletop a drop of his deepest blood, fallen from his lacerations and still lying there to be seen. She set her teeth to help curb her queasiness, and when that didn't seem enough, put her hand to her mouth.

"Are you going to be sick, lassie?" he asked, all his mockery cast off at last.

She shook her head, though she wasn't at all sure. He helped her undress as best he could, all the while murmuring, "Do no' fret; 'tis all right now, my lamb, my pet." He urged her into bed with him.

"Will you hold me for a while?" she asked timorously.

"That I will, gladly," He brought her close to his warm body and soothed her with his one good hand. She felt his lips touch her eyelids, and she rubbed her cheek against his rough chin. "Sleep sweet now, heart."

"Yes, I think I will." She reached up and touched his cheek. How was it that his closeness always helped to still the fear?


Flame realized that Cougar's battle with the bear had taken more out of him than he'd admitted when she woke early the next morning to a chilled cabin. It was his habit to get up once or twice in the night to tend the fire, but now the hearth was stone cold. He seemed lost in so deep an exhaustion that he didn't even stir as she unfolded from his embrace and crept from the bed.

She herself had to move slowly at first to avoid jouncing her sore muscles. She was as stiff from having slept coiled like a grub against him as from the recoil of the rifle. She found her dress and put it on, though the leather was so cold it felt wet.

Working the stiffness out of her bruised joints, she set about building a new fire. She stirred among the ashes, hoping for a few live coals. Shivering, she placed a handful of shavings over what she uncovered. A tiny flame ignited, flared, went out. Another glowed, then waned. She was shivering hard, chilled to the marrow now; her hands were going numb. She blew on the burning coals until she thought her lips would crack. At length they caught flame. The timid flames seized the pitch in a larger piece of kindling, and in another miraculous moment there was a pungent fire blazing.

When Cougar roused several hours later, he took for granted the warmth in the cabin, though he seemed surprised to find himself alone in bed. "Stay where you are," Flame told him. She was kneeling before her loud-sputtering fir-and-cedar fire, her long hair falling like silken threads about her shoulders. "I've got some hot broth for you."

"Broth! 'Tis only a scratch or two I have; I'm no' an invalid, woman."

"Nonetheless, you'll stay in bed today and do as *I* say for a change."

"Shall I?" He seemed amused. His smile became sly as she took a bowl of steaming meat broth to him. "All right, aye, I'll stay abed—if you'll join me."

She shook her head. "Behave now. If you won't think of yourself, at least consider me. If you die, I would be in a fine pickle, wouldn't I?"

"Such tenderness of feeling," he murmured, spooning up the broth with his uninjured left hand while she sat on the edge of the bed holding the bowl for him.

She took the opportunity to look him over. The scratch across his cheek had already dried darkishly, but the flesh around it was purple and bruised. His shoulder joint, where the bear had nearly wrenched his arm from its socket, was swollen and tender. These would soon mend, however. It was the cuts and tooth punctures that might fester and cause trouble.

"How is the broth?" she asked. She'd gone up the hill to the carcass of the bear for the meat, and though she wasn't much of a mountain cook yet, she thought she'd done very well this time.

"Grizzly is it? 'Tis generally no' so palatable as black bear—it tastes too much like coarse pork—but this is good enough."

"I thought it tasted very good."

"Aye, my sprite, that's the way of it when 'tis your own kill."

Her kill or not, she wasn't going to let that huge supply of fresh meat go to waste. In spite of the weather, which was an example of mid-autumn at its worst—rain, hail, snow, rain again—she spent the day laboriously fire-drying strips of bear meat. Cougar did no more than offer occasional instructions from his bed. When he wasn't sleeping away as if under a spell, he silently watched her work, so that when she looked up she was more than once surprised to find him smiling lazily at her.

As the afternoon began to wear away, she tried to think how she could save the rest of the bear meat—there was a quarter ton of it left—from the wolves.

She hitched Spot and the pack horses (she was afraid of Irongray) to ropes looped through a high fork in a tree and tied at the other end to the carcass. The horses easily pulled the meat up off the ground, where it would keep long enough for her to work the huge pelt free and save more meat from the unpredictable weather.

The evening darkened under the canopy of the trees about the cabin. Rain and sleet slashed at the door and drafts blew in and around its frame. Flame was still busy, now boiling down chunks of fat to make oil. (Bear lard was known, even in the East, to be sweet and long keeping. Many preferred it to butter.) In the windy pause that separated two downpours, she said to Cougar, "I couldn't believe how she kept coming back at you, even after you'd stabbed her and hit her with your tomahawk three times!"

"Aye, I tried to tell you. Grizzlies are nigh unkillable. Even a heart shot will no' stop the brutes. The only really vital spot, the brain, is guarded by thick flesh and solid bone. And only a perfect shot by a practiced rifleman is likely to hit home there."

"I was lucky."

"Nae, 'twas no' all luck, that; 'twas part pure gall—and part simple courage," he added. " 'Twas a fine thing to see your style, love. 'Tis a brave woman I've married." On his face was neither the look of amusement nor the jeering grin that she'd anticipated, but an expression of honest admiration, which unnerved her even more.

She was still busy at the hearth. She could tell that he was feeling better and she was therefore careful not to kneel too close to him. She'd just lowered another kettle of fat to cool when he said, "Can I be having another bit of that broth?"

"Of course." She brought him a bowlful. He ignored the wooden spoon and drank it like tea. "The morrow I hope you'll see fit to feed me properly. My belly's so empty I feel I could devour every living thing upon the land."

"We'll see if you're up to solid food—maybe a nice thick soup?"

He merely looked his protest, but after a long pause said, "Aye, we'll see."

He lingered over the last of the broth, watching her through full, gentle eyes. "What a bonny nurse you be, fair enough to make a man want to keep to his bed. My own good wet nurse never cared for me so well." He handed the bowl back to her, then quick as an arrow in flight, his good hand shot out and slid under her dress, up the back of her leg sending a little shock through her.

She scooted out of his reach, agile as a trout in a pool. "Behave yourself!"

"Sorry, the temptation was more than I could withstand."

He was smiling in a way that made her feel odd. She knew that smile too well. "You're incorrigible."

"Aye, and you're enjoying this. You fancy having me at your mercy."

Her dimples, that she so seldom showed, winked now. "It is a nice turn of events."

He grumbled, "Aye, a fine thing for you; smallpox would be better for me. I should've gone south for the winter. There are senoritas willing and lovely in Taos, with an appetite for desperate men in buckskin."

"Maybe that would have been a better idea," she answered blithely.

"Do no' be deceived by my present meekness, heart. I'm only letting you nurse me because you

245

want to that badly."

"Ah, yes, I knew it must be something like that."
She bent her head to hide her grin.

"Aye, laugh away. I'll no' be forgetting this." His
smile was full of mischievous pleasure.

A while later, when the wind rattled the door yet
again, he said with cautious indirection, " 'Tis getting late; the night is setting up to blow. Are you no'
tired yet?" His eyes intent on her face, he added, "I
can no' rest properly 'til you quit your fussing and
come to bed."

"Do I have your word that you will rest — properly?"

"You're a hard, woman, Flame. No' all that affectionate, I've noticed; no' exactly inclined to hop into
my lap everytime I make one." He was frowning
pitifully. "Mayhap I misnamed you. You're more like
the little white Scots rose that smells sharp and
lovely, aye, and breaks the heart."

"I think there's very little chance of my breaking
your heart." There was an edge in her voice.

He shook his head. "Blossom of fire, blaze of
brave light, will you no' come rest with me?"

She eyed him suspiciously, knowing that passion
always brought out the poetry in him. A quiet,
steady man, he was also a romantic. Yet with his
arm slung clumsily across his chest he was probably
as harmless as he could ever be.

As if to prove that notion wrong, he made as if to
throw the beaverskin back. "If you do no' come
willingly I shall have to come get you. I can handle
you with just one arm — you weigh no more than a
basket of eggs."

She put out her hand to stay him. His voice wasn't
unkind but closer to fierce than gentle. And she
knew he was capable of coercing her, even injured as

246

he was. He was capable of anything, anything at all.

Hesitant, self-conscious, she kicked off her moccasins, baring the pale stalks of her ankles. His eyes shone as her dress fell to the floor, as she shook back her hair so that it dropped shiny as sunbleached straw down the alabaster of her body. A flush from her cheeks spread to her proud breasts until they glowed, pink and reticent. They wambled in the light from the fire as she threw a new log on it and then moved toward the bed.

"Ah, you're that bonny," he said huskily, lifting the beaverskin to make room for her. The furs were warm with his body heat. "I can hardly believe the gods have thrown you to me. What was in their minds?"

Cougar's arm was out of its sling, and at the noon meal two weeks later he no longer used his knife awkwardly. Flame had treated him like an invalid long after he really needed to be. Shamelessly he'd accepted her attentions, and even exaggerated his injuries some.

"You enjoy being spoiled," she said.

"I admit it freely, aye, and can no' thank you enough for your kindness, heart."

But gradually he'd taken charge again.

He went out mysteriously right after eating today, and didn't come back for two hours. When he did, he gave her that brief Scots bow of his and presented her with a string of claws. "You've the rare right to wear these. A necklace of great grizzly claws is one of the highest distinctions a warrior can achieve."

"I'm no warrior."

She let the claws slide from one hand to the other. "I would feel silly wearing them." She dropped them

247

rattling onto the table.

"Why?" He shook his head fondly and laughed, after a fashion. "I was mighty pleased to see that beast go down." He gathered the necklace up neatly and handed it back to her. "Put it on, Flame."

With the claws dangling from her neck, she smiled one of her more elfin, dimpling smiles. (She wasn't aware of it, but those dimples were showing more and more often.) "Thank you," she said.

"Nae, thank you." He gathered her close in his arms. She put her hands on his shoulders and tucked her forehead under his jawbone. It felt right to do so, at least in this unique moment of accord.

"We're a pair, we are—I wear the scars and you wear the claws. 'Tis a thing for a man to think on seriously."

She spent most of the following days working on the hide she'd painstakingly taken from the she-bear. It took Spot's help for her even to drag the heavy thing to the cabin. There she tanned it and added the fur to her wardrobe, making herself a long, luxurious cloak, a hat, and a pair of fur-lined moccasins.

"I believe you would part with your hair before you would give up that bearskin capote," Cougar teased.

It was close to the truth. She'd become proud of her kill, and secretly satisfied to realize that Cougar now owed her his life as surely as she owed hers to him.

She was becoming so adept at finishing pelts from his traps and hunts that he gifted her with her own skinning knife, a lovely tool with a carved hawthorn handle. Sitting on a red-veined rock at the back of the cabin one afternoon, she was using the knife to skin the "braw little squirrel" he'd just brought her—

he never hunted squirrels, but occasionally one got into his traps — when she heard a faint commotion in the woods. She tensed. It was a dark day, the valley was shadowy under heavy snow clouds. A minute passed. She had thought Cougar was working in the shed, but perhaps it was him in the woods. For a man, he moved too softly, at too swift a pace. He was upon her sometimes like a mountain lion. Sometimes, thinking she was all alone, she suddenly felt a shadow at her side, and looking up, would find him there.

When no further sound was forthcoming, she went back to her work. But after a while the hush was disturbed again, and, out from under a tangle of small trees, a fierce-looking Indian materialized. He was mounted, and sat straight and motionless on his saddle blanket. In his free hand was a lance and a buffalo-hide shield painted with a design. The sinews of his forearms showed beneath his shirt sleeves, and the thick column of his neck spread down into his shoulders, down into the swell of his chest.

She rose slowly, letting the squirrel fall from her lap. Cautiously, she began to back away in the direction of the corner of the cabin, but the great savage was too quick. He urged his pony into sudden motion and blocked her way. In the same instant his lance was aimed at her heart. Deep lines, like cuts, were at the sides of his mouth, though he was still young. He made her think of an eagle.

There was a terrible silence before he spoke. "Who you?" he grunted.

Steeling herself for pain, she said, "I'm called Flame."

"You spirit woman. You kill the Waiting Cougar?" He jabbed the point of the lance against her breast.

"I haven't killed anyone."

"Where the Cougar?" As if to warn her to be quick with her answer, he raised the stabbing lance's point to puncture the skin below her chin. There it remained, slightly embedded in the satin of her neck beneath her jawbone.

She stood frozen, her head forced up, but her eyes fastened on him. "I . . . I don't know where he is at the moment."

"You lie." He increased the pressure of the lance fractionally. The point stung deeper into her flesh. "I kill you, spirit woman."

Then, with a movement as quick as the lightning in his eyes, he slipped over the side of his horse. He gave the impression of deadly suppleness as he came toward her. There was a dark force about him, an unfathomable depth to his face. She steathily slipped the carved handle of her knife out of its sheath at her waist. When she brought it up, however, it took no more than a flick of his forearm to disarm her: he hit her wrist so hard her entire hand went numb and the knife dropped from her tingling fingers.

Now he shoved her backwards to the cabin wall. He tossed aside his lance and put his own knife to her throat. He seemed as cold as ice, all his muscles rigid and tense. "Where the Cougar?"

"I . . ." She shifted the subject sideways a little. "I'm Cougar's friend."

Twisting one of her braids, he growled, "Spirit woman with yellow hair lies!"

"I'm not lying!"

Holding his knife hard against her throat, he demanded a third time, "Where the Cougar!" His lips were set in a thin line.

She mumbled something, half-choking from the

250

blade pressed into her throat. The skin beneath it had broken, and a warm drop of blood trickled down to gather in the hollow of her collar bones. She had not a single doubt that he meant to kill her—unless she did something to save herself.

She brought her knee up, hard, catching him in the groin, and she slipped out of reach as soon as he gasped and doubled to his knees. She raced for the lance he'd discarded, and now touched its point to his bent back. "Now you tell me who *you* are!"

That was when Cougar appeared at the side of the shed. His long rifle was raised and aimed; his eyes were blazing with cold Scots passion. "Flame, stand aside."

The Indian didn't lift his head, didn't straighten, didn't move. Not even a muscle in his face moved. Cougar, coming closer, burst out laughing. "So *you're* the commotion!" He lowered his rifle, calling to Flame, "Put down your lance."

She looked at him wide eyed, but kept the lance pointed at the Indian's back nevertheless.

Cougar, seeing her eyes shifting so uneasily, laughed again. He was close now, carrying his gun on his hip as he reached to take the lance from her. "Flame," he said, shining eyed. But then he saw the blood trickling down the column of her throat and he sobered. He bent to her quickly, and kissed her; then, fearless, blunt, outspoken as always, he turned abruptly to the Indian. "What do you mean, marking my woman?"

The Indian answered in his own language, rapidly, angrily. His face was flushed dark red. Cougar, somewhat appeased by whatever he was being told, nodded at length and said, "My love, may I introduce Dark Sun, my blood brother—and war chief of the Salish nation. Dark Sun, my wife."

251

Dark Sun, standing now (though still stooping some), looked her over suspiciously. He reached to lift and finger first one and then the other of the two flaxen plaits hanging over her shoulders. He touched the string of grizzly claws. His face was still flushed and angry with all he'd just undergone, yet there was something else there as well, a semi-doubtful respect.

As if to prove his control over this dangerous spirit creature, Cougar slung his arm around her. He said, "Offer him your hand, Flame."

She hesitated.

"You'll oblige me, my fair one." His tone was courteous, but signaled that he wasn't going to trifle with her just now.

Her face tightened, but she could only assume he knew what he was doing. After all, he seemed to have a sense for such puzzles as how to get along with Indians. Gingerly she proffered her hand. "How do you do, Dark Sun?"

Her finger bones creaked in the man's sudden grip. "Howgh," he said in his throat, "I do good." Then he threw his head back and screamed to the sky.

Cougar took her arm, motioning Dark Sun to follow. They walked toward the front of the cabin. Her heart was beating hard now, in reaction. "Are you all right?" Cougar asked her privately.

She nodded, touching the places where Dark Sun's weapons had stung her. Her fingers came away with traces of blood.

The muscles worked in Cougar's cheek, telling her that he knew how close the call had been for her, yet his words made light of it. "I did no' think such a small matter would faze you, but you've turned that white. You'll no' disgrace me by fainting now, will

252

you?"

She rose to the bait. "You know, of course, that if you hadn't come along when you did he would have slit my throat. I could never have held him off for long with that lance."

"I'm no' that sure, lassie. You forget, I've seen you stand up against Blackfeet squaws and mother grizzlies—and now you've bested a warrior known for his ferociousness—though some might say you fought unfairly. Still and all, you're that much alive. Scored a wee bit," he reached to blot away the blood at the base of her throat with his thumb, "but alive."

He held the cabin door open for her; then, with a smile, turned to make Dark Sun feel welcome.

She served a stew of squirrel and fresh grizzly meat. Dark Sun, though clearly nursing his injured pride, ate heartily. Before long the two men were talking casually, their tongues loose.

"How is your gosling cousin?" Cougar asked, moving from the table to sit before the fire.

"Huh!" Dark Sun joined him on the black bearskin rug. He took a pipe from the adorned case that hung around his neck, filled it and struck fire to it. "She sends me after the Waiting Cougar. She says spirit woman evil, will kill the Cougar."

His mind seemed to stray. He sucked on his pipe, blew out a puff of smoke. "Two-Edged Knife speaks to my father," he said at last. "He will give two horses for Lone Goose. I say, 'Two horses is not enough, but since thieves steal our horses there are not so many to use to buy a wife. Two-Edged Knife is an able strategist for a man of few years. He has cunning, craftiness, skill. Give him Lone Goose,' I say to my uncle. 'Do not talk foolishness,' Rotten Gut says to me. He is old, he needs Lone Goose to look after him. He waves Two-Edged Knife away."

"What does Lone Goose say?"

Dark Sun shrugged. He sucked into his lungs more of the killing mixture of strong kinnikinic, cedar bark, and willow. "Lone Goose says she will marry no man."

"And Two-Edged Knife?"

"He say Lone Goose wants to be the Waiting Cougar's wife."

Cougar seemed thoughtful. "Aye, well, she's a strong-minded lassie, full of high fettle, but I do no' think she's so foolish. Sometimes a woman gets notions about no' wanting a husband, and then she needs a man with a will stronger than hers to claim her. In all likeliness 'twill take Two-Edged Knife more than words and a pair of ponies to bring her to her senses."

Dark Sun sucked his pipe, nodding in agreement. Flame fumed in silence.

Outside, a mist had sagged down off the mountains, bringing a deep wintry hush. The fire in the cabin felt bright and friendly. After a while Dark Sun took up his bow and arrows, inspected the stone arrowheads, and began to straighten the shafts of those that were warped. He and Cougar exchanged stories. Cougar told how Flame had killed the grizzly. Dark Sun looked at her narrowly; she could tell he was impressed.

Speaking to her directly for the first time since entering the cabin, he told her of a time when he thought he'd killed a grizzly on an island in a lake. To get to his trophy, he stripped and swam to the island and was chased back ashore by a merely wounded and furiously swimming bear. Beached, he was forced to run naked through the woods until the animal finally weakened and gave up the chase.

By the end of this tale, Cougar was splitting his

sides. Even Dark Sun's mouth twitched. Flame smiled to watch them. She found she envied Dark Sun his friendship with Cougar. Earlier, with the Indian's knife at her throat, she'd claimed she was Cougar's friend, but that wasn't true: she was too intimidated by the man. Yet, she realized that she would like to be friends with him.

Cougar's laughter died down. The fire crackled. Outside in the darkness one of the horses whickered softly. Cougar looked at Flame across the room. His smile faded to something else. He seemed to pin her there with his glinting eyes and she abruptly experienced a sharp pang of lust. Hastily, she glanced away only to find herself staring straight into Dark Sun's eyes, which were gauging her. She was unnerved a second time.

A seemingly vast span of time elapsed. She cast about desperately for something to say, something that would fill the space between her and these two vital, virile men. But it was Dark Sun who broke the silence, saying to Cougar while still watching her, "My uncle is right."

255

## Chapter Seventeen

"You think Rotten Gut was right to make me accountable for this golden fury with her impudent blue eyes?" Cougar said. "Was he now?"

Dark Sun nodded, and the lines beside his mouth deepened. "Years make Rotten Gut wise."

"I hope so," Cougar murmured, his voice a purr.

Mystified and uncomfortable, Flame said, "Please, Dark Sun, tell me how Cougar got his name."

The war chief gathered his words. "The sky throws its clouds against the peaks and this thing thrills men. Two buffalo fight to the end, and this makes the bravest show on all the prairies. Are these things not true?"

She nodded; Cougar's eyes were twinkling at her.

"Flame, hear me when I say the clouds and the buffalo are as the sport of little children beside the Waiting Cougar's fight for life."

Cougar listened to these acclamations with rare signs of discomfort. He scratched the side of his nose and cleared his throat. Dark Sun ignored him. He was well versed in the art of story telling, and wove a vision of Cougar kneeling down to scoop up a drink of water from a rushing mountain creek. When he straightened, the cat was watching him, waiting for him.

"The cougar stalks its prey at watering holes. If a stream flows close to an overhanging ledge of stone, here the beast crouches and waits, and as animals come to drink, it leaps to the back of the deer, the antelope, the wild horse. It jumps onto its prey's shoulders, it sinks its claws deep, and reaches for the throat with its powerful fangs.

"The cold moon is close at hand. The cat is hungry. My brother stops at a pool to drink. He looks up, he sees the cat. He feels fear in his belly. The cat is going to leap. Its ears lay flat against its head, its legs bunch. Cougar searches for the knife in his belt . . ."

Flame saw it in her mind — the mountain lion's lips pulled back, its yellow teeth, and then its spring, long-reaching and beautiful.

"It comes into the air, fast, smooth. My brother feels both the shock and the pain at once. The cat throws him backwards so hard that the breath is sucked out of his lungs. Claws hook into his chest; he feels them scraping his ribs. With his forearms against the animal's neck, he holds the gaping mouth from his throat. They roll together in the brush, the cat's front claws still clenching the flesh of his chest. The animal's back legs curl in preparation to rake my brother's stomach. He twists futilely to keep clear of those huge clawed paws.

"Finally, finding his knife at his belt, he jabs the blade into the animal's back. It screams but its back legs continue to come up. The claws puncture my brother's belly and tear downward. The pain is

257

terrible. Everything he sees is light, a white shine that hurts his eyes. He knows he is badly hurt, maybe he is already about to die, yet the ripping hind paws are coming up again. He rams the knife into the cat's back a second time, slipping it between the small bones of the spine. The cat screams once more. Its body shimmies and its front claws curl even deeper into my brother's chest. He pulls his knife out and stabs a third time, and a fourth.

"When he rolls away, the cat is dead." Dark Sun pointed his pipe stem to the rich tawny-furred cap Cougar had tossed onto the bed earlier. Flame's eyes dwelt on it.

Cougar, not looking at either of them, uncrossed one leg, stretched it out before him, and studied the moccasin on his foot.

Flame looked at Dark Sun. He seemed to smile at her, although, with his impassive face, it was hard to tell. Then he rose. He and Cougar had erected a small shelter outside while she'd cooked their supper. Cougar made as if to walk him out to it, pausing to whisper to Flame, "I'll be wanting you as soon as I get back here—and no playing catch-me-if-you-can, heart."

He wasn't gone more than five minutes—just long enough for a variety of erotic pictures to teem into her mind. Then he was back, drawing her hard against him, both to gratify himself and to show her how unmistakable his need was. " 'Tis bitter cold out there." He laughed softly. "Poor Dark Sun, he's hardly gotten the sort of hospitality from us he might've gotten elsewhere."

"If you're talking about what happened when he tried to kill me—well, I'm sorry about kicking him like that, but I didn't know what else to do at the time."

Cougar chuckled. "Aye, I am talking about that. It put him out of sorts, it did—bested by a woman, even a spirit woman—"

"Please no more of that spirit woman business. I don't share your Indian friends' childlike belief in the supernatural."

"Still and all, 'tis well come by, and you should be grateful for it. Aye, blink if you will, but a war chief of Dark Sun's stature expects a deal of honor. He's a distinguished warrior and at home he has three wives to cater to him—none of whom would live another happy hour after unmanning him like that."

She now recalled the looks Dark Sun had given her.

"You can see now, can you no', how handy this notion of your 'supernaturalism' is?"

But another thought had intruded in her mind: "Three wives! What on Earth does he need *three* for?"

Cougar maintained a discreet silence.

When she started to move away from him, he closed his hand on her wrist, holding it tightly. "Aye, three, yet he says he's never seen anyone like you, with skin so satin and gold. He asked if you bring me pleasure. I took the liberty of telling him that you do."

"Should I be flattered?"

"Why no'? What's all this fretting about? And another question: Why did you keep silent when he came? He says you refused to tell him where I was." His lips were drawn back in a half-grin. "A man would almost think you were trying to protect him.

259

Is it getting to be a habit with you to try to save my life?"

She found herself without a reply.

"I think I want an answer, lassie."

"I—I was trying to gain time."

"Time? For me? He would have killed you in another moment, especially after you'd nearly gelded him with that tap of your knee. But you could've told him where I was before that; you could've screamed. Why did you keep silent, Flame?"

"Well . . . I didn't know he was your friend, so . . . what if I *had* told him? If he'd killed you, I would have been next anyway. Why risk both of us?"

Their eyes locked, and he threw away the key. When he spoke again, his voice had the softness of the wind in it. "Do you expect me to accept that as the whole of it?"

"That *is* the whole of it, so yes, I think you must." She found those gray-green eyes disconcerting. They looked too deep, they found flaws in her argument which she felt were better left unexamined.

Then suddenly he was smiling; it was his most irresistible smile. And he also began to swear, genially, monotonously, without anger, but keeping it up all the while he undressed her. He smiled and swore and opened her dress and pulled it over her head and let it drop to the floor so that she stood naked before him. She was so confused by this odd combination of pleased expression, censurous words, and demanding actions that she hardly thought to object.

He fondled a warm breast in each hand. "You may keep your secrets in your head, little demon,

260

but your body is mine to sound out." Quickly he undressed himself, and scooped her up and tossed her onto the bed. She lay limp with confusion. In contrast, there was a barely restrained eagerness in him. He'd told her that he would want her at once, and he seemed determined to satisfy that desire. He covered her with his own body, parted her thighs, and went in to the hilt with a single push. She roused now, but her flurry of shocked movement only drove him deeper. Sensation broke over her in waves impossible to deny.

"Aye," he murmured to himself as he lowered his head to kiss the places where Dark Sun had wounded her. The touch of his tongue made her shiver.

The rigourous unbroken rhythm of his thrusts quickly brought him to his apex. In a triumphant surge and burst, he crushed her to him, breathing brokenly. It was all so fast, so insistent, so scandalous. When he rose off her and flung himself onto his back on the furs, she wondered how he could be so urgent one moment and so langorous the next. She watched him through her lashes, feeling dazed and vaguely let down.

"If you're through, may I cover up?" she said irritably, tugging at the beaverskin robe on which they were lying.

He moved, but not to accommodate her. Though she already had the fur half over her, he pushed it down from her breasts and, bending over her on the rumpled bed, began to imprint delicate kisses on her nipples. "I left you unrequited, love. 'Tis a fault I shall correct."

"That isn't necessary."

261

The firelight caught the angles of his face as, with an air of complete absorption, he pulled the fur slowly away from her and began to explore her. "But it is. Aye, and 'tis bannock and cream I'll have for my dessert this night."

As if seeing her naked for the first time, as if just now coming to know her skin, its varying textures—in the crook of her arms, on her pillowy abdomen, in the folds of her groin—he mapped her body with his lips, tonguing where her waist started, and even rolling her a little to kiss the swell of her buttocks. What he was doing was unquestionably enjoyable—yet she always felt it shouldn't be.

A yearning, so potent it seemed beyond her command, saturated her, and, as if mesmerized, she lifted her head slightly toward his face, toward his mouth. A treacherous sliver of her wanted to kiss him, wanted to kiss him badly. She felt so fluid and vulnerable that she didn't even mind his tender, knowing smile.

When he took her beneath him again, and covered her nakedness with his big body, she was trembling, utterly enraptured by feeling. He gentled her with feather-light kisses until the trembling ceased and she lay with her face pressed into his neck. Helplessly she inhaled his exciting scent and felt the blood pound through all her veins.

"Hold on fast," he whispered, and then he enveloped her in a web of sensation. The world came forward in flaming sequences, in pillars and prisms, receded, and came forward again. Her climax, once it arrived, was silent and deep. Her body quaked under him and her nails nicked his back. The pleasure pulsed on and on, exceeded dreams, outlived desire, until at last she felt his own ecstasy flashed through him again like a bolt of lightning. Now she lay still and revelled in the feel of him leaping within her, filling her, deluging her a second time with the flood of his masculinity.

When he moved to lay beside her once more, saying, "Are you more comfortable now?" she was too encompassed by lassitude and too close to sleep to answer. She barely realized when he pulled her into his arms and murmured, "Alas, Flame, you undo me so, even I wonder if you're no' a spirit."

She said nothing; she was lost to a comfort as mothy and warm as an August night.


As the days passed, Flame learned to feel more at ease with Dark Sun. He took it upon himself to begin teaching her his language. And along with Salish she began to learn that he was a remarkable man with an innate dignity, even a certain courtliness, and, of course, plenty of self-esteem.

Three days loped away like gentle horses in fields of snow. Then one afternoon he asked her to walk with him. It was snowing, so she pulled on her warm bearskin moccasins and robe.

Outside, all she could see wherever she looked were snowflakes milling about. They were gliding and whirling and dropping in the white winter light. The cabin was soon separated from them by gauzy veils of snow.

Beside her, Dark Sun seemed large and powerful and mysteriously at home. The soft wind lifted his hair. She felt strange, as if they'd suddenly stepped out of normal time into a never-never land, and it was more than just being with him alone like this. She felt as if she'd stepped into the hold of something inevitable and tremendous, some white-gloved, iron hand.

In cautious spurts of words she ranged through all the obvious subjects: the snow, his plans for leaving tomorrow, the snow again. There had to be something in particular he wanted to bring up, and yet she remained chained to commenting on the snow once again, and to placing her feet carefully in it. Compulsively she said, "Cougar will miss your company when you go."

"The Waiting Cougar will not miss Dark Sun. He has Flame . . . who loves him."

Startled, she denied it. "He has been good to me—for the most part—but there is no love between us."

"You do not speak the truth in your heart. What you say and what you know are two things."

She wanted to say that was ridiculous, but since she couldn't risk offending him again, she settled for saying, "I could never love a man who treats me the way he does."

"What does he do to you?"

"He . . . well, he forces me to live with him as—as his wife."

Dark Sun glanced down at her quickly. Then he grinned, showing perfect teeth. She realized too late how he would view it: spirit or not, she was a woman, and a woman was property; a man might do as he pleased with his property.

"He beats you?"

She was for a moment struck dumb. "Of course not! I dare him to!"

He became almost paternal. "You love the Cougar."

She shook her head stubbornly.

"The Cougar is good husband."

She grudgingly had to agree with that, all things considered.

"Love is good thing for a woman."

There was nothing to gain by denying that—nor any call for extravagant rejoicing. "Cougar and I are too different," she said. "We want different things."

He shook his head. "The Cougar shows you the way home in the bed furs; you show him the way home in his heart. This is to be, Flame. My uncle, Rotten Gut, gives you the Waiting Cougar; you take good care."

They stood out on the floor of the valley, enclosed by the falling snow and by the mantled peaks of this bony land. Eyes shining, Dark Sun began to sing something in his own language. There was great emotion in his song, a feeling she understood even though she had only a spotty understanding of the Salish words. He put his hand on her shoulder, not speaking, but singing gently a mountain song and looking into her eyes. When he was finished, he fell back into silence. But after a while he said quietly, "I hear."

"What?" she asked in a sharp, thin voice.

His eyes were half-closed against the snowfall. "I hear Flame. She speaks in silence."

She was alarmed. And curiously anxious. Her face was turned up to his. She reached out her hand as if it might bridge the unbridgable. "Look, Dark Sun, it's not what you think. Cougar and I have an understanding. I'm only staying with him for the winter, and even then—though I can give him some things, others he must take. He understands that I will leave him the moment I can."

"What has been agreed upon yesterday has nothing to do with what you will do tomorrow, Flame."

"No," she whispered. "I don't belong here."

"The Cougar does not belong here. His home is far away, big stone lodge, much wealth. There he owns many horses and grows corn and drinks good medicine water."

"Grows corn? He's a farmer?"

"Big chief there, but raised like a girl. Sick all the time. The Cougar leaves his home for the mountains, to get strength from the mountains. He is strong now, he must go home. Good warrior—brave! hard!—but his heart lives with his own people. He should not sing his death song in The Shining Mountains."

His eyes looked into hers. She felt his fingers close on her jaw, lifting her face into the snow. "You send the Waiting Cougar home. You are Flame, spirit woman. Flame loves the Cougar, so she takes good care. My uncle sees all this."

Love Cougar. And send him home. Love him and lose him, all in the same breath.

*Flame loves the Cougar.*

But she wasn't really Flame—she had a name of her own!

Dark Sun was leaning forward to peer down at her face. She felt she'd gone white as milk. She pulled back, humiliated at having been trapped in such a ridiculous plot. She even said so now: "It's ridiculous!"

266

And yet it would explain why she responded to Cougar's nightly lovemaking in a way that often shamed her in the morning. Was love that sense of fulfillment, that wonder of feeling that repeatedly splintered her defenses and brought her an ever-deepening knowledge of what it might be like to be close to another human soul?

It had to be.

But how could she love a man whose name she didn't even know?

Details like names had nothing to do with it. It was love.

And she was possessed by it. Utterly possessed.

It wasn't yet sunrise, the sky was pale, colorless, cloudless. Flame had risen to say farewell to Dark Sun. Cougar, already standing down the slope, hadn't noticed her behind him yet.

The Indian and his horse were etched sharply against the whitened, still, half-lit landscape. He suddenly raised his hand with finality and rode away. Flame felt depressed, miserable, to see him go. For now she was alone with Cougar again. Alone with what she knew about him. Alone with what she knew about herself.

He turned, saw her standing there outside the cabin door, and started toward her. She waited, racked with anxiety. She'd slept little last night, but long enough to dream a nightmare of doors that opened merely to close silently again, with no progress made or path revealed.

She gazed away from Cougar's advance, at the valley white with snow. The far peaks were kindling.

Dawn was leaping into the sky. A red rim of the sun rose over the white shoulders of the land.

Finally, she had to look at Cougar again. She knew now that she was very much in love with him. How long had it been so? How long had she been throbbing with this powerful emotion? To think she hadn't even realized such a capacity lay within her; to think and to accept that it wasn't, after all, only some mysterious energy emanating from this valley, or from the mountains, or from Cougar himself.

She was afraid, now that she knew. Afraid and confused. Desperately, even as he came up the slope towards her, she tried to fill the holes in her armor. What should she do about this love? Certainly she couldn't just blurt out: *Cougar, I love you!* Only to have him say, *'Aye and that's nice, lassie,'* or something equally casual and cruel.

Better to do nothing. He would never know then. And she could leave him (somehow!) in the spring and resume her very private life, the sort of life she'd always preferred.

That decided, she felt immediately better, and congratulated herself that her thoughts on this most difficult subject were now in order.

Yet, again she hadn't considered emotion in her very reasonable decision, nor had she considered her invariable reaction to Cougar himself. It simply was not going to be the same now, knowing and living with him in such intimacy. Just watching him open the cabin door and stand aside for her to enter was enough to unnerve her. His barest touch at her throat as he helped her out of her cloak made her tremble.

And how could she help it? He was golden-tongued, classically handsome, every inch a hero. How could she help but love him? How could she possibly disclaim this love that was wedded to a physical desire so strong it approached pain?

They ate breakfast in silence, sitting at the table before the fire. She knew he was watching her, waiting for some explanation of the mood she'd been in since yesterday. She was reluctant to even raise her eyes to his, for she knew she had no talent for subterfuge. He was going to find her out; she wasn't going to be any good at hiding something this big from him. She only hoped she could keep herself from throwing her hands around his knees and clinging pathetically.

"You're no' eating, Flame. There are few delicate feeders in the mountains. Do you know why? They weaken and die off."

"I — I'm just not hungry right now."

"Is there something you want to tell me, lassie?"

She shook her head. And that motion seemed to free something in her — something running beneath all this confusion of love. Something silent and profound. Anger.

She turned a suddenly fulminating gaze on him. "You have all the secrets to tell, not me."

The fire's reflections glanced in his eyes.

"Who are you, Cougar? Tell me about yourself — your real self — the real life you've kept covered up so I couldn't see. You've had everything from me — everything! — without giving me so much as a glimpse of you. Who *are* you? *What* are you? I want to know about the Scotsman, the 'big chief.' Tell me about the wealth and the corn and the good medicine water, tell me about horses and the mighty

269

lodge built of stone!"

"Dark Sun." His voice sounded like icicles breaking. Anger made his gray-green eyes shine radiantly. She shivered, wondering what he would be like if he really lost his temper. And she felt a presentiment prickle along her arms and lift the hair at her nape.

In the dramatic pause nothing moved in the room but the flames of the fire. Minutes passed, and finally he spoke:

"I was born thirty-one years ago, the fourth son of the sixteenth Viscount of Lanark—that is, including the other three sons of my father, none of whom lived to be christened."

*A viscount! An aristocrat! A lord of the British realm!*

"I'm Colin Roy Craigh—if you will. I have my blood from kings. But to my people, as head of my clan, I'm known as the Drummond."

She sat very still, her eyes gaping with shock. As he threw out so abruptly all that his life had been and what it promised to be, her own shriveled to embers. To cinders. "The Dr—"

"Please do no' interrupt. You wanted to hear this—*had* to hear it—and now you shall." He got up to prod the fire, then leaned against the mantle, his back to her.

"Like my predecessors, I was born weakly, but somehow struggled to suck and survive, though I continued frail through my boyhood. My father died then, when I was yet a bairn. There would be no more sons got from him. I was the last of my line. I *must* live to be the laird of Clan Drummond.

"To guard me, my mother shut me up in nurseries and schools and recitation halls, and I came out of

270

them with a bellyful of words, though I did no' ken a thing." He was shaking his head, slowly. "Education sometimes only discloses from the foolish man his lack of understanding."

He faced her obliquely. "You see, I was trained for naught but to be a gentleman-poet. Oh, I did well enough at that, I suppose, aye. The verses came easily, spouted out of me, conceits and figures — I spent my youth writing poetry like a madman, describing sentiment like a turtledove. I was naught but a little scribbler, who'd never worked a day in his life — who'd never thought to.

"Then realization came bursting in the door one morn: I was no' a man. I had much erudition, aye, that much dust shoveled out of all those libraries into my empty skull, but I could no' use my hands, my eyes, my feet, or my arms." Now his bearing became, gradually, less formal and more gentle. "I did no' ken the simplest things — which roots in the woods are good to eat, how to map a course by the stars, or tell the time of the day by the sun. I could no' swim, I felt afraid of a horse, of a sheep . . ." he was nearly whispering, ". . . of a spider."

When he went on, his voice was stronger. "There were many questioning my fitness to be the Drummond. Oh aye, there were, as you can imagine. Few had any confidence in me; my clansmen were that wary, that skittish. 'Twas the great cholera pandemic, begun in India in 1826 and spread from Russia into Central Europe, that brought the matter to its head. The plague gained Scotland in 1832, and one day a delegation came to the castle and asked me point-blank to leave — to run for my life, as it were. They knew, sickly creature that I was, that I would no'

271

survive even a touch of Dame Cholera."

Flame was finding all this so hard to envision. There was very little this man couldn't do. He looked so right holding his gun, riding his huge horse, surviving by his wits and his abilities. He was tough; he could hold her with a look; he was doing so this very moment.

"The Drummond, you see, is only as powerful as his clan, and the clan only as strong as their laird. Scotland is no' a soft land. My people need strength to survive. They needed *me* to be strong. My last tutor told me a thing, a Roman rule: Teach a lad naught that he can no' learn standing on his feet.

"It came to me that day that I must learn to live on my feet."

## Chapter Eighteen

" 'Twas in the autumn of 'thirty-two that I came to the mountains of North America," Cougar said. "I traveled with some fur traders at first, and found that here was a place to fight against hunger and cold, all right. Here was adversity enough to tool my wits and mold my body. 'Twas all going according to plan—then the cougar got me. My white friends abandoned me for dead, and dead I would've been, but Dark Sun found me. He took me to Rotten Gut.

"As I recovered, I sensed there was a change in me. I knew somehow that the long, tedious fairytale had ended, that abruptly, youth lay forever behind me. I was in a new place where only manhood was valid. Yet I had a new feel for life, 'twas lovely and intense. Rotten Gut says the spirit of the cougar had seized me, entered me, he says it's in me yet. Mayhap he's right, for I do no' even think like the boy Colin Roy Craigh anymore: I've become the Waiting Cougar, a man who stalks the mountains, making up his laws as he goes along. And I'm no' sure anymore if I ever want to be anything else."

Flame sat in a stupor. Nearby a very large man was saying to her in an unconcerned way, "And there

273

you have it, lassie. Do you know enough now?"

After a long silence, she asked politely, "Do you own much land? In Scotland, I mean."

"A fair amount. 'Tis dotted with crofts. The people who live in them are descendants of those who've worked the farms for the Drummonds since long ago. The way of life there has a continuing pattern."

"You mean it's feudal. You're a kind of overlord. You take what you want and people kneel down to you."

"No Scotsman kneels down to anyone," he answered curtly. "I had title to every rood of the land but I took no more than my share from those who worked it."

American stubbornness crept out with her lower lip. "Still, your word is the last word, isn't it?"

The breath between his teeth seemed to tear the awkward stillness. He took two slow steps to stand before her — and she waited, like a bird waiting for the approach of the viper, unable to move.

"I'm tempted to teach you all about the Scots." There was in his face a look of offended honor. He reached for her wrist and pulled her up to him. (She felt a warning in the grip of that hand — he could crack her bones.) "How much you have to learn about me still. About the overlaird, the feudal master."

She wanted to tell him she was sorry for her remarks, but was too afraid of his fury, too unsure of his mercy. In her eyes he could never again be the mountain man he claimed to be. He was the seventeenth Viscount of Lanark, the solitary leader of his clan, the Drummond . . .

It was then that the horror of her situation over-whelmed her afresh. She'd thought it bad enough to know the mountain man Cougar might treat her love with callous indifference, but . . . It was then, in that instant, that she knew: The Waiting Cougar would someday soon vanish from the mountains, while in Scotland, Colin Roy Craigh would reappear. And he would almost certainly begin to look about for a suitably grand woman to be his bride, to become his countess, to bear him honor and heirs.

She leaned dumbly against him, too shaken to hold herself erect. He made a little sound of surprise and abandoned his provoked grip on her wrist in order to embrace her. His arms were so muscular and his mouth was so strong as he bent to take hers — so enthralling and yet so supple. And his fingers, his noble fingertips, were so perceptive as they gripped the back of her head. She knew a moment of intense doomed loved . . . followed by such a heat of desire that she would have fallen to her knees if he hadn't been holding her firmly.

"Aye, Flame, you learn to know me — and to want me."

She gasped. Her face flooded with color. Defensive anger spurted through her veins. She raised her hand to slap him, and was stopped only by the look on his face.

"Aye, go ahead," he said, and there was in the way he said it a blend of benevolence, gleeful anticipation — and the promise of inevitable retaliation.

In a panic she backed away, using her hands to curtain her cheeks. "It's not true — I *don't* want you! You're really too outrageous! I don't know why I try to carry on conversations with you!"

His strong fingers gripped her forearms and pulled her hands to his chest. His extraordinary eyes, fierce with devil-may-care emotion, blazed into hers. "Do no' lie to me anymore!"

Suddenly she felt aghast with the sheer power of her emotion. She was blistered and clubbed by it; her old techniques of holding him off were shattered, her past resistance was blown to bits, all her defences were incinerated by the white-hot heat of her love. "No," she said weakly.

"Woman!" he groaned. Pulling her closer, he buried his hands in her streaming hair and brought her cheek against his hard shoulder.

With a gesture so simple as that he could make her cease thinking and *feel,* make her conscious of life itself, warm, urgent, to be sensed wholly. It was delicious, exhilerating, irresistible. She knew with apolcalyptic clarity that she did want him. She wanted him more than she would want any other man as long as she lived.

"All right," she said, her voice muffled in his shirt, "I won't lie. I—I do want you. I want to be your wife—the wife of the Waiting Cougar," she added quickly, looking up at him. She would allow herself that much. She wasn't looking very clearly into the future, but that there would be a future, she was sure. A future without him. For she could never ask him to take her with him. To grovel and plead was not part of her nature, so she fell back on her pride. "For now," she whispered, "for now, as long as winter forces me to stay, as long as I'm called Flame, I'll be your wife."

His eyes had taken on a peculiar expression. He said nothing for a moment, asked no questions, made no comments. Then, after what seemed an eternity, he said in a cold treble, "As long as you're Flame, is it? Do I hear the hounds of spring baying on the far side of winter? I'll make the best of the snow then. 'Tis just as well; anymore of you and you're bargaining ways and I'm afraid I might go daft with euphoria."

The cabin was fire lit. Flame lay naked with her head on Cougar's shoulder. She was trailing her hand bravely across his chest and knew it was something she'd wanted to do forever. Outside the breathless day moved toward cloudless high noon, surrounding the cabin with fierce winter cold, yet she'd never felt so warm in her life.

With simple innocence and openness she was exploring his body. She trailed her hand over his scars, flinching from the pain they had once meant to him, then trailed lower. After a moment, he caught her fingers and brought them to his mouth, kissing the tip of each one. "You grow bold-hearted, my rose-lipped wife."

He turned onto his side with a kiss in his eyes and a suggestion of passion about his mouth. "I recall the morning after I bought you, I sat upon our lumpy pallet to inspect my merchandise. You were slumbering on your back and looking that rumpled and dear. Your hair was untidy, your face sunburned, 'But this is a bonny woman,' I told myself, 'and I'm the luckier for that.'

'Twas a miracle to find such a tender maid in such a place as I'd found you. Still and all, that was what you were—tender, a maid, the prize waiting for the

277

man who came first. Rotten Gut had told me I would find a woman among the Blackfeet. He said she would fight me, but that I had to make her mine. 'Well,' I said, ' 'twill no' be hard to take this lassie'—which was another way of saying I had to have you, and I stroked your uncovered breasts—carefully, so you would no' waken—"

"You didn't!"

"Oh aye, I did. And now I think you like me to stroke them."

She lowered her lashes.

"You're no' going to deny it then? No more shutting up your doors and drawing your shades in self-protection? No more fear of me warring with your desire?"

She shook her head on his pillowing arm, though her heart was fluttering.

"No?" he teased in a deep voice, rolling to place her half-beneath him. "No' even knowing that I hold you fast and at any moment can press my advantage as I wish?"

Again she shook her head.

" 'Twould make no difference, for I should win my way regardless."

Her mouth curved into its most dimpling smile. She had always been somewhat terror-stricken of him, but now with his hardness pressed against her thigh she swelled with a glorious sensation of power. It gave her enough courage to say, "And thus I should win *my* way, my formidable husband."

He raised his head, his eyes shiny as he looked down his nose at her. "Hmm . . . you smile and call me husband this day, but 'tis a tardy smile, I'm thinking, and a tardy hearkening." His mouth twitched. "Yet 'tis of no consequence that, I suppose. Better tardy than never." He dipped his head to kiss her.

*And better for a little while than not at all,* she added privately, as she opened her mouth to his insistence.

When he lifted his head again, her smile was small and painful.

"My heart?"

"Cougar, do you . . . care for me?"

"Can you no' feel how much I do?" He pressed his loins against her hip.

It wasn't the answer she'd hoped for, but she didn't have time to consider that, for he was gathering her further beneath him, his legs straddling her so that he could rub his manhood in the crease of her closed thighs. His pale eyes went dark.

"Tell me about your home, Cougar."

"By and by I will, my white, white petal, my mystical spirit woman with opalescent skin."

"Now Cougar . . . please?" She felt it best to know everything at once. Tomorrow, or even an hour from now, she might not be strong-hearted enough to ask, and might even begin to delude herself. Best to know it all to begin with. "You said you would tell me anything I wanted to know."

"Aye and I will, but later."

"No, tell me now."

He wasn't pleased. "Castle Drummond then." He heaved a sigh of impatience, holding himself over her on his arms. "Castle Drummond, seat of the clan, across the wrinkled sea. Set in a world of moor, glen, plunging burn, cloud, snow, forest, waterfall . . ." He seemed to have to search his

279

mind, perhaps because he'd never been asked before to describe what was so familiar to him. " 'Tis a fine castle, with a double square tower—a notable example of Gaelic baronial style, that. 'Tis rich in turrets and gables and vaulting windows that let in the afternoon sun. Aye, 'tis famous for its woodwork, too, and for several painted ceilings, and some of the antiquities—furniture and such—preserved inside.

"Westward its windows look out to yon high road—is all this what you want to know? Mmm . . . and I was afraid so. To the east through the tall trees, pastures stretch with clover and sweet grasses; far off you can glimpse the sunlit river. There are walled gardens, and massive yew hedges . . . 'Tis all surrounded by green hills, you know, well-made for walking. There is an ancient stone pillar . . . and Tower Dunrobin—all that's left of an older castle. Let's see . . . our dungeon is called Auld Nick's Hall—"

"A dungeon!"

"Aye," he grinned down on her, "and just outside stand the old stocks."

"Do you use them?"

"Oh aye," his face went straight, "I did. Do no' forget I was an overlaird, my word was the last word. I sometimes even ate small town-children. I liked children better than walnuts, I did. But your fine white flesh tastes far sweeter. I would wager a thousand pounds on it." He bent to kiss her mouth. "Aye, you're that delicious."

"Cougar—no," she wriggled beneath him, ". . . tell me about—about the town."

"Why?" He was growing restive. His knee slipped

between hers.

"I'm curious."

"I've always heard curiosity is an objectionable quality in the female mind. Now I know why." He kissed her again, trying to open her mouth for his tongue as he had before, but all she gave him was her puckered lips. He made an impatient growling sound in his throat. "All right, but briefly: 'Tis a pleasant village of sixty souls, give or take a few, with a coaching inn. It stands on the river. The kirk porch faces the shaft of an old parish cross dating from the thirteenth century . . ."

He couldn't know that each word he spoke was a thrust that went through to her heart. It was clear to her that he knew and loved every foot of his land. "So much history there," she murmured when he paused.

"Aye, prehistoric cairns and remnants of stone circles—and standing stones." He caught her eyes and smiled wickedly as he pressed the tip of his stone-hard flesh against her.

"Do you have mountains?"

"No' wild ones like these. No' mountains where all trivialities and irrelevancies are cauterized. No' a place like this one where a man really feels the satisfactions of being a man among men."

"That's different, I take it, from being a lone woman among those same men?"

He looked down on her for a terrible and wonderful moment. "But you're no' a lone woman; you're my woman. Must I always be reminding you? Can you no' remember from one moment to the next? Or is your design a cunning one, meant to wear down my strength, my virility? If so, I must warn you

281

'twill no' work. No, Flame. And now the questions and answers are done with; you shall rend honey to your laird. Aye, my thirst for honey is frightful just now. But 'tis a thirst easily satisfied. All I have to do is touch you here . . . and here . . ."

She stiffened and inhaled as his second knee parted her legs further, as his thighs stretched her wide for his pleasure, as his thumb and forefinger opened her. But then she subsided gently back into the furs. For the first time she greeted surrender.

"Aye, you see how 'tis. And now I must kiss you, and have you, lassie." As his mouth took hers, he pressed into her. His tongue and his flesh invaded her together, so that she was doubly taken.

A little feeling of disgrace shivered in her mind, but she cast it off with his slow, deepening penetration, his equally slow withdrawal, his penetration once more. Again and again that slow stab of passion. His hands were clenched around her back, holding her fast to receive his strokes.

She pulled his head down and kissed him, and put the point of her tongue in his mouth. Almost immediately he jetted his ecstasy into her, his loins jerking convulsively and his heart drumming against her breasts. She joined him in a glittering stream of pleasure, the velvet sleeve of her embracing him with rhythmic spasms. She welcomed that burst of rapture like an old friend.

When it was finished and they were peaceful again, lying side by side, she stroked his back, until after a moment, her hand felt still. Her eyelids were heavy.

"My bonny, my beloved, are you going to sleep? 'Tis the middle of the day. Well, you'll no' mind if I kiss your white breasts? Nae, do no' mind me; sleep."

And that was all she knew for a while, his words and the warm tug of his mouth at her body as she hung above sleep, before she fell into its comfort.


Flame felt she was doing fairly well on snow-shoes—at last. Cougar was teaching her many of his skills now, and today, as soon as they stepped under the trees, she was aware of when he became suddenly silent and totally attentive. He saw something, and indicated with a grin and a little jerk of his head for her to look up. Then he waited.

He'd told her that the goal wasn't to look for a specific thing, but to catch movement. "Once you've caught a movement, you can focus on what's causing it." She was learning to catch the tail-flick of a deer, the muscle-ripple of a fox, even the twitch of a chipmonk's nose. She was learning not to strain for anything; she was learning, instead, to see.

Conscious of being demanded upon now, she searched out the red squirrel he meant for her to find in the branches overhead. He nodded, satisfied, and they moved on. She breathed deeply, trying to flow as she moved. She gently blanked out her thoughts so her senses had full sweep, and soon she found herself—it seemed a contradiction—more acutely aware and wide awake to everything around her than she'd ever been before.

It wasn't long before they discovered what they were looking for: the hiding place of the mule deer Cougar had first pointed out picking its way warily out of the thick cover by the eaves of the forest.

Evidently this was where it slept. The snow was trampled and scattered with droppings, and there was an indentation of the deer's body. Cougar knelt and picked up a few loose hairs tipped with red.

It was an old buck, too drained after the autumn rut to migrate to warmer climes with the rest of his herd. He'd been defeated and routed from his harem and now was too weak to go lower for food. Winter would be asking everything he had. Flame's reason assured her that it was a mercy they were on his trail; otherwise the deer would no doubt starve, slowly and horribly.

The deer's age, however, wasn't keeping Cougar from using every gambit he knew to reduce it to a fresh supply of venison. He'd been teaching Flame to use a bow and arrow. (He was a good teacher, but a strict one. When she was careless or inattentive, he tended to use language as vibrant as red baneberries.) He wanted her to kill this deer, and she was willing to try, to please him. She carried her bow on her back, along with a light quiver holding eleven arrows.

They moved on as silently as they could in the fading day, snowshoes making their footfalls mere whispers. The icy rime of early December lay on the brittle stalks of the sedge where they expected to surprise the deer. The ice cracked and broke off at the slightest brush of her bearskin. Cougar wasn't wearing his capote, and she noted that his braintanned buckskins made no noise when they touched the brush. She shrugged out of her cloak. Surprisingly, she didn't seem to find the cold much of a factor just now; the suspense of the hunt was keeping her warm.

Now they both moved across the landscape like shadows. They moved with the other mountain sounds—the wind, the ebb and flow of the light. They stopped often to look and wait, hardly breathing, so that then there was nothing but the soft white move of their eyes in the closing twilight.

A new storm had been gathering all afternoon. Large snowflakes began to pelt Flame's face. Soon the ground was freshly covered and all evidence of hoof-print was erased. They were moving at a pace that seemed painfully slow. If they didn't find the buck soon it would be too dark.

Suddenly the mule deer shivered, and Flame saw it. He was lying down, his neck stretched out flat along the snow, his antlers motionless—she would never have seen him except for that tiny, mortal shiver. Evidently the snow had chilled him in spite of his dense red-gray fur. His head was less than ten yards from her foot. She froze as he looked her way.

When he detected no motion, the briefly alert gleam faded from his eyes. They went dull and gray, old and weary. A spasm of pain seemed to twist him as he turned away. Flame could move again, but she didn't.

Cougar made an expressive gesture with his eyes. It was as explicit as handwriting: Kill him.

Still she didn't move. She was struck by the look she'd seen in the creature's eyes. He was a living thing, trying his best to survive for as long as he could. What right did she have to decide he would be better off dead?

Somehow the deer must have sensed he'd been discovered. He leaped up with more agility than she might have expected, and began to thrash out of the

285

undergrowth.

"Aim, lassie!" Cougar said in a low tense voice. "Do no' let him reach that gooseberry patch."

Obediently she brought up her ashwood bow, aimed, pulled back the rawhide cord. The deer broke out of the cover, he sprang into the open with his nose raised. Flame's body and bow pendulated with his run. The tip of her arrow rode on his shoulder.

"Now!" Cougar urged.

She let the arrow fly. The bow twanged in her hand. It would have been a heart shot had it had more strength behind it. As it was, it merely pierced the animal's hide and tough muscle and bedded in his lungs. Still alive, the deer went down, bleating like a lamb in the snow.

Cougar brought his rifle up. He leaned forward against the recoil, waited with his forefinger on the trigger while he aimed, then fired. The deer stopped kicking.

Flame ran to the barely struggling body. She got there in time to see the tender beauty in the old deer's eyes gradually take on the emptiness of death.

Cougar thumped her affectionately on the head. "Good shot, lassie." He winked glitteringly. "A wee more practice and you'll know how to put your power behind it better."

She felt like a little girl staring at an empty birthday box. "I don't think I like killing things."

Flame was warming the midday meal when a strange voice came from outside the cabin: "Anybody t' home?"

Her heart leapt into her throat. Cougar was off

checking his traps. He might not even return for lunch. Sometimes he didn't return until dark, exhausted after walking miles along the streams to empty and reset his traps.

Uneasily, she opened the door.

It had snowed earlier, but now the gray sky had opened like a rent veil, so that the valley floor glowed in brief brilliance, while the surrounding peaks towered like sentries into the remaining clouds.

Beyond the threshold of the door stood a tall white man with an ugly unshaven face and sharp Mohawk nose. He said in a great bass voice, "Good afternoon to ya', ma'am," and reached to take her hand. She put it behind her quickly. He smiled anyway. "Name's Bohn, Filbert Bohn. And this here's Louie Orangewood. We're two of Bridger's men, or used to be." He brought his companion forward, a man whose eyes were jaded and flat. Flame took him in at a glance: burly, going bald, massive jowls, probably forty-five years old, but appearing sixty.

"I b'lieve you know these other three varmints," Bohn went on. He gave the three "varmints" a backflung smile. They stepped forward: the two squat Reade brothers and their youthful ward, Jack Goodspeed (upon whose downy-bearded face was that deceivingly boyish grin).

"There now, didn't we tell you?" Hosea said to Bohn and Orangewood. "Pretty as petals — and glad to welcome a bunch of old campfire friends into her lodge, ain't you, Miss Flame?"

She looked from face to face. They all looked back, except for Radford, who seemed to see some-

287

thing to smile about in the snow at his feet.

They had come on foot, leading their horses through the deep new snow accumulated on the valley floor. As they began to kick their snowshoes aside in a whisper of leather ties, she thought quickly. If she tried to slam the door and bar it, she might not succeed — and would certainly precipitate a feeling of ill will, maybe even a show of violence. Also, she would be locking Cougar out with five potentially dangerous men. The best course seemed to be to invite them inside and try to maintain a pleasant atmosphere until Cougar returned.

Bohn's fierce eyes were watching her. "I'm sure pleased t' meet ya' ma'am." He was shaking the snow off his buffalo-hide coat, slapping his shoulders and thighs. "These here varmints been talking nothing else but white woman since Louie an' me met up with 'em a month or so back — an' o' course we didn't believe a word of it. We don't meet many white women — so nothin' would do but we come up heres to take a look-see fer ourselves."

How had they found this place? she asked herself wildly. Cougar believed it was his secret alone. Had Hosea and his partners followed them here, then gone for the extra two men? Why?

Clearing the twigs from her throat, she said, "Won't you come in?"

They headed directly for the fire and stood crowded shoulder-to-shoulder around it, warming their faces and outstretched hands. The single room seemed suddenly about to burst at the corners with so many fur-cloaked intruders.

As they began to shed their wraps, tossing them in a pile on the bed, she said, "We haven't much in the way of hot food, but you're welcome to share it. And I'll get out some dried buffalo meat. That ought to fill you. Have you traveled far today? I imagine you're hungry." She was babbling, trying to cover her trembling with a show of casual hospitality.

"We are hungry — we're men, ain't we?" Bohn nudged Orangewood and Hosea, who stood on either side of him. "We ain't had a bite since day 'afore yesterday. Game's awful scarce, ya know."

All five were turned to watch her every move now. She crossed the cabin to get a parfleche of buffalo meat and placed it, opened, in the center of the little table. The men remained entirely silent. She sensed what was behind their muteness and considered bolting for the door.

She knew she would never make it, though.

# Chapter Nineteen

The stew on the fire made a gurgling, bubbling noise. Since the five trappers formed a solid wall of masculine bone and tissue between Flame and the hearth, she had to ask, "May I get through, please?"

Bohn and Hosea immediately made way for her, Bohn saying, "That smells right fine. Be it venison?"

"Mule deer. We shot it last week. Cougar killed it, though I took the first shot at it with my bow and arrow." She prattled on, "He's teaching me to use a bow, but so far I can hardly do more than pierce the hide—"

"Next time 'twill be a heart-shot. She has as accurate an eye as the best of men. 'Twas herself that killed the grizzly whose claws hang 'round her neck."

Cougar stood in the door, his rifle in his hands and a strangely prismatic glitter in his eyes. His gaze fixed on Bohn, on Orangewood, then on the others. There was nothing in his face except quiet, yet he looked so confident, so certain of himself that Flame felt weak with relief. She couldn't restrain the sigh that escaped her.

He closed the door and shed his capote, then shook hands with each of the men in turn. It was a moment to reveal to Flame how admirably he'd been schooled in all the graces. He was correctly courteous, polite to a downright courtly degree; yet, although none could have faulted his behavior, the air in the crowded cabin remained subtly cold, indefinably amiss.

"What brings you so far north?" he asked Hosea.

"Oh, we decided to do a little trapping. Been fighting Blackfeet, too, just for the fun of it."

"The fun of it?" Cougar said with slow, philosophic calm. His pale, cool eyes became paler and cooler.

"That's right," Bohn said. "But we got us some beaver, too. Took one t'other day so big it left pawprints big as postholes on the riverbank. I guess you been out checking your own line? Gettin' anything worth skinnin'?"

"We've taken a plew here and there," Cougar answered cautiously. "No' that many, but a few."

"Much the same ourselves."

Radford, his eyebrows raised, put in, "But Bohn, we ain't done no trappin' fer weeks."

Hosea clapped his brother on the back. To Cougar he said, "You remember how it is with Rad here." He winked hugely, while his glance to his brother contained a warning.

"Hosea," Radford went on childishly, "you oughtn' to tell people things that ain't true."

For a moment the situation seemed to hang like a rock teetering on a cliff. Jack Goodspeed spoke up.

"I would sure like to see some of your pelts. Got any handy?"

Cougar looked at him without speaking, then gestured Flame toward the door with his chin. She grabbed her bearskin and went out.

The cold air startled the sheen of sweat that had gathered on her forehead. She slipped on her snow-shoes and trudged past the visitors' horses to the shed. The cold seemed to clear her mind. Rummaging through the lustrous pile of pelts at the back of the shed, she found a small one on which she'd practiced her first attempts at dubbing. Since then she'd spent hundreds of hours at the tiresome and painstaking task of removing the fat, meat, and blood from pelts with pieces of sharpened elk horn, and she'd become expert. But this early one was unevenly finished; it was shedding some of its fur already.

The small cabin seemed stuffed with men when she squeezed back in the door. She immediately felt engulfed in the visitors' stale personal odors—reeky woodsmoke, rancid tallow, and sweat. She handed the pelt to the boy. It passed from hand to hand. Bohn said, "That's purely nice work." His look told Flame that he thought she was a very shrewd customer. She looked back at him innocently.

The burly Orangewood echoed with, "Right nice work for sure." His voice was cynical. He looked sideways at her and contorted his face by lifting one side of his mouth into a contemptuous sneer.

"Won't you have something to eat?" she said, indicating the table.

As they scooped themselves bowlfuls of the stew it was Jack and Orangewood who took the two stools. The other three sat crosslegged on the floor rugs.

Cougar took a casual seat on the edge of the bed. Flame sat near him, hoping to become invisible. He picked up a rag and went to polishing the barrel of his rifle. The strangers had left their own rifles outside, though each carried a long, murderous-looking knife at his belt. Flame felt the tension mounting, each moment climbing with it, as Cougar continued to wipe his rifle almost lovingly, his eyes on the men all the while. They, in turn behaved much like fencers who were gauging him with passes of their foils preliminary to the real bout.

"Say," Bohn said out of a full mouth, "I got me a new plumb-center rifle at last rendezvous." Pieces of food dropped out with his words. "Made by a fella name of Joseph Manton. Cost me a lot less than I expected. Uses balls that run twelve to a pound."

"Bring that in and show our friend here," said Hosea, a grin on his pock-marked face.

"I would be obliged if you would leave it outside," Cougar said quietly. "I'll have a look at it as you leave." That they would be leaving soon was implied.

Bohn and Hosea passed glances back and forth. Everyone shifted a little. "Sure thing," Bohn said with a show of unconcern as he went back to his stew.

Radford brought out a Jew's harp and began to play it, holding it in his one good hand. Hosea said over the music, "We hear there's bad doin's back in the States, a bad winter, bread riots in the cities—"

"Riots!" Flame said.

He nodded, satisfied with her response. "Well, what more can you expect with the same old gutlessness of the fee-nanciers, always making trouble for the little fella?"

"They got theirselves a new president," Bohn

293

added. "Man called Van Buren."

So there was a new president in the capitol. Andrew Jackson had chosen his successor and gone back to his Hermitage in Tennessee. Martin Van Buren — and politics in general — didn't interest Flame, but naturally the condition of the nation did.

"Still, new man or not," Bohn was saying, "they're crying that doomsday's about to come. The West is broke, they're saying — though I ain't noticed that so much myself."

Orangewood spoke up. "With whiskey four dollars a pint? Nigh a plew a pint! Now you can't ignore the poor doin's we got going fer us, Bohn. I be dogged — I am, now! The fur companies are just in a pitiful fix. Thing's 'r gettin' worse by the year." He took his knife from his belt and started jabbing the wooden tabletop with it, as if to relieve his feelings.

"What do you think, Cougar?" Hosea asked.

"I think it could possibly lead to a festering appreciation of one's dispensability."

Grinning around his harp, from which saliva dripped, Radford said, "Don't he talk nice?"

"Yessir," answered his brother, "he's a gentleman all right, from heel to crown."

Now that the men were finished eating, Flame felt rescued from the necessity of squirming a moment longer under their prodding eyes by the need to clear the table. She tried to move around Orangewood, who lolled on his stool in her way, but he reached out suddenly and slid his hand around her waist, saying, "Come sit here on my knee and tell me all about yourself, girlie." She toppled onto his lap and was captured in a bruising grip. His fingers moved up from her waist to clench onto her breast. At the same time she saw his knife was coming up toward her throat. Cougar moved with lightning speed, tearing her from his hands and thrusting her behind him. The barrel of his rifle was pushed into the burly man's nose.

A tight smile thinned Cougar's mouth, and his eyes burned from under his narrowed lids with an intent, killing light.

Silence settled on the assembly. Orangewood tried to laugh, then stood up slowly and stepped back from the gun's barrel. His jowls had turned scarlet.

Cougar's rifle followed him. Every muscle and vein was taut. The rest of the men sat motionless, waiting for what would happen next, their faces sober and eyes sharp.

"I just believe you travelers might be straining your welcome a wee bit. Aye, I just do think that," Cougar said with seemingly easy confidence. " 'Tis time to strap on your medicine bags and go."

Jack said, his words tumbling with injury, "W—well, be goddamned! No need taking on like some sore-tailed bear."

Hosea, in a faint forestalling of the inevitable, muttered, "We just come by to be friendly and warm ourselves. I told the boys here you was a nice fella, that we liked you from what we know'd of you. Thought you liked us."

Cougar answered huskily, "No doubt someone has liked you during your lifetime—some woman must have mothered you, at least—yet, none with any sense could like you now."

An incongruously wistful expression unfurled on Hosea's coarse face. "Are you insulting my mother?"

"I'm insulting you, man."

Flame thought this candor a bit imprudent. After all, there was only one of him and five of them.

Hosea stood perplexed and still, then burst out with, "Why—why, I'm a mountain man . . . like you!" The very air was stirred and shaken by his outrage.

"Indeed, you are." Cougar's voice was still full of lazy self-assurance. "But I've found little to praise of the morals, intelligence, or even the companionability of us mountain men."

Getting to his feet now, Bohn said, "Well, it's poor doin's makin' up to trouble, so I b'lieve we'll be heading out on our way."

"And have a good journey," Cougar said, moving without strain to shepherd them out at rifle point.

Radford was last to move. He stood there, not quite understanding. His eyes had gone big and his mouth hung open.

"You too, laddie," Cougar said, not unkindly.

Though it wasn't long past noon, the day was already in its waning, with shadows of night coming on. It promised to be the darkest evening of the year. Getting into his snowshoes, Bohn flashed Cougar a tough look. "We'll be around ag'in."

"You're warning me?" Cougar said.

"Just tellin' ya, squaw-man. I been in these parts since Laramie Peak was a deep hole in the ground, and—may God twist my tripes!—I'll be here long after you're gunshot and gone under."

Cougar laughed in a calm, unafraid fashion, so that Bohn had to struggle with his temper.

"Good-day to you, ma'am," he said, reaching for his horse's lead reins.

She inclined her head stiffly.

Jack Goodspeed was the last to pad off. He paused to say to Cougar, "I don't like you. And I don't like the idea of Miss Flame being married to you."

"Leave it, laddie."

"And I don't like taking orders from no foreigner."

"Come on, Jack," Hosea called. He held the boy's horse as well as his own.

Flame heard the boy mutter to the older man, "I'm bound to rub that faker out one day."

Orangewood looked back at the boy with a gleam in his eyes. "Sic 'em!"

The afternoon was turning frigid and the snow was crusting over. It crunched under their feet as they tramped off single-file. Their footfalls grew fainter, fainter, until at last there was silence again in the empty snowfields. Flame whispered, "Will they really come back?"

Cougar looked at her in a way she'd never seen before.

"I don't understand. What do they want?"

"They want everything. Our pelts, the horses, the cabin—'tis cold out." Every word dropped echoing through the shadowiness of the day. "And they want you. Mostly they want you. They'll no' have you, though. I keep my own with a tight fist. 'Tis the Scots in me." He turned to put his hand on her shoulder, then smiled down at her.

She whispered, "Tell me what we're going to do."

He gave her a considering look now, and at once she knew he was about to manipulate her toward some uncomfortable fact. Suddenly he became legendlike again, became that figure of mystery who had mesmerized her from the first. His eyes were like gray forest fog, and again the haunt of prophecy seemed to touch him.

"You must try no' to think of them as men. Think

of them the way you did the bear." He touched her cheek with his hard fingertips. "They'll come again, aye, and when they do, we must kill them."

With endless patience he seemed to mark the time it took for her to react. Already shaken, she felt her composure deserting her completely beneath his still, considering gaze, until she was quaking like an aspen in the wind. She retreated from him slowly. "No—no. No, I won't help you." White to the lips, she said, "I can't! And I won't let you either! Let them have the cabin, the pelts, they're not that important!"

"And you, lassie? Shall I let them have you, too?"

"We can leave."

" 'Tis cold out, my heart."


A week passed, and another day, and there was no sign of the five trappers. Cougar had kept Flame so close in the cabin that she was in serious need of some fresh air and freedom. He had barely slept at all the first few days, and even now was on watch the whole of every night, waiting for an attack of some kind. His mouth seemed permanently set in its starkest, most implacable lines, so that Flame felt half-afraid of him again. Nevertheless, she tried to reason with him:

"You have to get some sleep. I don't think they're even in the area anymore. They've probably been miles away for days and would laugh to know you're still doing twenty-four hour guard duty this way."

"They're gone, are they? There'll be no attack? As sure as ripe fruit never drops from the bough?"

But he was tired; his eyes were sunk deeply in their sockets; in the firelight his face was stripped down to

298

golden bone. She could see her argument was having effect. He turned toward the door with a droop in his whole body, then turned to look back longingly at the bed. At last he sat down on it heavily. He said nothing for what seemed to be an age, then, "Aye, lassie, all right." He sighed. "I'll just have a nap then. I suppose I've got to rest some. But if you hear anything—*anything*—you wake me. Give me your promise."

"I *will,* she answered with strained patience.

As he stretched out, she placed a light hand on his shoulder. Her impatience died in wistfulness.

At first his rest was light and broken, punctuated by jaw-cracking yawns, but then he rolled onto his side and seemed to drop into a deep slumber. She saw it with satisfaction. It was reassuring sometimes to see these evidences that he was only human after all.

Asleep, he looked younger and defenseless, his disshevelled hair curling onto his forehead and his finely shaped mouth mellowed to boyishness. The severe lines of vigilance were no longer there. Such a handsome man!

The valley was awesomely quiet all that morning. In the cabin the occasional spark from the fire seemed loud. Near noon she heard the horses whinnying in complaint and she realized they hadn't been tended since yesterday evening. She moved quietly to pull her bearskin around her and take up a bucket of melted snowwater. Flicking her thick plaits over her shoulders, she unbarred and opened the door, inch by inch, watching Cougar's face all the while. So lost to sleep was he, he didn't so much as move an eyelash.

Outside, she looked across the frozen, silvery

299

world of the valley. Snow had fallen heavily in the last eight days, but the nimbus around the sun was a sign that the weather was changing yet again. The temperature was going to plummet. Cougar had told her that in this area it sometimes fell to thirty, forty, even fifty below; sometimes there were winds that not even the wolves could endure. She'd already heard the cold split trees open like rifleshots, and had seen it freeze the streams bank to bank and clear to their bottoms. Now she felt it; a cold was coming that could weld a man's hand to the steel of his rifle — or a woman's to her knife — if either was idiot enough to touch them.

She drew a deep breath, like a sailor about to plunge into the sea, and then literally flung herself forth out of the shelter of the cabin's shallow doorstep.

She kicked off her snowshoes as she entered the shed. The low-roofed shelter was somewhat warmer than the open air, holding the collected body-heat of the five animals. Still, its walls were bayonetted with ice, and from the roof across the open end more ice hung, like crystal prisms dangling, catching the light from outside and refracting watery rainbows. She poured the bucket of water into the hollowed-log trough, put out fresh feed, and moved between the horses, talking to each of them, murmuring as if to pets or to children. Their warm grassy breath misted her face. Her own pony snorted and nodded at her and she laughed. She often boasted to Cougar that the little horse understood English perfectly, and probably Flathead as well. As she spoke to it again, it kept its ears pointed forward, but held its head daintily to one side, as if listening.

That was when she heard the men approaching,

moving toward the shed in a pack. They were on showshoes as before: she heard the soft whisper of their steps coming, not quickly, but at a steady pace, a confident pace. *They've been waiting a long time,* she thought.

There was no point in her trying to make a dash for the cabin. They were too near; already she could hear them just outside the shed. She stood where she was, between Spot and Irongray, motionless. Her whole being was as fixed as a deer's at that moment when it takes fright and is about to flee.

They had waited for just this, for the moment when they could get her separated from Cougar, they had waited eight days for it. And eight nights. Waited through wind and snow and freeze. The idea of such monstrous patience chilled her to the marrow.

Briefly she considered screaming, but if Cougar came bursting out of the cabin now, fuddled by sleep, she feared they would cut him down instantly. If she kept her head, though, perhaps she could bargain for time. Perhaps she could save him, or at least give him a better chance at survival.

She couldn't help an involuntary shiver as they formed a semi-circle around the open end of the shed. In that moment of most awful quiet they were, all five of them, grinning. There was a glitter in their eyes, like hounds close upon a fox. Bohn even laughed, softly.

Louie Orangewood said to Hosea, "Me and you better go see to the Scotchie bastard."

Hosea, after clearing his throat and adjusting his beaverskin hat with his thick-fingered red hands, agreed. "I aim to lift some hair. I want a Scotchie scalp to hang on my old leggings."

The younger three, that greedy glitter still in their eyes, entered the shed. One by one, like muslims into a mosque, they filed inside. Again came Bohn's laugh, a louder chuckle now, as they closed in on her. The chuckle ended with a loud hawking in his throat.

Belatedly Flame realized what Orangewood and Hosea had meant by "see to the Scotchy," and she now cried, "Cougar!" Her voice was frustratingly thick with cold.

"Shut up!" Jack Goodspeed stepped forward quickly and whipped her face with his hand. She stumbled back between the horses, both her cheeks stinging. The boy followed, grabbed her wrist, and dragged her out into the open floorspace. She opened her mouth to scream Cougar's name again, but Jack raised his fist this time. The edges of his nostrils were blenched and flared. She flinched in anticipation of the blow.

"Hold on, now!" Bohn said. "I want her awake and kicking. That's half the fun of it." He looked at Flame avidly, grinning with delight. To Jack he said, "Let's wait a minute and take her inside. It's cold out here." The eight days of harsh weather had been at him. His lower lip was swollen and cracked and clotted, like a half-grilled sausage.

"I want some fun now," the boy said softly. "If you're too cold, go on. I'll bring her in directly."

"I want some fun, too," Radford giggled. Spittle dripped off his lower lip.

Bohn's laugh came again. "A'right, sure, you want to get your baby peckers frostbit, it's a'right with me. I don't mind watchin'." He leaned his rifle against the wall (his new Joseph Manton, decorated with brass tacks and vermillion) and he moved to

302

grip Flame's arms from behind with ungentle fingers.

The boy leaned his rifle next to the Manton, and took his knife out. He used it to cut the ties holding her cloak closed. Humiliatingly pinioned as she was, there was nothing she could do to protect herself. He passed the knife before her face, slowly, obviously hoping to see her flinch again. She stared at him stolidly, though the honed blade was a mere hairsbreath from her skin.

"Let go of her," he said to Bohn. "I want to do it by myself."

Bohn released her arms with another chuckle. The bearskin fell from her shoulders, exposing her to the chill.

The boy said, "Take your clothes off—all of them."

Though he was barely as tall as her, he suddenly seemed a monster. He was so young, and seemingly from a decent middle-class family, probably brought up to be a gentleman. He was even handsome in a boyish way. A few flakes of angelic snow clung to his long eyelashes. Yet he meant to handle and use her body as he chose—to rape her cruelly. She thought she'd grown immune to horror, but now she felt it batter her afresh.

Shaking violently, as much from fear as from cold, she removed her knife belt, unlaced the top of her dress, touched and then gripped the bottom of her skirt. She paused for one suspenseful moment, then drew the hem upwards.

She jerked and let go of it as a shot rang out through the valley—and jerked again at the sound of a man's strangled scream.

Jack was grinning at her obscenely. "That's the

303

end of him."

Radford, who had lost his foolish expression, seemed more sharp and alive than he ever had before — like an animal waiting quietly.

Jack prompted Flame with his knife. "Come on, strip! There's five of us, you know. They'll all want their turns."

She hardly knew what she was doing. Her mind was in the cabin, her whole soul and being were fixed in the cabin: *Cougar!* The bear claws of her necklace fell back coldly onto her unprotected breasts as she pulled her dress over her head.

"Not bad." The boy was studying the vision she presented to him.

"Toothsome," Bohn agreed.

Their voices seemed a long way off to her, the scene was confused, pale, fantastical. Her cloak and dress were at her feet. It was much colder than she'd realized; her skin was pricked with goosebumps, her nipples puckered to little pink berries.

"Now lay down on that bearskin."

"Look," Radford said, grinning like an idiot, his eyes riveted on her lower belly, "she's yellow-haired there, too!"

Jack laughed lewdly. "That's right. Pretty, ain't it? I'm going to be happy as a moth in a yellow mitten — and just as busy. *Lay down!*"

She knelt on the fur.

"You're a fool," Bohn muttered. "She's colder than the north wind, shivering so hard she'll unseat ya. I'm waitin' till we get her inside."

"I'm right after Jack!" Radford whined eagerly. "I'm second!" His deformed hand waved in the air. An image of him reaching with it to take hold of her flashed through Flame's consciousness.

304

Jack bent over her in gathering impatience, wielding his knife around her face again. How thin the blade was. How cold the steel looked. How eager for blood, how blue with malice—like a madman's glinting eyes.

"I ain't telling you again, now—lay down and spread yourself! I want to have a nice look at those soft parts between your legs."

*Chapter Twenty*

Jack Goodspeed grinned in greedy glee. "That's right, down—"

"Bohn was right," a voice came quietly from behind the boy. "You are a fool, laddie. Aye you are, just."

Flame whimpered in relief. She felt relief like a thrill, starting in her fingers, tingling up her arms, and squeezing her ribs. Tears welled up, prisming the beautiful sight of Cougar, alive, with his rifle-barrel touching the back of the boy's head.

He started to speak again in that same low passionless voice: "Stand up, slowly, and toss the knife down under yon horses."

Jack looked sick-scared as he did as he was told.

"My heart, put your dress on before you take ill." His gray eyes burned with incandescence. Flame continued to stare at them for a moment, then she scrambled to pull her dress on and tug the bearskin around her.

"We didn't hurt her none," Bohn said. His eyes

slid to his rifle, leaning with Jack's against the wall.

"You're lucky in that," Cougar said. He gave the man a bright false smile. "If you'd harmed her I would cut you apart slowly 'til there was no' a piece of any of you the size of a five-penny bit."

To Flame he said, "Leave us, lassie."

"Tell him we didn't hurt you none, girl."

"Your chafing sighs hew my soul," Cougar taunted. "But 'tis a merciless world, you ken." His mind seemed to be working as quickly and as grimly as a guillotine.

Bohn drew in a breath with a hiss. He'd gone pale, though his Mohawk-nose was still red and painful-looking.

"Flame, my love," said Cougar with most exquisite courtesy, "would you be excusing us?"

She made an irresolute gesture with her hands. "Cougar . . ."

Bohn muttered, "I ain't skeered of you."

Meanwhile, Jack could only glare straight ahead of him, for the rifle barrel was still touching the base of his skull. Radford had a dull, silly, friendly expression on his face, but his eyes were tearful, as if he knew. He said, "Hosea said I could, Hosea said so."

"Shoot him, dummy!" Jack said suddenly.

Cougar reached an arm out and took Radford's rifle. He gave it up without resistance. "That's it, laddie." Cougar leaned the gun with the other two.

Jack made a disgusted sound.

Bohn tried, "How 'bout if we just go on our way?"

Cougar, still with that deadly amiable look about him, turned to Flame and smiled, but his voice was a shade less patient this time. "Go back to the cabin, my heart, and close the door."

She looked at him an instant longer. There was something ancient and tenebrous in his eyes. When she glanced at his hand she saw his finger on the trigger of his rifle.

As the silence lengthened she wildly groped for the emotional key that would reduce this scene to order. All she could think to say was, "You can't, Cougar."

There was no real expression on his face anymore. "I'm that sorry, but do no' argue this time. I've asked you to go. Leave us—*now!*"

She'd occasionally suspected that his temper would be a terrible thing. Now she knew it to be true. Involuntarily, she backed against the flank of Irongray. The horse leaped away. She stumbled, unbalanced for the moment . . . and then she was running out of the shed. She didn't stop for her snowshoes, and didn't look back. There was no sound other than the snow-crunch under her feet and her breath going out and in, crisply, like the crumpling of parchment.

Two bodies lay on their backs in the cabin door, one gun-shot, the other stabbed. She reeled back from the odd, frozen-in-stupifaction expression on Louie Orangewood's face and from Hosea's lips twitched back in a dead man's grin. A moan was muffled behind the fist she pressed against her mouth. She stared, nauseated. She thought of Cougar's hands, which caressed her with such tenderness, appalled to know they could have killed these men.

The bodies were blocking her way: she couldn't enter the cabin without stepping over them and couldn't close the door without moving them. She waded around them instead, around the open door,

308

around the side of the cabin, and headed for the woods.

Here the snow was untramped and unmarked, about three feet deep. Though her legs soon ached with the effort, she struggled on through it, until she was breathing in shallow gasps and there was a light film of cold perspiration on her lip. She stopped, to hug the upturned root of a great tree. Hard ice flakes pressed into her cheek. She took a deep breath and held it. The silence flooded in so suddenly she heard it.

She looked back in the direction she'd come from. She could still see the shed's roof. What was happening there? A breeze gusted, unseen but penetrating. She looked up at the sky between the trees; it was pale blue with thin clouds. She needed to breathe again. Her mind spun in confusion for lack of oxygen, but still she held her breath.

At last she heard what she'd been listening for: a shot. And after a while, another one. Then a third. Cougar had used his own and two of the other rifles, one to kill each man.

She didn't hear anything more from the shed because she was running once more and making too much noise herself — for now she was sobbing.

In the purpling light of the sunset the view of the Drummond's Seat dropped westward. The icy wind made Flame's eyes tear; it hummed in her ears, up from the sheer ravine below, pregnant with the scent of junipers.

She could go no further. Besides the impossibility of the terrain, her feet were numb, her knees skinned, and her thigh muscles quivering with cramps. She'd been floundering in the snow for well over an hour, but now her senses were returned at last — and she realized she'd done something very foolish. "Stupid," was how she put it, muttering aloud to herself. Her face reset itself in an expression grim stoicism.

The cold had already intensified its terrible simplicity. And in the state she was in — soaked and exhausted — it was going to take her much longer to retrace her steps than it had taken her to get here. It probably would be dark before she regained the cabin.

"Stupid, stupid."

Her voice was lost in the last stand of the day. The wind hummed again out of the vast lonesome landscape, and the setting sun shone sternly on her hair.

She wished she didn't have to go back. If it only weren't so cold she could no doubt fashion herself a shelter, rest, and regain her strength. But she couldn't dry her clothes without a fire, couldn't feed herself without so much as a knife.

Her knife was still in the shed, on the belt that Jack Goodspeed had forced her to remove. What else was in that shed now?

Suddenly she hated these mountains, hated this unfriendly, frozen void where she'd been compelled to feel things she didn't want to feel and ask questions about herself she didn't want answered.

She stiffened her shoulders; it wasn't going to do any good to start whining and complaining now. She had to get back to the cabin. A night spent in this deepening cold, already wet and tired as she was, already on the very edge of her endurance, would be fatal.

She sighed. She was being melodramatic. There

310

wasn't any real danger of dying. She knew that Cougar was probably on her trail even now. Humiliating as it might be, she'd always known he wouldn't let her run off like this. All she had to do was turn around and retrace her own tracks and sooner or later she would meet him.

Yet how she dreaded that meeting. Dreaded that deadly presence she'd last seen in the shed. Dreaded seeing his face, his hands that had killed five men this day. Tonight perhaps, or tomorrow, he would put those same hands on her, mold her breasts with them, and—God help her—give her pleasure. She'd often wondered what kind of man he was. Now she asked herself what kind of woman she was . . . to love him.

Hadn't she always been aware that he was capable of anything? Hadn't she felt disaster coming from his direction since the beginning? She'd been too frightened to dwell upon it before . . . and now she was near to gibbering with terror.

She comforted herself with the idea that there must be a current, if she would stay ready and have the patience to let it take her, which would deliver her beyond this day to another dawn and a useful end to all of this.

She was following her own footsteps when she first saw him among the trees on the slope below. She stopped where she was, nearly waist-deep in the snow, and watched as he shuffled forward on his snowshoes. He had her shoes tied to his back, along with a small bundle. He was concentrating on her trail and didn't seem to see her at once, though she made no attempt to conceal herself. She merely stood there, inert, waiting until at last he stopped before her and met her gaze.

"You were thinking of abandoning me, my love?" Bright ridicule shone in his eyes. "But I should be so desolate." He untied his burden and laid her snowshoes side-by-side on the snow.

"Don't touch me," she said.

He regarded her with almost a sneer before he calmly took her hands and helped her climb out of the snow onto the snowshoes. From the bundle he brought out a dry pair with fur-lined leggings. Then he went to his knee to remove each of her wet moccasins in turn, taking each foot between his hands and massaging it as she placed her hands on his shoulders for balance. He eased her feet into the dry moccasins. Finally, he strapped the snowshoes onto her feet.

The wind had whipped her hair into untidiness; shining strands had escaped their plaits to blow across her face and around her long lovely neck. When he stood again, he took off his cougar-skin hat and fitted it over her head.

Tears sprang into her eyes at his thoughtfulness and care for her. But, seeing them, he raised his eyebrows and spoke again—repressed but authentic anger: " 'Twas a daft thing to do, this!"

She had already told herself the same thing—and had even expected his scorn—yet she felt annihilated by it now, all the same. She found herself wanting to cry outright. His contempt was really too much, on top of what the day had already heaped upon her. To hide her hurt, she turned her face from him.

As she took a step down the slope, his dry dreadful voice pursued her: "I would like to shake you! Nae, I could strangle you."

The muscles stood out in his neck. She sensed how close he was to violence. She was frightened, yet still defiant. She said over her shoulder, "Perhaps you should just shoot me—as you did those unarmed three in the shed. Tell me, was it easy killing Rad—"

He caught her shoulder and swung her about. His face was horrible. Never had she seen so much feeling there. What was it? Revulsion? Regret? Rightousness?

She whispered, disengaging her arm and taking several steps backwards, "I suppose you feel you did what you had to do."

"But I did no' do it! Because of you! Because I was too much the coward to face again the look you gave me as you ran off. Nae, I let them go. And now they'll be coming back again and again, if necessary, for that boy has the lust of the huntsman on him." He was storming, giving out lightning and thunder. "He wants you that badly. Ah! but a boy's desires *should* exceed his arrow range, say the Indians—"

"You—you let them go?"

"Aye, and mayhap they'll kill us both after all— me quickly, you more slowly, with more care, more thoughtfulness."

She listened in stunned silence. Too late she realized the danger of her delusive wish for him to show them mercy: She'd been wrong to stop him!

He was giving her a long, measured look. "Oh aye, now you see, lassie. You wanted me to do it— but wanted to have me to blame for it, too," he said bitterly.

She felt a sickening jolt, like a blow to her numb face. She gathered her cloak about her, aware (and not for the first time) of the extreme clarity of his mind. And at this moment his sight was an icy probe into her dark secrets.

313

"No, I don't think that's true, I—I just didn't realize . . ." She looked about her quickly. "Where are they?"

He gestured eastward. "Across the glen they headed—without guns or snowshoes or horses. They'll be no threat within the hour, but in a day or two . . ."

He left the sentence hanging ominously as he took a slow step toward her, and another. He was at his most overpowering. His eyes were steel gray. He was ready for a fight, and she had to maintain considerable effort not to break and run. As it was, she couldn't stop her teeth from suddenly chattering spasmodically.

The pathetic sight of her shivering there seemed to jar him. His face changed, not all at once, but little by little, until he said, "My God! Flame!" His ragged voice came close to breaking. "When I saw what they were doing to you!"

The spell of her fear was broken. This was Cougar. This was the man she loved. Time stopped its shuddering pace as she felt the magnitude of her emotional and physical connection to him. She reached to take his shoulders in her hands; her unconscious strength was in the steadiness of her look. "I'm all right. It's over for now. We'll get out of this all right."

They would, wouldn't they? she asked him with her eyes.

Taking her into his arms, he pressed his lips to her cheek. "Aye, lassie, we'll be fine, you and I. We'll be fine."

There was a small wind, a small, tenuous, cold

314

wind. It whispered across the icy valley floor and its susurration was a sad sound.

"There are happy places," Cougar said. "Here is no' to be one of them." He turned to Flame, "So, woman, what are we to do?"

They were on the slope above the cabin. The roof seemed forlorn under the trees. Flame felt the presence of the two dead men, steadfast and watching, as well as the eyes of the three Cougar had spared. Without realizing, she hung back a little.

His arm encircled her back and pulled her to his broad chest. He held her protectively. "The bodies are beyond the shed. You need no' lay eyes upon them again."

She escaped his arms — and any eye contact with him — and went on down the slope. The first echo of starlight was shimmering on a field of overflow ice on the opposite side of the valley. She kept her eyes on that.

Cougar seemed completely recovered from his show of emotion earlier. But then, as she had long ago discovered, he was above all rugged, even in his moods.

He was always the man of the tight bargain, the crafty lure, the affection that would not be gainsaid. While she was always the woman of doubts — the doubts of day and the doubts of night. It appeared that she loved Cougar, but was love really the right word for those strange, deep, primitive affections she'd felt, which had got mixed up with so many other important considerations, such as the struggle to stay alive?

At the cabin door she paused, her lips pale and still. Cougar opened the door; she entered before him. All seemed normal, except that the fire had gone out and the place had a smell of ashes. He went to start it immediately, while she stood close by to warm herself. Her hands trembled as she held them to the catching blaze. Squatting on his heels, he looked up at her through his eyelashes.

She felt so shattered by the whole episode she could hardly nerve herself to speak of it, yet she knew she must try. "What . . . what will we do with them . . . Hosea and Orangewood?"

He considered her. "We can no' bury them. The Indians would burn them."

"I suppose that's as good a method as any, under the circumstances." After another moment, she said, "Would it be wise . . . I mean, considering what you said—that the 'hunter's lust' was on them—for us to stay here and wait for them to attack us again?"

He didn't answer. And she found she didn't have the strength to pursue it. She felt so very tired. Almost before she knew what was happening, he was taking her bearskin cloak from her and undressing her. He picked her up and placed her in bed.

He didn't join her right away, but stayed on by the fire, staring into the flames until the evening logs burned down. When at last he undressed, she pretended to be asleep. She didn't think she could suffer to be touched by a man ever again, but especially not tonight.

She felt him pull the furs open, felt him slip in beside her. She was lying on her side, facing away from him. Her hair was all loose and she didn't move as he brushed some of it off her cheek and kissed her there. His lips were warm.

His arm stole around her hips. She tried to maintain the impression that she was lost in slumber.

His hands began to explore each part of her.

Despite her unwillingness, his touch was so effective that she was all tremulous. His hands were on her bare thighs, stroking them as if he were stroking a nervous horse. Only when she was in a state of intense anticipation did he move on to another part of her. Now it was her bottom that he was smoothing and caressing. She resolved to let him do just as he liked—as long as he didn't ask her to become involved. Even when he urged her onto her back, she continued her pretense of sleep.

But then his knees got between hers and he was over her, so large that she felt small beneath him. A warm and blunt part of him grazed her inner thigh. The touch was fleeting but the image it made was one of solidity.

There it was again, that tantalizing touch. Then his lips met hers for the first time.

Affecting to just now awaken, she tried to push him away.

"Be still, Flame," he ordered. His arms tightened. "How can you—tonight—after what I was forced to do?"

"But I thought you were fast asleep, wench." There was no humor in his words, only mockery.

To no avail, she tried to pull away from his clutches. But then her energy seemed exhausted, and she lay at his mercy as he calmly sank himself into her warm flesh. "Sweet bitch," he sighed, nudging deeper, "how I need you."

She tried again, though knowing that her will had failed her. "Cougar—"

He stopped her mouth with kisses until her resistance was lost. Her eyes softened and became unfocused, they shone with the soft radiance of the evening stars in April. Her hands were on his shoul-

317

ders, her fingertips digging into the muscles there.

He was in utter possession of her again, enjoying a deep and satisfying penetration. He began to move, and, cradled in his arms, she couldn't help responding to his lovely thrusts. She felt that familiar and delightful surrender of her senses and moved to meet each returning intrusion of him. She even kissed him back now, insistently, to encourage him on. She found herself overcome by a furious impatience, so that she was abandoned in her wordless entreaties for satisfaction.

"Aye, my heart," he murmured, "you must cling to me always."

It was a disconnected rhapsody that nevertheless ended in a pinnacle of bliss. Her head went back, her mouth opened, and she uttered a series of staccato cries.

He left her lying in a listless state of enjoyment. After a while his voice sounded in the semi-darkness. "You see, Flame, you still want me."

"If you'd only asked I could have told you that," she said dryly.

He leaned on his elbow to look down at her and a puzzled expression crossed his face before he smiled. "But your words, your mind, are no' always the purveyors of truth. I wonder sometimes if you yourself have any fancy of what's really going on inside you. 'Tis your body that has always been my lodestar."

She turned her back to him and pulled the beaverskin robe up around her chin. She felt frightened, felt a sensation of danger, felt all the impending agony of his eventual but certain abandonment of her. Her mouth quivered on the verge of crying. In anticipation of the pain to come, she crept away

318

from the closeness of his tender embrace. It was self-defense that prompted her to say, "You're insensitive and crude."

He pulled her back toward him in a peremptory manner, and held her hips and thighs to his own. "Lassie, lassie." He shook his head in mock sorrow. "After the time I've spent on your education, and you still have no' learned a thing. You think I took you without sensitivity? I know you were that abused today. I had to show you it can make no difference to us."

She turned to him, the long held-in tears erupting. "Please, Cougar, don't keep me in this valley, this cabin, any longer. I hate it now!"

His voice grew caressing. "Then we'll leave it, we'll leave this place forever."

"Really?" Her tears halted abruptly. She felt an excitement, even on the surface of her skin. "Really? You . . . you'd do that for me?"

"Aye and I would." His eyes spoke words. His kind, large smile gave her a thousand assurances. "We'll go to Rotten Gut's camp for the rest of the winter."

Rotten Gut's camp.

She had read too much into his first willingness. Her thoughts had flown out of the mountains, across the prairies, all the way to Philadelphia . . . and yes, for a mad instant she'd even allowed herself to dream of Scotland, of him taking her there to make her his true wife.

But no. To Rotten Gut's camp. He was still not offering her a future with him. He had never offered her a future with him.

And he never would. She had to wrest her mind away from that seductive oblivion. One couldn't ignore the facts.

Only, since she'd become the bride of the Waiting Cougar, she'd discovered that there was no ecstasy to be found in the facts.

# Chapter Twenty-one

The next morning Flame packed her accumulated gear at Cougar's direction. His mind was rapier sharp, while she followed each command with dazed obedience, answering when he spoke, but otherwise remaining withdrawn behind a shell of silence. He hung a hatchet and a knife from her slender waist and fastened her bearskin about her, picked up her bundles and marched her out to where the horses waited under the chill gloom of the pre-dawn.

As they passed out of the valley, they left the cabin and shed ablaze. Flame didn't look back, but Cougar did. His face caught the dim winter light without expression, then, as he turned away from it, he gazed eastward, shading his eyes as if he saw, far away, things she couldn't see. He suddenly looked very jaded. " 'Tis a long road; we'd best begin."

They were taking very little with them. Cougar had rigged the packhorses each with a travois. Their two saddle horses carried light packs. He planned to scatter the five horses of the trappers as soon as they were out of the valley.

The travel was arduous as they marched day in and day out in snowpaths too deep for riding.

Cougar followed the windbrakes down the canyons but even so, they both wore out a pair of moccasins a day. They were in some of the finest beaver territory in North America, and if not so preoccupied, they could have reaped an enormous harvest of pelts. But they were preoccupied—with moving forward, keeping warm, staying alive.

After three days they spotted a large, solitary tepee pitched beside a river bank. They left the horses and worked their way to where they might see without being seen. The tepee was about twenty feet in diameter and had a round entrance of a type Flame hadn't seen before. Smoke wisped up out of the smoke-hole. It was occupied by at least nine Indians, all men.

Flame smelled roasting meat. Tripods of green trees had been erected and carcasses of game animals hung from them slowly roasting in the heat and smoke of the fires beneath. Her mouth watered. They'd missed their noon meal, and she was as famished as a January wolf.

"Would they be friendly to us?" she asked.

Her words were met by silence. In fact Cougar stared at her for so long it almost sapped her. Finally he said, bitingly, "Oh aye, as friendly as my cousin Donald, every one of them. These are Piegans, heart, one of the three Blackfeet tribes. This looks to be a hunting party, which means there are more of them around somewhere, mayhap a small village wintering in the area."

He took her away from the spot, and when they looped back to their route along the river the next day, he was still cautious. His eyes disregarded nothing. How could he be so infernally careful over every stick and stone, every noise and sight?

They continued downriver and camped within a

322

narrow gulch. The place was only a sling-shot wide and walled on two sides by towering stone. It felt safe to Flame, yet her sleep was full of confused visions and punctuated with sharp jerks back to wakefulness.

Her unease was justified when the next noon Cougar scouted out an Indian village only three miles from where they had camped. The tepees all had the round entrances distinctive of Piegans.

" 'Tis the main encampment. I estimate forty warriors."

He and Flame were crouched within a thicket of lodgepole pine. She could see several of the warriors, as well as several women. She even heard the sound of a baby crying, exhaustedly and hopelessly, and the sound of subdued voices, male and female, in argument.

Several men were cutting and trimming lodgepoles, so plentiful here. The air was filled with the sweet aroma of pine and blue spruce, bark and sap. And there was smoke, for one man was burning a hole near the end of a new pole so that it could be lashed to the side of a pack saddle.

The few horses the village had stood slack, their eyes sad and lifeless, their ribs revealed through their long winter hair.

None of this made the situation look dangerous. These were only people, surely, with enough worries of their own to be uninterested in a pair of passing travelers.

Leaving the animals with Flame, Cougar scaled the highest nearby rock to better observe. When he'd been gone for ten minutes, there was a change in the horses. Irongray's ears were now up and forward, and his eyes were standing out a little; and there were little spasms in Spot's nose and neck muscles.

While Cougar made his way down again, Flame stamped her feet to keep warm. She had a clear view of his descent, and was amazed to see him bring his rifle up to his shoulder. He seemed to be aiming right at her.

He fired. She heard a *splut* and spun to see an Indian behind her clutch his head. He screamed, and his voice was like a sword of ice that went right through her. He fell out of sight behind the snow-bank from which he'd been preparing to attack her. She felt instantly frenzied and began to run, as well as her snowshoes would allow, toward Cougar.

The horses threatened to bolt behind her, but she paid them no heed. She clambered up the rocks, past Cougar, who, with his rifle and shot pouch in one hand, gave her a boost with the other. "Climb!" he ordered, and sent her on. He stayed to protect her retreat, and even in her panic she recognized it as a gesture sure and noble.

More Indians were appearing from the direction of the village. Cougar grabbed the horses' lead reins and half-dragged the entire packtrain up into the rocky ledges where Flame waited for him anxiously, holding her chest as though afraid to breathe.

One Indian caught up with him, a warrior over six feet tall, broad and well muscled, with the feathers of a sub-chief. Once again she saw Cougar's tenderness twisted into the hands of violence: there was a screech from the Piegan as Cougar drove his knife high into the man's side, striking his heart. The Piegan stumbled back about fifteen paces, then fell dead.

Cougar shot another in the belly, but that Indian, falling to his elbows, returned fire with a rifle so old it might have been one brought down from Canada by the first voyageurs. Even so, the ball came so close to Flame's head; she felt the breeze.

While this wounded man crept behind a rock to reload, Cougar gained more distance from him.

Wedged down between protecting rocks and a winter-broken cedar, he and Flame watched the Indians gather in the snowy trees at the base of the promontory. Most of them were armed with nothing but shields, bows, and quivers full of arrows. One boy had only a stone hatchet with a broken handle. Yet several had guns. Cougar assured her, "At three hundred yards an Indian weapon will no' hit anything. Such as they have are of poor quality, and their ammunition is likely to be scanty."

She saw the truth in this, for when the warriors shot at them, their guns produced only a faint pop. The lightest wind carried the meager sounds away.

"But there are so many of them," she said.

"In a fight like this, arms matter a deal more than numbers." Patting his own rifle, he added, "This is enough to keep them at bay for now. At worst, we're at a stand off."

Nonetheless, the Piegans were a war-loving people, and they squandered ammunition on the pale faces for a long while, then spent the rest of the day stirring up their ferocity by prescribed ceremonials. As the sun went down and the moon drifted overhead, already at its full height, the singing of the Indians changed tone: the bass-voiced chanting quickened, climbed, became a blood trill. It made Flame's skin creep. She could see a chief's hands rapid in a narrative urging his braves to annihilate the party cornered in the rocks. Despite Cougar's confidence, her spine tingled with fingers of fear.

"They're rousing themselves to arrow deeds," he told her. "They'll no' attack tonight. Still and all, I'd rather no' be here tomorrow morning."

The baby she had heard earlier squalled even louder now, as though indignant at all the noise Finally, one Indian, a man with tufted eyebrows showed himself openly in the moonlight and shouted up, seemingly almost in a rage. He looked as tall as a ponderosa, a gigantic figure, and had a voice that could be heard around the world.

"What's he saying?" Flame asked. Her own voice was no more than a thin thread of sound.

A glint of amusement relieved Cougar's rather dour face. "Now the fun begins. Indians have a childish fondness for insulting words. Our man there is saying that I must be a woman and should dress myself like you, since I've crawled into the rocks to hide with you."

As a Scotsman, he seemed to have no doubt about what the next step should be: He took out his silver flask and urged it on her. She took a sip, while his own drink was considerably deeper. Warmed, he shouted back at the Indian, saying that the man was "naught but an old coyote, spotted with wood ticks and scabs." He enlarged upon the subject: The whole tribe were "naught but rabbits"; the whole Blackfoot nation were "crows with broken wings."

The Indian responded in kind: He and the men with him were the bravest on earth; they had only scorn for this womanish creature who had gone pale the first time he'd faced an enemy and had never regained his color since. He claimed that the blood in the Indian men was scalding and their honor was crying for battle.

The moon set about halfway through the night, leaving the stars alone to wheel overhead. They were able to slip away then. Cougar transferred their most vital supplies to Irongray and Spot, leaving the three packhorses. By picking a path through the snow-covered rocks, Cougar found them a narrow way up and over the top of the promontory. He moved through the night like a cat, never faltering, never doubting his footholds, never looking back except to help Flame and the horses along behind him. She followed him with complete trust, though her heart was throbbing with fear.

At dawn the sun returned, filling the world with light that found them three miles from the Piegan village. They traveled on all that day, until Flame was hideously tired. She didn't complain, however, for she understood that he wanted to maintain their lead.

They made perhaps nine miles all told. Unfortunately, it was thawing that day, so the path they left behind them was distinct when the freeze came that night.

They camped in a hollow under a thicket of leafless aspen. Cougar petted her extravagantly for making a singularly tasteless broth from a thin snowshoe hare she'd brought down with her bow. It was blowing hard from the southwest at sundown, a night of moonlight and starlight and clean, biting air. She felt the cold intensely, and in the face of it she felt discouraged, frail as a reedy stalk, white and blown.

The hours passed without incident, though Cougar was cautious enough to fear that the Piegans hadn't satisfied their honor. He left their bed well before morning hardened upon the shelter's sides. "to take a scout 'round."

Returning a half-hour later, he appeared easy of mind. "How are you feeling, lassie? Well, I hope — because we're in for a bit of trouble." He said it casually, stretching from the buffalo robe he'd taken a seat on to accept the hunk of dried venison she was handing him. She was confused for a moment; his attitude belied his words.

"I don't understand," she said soberly, trying to keep the panic out of her voice. "What do you mean when you say 'a bit of trouble'?"

A grin lifted the corner of his mouth. "I mean they're out there—but be calm," he said through a yawn. "Do no' show any fear; do no' even look about. We're going to have to out-fox them again. Your part is to act as if you suspect naught."

"I don't know if I can do that," she said with careful understatement. She was more than ordinarily nerveless this morning, the effect of the events of the past week: the attack of the trappers, the hard journeying, the short amount of rest she was getting . . . and the trailing flotsam of her continuing bad dreams.

"You can. I think you were most succinctly bred to disguise your feelings. Remember how you pretended to be asleep while I loved you a week or so ago? You were that good, aye. Once or twice I almost believed you really were no' wide awake to me all along."

"I—I don't know, Cougar . . . I don't feel very brave right now."

"Do you no'? 'Twould be a change for you then. Though you've long lived in the cruel clutch of circumstance and under the bludgeonings of accident, to my knowledge you've yet to wince or cry aloud. I've come to consider you a creature of the highest courage. You might as well proceed with your colors flying now."

Her eyes were very wide. She sat mousy-still. "But what are you going to do?"

"Well, polite parleying obviously will no' shake them loose. But 'tis my experience that anything unforeseen always takes the fight out of an Indian. Mayhap I can use that to give us an edge."

As he finished eating, he rose to put one arm about her, and with his other hand he pressed her bright head against his chest, stroking her lustrous hair. He framed her face and kissed her forehead, eyelids, cheeks, mouth; he opened her bearskin to caress the leather over her breasts. Looking into her eyes, he murmured, "Wish me luck, lassie." Then she saw him slip five or six rifle balls into his mouth. She knew he did that for quick reloading.

He took up his rifle and moved off, as if intending to make a nature call within a tangle of saplings bent and white-haired with ice. She went back to work briskly, striking the shelter and pretending to tranquilly pack the horses. She was shaking violently, yet somehow kept her head.

The minutes screeched by slowly. *What was he going to do?* As she tightened the horses' pack ropes and stooped as if to examine Spot's knees, suddenly she heard Cougar burst out with a hurried yell about thirty yards away. After that everything seemed to take place in slow motion, like one of her bad dreams. The scene seemed far away; she felt almost as though she were looking at it through the wrong end of a spyglass. She barely was aware of turning, of calling his name: *"Coouu-ga-ar . . ."*

A clutch of Piegans stood up as if quirted, and lit out, wading through the deep snow. Cougar stood, too, and exploded into a crazy hallooing that sent the Indians into further disarray. Flame screamed, her clenched fingers beating against her breasts. Cougar chased the warriors, staying just out of rifle shot and firing every few minutes to keep them running. All the while he went on yelling and thundering like ramping hosts and warrior horses; he turned the air sulphur-blue with his cursing, in English, in Gaelic, and in several Indian languages.

Flame stood like one stricken, waiting for him to return. When he did so, he brought with him the pervasive odor of gunpowder. He gave her a brilliant grin, unable to keep the gloating out of his face. But when he saw the tears on her cheeks, he was shrewd enough not to laugh. He framed her fatigued face again with his big hands and lightly touched his lips to her forehead and hair. She was still shaking, her lip was trembling uncontrollably, and he held her hard to stop her shivering.

"My heart," he said gently in her ear, "we must go now, while we have the chance. I'd like to say the hot-blooded fools will sheathe their knives and run all the way home, but I can no' promise that. Red people are like the Scots—they love quarrels and warpaths and undying hates.

"If it's any consolation, I doubt they'll take to our trail again before the morrow. They'll believe they can catch us easily enough in a day or two. But if it storms they might no' be able to tell which way we've taken. Their dogs would know, but they've got no dogs with them."

She fell in behind him as they moved out, down long snow-covered slopes, through alleys of bending boughs, with the cold wind stinging their faces until hers felt frozen brittle. She was so despondent she didn't even glance about her until high noon. Snow was starting to settle on the ridge they were descending. A first flake melted against her palm . . . then it was snowing hard. She gazed at the myriad flakes until her senses swam. Before any time at all had passed, the soft new fall was a foot deep.

All the rest of the afternoon they shuddered through the ghostly blizzard. Now and again she thought she heard faint voices, but she wasn't sure: it might only be the cold wind coming down the mountains.

Flame woke struggling for breath. A hand was clamped over her mouth.

"Wake, my heart — but quietly."

Cougar. She nodded and he lifted his hand.

"Here's your dress, put it on, and here —" He put her fur-lined moccasins in her lap.

"What —?"

"Shh . . . trouble's coming and we'd best be ready when it arrives."

Fully awake now, she found herself sitting up in the dark buffalo-hide shelter, frightened. She heard a whicker from one of the horses outside, but nothing else, nothing at all alarming.

She dressed as silently as she could, and as quickly, while he peered out through a crack in the shelter's opening. She could smell the pine-sharp night, though it was black as a pit. With no moon or stars overhead, the white snow gave off very little light, yet she could see well enough to tell that Cougar was already dressed.

He'd said that danger was approaching, but not knowing its form or direction struck her with panic and made her fingers stiff and uncooperative at the lacings of her leggings. At last she got them tied and gathered her fur cloak about her. "I'm ready," she breathed.

He left the shelter first, crouched to strap on his snowshoes, then he signaled her out and helped her with hers. He put something into her arms — her bow and quiver of arrows — and with his hand at her waist, he ushered her up into the trees.

Behind a hillock of snow they burrowed down to wait. He didn't need to outline the situation for her; she could guess for herself: He had heard something untoward, something he couldn't actually put a name to; yet, his most acute ear — or his intuition — had told him that trouble was afoot. Flame knew that intuition of his by now, and she'd learned to respect it absolutely.

So they waited in the trees, waited under the immaculate sigh of the frozen forest. The hours passed, the sky paled minimally. The horizons of her vision relaxed. It was still dark, yet not really night anymore. Low light, pearl gray, showed behind the eastern clouds. A flock of ducks passed low overhead, quack-quack-quacking.

All this time Cougar's eyes were busy, looking for motion, looking for color, looking for anything out of place. Flame had heard the horses stamping the snow in the darkness, trying to get to the grass buried beneath. She sat and shivered, holding herself tightly with her arms.

At last from the left of the campsite came a sound. She heard light scuffling steps and soft breathing. The shape of a man wearing a tall beaver hat emerged into the clearing. Another man took shape, then a third.

Who would think they would follow so doggedly?

Cougar. Cougar had known. That was why he'd been so willing to give up his glen, his ethereal valley, misted like myths. His sensitive instincts gave him an understanding of emotional truths beyond her own analytic mind's reach. He'd said there was a law ruling their lawlessness: a desire was on them, the hunter's lust.

The three men looked like three filthy scarecrows as they surrounded the shelter in silence. They moved in close enough to touch it, and on signal they attacked. Flame looked on in horror as they raised knives and tomahawks and brought them down, raised them and brought them down again . . . and again, stabbing, slitting the hides, smashing the light framing.

Cougar was aiming his rifle. Suddenly he fired. The explosion was thunderous in her ear. In response, Filbert Bohn arched his back awkwardly, threw up his arms—"Huh!"—and fell to his death.

Young Jack Goodspeed shouted, "They're in the trees!"

Flame watched them coming. For a second she crouched as if to hide, dazed with the speed at which these things were happening.

Then hatred burst upon her. It came with a violence, twisting her stomach. "I hate you." Her lips shaped the words. Her face felt cold. Her face was horribly wan, her lips were tight, blue, but there was solid, unflickering strength in her eyes. Calmly she notched an arrow and pulled back her bowstring, pulled it back hard, harder, until her straight left arm was shimmying with strain. Then she let the arrow fly at the nearest oncoming target.

He stopped. It was Radford Reade with a blanket draped around his shoulders. He stood with her arrow's feathers protruding from his chest. (A heart shot, she thought vaguely). He was looking at her. His mouth hung open, his teeth were stained with blood; a little blood spilled out onto his lips as he spoke: "She got me, Jack." He said it dully.

"You forced me to do it!" Flame shouted. Her face felt like a hardened mask of ice, and she was sobbing now—with fury and agony and terrible regret. "Oh, God, I hate you, I *hate* you," she whispered through the pain.

Radford answered with a grunt and stretched forward his beastly claw before he fell sideways into the snow. Blood continued to pump out of his pierced heart, dark and thick. In contrast, there was no color in his face. His eyes were wide and glassy. She could only stare at those clawlike fingers, mesmerized. She knew he must be dead, yet they seemed to get closer, closer . . .

There was still enough of the confused young woman from Philadelphia in her to feel that she must somehow be responsible for this whole terrible thing.

She stood abruptly, and in doing so, she jogged Cougar's arm. At the same instant she heard the boom of his rifle once more. Because of her the shot went wild, and in the flick of an eye Jack Goodspeed was among them.

Cougar's rifle was useless now. He reached for his belt-knife, but his snowshoes stuck on something, a twig or a rock buried in the deep snow, causing him to lose his balance and fall backwards.

Flame saw the boy standing over him, swinging his arm back over his shoulder. A knife was in his hand, that thin-bladed, starved-for-blood knife he'd threatened her with so recently. She leaped to grab his arm. He flung her off with a curse, and without a moment's hesitation brought the blade down on her. His eyes seemed to sizzle as they blazed at her.

She felt as if she'd been punched, hard, and her side burned. She found herself looking up at the arc of the clouded sky. She felt sick and full of burning.

There was a horrible swishing sound, and then a sound like wood thunking against the side of a ripe pumpkin. Cougar had hit the boy with the butt of his rifle. Jack was still standing, but he dropped his knife hand as he swung drunkenly to face his attacker. Cougar clubbed the side of his head once more. *Thunk*. Now the knife slipped from Jack's fingers and was lost in the snow.

Flame tried to sit up, but the pain in her side was too great. There was a tremendous roar in her ears, like the growl of a rain-engorged stream.

Like the end of the world.

Now Jack was on his knees. She heard him pleading, "Don't hit me—don't kill me!"

"Cougar?" she said in a small, dry, seed-hull of a voice. She still couldn't seem to rise up from where she was lying. Her hair had fallen back across the snow, and her robe was twisted askance. Her dress was stuck to her side, sodden with gore. She could feel the blood soaking down under her back.

Dragging the boy up by his collar, Cougar flung him down again.

"Tell him I'm hurt!" Jack whimpered, scrambling on his hands and knees to lean over Flame. His breath carried the strong scent of belly-staled whiskey. "Tell him not to kill me! Please, Miss Flame, tell him not to hit me again!"

She mumbled, "He let you go once, but you came back . . ." She couldn't begin to describe her feelings anymore. She'd killed a man, and now wanted to see another die.

"You're injured!" Cougar exclaimed.

Jack began to cry. "It was Bohn's idea. He wanted you real bad. You're a pretty woman. And white. You know how it is. You won't let him kill me, will you?" He begged the favor with tears and a tombstone grin. "Why, I'm just a kid; I'm only nineteen." He tried harder to smile; he looked pathetic in his desperation. Yet Flame saw his eyes flick restlessly for some weapon, and his hands were searching the snow for his knife.

335

Cougar said, "You're the gutsiest pup I've ever met. Now *get up!*"

"No—Miss Flame!"

She turned her face away from his pitiful expression. She would live through this, she told herself. Yet when it was over she would be young no more. She knew it, and her heart ached peculiarly within her.

"You'll suffer if you let him do this! As certain as winter!"

" 'Tis no' her decision—and this time I will put an end to you, though the heavens cave in," he finished dreadfully. His face was like some carved, cruel titan's face, heavy and powerful. "Now get up!"

He dragged the boy a little way off down the timbered slope. The last Flame saw of him, Jack was blubbering, chewing at his lips to stop himself.

Cougar used his rifle. She heard the shot, saw the butt jump back against his shoulder and gunsmoke whiff away.

## Chapter Twenty-two

Cougar turned, fastened haggard eyes on Flame, and came back to her side. (He limped badly, holding his knee; he must have twisted it earlier, when he fell.) His anger had been quick, hot, and violent; but she saw that he'd taken no pleasure in what he'd just had to do. His face seemed sorry for everything as his big hands hovered, uncertain, over her.

"What can I do for you, my fancy? How can I help you? How bad are you?"

"Not bad, I don't think." She was pale and her eyes were big and underscored in blue. She watched his face intently as he opened her robe and examined her side. He betrayed no emotion; only the tiny movement of his jaw muscle warned her.

He shrugged off his wool capote, cut a wide strip from the bottom of it, and eased it beneath her waist. He put a pad of the material over her wound, then twisted the bandage tight. She wanted to thank him, but for the moment she couldn't speak; she could only look at him in trust and suffering, like an animal. With his eyes riveted on his handiwork, he held out one hand, groped for hers, took it.

She made a supreme effort and managed to sa
"I'm not going to die." Despite her words, she foun
herself clasping his fingers as though her life de
pended on his steady answering grasp.

He sat back on his heels, still holding her hand, t
which he gave a squeeze. He reached to cup her fac
and smiled his soul-sundering smile. "Aye and
should no' think so." His manner was especiall
hearty. "You'll need some time to recuperate, bu
soon you'll be back bestride your broomstick."

When he lifted her, the world slid sickeningl
sideways. She felt a landslide of tumbling sensation
Her legs swung loosely, and her long yellow hai
streamed over his arm like a flag. She glimpsed
little of her own blood, a stain of brittle red color, a
red as danger, soaking into the white snow where sh
had lain.

He carried her down the silvered slope to th
flattened and ruined shelter, laid her atop the thic
hides, covered her with robes, and paused to strok
her head, to call her loving names—lark, lamb
pretty—then, ignoring his own injured knee, he se
about building a fire near her and dragging th
bodies of Radford and Bohn out of her sight.

She felt herself failing. The cold was seeping int
her like a fluid. When he bent over her next, sh
clutched his arm with what strength remained to her
"I wouldn't leave you this way."

He was still smiling at her in that heartening
manner. "I ken you would no'; there's too much
loving ahead of us yet. 'Tis no' spring yet anyway.'
He knelt by her.

She raised an arm, put it around his neck
brought his face down and kissed his mouth gently.

"Nae now, you must lie that still." He touched her
forehead lightly with the tips of his fingers—and no

338

doubt felt the chill of her skin.

Her eyes were blurring. Perhaps the dawn light was playing tricks with the snow. "I care for you, you know. I've never said so, but I do."

"You've said it, many a time; you just did no' hear yourself as I did."

That was what Dark Sun had said: *"I hear Flame; she speaks in silence."*

He left her lying there, her head pillowed on his cougar-skin hat.

By now the air was full of the fragile white frost of dawn, causing an uncanny glow. The eastern clouds were swollen with light, ready to declare the new day, while the west was yet purple with storm and night. For the moment everything stood out in sharp prominence. There was something in the air, making every sound, every shape etch itself deeply in her mind: the high glistening crowns of trees; the snow sky; the forest shadows of amethyst and blue. When Cougar looked at her from across the fire, the gleam of the blaze shone on his face. The light was suddenly so dazzling that she could hardly see him through it — only his eyes, which were for once a bright green, an extraordinary green. It was almost unnatural. Then she thought she saw a rippling of bright muscles, like a cat's, and the rose barbs of bright paws, a numenous tawny incarnation . . .

It was Cougar's familiar voice, however, that said, "I think what you need is a drink to help you rest better." He came to hold her head while he put the silver flask to her lips.

She took a sip, and at his urging, took a second, then a third. She felt the liquid choke off the air from her head, and it soon enough clouded her thoughts further. The situation became so unreal in her mind she could scarcely believe it. Especially

when the whiskey dulled the pain in her side. "Cou
gar . . . tell me . . ."

"Shh . . . breathe softly, softly now, my love."

"But . . . do you care for me?" She gripped hi
hand with ice-cold fingers. The pain was mountin
again, and she had to struggled against it. "Tell m
you do, even if it's not true."

He smoothed his hand back from her forehead
"Ah, but 'tis true. How could I no' care for
woman with eyes clear as dew on blue columbines —
dewdrop gems, those eyes. And hair of light yellov
corn tassles; and red lips that taste like woodber
ries," he murmured.

Deep inside herself she wept with terrible disap
pointment. A deep, waxy chill splayed through her
body. The wound under her ribs throbbed and grew
more painful, slim and lacerating and penetrating
ever deeper. This time when he pressed his silver
flask to her lips the pain didn't ebb, but lay like a
long metal spearhead embedded in her flesh.

He said in a whisper, "Stay." That simple plea held
all the gentleness of which he was capable. "Please
stay, stay with me, my fragile Flame; you hold the
whole heart of me in your hands, you ken. Stay, and
I will make amends, apologies of caresses . . . Tenacity, tenacity is all I ask of you now. Stay . . ."

But he was struggling to hold open a restive gate.
Already her look ignored his existence. She gazed at
him without really seeing, no longer even agonized
by the pain in her side. "Sleepy," she murmured, or
meant to. She felt something move inside her, a
fluttering behind her eyes, like the wings of a moth.
Her vision grayed; she was in a mist which gradually
thickened and blotted out all sight and noise. It
wrapped and protected her, and she went into it

willingly, for it was safe there, and she was so weary of this mighty landscape that had no fenced niceness.

"Oh heart! *heart!*"

It was a piercing cry, with a peculiar lost-soul sound; it flashed upon her mind the instant before she lost all consciousness.


The stars gave out little light. It was cold, still, wintry. The coarse snow was frozen dry. The day had thawed, the night had brought a new freeze, and now Cougar had a crust to tramp on. He gave half his hearing to the squeaking sound of his snowshoes crunching out the limping rhythm he'd kept up since noon. The other half he gave to the travois sliding along with a steady scraping noise at his heels.

He'd waited until noon to move Flame, for he'd wanted her wound to have a chance to close up. When the bleeding finally stopped, he'd eased her onto one of the travois. (How light she was! How terribly vulnerable with her sleep-softened face, a fragile thing of flesh, bone, and flowing blood, barely burning with life.) Then, with a single parfleche of dried meat on his back, he took the poles of the travois up into his own hands. He knew he could make better time pulling her himself, without the added drag of the horses to be led.

He'd hated letting the horses go—poor Irongray and little Spot (daft name for a horse, that; 'twas a name for a dog)—but it couldn't be helped.

His head was a little light with fatigue now, even though he was trying to pace himself. His eyes glinted upwards under their brows. The constellations said it was about midnight. At this rate, and allowing himself no more than a few hours sleep

during the darkest hours of each night, he figured h
could make Rotten Gut's village in four days.

Always before when traveling he'd taken pride i
his power to keep his head, no matter the ever
changing beat of the terrain, no matter the weather
He'd been struggling along now for twelve hours
but he felt no pride in that—only a belly-clenching
urge for more miles.

Skirting an overhanging rock, he heard a pack o
timber wolves ahead. When he topped the ridge, h
saw the first of them. They had slain some smal
animal and were yapping and fighting over th
carcass. They were terribly hungry, for they were
growling and snapping, primed to kill even each
other.

He saw, too, how big they were, and for the
moment he was glad Flame was unconscious. Sh
would be frightened, though likely she would try no
to show it. Yet there would be that certain uneasiness in her sea-blue eyes to give her away.

He didn't moderate his pace but continued moving
steadily forward, the travois skidding behind him.
He knew of no attack against man by these western
wolves. He'd been followed by them on occasion.
They'd trotted after him for days and nights at a
time, and when he slept they'd stolen up close to see
if he had anything they could eat. But that was all.
Still, hunger, if violent enough, might force them to
attack. Hunger had made more heroes than courage
ever had. If they smelled the fresh blood of Flame's
wound . . .

He kept on toward them. Maybe he should be
more cautious; he wasn't sure. All he was truly
certain of was Flame's time clicking away, seemingly
faster than the tread of his feet.

When the wolves saw him, they stopped their

quarreling. The remains of the small carcass lay among them, temporarily forgotten. At least thirty eyes (the abandon in those eyes!) watched him as he came on. The air cracked like sheet-ice; the stars froze.

They began to warn him with growls and snappings, their spines steadily arching higher. Both male and female showed fangs over two inches long and jaws powerful enough to splinter the fresh shoulder bones of an elk.

The leader of the pack crouched her long gaunt body low and moved forward, unhurrying, her silvery fur bristling. Cougar caught a glimpse of four needle-like teeth. His muscles tightened slightly when she growled at him. She hunkered down further, and snarled, and exposed a few more of her lethal fangs. All the others moved up and formed a half-circle with her. But Cougar came surely on.

They were all showing their teeth and hunching. Their eyes were like black pearls in the snowlight, with irises that flashed pale green. Cougar neither slowed nor turned aside. Their heads bent low, thrust out, they breathed shallowly in the dark. He came on.

He passed the wet bones of a long-legged hare. The wolves had stripped them clean. Even the hide had been eaten. It was then that he loosed his only parfleche of food, dropped it, and trudged on.

The wolves watched him disappear over the next ridge, then, with a scuffle of paws, they pounced on the tightly-tied envelope of rawhide, losing interest immediately in the brave, if foolhardy, man who had walked among them, dragging his odd burden behind. Later, when he was already gone and it was too late, their splintery eyes looked about for something else to kill.

The darkness had dissolved into grayness. Though it must be eight o'clock in the morning, there was only a hint of daylight. This new snowfall was fast covering the crust. Cougar shook some of the snow off his caked head absentmindedly. He blinked often, yet still the flakes kept piling up on his frozen eyelashes. Small drifts of it were quickly covering everything. Snow on snow.

He listened attentively, as though to the wind. The wind seemed to utter something, again and again, in a husky whisper; he could not quite decipher it.

Behind him Flame lay strapped on the travois as silent as the snow. Flakes swirled over her in high chimneys of wind; they filled the trail made by the travois and Cougar's snowshoes, and they lay like sprinkled pollen on the robes covering her. They compacted under Cougar's feet so that his steps now made a hollow sound near her head. Big flakes crowded down like diaphanous curtains, shutting the two of them off from everything.


The cold wind was cutting through Cougar's bones. The air was almost too cold to inhale. Even walking steadily didn't prevent the penetrating cold from crystallizing in every sinew. He rebuffed it as best he could, yet he almost didn't know who he was anymore. He'd become remote and dim to his own senses. How long had he been traveling? He didn't know. He'd walked on ice crusts and he'd waded in soft snow, knee deep. Now he observed his feet dully, with a blind-eyed stare. Each step felt like something done, like one more chore put behind him and one less lying ahead. A blinding white sky arched over the silver trees on either side of him. The day crackled. Suddenly through a rent in the clouds a single shaft of powdery sunlight stabbed down. Looking ahead through the haze, he saw a misty rainbow curve over the steep face of a stone barrier.

Stone, his mind registered. That meant he would have to make a detour. He would go up through those runty trees. He stumbled slightly, his knee slipped painfully as he changed direction and began to climb.

He topped the shoulder and looked down . . . swaying a little. He felt a lackluster disappointment. Not this valley. Maybe the next one . . . or the next. He must keep going; he would not bury his hopes and affection on this windy hillside. No, he would not.


The brush walls, built around the winter lodges as weather fences, were covered with snow; they gave the village a humped and mounded appearance. The wind blew cold across this scene, a scour of reality, scraping optimism from the face of the land.

Several of the villagers had wakened at the first sound of the dogs and now were standing in the dark, quiet and anxious, their faces turned toward the silent limping man and the travois he was dragging.

Who is this? they murmured. Who has walked down out of the eternal wind, out of the embrace of death? He seemed a specter to them; he had the face of one who had looked the wind in the eyes; he had seen things that few see and live through, and he was changed. Thus, when he dragged himself into the Salish village following his terrible walk through the blizzard kingdoms of the mountains, with the body of his woman on a travois wrapped in ice, the first Indians looked hard at his desolate face and said, "Who are you?"

They didn't recognize this terrible-looking whiskered man who had just walked into their village off the mountainside. They asked again, "Who are you?" And the terrible whiskered man said, very quietly, "I am called the Waiting Cougar."

He put the poles of the travois down at last before the large central lodge, and stooped to untie and lift Flame's robe-wrapped body. Someone asked softly, "The spirit woman?"

"Aye," he answered gruffly.

The village dogs watched, sitting around in a circle, their tongues hanging out pink and wet. More people came out of their tepees, and every face wore an expression of concern. The silence was broken only by clucking sounds of compassion.

Another voice called, and Cougar responded: "Aye, she's alive."

He carried her through the doorflap, stepped to the low-burning fire, and stood in the center of the tall lodge. Lone Goose and Rotten Gut stared up at him from their pallets. At a sign from her father, the girl quickly rose and moved to put fresh furs down for a temporary bed. Cougar laid Flame down on it.

Her face was alabaster and lifeless. Rotten Gut bent over her, drew back the robes. He loosened her bandages, stared at the wound, then called for some balsam sap to fill it. When he gently covered her again, he looked at Cougar. He didn't speak, but his eyes had gone terrible. Cougar couldn't meet them.

"She is so young," the old man murmured.

"Aye, well, you're to blame." Cougar's anger flared up, then waned as quickly. "And I'm to

346

blame."

His shoulders sagged wearily as he sank beside her pallet. Lone Goose petted his cheek with a slender bronzed hand. "I will sit with the white woman. You go to my bed. You need sleep."

"Nae," he said. But he did accept a large chunk of roasted moose. He hadn't eaten in four days, and by the time his hunger was appeased, there was nothing left but bone. After a while he slept, too, huddled there beside Flame's pallet.

Rotten Gut's hand, so grisly and old, lay over Flame's with what he hoped was a light kind of comfort. The chief, white-haired, bent, dozing half of each day away against his willow backrest, knew he was very near to leaving the world himself. He felt very peaceful, frail, gentle. He didn't fear his departure, nor the things that might be waiting for him beyond. He hoped that this, too, was a comfort to Flame. Perhaps her fever allowed her brief moments of semi-lucidity, and at such times she might be glad to sense an old Indian propped near her, his hair so wispy-white and thin. If she was going to die, it might be a comfort to her to know that she would soon have a friendly companion to share her journey.

She was not dead yet, though. No. Rotten Gut sensed that she was suspended between life and death in some unfamiliar way. However, she was dwindled down to a tiny tongue of fire. Did she feel herself flickering, flickering, ever threatening to pull free of the wick?

Despite her grave illness and injury, Rotten Gut was equally worried about the Cougar: His face was too emotionless, or too full of good cheer, or too full of self-blame. Always his eyes were burning, and he held himself very carefully, liked cracked pottery. The Waiting Cougar, Rotten Gut knew, would not fare well if his spirit woman were to leave him just now.

As usual, his intuition was strong and right. Cougar was not faring well, not at all. As near as Flame was to death, that near was he to madness. All through the remaining days of snowy January he seldom moved out of the small lodge Rotten Gut had provided for them. He squatted on the buffalo skin rug next to Flame day and night, wiping her brow, holding a cup to her lips, or just sitting and watching her.

He suffered thus into the month of February, as the river by the village suffered to break through its ice into a run. In a brief moment outdoors he squatted at the edge of the dashing, swirling water. He dabbled his hand in it. It's ice-coldness felt pure and clear, like the ice that clung to the boulders in its midstream. When he pulled his fingers back they were stiff.

He remembered then another river, a strath in Scotland, and his boyhood explorations of gentler more familiar wilderness, his very own moors and woodlands. Those sweet days glistened back in the distance like dreams of summer dawns. They were breaking through the ice in his heart, along with something that wanted to live free once more, wanted to send down roots and form buds and bloom once again.


Flame's hand was the first thing to come back to life fully. Her hand in Cougar's. She was still mostly blind and deaf and mute, but she could distinctly feel his forefinger caressing her wrist.

She had long imagined herself lying on an ember, but now discovered, without opening her eyes, that she was enveloped between furs, her body wet with perspiration.

"If I could only prod you from this sleep, my mourning dove." Along with the words, Cougar was trying to spoon something into her mouth. It tasted vile.

She wanted to awaken, she really did. She'd dreamed so long a dream, and come so near to death in the dark . . . "Wh-what is that?" she said, and was shocked at the hoarseness of her voice.

From under the first flutter of her eyelashes, she saw him freeze, and then saw his lips twitch with a sickly grin of relief. " 'Tis a decoction of choke-cherry twigs — for fever . . . and it must be effective, for here you be, awake."

"No thanks to you . . . ladling horrible stuff down my throat when all I've wanted . . . was water . . . gallons of cold water."

She thought vaguely that he had probably saved her by his constant care, yet with the taste of his vile medicine still on her tongue, she felt irritable.

He laughed. "Lucky for you I did no' spoon calomel into you — as they do routinely at the trading posts — and added another terror to your sufferings."

Suddenly she was glad beyond bearing to see his smile. Her slow eyes saw past his nonchalance to the lines of stress and the way his cheekbones now angled his once full face and how his wide shoulders were bent.

"Cougar," she said softly.

She thought she recalled now a familiar but drawn face hanging above her these past . . . days? . . . weeks? How long had she struggled in that place

349

dark as a hole? However long it had been, somehow she knew that he'd been with her, he'd encouraged her, comforted her, pulled her up out of it. As her mind cleared further, she remembered days of painful movement, which she had resented at the time, and had blamed him for. That willful journey of his must have saved her life. He'd got her to this clean tepee, this warm fireside, this safety. And she was going to get better now, soon it would be finished.

Grateful as she was, she didn't have the strength for any great show of emotion; she only stared up at him as the tears slid down across her temples. "When did you last eat?" was her only question.

He shrugged. " 'Tis no matter."

Kneeling beside her, he looked phantasmal, too good to be true. With more effort than such a simple action should have required, she raised her hand, put a finger on his cheek, and slid it to his mouth. When he took her in his arms, she clung to him and moved her lips against his throat. The mountains receded and left one tepee standing in the pale winter daylight, lit by love.

Then she saw Lone Goose. Shaken, she drew back, breathing fast from her exertion. The girl was standing in shadow, a dark silhouette against the lighter tepee walls. She held a bowl in her hands. As if only now remembering her presence himself, Cougar turned and handed her the wooden spoon he'd been urging Flame to drink from.

"You health returns, Flame." Lone Goose said in her clear, pretty voice. She was smiling at her a bit sheepishly. "This is good. My father will be very happy to hear it."

Flame tried to sit up.

"You'll be making no stir now!" Cougar commanded harshly.

350

She stared beyond him at the girl, at the serene line of her mouth and the curve of her cheek. Her dark hair dangled to her waist in a plait as thick as Cougar's wrist. When she stepped forward, Flame knew she'd never seen a young woman hold herself so well. But Flame remembered also what she'd seen in Lone Goose's eyes last autumn. And she remembered that she'd sent her cousin to kill "the spirit woman." Again she tried to sit up.

"Have a care, wife!" Cougar said in a parade-ground voice. "Go on like this and I might have to strap you down." His deep gray eyes shone with resolve, with hard masculine intention. Then he softened. "Heart, my heart, but you're a foolish one."

*Chapter Twenty-three*

Flame had no choice but to stay where Cougar demanded, for she was frail as withered branches. Outside spring was about to unfold any minute. The enduring crags were about to rise out of their receding layers of white, and the heavy frosting on the fir trees was about to shrink and fall so that their dropping limbs could spring up to their normal symetry, ready for the new season of life; but inside her tepee, Flame was still weak. Just being alive, however, filled her with awe, left her open-eyed and reverent. She did all she was urged to do: rested, ate, drank, rested again. And after eight dreary days of this, Cougar let her have a taste of daylight; she was allowed to sit in the tepee door for an hour during the warmest part of the day. Here she listened to the earliest of the returning birds who were shattering the silence of winter with song. And gradually the prospect of being strong and really well once more became a reality.

The afternoon came when she was able to persuade Cougar to let her take a walk. She felt lonesome and hungry for the sight of human beings. "I'm no' sure about this. Mayhap you'd best stay in for another day, fancy," he said thoughtfully, pausing as he helped her tie her leggings.

She pulled a face at him and lifted her foot to continue dressing herself. Leaning forward to where he was squatting before her, she ruffled his hair affectionately, to let him know that his second thoughts were in vain; she was leaving this tepee today. She'd recovered and she was going out. The pallet, the immobility, the grizzled chief who came to visit — those were done with. She was eager to fill her lungs with fresh air. Life had somehow endured in her, was somehow renewed, and she was going to rejoice, she was going to let the sun melt away whatever last traces of sooty blackness still lingered in those drifts at the edges of her mind.

Yet only moments after leaving the tepee she murmured in a threadlike voice, "I must look awful." She felt self-conscious under the stares that met her everywhere. Braves with feathers in their glossy hair and women in scarlet blankets all stopped what they were doing to stare at her.

Cougar gave her a knowing look. Her hand was on Cougar's arm and he was leading her through the concentric circle of tepees to the edge of the village. "You're a trifle thin mayhap, and there are those bruises under your eyes . . . but to me you're that lovely. Aye, I still have a stunning piece of porcelain for a wife."

He'd set himself out to be as charming as possible to her, and she knew he was being gallant in not mentioning her slow, trembling steps. She was discouraged to find herself so frustratingly weak, and was grateful when he stopped at the edge of the village, ostensibly to watch the light distill into a water of gold as the evening sun dropped.

A pair of children, toy bows dangling at their shoulders, ran up to tug at Cougar's sleeve. He gave them a flashing smile. He was popular with the children; she'd noticed it before. Probably because he wasn't affected and mannered the way most people were. He didn't fuss over them, was perfectly direct and spontaneous. They seemed to love him. As he hunkered down now, they were right at his knees, adoring him.

A sudden desire to present him with a child of his own welled up in her.

But no. She reminded herself that she wouldn't be with him that much longer. And he wouldn't be pleased anyway. Hadn't he insisted on being very careful about keeping her from conceiving?

Yet, she found the idea didn't fade with reasoning. Perhaps because it was a personal wish. Perhaps it wasn't him she wanted to please. Perhaps what she really wanted was to carry something of him away with her. Once she left him, she would have so long to live without him, possibly even forgetting what he looked like in time, the image of him in her mind's eye getting dimmer and dimmer until he was only a mythical being she couldn't picture at all.

If she had his child, however . . .

She realized instantly that a baby could not make a difference in the way she was bound to suffer. Nothing would make that any easier. A child wouldn't change it at all. She would feel his absence in her life just as much, no matter what. No, her love for his child would grow separately, a lovely but different emotion alongside the feelings she had for its father. Her love for Cougar—and her grief when she lost him—she would live with always, all her days. And she wouldn't want it otherwise.

She shivered in the first flutter of the night's wind. He saw it and stood. "Time for you to have your supper and get back to your bed."

"Will you share it with me tonight—my bed, I mean?" she murmured shyly.

He smiled, and she was aware of his scrutiny. "Well now," he said, drawing a long comfortable breath, "let me just think: I suppose you've been a reasonably tractable patient; you feed well and have been sleeping tolerably. Aye, all and all, you've been a fair patient. I suppose you deserve some reward." His grin widened. "I'll lie with you, and hold you close, that willingly. I've missed you. But remember, you be a sick one, just getting back your strength from a hole in your side. You must promise no' to tempt me further than just cuddling a bit."

"Must I?" she said impishly.

A little while later she lay watching the propped tent of split wood burning in the fire ring. The dew-cloth lining of the tepee was running with light and shadows; the lodge was alive with crackling pine and sweet smoke. Flame was learning to appreciate these ingenious conical tents. They stood firm against the wind, were well ventilated, yet warm and draft free. The air inside was so quiet just now that the fire smoke climbed straight as a stem to the open flaps provided for it. She heard the fire murmuring at the wood, and once in a while the sound of a passing dog, but that was all.

She and Cougar had eaten. She was still allowed little else but cracked corn soaked in clear water and roasted in ashes, but even that had tasted good.

Rations were lean in the village at this time of

year. Early spring was a difficult time, since the buffalo had moved out onto the plains and couldn't yet be followed because of the snow. Dog meat was abundant, and she'd been encouraged to eat it by Rotten Gut, for it was highly esteemed as a restorative for invalids, but she hadn't ever learned to get it down. Therefore, Cougar ate all the dog meat dishes Lone Goose brought them. He claimed it resembled beaver, which he liked. "Anyway, 'tis far superior to the diet of horse I was on once," he said.

Lying in his arm, she mentioned, "I haven't seen anything of Lone Goose for several days."

He chuckled, "Nae, and because of Two-Edged-Knife's attempts to pull her off by herself. Rotten Gut watches her all the day, and as soon as supper's over, he sends her to her bed."

Flame recalled the alarming scene she'd witnessed between Lone Goose and Two-Edged-Knife last autumn. She remembered the warrior as being strong and ferocious and frightening. Lone Goose must be terrified of him. "I take it she's given up her notions about me being a threat to you?"

"Aye, Dark Sun had a stern talk with her after he visited us. I think she's put away her foolish notions."

"I hope so. She's a lovely girl, isn't she?"

"She's that."

Flame stiffened and added crisply, "But very young — not much more than a papoose really. Certainly too young for grown men to be pulling her about."

"Nae; according to her people's ways she's fair old enough to make a man a fine ripe wife, a fine soft wife." As he said this his fingers were stroking the upper slopes of Flame's breasts.

She said nothing. Jealousy was running like fire

through her veins. She was discovering that she didn't like to hear him even speak about another woman.

"Tired, my sweet?" He was still fondling.

"Very." She put all the chill she could muster in that one word.

"Aye, I thought so. A good night to you then." She was taken by surprise. All evening he'd been silenter than usual, cajoling her into bed earlier ordinary, and now coaxing her off to sleep so abruptly. She worried about it a little before she drifted off.

She'd fallen deep into her dreams when she was awakened by the sound of someone screaming. She opened her eyes to find Cougar's side of the bed empty. It added to her disorientation and alarm to find him dressed and peering out the lodge door, shaking his head in disgust. She was sure she heard him mutter a curse, and something that sounded like: "What a cack-handed lad that one is!"

"Who is? What's going on?" She rose and pulled on her dress.

There were more yells — an old man's now — as she joined him at the door. She definitely heard him curse this time, not loud, but evidently with deep feeling.

When he went out — reluctantly, she thought — she followed him. A little bit of moon had come up, though hardly enough to give out any light. Rotten Gut's tepee was next to theirs. Out of it burst a man — at least it was the shape of a man. He was entirely naked except for white stripes painted all over his body. He seemed to hesitate at the sight of Cougar.

Flame heard Rotten Gut yell again, in fury it seemed, and the painted man tore away between the

357

tepees. Other people were running out of their homes all over the encampment now, with lances, bows, tomahawks . . . everybody shouting. Yet the sight of the painted man was so astonishing that they all shrank into their blankets out of his way, allowing him to escape into the woods with only a shuffle of spruce needles to mark his final disappearance.

"What is this all about?" Flame asked Cougar again, tugging at the fringe of his sleeve. Unsatisfied with his shrug, she started past him, moving closer to Rotten Gut's tepee on her own. He followed at an unperturbed pace.

The old shaman was surrounded by people and was speaking and gesturing more rapidly than Flame would have believed possible for a man of his age. His normally impassive face was hard with excitement. Lone Goose stood behind him, her head lowered and her eyes downcast, as if in modesty.

"Dark Sun," Flame said, spying the war chief nearby, "what is happening."

His eyes were stretched with watchfulness. "Something tried to spirit away my little cousin. A white and black spirit. It cut the tied rawhide thongs of the lodge door and crept in. My cousin awoke to find it over her. It tried to lift her, to carry her off, but she cried out. My uncle awoke and yelled. The spirit ran away." He didn't seem to be affected by the general attitude of astonishment around him. He was leaning on his lance, his expression calm though watchful; his eyes slowly shifted to Cougar. "Did you see anything?"

"I saw something," Cougar said brusquely, irritably.

"So did I," said Flame, "but it was only a—"

"I'd best get you back inside," Cougar interrupted

358

with a hard squeeze of his hand on her shoulder. " 'Tis too chill out here for the likes of you. And barefoot you are!" He swung her up into his arms.

On the way to their tepee, she said, "But Cougar, that was no spirit."

"Was it no'?"

"Of course it wasn't—you know it wasn't!"

"It appeared to be."

"Oh, Cougar!"

"Have you no' learned, love, that you're always fooled—'tis no' what you prepare for that awaits you."

"But—be reasonable now—what did that man want, what was he up to?"

He raised his eyebrows in exaggerated innocence as he put her on her feet within their lodge and started to strip her dress over her head. "Who can say? Mayhap 'twas a deed without a name." He suddenly chuckled. "But did you see Rotten Gut? Who would have believed the old man to have so much blood left in him?"


It was deep dusk a chaste week later. Outside, the world was a dark blue. Light raindrops had drenched the village all afternoon. The trees looked like quenched torches in the dark. Occasionally, the moisture found its way through the smoke hole to sizzle in the fire burning low in Flame's tepee.

She generally felt well enough now, though she still weakened easily. Sometimes a tremor would shin through her, vicious and uncontrollable, to be put down neither by grit nor self-reproach. At those times she simply had to rest.

She was with Cougar tonight, her head on his shoulder as they sat staring into the fire. He smelled of soaproot and clean ice melt, for he followed the Indian custom of river bathing regularly, even in cold water, even in March.

They were talking aimlessly, going from this subject to that to something else. "Remember apples?" she said musingly. Her mouth watered just to recall the crispness and fragrance and juice bursting under her tongue as she sank her teeth into one. Acorns, pine nuts, chestnuts, serviceberries, thimbleberries, chokecherries, big yellow currants, wild plums— none could satisfy like a single ripe red apple. If only she had one now.

Well, it wouldn't be long.

She decided that this was as good as time as any to broach the subject that haunted her. Lifting her eyelashes, she began: "You know I must leave you soon." She had wondered if her nerve would hold, and now was conscious of an almost fanatical determination to have this over and done with, as quickly as possible.

"Must you?" There was an odd quality in his voice, as if he'd expected this and prepared himself for it. His smile was so slight as to be a reproof. There was something astringintly shocking about it, too, like the slap of a cold, salt wave.

He had seemed somehow different since her recovery. Sometimes he'd been almost tentative with her. Now she sensed that that had only been in consideration of her health.

He looked down at her and his gray eyes stabbed her with their sudden intensity. "You're still no' completely well. We'll discuss it when you are."

"But . . . I told you I'd have to leave as soon as the winter was over."

*As soon as the winter is over.* It was a repellent refrain, as ugly as: *And she never heard of him again.*

"I thought we'd agreed . . . I can't live here, Cougar. This is no place for someone like me." It was a half-mad world where nothing was safe, nothing was sure, where anything could happen. She was wearied and discouraged by it. Her casual optimism had pushed up obstinately again and again, but now, like a flower plucked over and over, it was gone. "I belong in Philadephia, where — where I'll never have to kill a man, or condone the killing of a boy in order to survive."

"You must no' think of that; we must start all over fresh and forget that."

*"Forget it! I have killed a man!"*

"Aye, forget it," he said sharply, "and forget Philadephia, for you'll no' be going back there."

"But . . . but you must let me go," she whispered.

His chest swelled with his emotions and unwittingly revealed him. With deceptive unconcern, he turned to unlace her dress. "You're that impatient to be gone?" There was an undercurrent in his voice. "Indeed, my good wife? You think to leave me, but do you think I'll permit it?" He was pushing her dress off her shoulders, tugging it down to her waist, exposing her breasts.

"I must — I have to!" she said, struggling now against his busy hands, which seemed dangerously intent all of a sudden.

"Nae, I find I can no' allow it after all. You're meant to be my wife, and I'll husband you for as long as my strength is greater than yours. You'll remain with me, do you hear?"

He suddenly put aside all pretence of good temper and gave her a little shake. "Do you hear? Bring up out of that profound, considering mind of yours all that you've discovered about me. Look at me! Do

361

you see a lap-cat with claws that have been clipped? Do you see a man who has yielded to the thongs and knife of the gelder? Will I let you go, my brave Flame, now . . . or ever?"

As his head descended to her breasts, she lifted her hands in horror. "No! Cougar, don't, I don't *want* — "

"What you want and what you get in this life are oft' two different things!"

He pushed her back onto the furs of their pallet with firm purpose. Though his strength was controlled, he seemed so near to some truly violent outburst that she was afraid of him.

"Not now! Not like this!" She fought against his hands that were tugging her dress down her legs. When it was completely off her, she kicked at him and tried to scramble away. He caught her and lapsed into Gaellic for what she knew wouldn't be fit for a lady to hear in English.

It wasn't hard for him to capture her hands and lay heavily over her, pinning her beneath him. She stopped fighting and lay staring up at him, her eyes hot with outrage.

He sighed now, and visibly tamped down his fierceness. "Do no' make me force you," he said, and added more kindly, "Come, heart, open your delicate blossom. 'Tis no use, this — 'twill do you no good."

He was right, of course. What would defiance accomplish? She was helpless. They both knew she was.

With a breath-stealing lurch of heart, she willed herself to relax into the furs, opening herself as he wanted. "All right, go ahead, do it. This will make leaving you easier. It will be so much easier if I can hate you."

His hands left her wrists, slid down her arms to her shoulders, down the curve of her ribs, and closed over the roundness of her buttocks.

But then he gave a wordless cry and sprang to his feet.

She rolled onto her side in relief, her face hidden in her arms; she lay slumped and broken, as though dropped from a great height.

After a long moment she felt him kneeling beside her again. His fingers tightened about her wrist and pulled it away from her face so that she was forced to look at him. "Hearken, Flame: You belong with me. You can no' take yourself away from me."

"You can't keep me . . . you can't, Cougar. I won't stay—not a minute more than I have to. I *will* leave you, somehow!"

She was gratified to see how hurt he looked before he strode from the tepee. A man with the eyes of a tortured animal.

Cougar rose early in the icy dawn. He dressed quietly and stood looking down at Flame, who was still fast asleep in the silvery morning darkness.

Watching her, he was transfixed. He regretted last night, deplored what he'd nearly done. His heart squeezed painfully under his ribs to remember it. She deserved better.

Mostly blinded by his passion for her, he'd rarely observed her in a detached way. But now he did, and suddenly he saw her not as the wife so familar him, so sexual and exquisite, whether wearing fur and claws or wearing nothing, but as a woman of twenty-four, brought up within a somber, poor home and catapulted into a terrifying alien world. A world of knives and alcohol and destruction, where white men, seeing her, inevitably whispered single-minded words.

He thought of her small wringing hands overcoming crises that most others of her type would find not only unsurmountable, but unimaginable. He saw her picking herself up from the stones of Fate and making efforts again and again to make peace with her predicament.

He saw her standing up against a grizzly bear ten times her size to save his own life. Any lesser woman would have run sobbing for her own safety.

He thought of her sticking by her agreement with him despite all difficulties, under all conditions, unwaveringly.

He saw her knowing him far too well for his own conceited contemptible comfort. And now, for the first time he realized some of what she must have suffered from the man who had called himself her husband, the man who had claimed to prize her relentlessly, the man who had promised to watch over and protect her in return for her favors.

He had not protected her from anything, least of all from himself.

He bent to kiss her lips lightly, then left the lodge.

Last night's rain had diminished to a gray moistness. He left the village in this ghostly mist, worked his way through wet undergrowth as dense as walls, and climbed to the top of the highest cliff. There he stood, outlined against the sky, a man alone.

The sun was trying to rise behind the thick, wet haze, trying doggedly to open the veins of dawn. He watched for a long moment, then, all of a sudden, threw his arms wide and shouted, "Cougar! Hear me! I cast you out! My terrible brother, I renounce you. You can no' be spirit-twin to me anymore.

"Do you hearken? I release you; I'll no' be afraid

to walk without you; I'll no' be afraid to rejoice without you; I'll no' be afraid to be myself anymore.

"You clawed into my life; you gutted me and made me over, a stronger man. I thank you for that. But now I must walk alone. You can no' live in my belly, in my heart, anymore. I am Colin Roy Craigh, Viscount of Lanark . . . the Drummond!"

He felt drained, so weak he actually staggered. And turning, he saw the cat. It stood fifty feet away on the edge of a rock, observing him, poised elegantly, long and sleek in body. They watched one another for a drawn-out moment, even until the air changed its texture, becoming as explosive as gunpowder. Then the animal moved off, without haste, touching the ground lightly with its big paws as it trotted soundlessly away.

Such dreams Flame had had in the night! And when she woke, immediately the scene between her and Cougar came back, very clear. She was sure something important between them had been destroyed.

Though he hadn't actually done so, he'd meant to take her without care, with force. And it had left her feeling as badly as if he'd reached out and grasped her by the scruff of the neck and given her a violent shake.

She was pulling her dress on when he stooped into the tepee. He was shaved and washed, shining and calm. She knelt on the bedfurs, head lowered, waiting, as if for some kind of blade to fall. When nothing happened, she pushed her hair back from her face with both hands and nerved herself to look at him.

His face was expressionless, but his gray eyes were

shrewd. When they searched hers, she felt herself crumbling. A wave of fear, which she'd denied last night, engulfed her.

The first thing he said was, "I'm that sorry, lassie. I had no idea such a thing could ever happen. I knew the cougar in me had grown jaws and fangs, but I never meant to seize you with them. Nae, never you, never like that, love." He crossed to her, and sat on the edge of the furs. " 'Twas an unequal contest. I must beg your forgiveness."

He drew her to him, and when she resisted, he exerted his easy strength in a way she suddenly found hateful. She found herself in his embrace against her will again. His tone, his smile, the softness in his gray eyes said that he wanted her to forgive him, yet she wasn't able to do that, not when he was forcing her into intimacy again this very moment. "This is what you enjoy most, isn't it?" she said bitterly, "proving that you're stronger than me."

He smiled, without humor, and tipped her face toward his.

"Don't!" She twisted her head away.

He ran his hand in a caress down the length of her hair. His smile faded to soberness. "Are you afraid to even let me kiss you, lassie? Mayhap because a kiss would weaken your anger?"

After that dare, she refused to so much as flinch as his mouth closed over hers.

He took as long as it pleased him over kissing her lips and face, her neck and ears. He pulled her onto his lap and slipped his hand down the front of her dress to use her small breasts and tease the nipples.

She shook with anticipation when his hand stroked her knee and began a slow passage under her dress to fondle her smooth hip above her leggings. Her sighs grew shallow when at last he reached her secret place. Within moments she was quaking in long, drawn-out pleasure. She was drawn slowly, irrevocably, up the lesser slopes to the peak. Her sighing became panting, and then hard gasping, as his sounding fingers eased her over the verge of ecstasy. Her entire body churned in the hold of unimaginable pleasure.

After continuing to touch her for a long while, he allowed her to rest against him, and kissed her as if in gratitude for the pleasure it had given him to watch her abandon. She realized that he was taking an inordinate pride in knowing that he'd conquered her again.

"That was no' too much for you?" he inquired. "No' too much exertion?" He seemed amused because her face flushed a pretty pink.

The rest he allowed her was short. He turned her on his thighs, positioning her so that she faced and straddled him, her dress falling around her bared legs. After a small rearrangement of his clothes, she felt his bold member at the join of her stretched loins. He took her by the hips and urged her downwards, so that she impaled herself on him.

She began to move slowly, her hips swaying backwards and forwards lithly, as if refamiliarizing herself with the snug fit of him. And with her movements ecstasy rose and fell in billows, until she was uttering cries of pleasure. It broke over her as though she were lying on a sea beach and white-capped waves were smashing over her. In the end her breath was driven out of her body and she went dizzy with the violence of it as, with a soft cry, he jabbed quickly upwards into her one last time and found release.

When he lifted her off his lap several minutes later, and sat her beside him, she found herself beyond spoken words. Though her anger was indeed weakened—as he'd predicted—her fear went deeper than ever. She listened as he said with perfect composure, with the composure that comes only with the utmost self-assurance, "Aye, 'tis as I thought. Your body still speaks to me."

# Chapter Twenty-four

"Look at me, lassie. There—that's some improvement, at least." Cougar's mouth was sympathetic, yet his smile, seen close, had a certain desperation. "This pretty head of yours confuses you about life, confuses your own emotions. Your body is no' so addled, though—that I've seen. It knows its own needs and knows enough to satisfy them, simply and honestly."

Wordlessly he handed Flame her comb. But there seemed something about even combing her hair—sitting straight-backed, moving her arms about her head, the delicate shift of her breasts under her dress with each stroke—that was for the moment too suggestive. He was watching her too intently; his mood was too enigmatic; there were too many lights and shadows in his eyes.

When she was finished, he said in the same mild, maddeningly neutral tone he'd been using all along,

"I'll be leaving you for a time, while I see to some unfinished business."

"What business? Where are you going?"

"I'll be back soon." He offered her his hand. "Come, let's walk before the village is all astir. I have a little time left before I go."

Emerging from the tepee, she asked, "What are you up to, Cougar?"

" 'Tis naught for you to worry about."

"You didn't say anything about going off before."

"I'll be gone a few days, mayhap a few weeks—I can no' say offhand." He seemed to relish this mystery.

"You're trying to frighten me. It's because of last night, isn't it? Because of what I said—"

"Last night you said you would leave me—and tear my life tatterdermalion." The very idea seemed to reignite his anger; their unresolved argument seemed about to boil up again. "You've never felt bound to me—but mayhap I can remedy that when I get back. And when I do, you'll be bound to me wherever I go."

She saw that his now so-very-civil manner was a thin disguise for some clearly unrelenting purpose. A light breeze ruffled his hair and emphasized his appeal. She was unnerved. Never had he seemed more in control, more determined. "Cougar, you can't really keep me."

"You think no'? Truly? Well, I've considered, and I see that I have a means. 'Twill take a little time, but I have hands enough to hold you—until you grow docile."

His face was unusally grim and resolute; he'd come to some conclusion and she sensed that learning it would not be a pleasure.

He was guiding her out of the village. The sun

had vanquished the haze; the air was clear and the trees threw stretched shadows. Everything stood out in fine-edged relief. She hadn't been up so early in many weeks and had almost forgotten how fresh and deliciously colored a new day could be.

After the rainy night the hills at the valley's edge were brimming with dark seeps and trickles, all massing along the creases into rushing streams. One of these glittering streams lay beside where they were walking, catching them, and going by, a thread of light and sound. Yet the atmosphere struck damp and dank through her moccasins to the soles of her feet.

The sun's light was cool and watery. In contrast, Cougar's hold on her hand was solid and warm and firm. He'd brought her far enough out from the village so that if she called out, no one was likely to hear her. They were alone again, in this land as vast as solitude.

"Are you sure you even want to try to keep me?" She kept her face averted, seemingly watching the sky-colored brook. In a small voice she added, "Why not let me go while we still feel friendly toward one another?"

"Friendly?"

She felt the hackles rise on the nape of her neck. "All right, just what is this devious means you think you can use to make me 'docile'?"

He looked so blank about the eyes, his jaw was clenched so hard and his mouth was so tight-lipped that she knew that he truly was settled on something. She pulled her hand out of his, stopped and stared at him, for she had to know, of course.

When he didn't speak for a long moment, she felt more certain than ever that what he was about to say would change her feelings for him. Until now he'd been ruthless about everything; why shouldn't she expect more of the same?

"A bairn," he interrupted her thoughts. "I want a bairn from you, after all. I've a thought to see you bloom like a pod-burst leaf in May. A son—or a daughter—that makes no difference. But when you conceive, then you'll have to depend upon me; you'll be bound to me."

She stared on at him, her mind jarred beyond thought. It seemed as if a shutter had clicked open. Was it just yesterday that she herself had considered bearing his child? But put to her this way, as a means of coercion, the idea was totally repellent.

"I'll be counting your days again," he was saying, "but for a different purpose now. I'll love you each night, 'til I'm too exhausted to love you again and want only sleep. I see no reason to waste time; indeed, the sooner the better for we've traveling to do, and 'twill be easier for you in your first months. I want to get you home and set up and all 'afore—"

"Home? What do you mean?"

"Why Scotland, of course."

Her lips parted with shock. If "home" meant Scotland, then "set up" could only mean that he was planning to install her in some cottage convenient to his castle as his mistress!

She tried to remain cool. "I understand that you can't respect me much, but you mean to tell me you would . . . and all by force, I suppose—like last night!" There were tears in her voice, and she already felt damning wet patches under eyes. She didn't want him to know how deeply he'd wounded her, yet her mouth trembled.

He softened. "Nae, no' by force. You know full well I need no' use force on you."

She swallowed back the humiliating memory of

372

what she had let him lead her to only a short time ago. "You think you can drag me across half a continent and the Atlantic Ocean by beguilment and seduction?"

"Once you're carrying the bairn you'll see you must come with me. 'Twill be clear to you."

Her blood called for action. She swung her hand up. Though he must have seen it coming, he didn't move to defend himself. Perhaps he felt she deserved this much retribution.

Yet as soon as her palm connected with his cheek, she was overcome with confusion. She had a brief impression of the well-defined world slipping inexorably out of focus. She wasn't so long out of her sick bed that she didn't still feel the occasional tremor, the occasional faintness. Nevertheless, she raised her hand once more.

But this time, quick as lightning, he caught her wrist. "I think no' again," he said in a voice of flint.

Her heart paused in the crystalline silence. An insistent whisper warned her to go no further; she was in an overstrung, unreliable frame of mind. She wasn't completely recovered yet. Her body was sending her certain sinister warnings, like this sensation of the stable world trying to slide furtively out of control.

"I think you're overwrought."

*"Overwrought?"* Waves of faintness rode over her. "Oh, yes, I daresay! The way you treat me!"

"Flame—"

"I won't! No! I won't have your baby! And I won't follow along behind you to Scotland—never!" A deep horror that was nearly awe had stolen over her. She was shaking her head wildly in an effort to speak through her emotion. "I won't let you touch me! You've always had your way and never mind me and what I might want, and—and . . . I resent it . . ." Suddenly she was so weak she could hardly speak above a whisper. "I *resent* it!"

He was ashen himself. His face was battered with feeling. "Lassie," he said soothingly, "would it be so bad then, to live in Scotland with me and mother my bairns? You've no' been that unhappy with me, have you? You seemed content, at the end, to be the Cougar's winter wife. Can you no' trust the Drumond to mate you as pleasurably?"

Her response was cold, tremulous, still on the verge of rage. "Mother the child of a brutal overlord, a man half-savage animal, half-tyrant?" She felt again, for a blink of a second, that sick, lost dizziness, and her shoulders swayed with it.

He took her arms to steady her and said in a low but flat voice, "You're going back to bed."

"So you can rape me?"

That word affected him. Despite the fact that the whole world was swimming, that her head was full of rocking, sick vertigo, she saw him wince. And she felt his hands tighten on her arms. Even while her fingers clutched his shirt sleeves for support, she cautioned him anxiously, "Keep away from me! If you ever touch me again I'll . . . I'll find some way to injure you!"

Abruptly the world went dove-gray. She felt him swing her up into his arms and turn back toward the village. She was too weak to oppose him, so gave him no trouble as he strode along.

But once inside their tepee, as he put her down on the furs, she found the strength to speak again. "What you plan to do to me is absolutely unforgivable. That you could even *think* it . . ."

He stood over her. His face was ghastly. "You look so distraught, my heart—I do wish you would

374

sleep a while."

"It's vile, the worst possible thing you could . . ." Her voice failed. She turned her face away. Slow tears crept to her eyes.

"You must no' think I'll hurt you. And long 'afore your time comes, I'll see you settled comfortably, with women and servants to help you . . .

"Flame! I'm only doing what I must!" He was kneeling, pulling her up to his chest so fiercely that she cried out with shock. He kissed her hard. "I can no' let you go—I will no', nae, never!"

She stifled the little cry that sounded in her heart. "Please," she pleaded, her voice sodden and choked, "go away. Just go . . . please." Her tears were brimming over; she knew she looked wretched and white.

He laid her back gently and took his arms away. "Aye, 'tis best I do go for now, I think. You'll be sick again, getting this upset." There was a dry, wrenched pain in his voice, as if his throat had tightened. "I wish I could make you see—I only want to keep you. Please, my heart, say you'll never leave me and I'll take your word on it. 'Twill no' be necessary then for me to insist on anything. We could just let the bairns come when they would."

She felt trapped. There was no place to go, no safe place to go—except into his arms. As if to deny this, she turned on him with, "I *will* leave you! You'd better never stop watching me for a moment, for that's the moment I'll be gone! I loathe you now. Do you hear me? I *loathe* you!"

He stiffened and stood. "A woman like you should have a latch on her cage: She bites." He seemed to wait for his anger to pass, for his voice to steady. "If you try to run away, I promise I'll find you. You know I will; you know you've no' the skill to evade me for long."

"I'll find someone to help me—no matter what his price!"

"You would no' risk another's life that way," he answered thinly. He made a fierce little sign with his hands which she interpretted smoothly.

"You wouldn't!"

"Aye? You think no'? Would it be the first time I've killed to keep you to myself? Think of Hosea Reade, of Orangewood, and Bohn. Think of young Jack Goodspeed."

With that he strode from the lodge, without another backward glance.

Cougar found Two-Edged Knife where they had arranged to meet. "You bungled the last one, laddie," he said curtly in English. His mood was sour. He had a burning devil inside him. "A fourteen-year-old stripling could do better."

The Indian said nothing, though he must have understood Cougar's intent, if not his foreign words. He returned the white man's regard unwaveringly, with a kind of cool pride.

" 'Tis a stupid stallion who does no' ken how to kick down a mare's fence." He shifted to the Salish language. "Why did you no' carry her off? You had the chance. The old man could no' have stopped you."

"She cried," the Indian said, as if that explained everything.

"Aye, they cry—at first—but you can no' let that stop you. A woman does no' ken what she wants. 'Tis a man's task to teach her." His face was sardonic and rather gloomy. Why did the words ring so hollowly in his ears? "Well, you'll no' get another

376

chance like that one so we'll just have to try something else."

The old man was singing. Now that Flame understood the Salish language better, she heard snow in his song—sounds as soft and cold as snowflakes—and then there were spring rains, and ducks returning. His voice became the evening wind, high-pitched and whining through the trees. It was a lonely song, and it matched her mood.

Cougar was gone. His gray eyes and slow smiles and knowing ways were gone. At first she'd felt glad; she'd actually hoped to never see him again. But then gradually she realized that she'd never felt so sad and lonesome with him around. Infuriating though he was. Possessive though he meant to be. It was as if all her confidence was gone with him, and all her pride as well, and all her capacity for happiness.

She looked down at the leather-work in her hands. A shirt . . . for him. She'd worked hard tanning the leather yellow. The day of his going she'd found his spare pair of breeches and his best shirt crumpled in one of their parfleches. There were white and black stains on both. The shirt would be unwearable; he would need a new one when he returned.

She knew that Two-Edged Knife was gone from the village, as well. There was a connection to be made between Cougar's stained clothes, Lone Goose's black-and-white striped spirit man, and Two-Edged Knife's courtship of the girl. It had taken Flame all of an hour or so to figure it out, but then it seemed transparently simple.

The exact reason for the two men's absence wasn't quite so transparent, though Flame had no doubts that it, too, had something to do with Lone Goose. It was five days now since they'd gone. No one but Flame seemed to connect their simultaneous disappearance, and she was still amazed by Indian naivete.

Rotten Gut's song ended. In its wake the sounds from the surrounding village were the small sounds of calm. It was early evening. The sun was going down. It was getting chilly, with the light slanting in so horizontally. Too chilly even for the newly hatching mosquitos. A little breeze ran along the ground making Flame draw further into herself.

The haziness of the tender March day had lifted in the changing light, and the view of the river valley stretched with eerie precision before her eyes. To the east, where a hill met the sky, she saw a surge of motion and wondered idly if it could be deer, or perhaps a herd flowing down the slope? No, more like a horse herd, she thought vaguely. Maybe the hunters had found the village some new stock to replace what was stolen last summer. Ordinarily, she would have said something to Rotten Gut and would have drawn his attention to it, but today she was too listless to even think much of it. Without interest, she watched the horses coming up the valley fast, prancing and kicking like colts in the day's coolness.

Meanwhile, the light in the west went out; low on the horizon one star burned faintly. The sounds about the village were still little sounds: a dog giving a halfhearted bark now and again; children's cries of delight coming to color the evening a little. Flame supposed she ought to go to her own tepee.

During the first days of Cougar's absence, Dark Sun had stayed in the village. She'd felt his eyes upon her constantly. Obviously, Cougar had told him to keep an eye on her. And so he had—such a

378

watchful eye that she'd begun to feel unnerved. Briefly the urge to escape became overwhelming. It made her angry being watched like that, and one day, impulsively, she set off at an agile pace out of the village. When, as she'd fully expected, Dark Sun appeared, spear in hand, to block her path, she went up to him and said point-blank in his own tongue: "You do not have to do this. You can just let me go. He is planning to go home now. I loved him, and now he is leaving. Isn't that what you and your uncle wanted?"

He stepped closer, warning her silently. His free hand reached out to clamp onto her forearm like a manacle.

"All right." In spite of herself, she was still a little afraid of him. "I will not try to run away—if you will just stop spying on me."

"I would have to bring you back, Flame. I have promised my brother—"

"Yes, I know."

"I have your word?"

"Yes," she answered sourly. When she made her escape, it would have to be from Cougar himself. She wouldn't leave anyone behind to take the blame for her.

She had calculated all the risks, and concluded that simply slipping away was going to be her greatest challenge. She wasn't too worried about starvation anymore. She could get her hands on roots along streams, new berries clinging to bushes, rose hips, and there would be the occasional small animal brought down with her bow. Slipping away from Cougar, however, and eluding his tracking skills— that was going to prove to be difficult. (She steadfastly refused to think about what he might do if he recaptured her.) Nevertheless, she was making her

379

plans, and the beginning of the new moon would see her on her way toward the Missouri River.

Of course she didn't confide any of this to Dark Sun, and after their "talk," he'd gone out hunting as usual, only stopping by her tepee at odd times to reassure himself of her continued presence.

She sighed. Nighthawks whimpered in the deep sky overhead. Still she lingered on before Rotten Gut's tepee, watching the lazy plume of smoke from Lone Goose's outdoor cooking fire. Rotten Gut was dozing at the edge of the fluttering light. Flame sighed again.

"You pine for The Waiting Cougar." It was Lone Goose who had spoken.

The truth rankled. "As you pine for Two-Edged Knife?"

The girl's back stiffened, then, glancing at her father to see that he was sleeping soundly, she seemed to forget the camas root she was peeling and said, "He crushed me utterly with his embraces until I fell in love with him."

Flame was struck dumb. She'd meant her comment to be a jibe. She'd seen Two-Edged Knife's treatment of Lone Goose first hand, seen her fright . . . but evidently the girl had gotten over that—or learned to thrill to it.

*As I did,* she spoke silently to herself.

"Was it so with you and the Waiting Cougar?" Lone Goose asked shyly.

"Yes, I suppose so." Was there any point in denying it?

Lone Goose nodded. "At first I was afraid." She smiled musingly. "He is so strong; I still fear him a little. Is it terrible to be taken . . . I mean . . . the first time, Flame?"

She swallowed. What to say to this enchanting

380

mixture of woman and child? "Not terrible," she began with an almost maternal tenderness. "I suppose every woman is afraid at first, but . . . if the man is gentle . . ." *If he is gentle, a feeling climbs in you the way a wind climbs—an early stirring of reeds, hardly noticed; then the air moves faster and harder, and there is no calm left; the blasts become hard; then you know this is something like a tornado.*

"Is it wonderful?"

Flame swallowed again, then whispered, "Always." She couldn't deny it. It was much too late for that. And what terrified her most was the realization that she would carry this torment with her for the rest of her days.

Lone Goose nodded as if she had suspected as much. But then she sighed. "My father needs me."

They both glanced at the helpless-looking, dozing old man. He did indeed look as if he needed someone to take care of him, and Lone Goose supervised his domestic routine with a deceptive absence of fuss.

"If Two-Edged Knife steals me—"

"Oh, he can't do *that,* can he?"

"He tried once already."

"Was that what that striped-spirit business was all about? He was trying to steal you? Really?" Flame was reconsidering Cougar's part in that affair. Until now she'd assumed it was only some harmless courtship rite, but to look at it in the light of an attempted abduction was something else entirely.

"If I hadn't cried out . . . but I was startled," Lone Goose said regretfully.

"But what if he *had* stolen you? Surely the men of the village would rescue you."

"They would look for me, yes. But if Two-Edged

Knife could keep me long enough to make me his wife—and he is very strong and very clever—I think they might not have found us, not before . . . I could not have withstood his strength for long. Of course I would try—a woman must try to protect herself or be shamed—but he would soon conquer me with his strength. He would have made me accept him."

Another huge sigh. "I think he has given up on me now. I think he has gone to look for a wife in another village. I feel much sadness." She spoke slowly, "Like you, Flame, I pine."

Flame looked up. She'd been half-aware of a growing ruckus, and now the sound of approaching hooves passed over the borders of her hearing, becoming louder, closer, until they hammered upon the village. Women had already left their cooking fires, men had set aside their wooden plates. The pounding hooves were reaching even into the tepees, bringing the old people out. It was a sound like distant breakers, rising sharply. The whole herd seemed headed right for the village. Their coats showed many different colors—honey skins, reddish-brown spots . . . Mothers ran to catch their children up into their arms as the hoofbeats crescendoed, thundering close between the tepees. Rotten Gut struggled to his feet, blinking his eyes hard and trying to pry with them into the twilight.

It soon became apparent that though the horses appeared to be stampeding, the danger was in truth minimal. Two-Edged Knife was driving the herd, and each horse was tied to the others on a long lead-rope. Thus he drove them right up to Rotten Gut's tepee, where he called out imperiously, "Will this be enough horses for your daughter?"

The men of the village were ringing around the

herd to keep them corralled. The women shouted and chattered like children at so much wealth being brought into the tribe. Old men waved their hands and talked fast, trying to be heard above the shouts of the younger people.

Two-Edged Knife's bow dangled in his hand. His exquisitely muscled body was gleaming with sweat. He seemed very sure of himself.

Rotten Gut gave a little surprised grunt. Flame thought she saw something bright and completely pleased in the old eyes. But they were carefully focused on one big red horse.

Two-Edged Knife dropped off his pony. He caught the rope around the red horse's throat; it snorted loudly, backed away, and tried to spin. He held on while the animal reared and pawed the air. The muscles of his bare back undulated as he brought the animal to heel.

The interest rose higher in Rotten Gut's face. He took a step forward. His hand went out to stroke the horse. The animal's whithers quivered; it inhaled with a long tremble.

Two-Edged Knife's face showed no expression; only his eyes seemed alive. The wrath that seemed always lurking under his brow came into play as he regarded the old shaman. "Two-Edged Knife wants Rotten Gut's daughter for his wife."

The old man's face went stubborn and blank again, as if he were putting all the horses aside and closing his ears to any further temptation. There was no sign of that pleased, dancing light in his eyes now.

Two-Edged Knife's gaze left that stony expression and searched and found Lone Goose. "Lone Goose, will you be my wife?" he asked in a surprisingly gentle lover's voice.

The girl went pale. She stared at him, then let her eyes slide away. "It is not for me to say."

Flame felt the bottom drop out of her stomach.

## Chapter Twenty-five

Rotten Gut shouted furiously, "Lone Goose will not marry anyone. Get away! Get away!" He placed himself between Two-Edged Knife and the girl.

"Rotten Gut," Flame said softly, knowing that she was treading on dangerously cracked ice, yet unable to stop herself, "he loves her."

The old man looked at her in contempt. "Love is a woman's word." Yet he turned to look briefly at his daughter. Though her face was impassive, tears stood in her eyes, glittering. "No," he said to her, almost regretfully, and turning back to Two-Edged Knife, he said it even louder: "No!"

"Then I will take her!" Two-Edged Knife ki-yied and tried to dodge around the old shaman.

"You leave her alone!" Rotten Gut yelled desperately, side-stepping to cut him off.

Lone Goose made no move; she only stood stoically behind her father. Flame was incensed. With a choked cry of disgust, she said, "Yes, you must take her, Two-Edged Knife! Take her!"

As if needing but that small spur to action, the warrior threw himself onto the red horse's back. He charged right at Rotten Gut, making the man stumble back. Leaning out and down, he circled the girl's waist with his muscle-corded arm and plucked her off the ground. She struck out at him. He seemed not to feel it. She struggled wildly, but he held her. With her kicking angrily under one arm, he *ki-yie*d again with victory. In another moment he was galloping out of the village with her thrown across his horse like a Sabine woman.

"Take your hands off her!" Rotten Gut called after him. Then to the other men, "Stop him!"

It seemed to Flame that the men were a trifle slow in following his command. She had an idea that they would not give their best effort to chasing down a man of Two-Edged Knife's fierce reputation. She had an idea, too, that Lone Goose would be a woman and a wife before the sun rose again.

Rotten Gut watched the half-hearted rescuers ride away, then he went wordlessly into his tepee. There was nothing left but for Flame to return to her own tepee. She had expected Cougar to show himself sometime during the emotional scene just enacted, but there was no sign of him. Perhaps she'd been entirely wrong about his collaboration with Two-Edged Knife.

Or perhaps he'd decided not to return to the village at all. Perhaps he'd taken to heart her final words to him and, rather than bother with her, he'd decided this was as good a time to be rid of her as any.

Perhaps love was only a woman's word.

Despite the stars overhead, the evening seemed very dark, and she knew it would be even darker inside her empty tepee. It was a ravaging thing to contemplate, that darkness and emptiness. She ducked inside, longing to release the tears that were making her heart ache.

Flame straightened to find the place lit by a small fire of aromatic fir. Cougar, who had just lit it, was squatting behind it, a grin spreading over his face. He looked slyly amused, watched her with a kind of mischievous expectancy. And he was so handsome that her knees turned to water. She found her gaze drawn inexorably to the taut strength of his shoulders. She thought, *How beautifully he's made!* The muscles of his torso rippled under his shirt; the planes of his face were accentuated by the flickering bloom of the fire. Why couldn't this be like a melodrama, where she could recognize the villain the minute he stepped on the stage. Why couldn't he be like that? Why did he have to look so agreeable and have those truly aristocratic manners?

His own unhurried consideration of her could almost be checked item by item: His gaze moved to her shoulders, to her head, to her flaxen hair, and back to her face, her cheek and jawbones, her rose-colored lips. Without a word he stood and came to take her into his arms. Her eyes remained blank and stubborn, holding him off; yet he kissed her deeply, a long kiss of passion and desire.

She had to dredge up the will to pull her mouth free. It was on the tip of her tongue to lash out at him, while at the same time she wanted to tell him all she'd felt during the past five days. In the end she did neither; pride erected its familiar barrier.

"How have you been feeling, lassie?" he asked gently, taking her face between his palms and kissing her brow.

"I've been fine."

"I expect you kept Dark Sun busy squelching your

387

plots for liberation."

She didn't answer. She wished desperately now that she *had* made some real attempt to escape, for the sake of her own self-respect.

"I'm that sorry I had to leave when I did, and without telling you why. The decision was no' come to impulsively."

"I know why you've been gone. Did you see how it turned out?"

"Aye. Rotten Gut's a stubborn old man, but he's no' as unhappy about it as he's trying to look. 'Tis an act to save face, that's all."

"Surely he can't be happy about having his daughter carried off like that, to be molested and violated."

His grin was lopsided. " 'Twas Rotten Gut who sent me to carry you off. 'She will fight you,' he said, 'but you must insist.' "

"If you're trying to excuse yourself by laying the blame on a half-crazy old man who has too many vivid dreams—"

"Did I say I was trying to excuse myself? I did just as I wanted to do. Once I saw you I did no' need any man's prompting. Nor do I need it now. 'Tis the moment, I think, for you to welcome your husband home rightly. Brace yourself, lassie." He made as if to kiss her again.

"No—don't!" She tried to escape his arms. "I warned you . . . don't touch me!" He pulled her closer though she pumelled his wide chest.

His kiss was devastating. She leaned weakly against him when he was done. But then her outrage was refueled. She felt fury, clean, white, and hot. She straightened her spine. "I demand that you let me go."

A gleam had come into his eyes that made her

heart jump. "You do no' really want that." He moved against her so that she couldn't help but be aware that his desire was at full stretch.

Now real fear shuddered through her; her eyes went wide and fixed on his face. She remembered the night he'd nearly forced her, her helplessness, his strength, and she felt sick to her stomach. If she pitted herself against him, was that how it would be? An act of violence that would leave her feeling used and soiled? Her fury was gone as quickly as it had come, replaced by something more primitive.

"What's this now?" he said, peering down at her.

He set her from him, keeping his hands on her arms, however, as if he felt she needed steadying. "You think I mean to harm you?" When she didn't answer, he spun away as if he'd been punched. "Aye, you do! Well you can stop looking so frightened — I'll no' be touching you then. You have my word on it. Why would I want a woman who loathes me? That was the word, was it no'? *Loathe?*"

The silence was heavy between them. Now that his back was turned she saw how worn he looked. His breeches were dusty and there were several rents in his shirt; but more telling was the slump of his brawny shoulders and the way his hands hung so loose and empty. "Are you tired?" she asked in a conciliatory voice. "Hungry? You're well, aren't you?"

"Do no' tell me you're anxious for my health?" Looking back over his shoulder, he quirked an eyebrow at her.

Now he was being callous, and she'd hoped . . . hoped what? "Oh, Cougar, I . . . I don't know!" She put her face in her hands. A shiver ran through her as in one stride he came back to her. His outstretched hands touched her shoulders, then dropped away again. Yet feeling him near, she realized exactly what she'd hoped—to be taken into his arms, to be held gently, to be needed by him, *loved* by him.

He inched closer and stopped, waiting, as if for her to get used to him, as a hunter waits to calm his quarry. He must have felt the little flutter of uneasiness that rippled through her. She was still afraid of him, yet expectant at the same time. Oh! what kind of curious emotional bondage was this?

"Flame." He was close enough now that his lips stirred in her hair when he spoke. "Do you really want to be free of me?"

At some level she was aware of the hazard lurking in that question, and so answered it with one of her own: "Will you let me go?"

"Aye," he breathed.

"Oh." Her heart stopped and began once more with a slow hard beat; she felt unexpectedly hollow and wanted to sit down.

"I'll no' make you stay with me anymore, no' if you truly want to go. How could I demand it when I love you so."

"*Love* me!" Her head jerked up. "You don't love me! You like to *make* love *to* me, but that's hardly the same thing."

"I can no' blame you for doubting it. But 'twas like lightning. The first time . . . seeing you, and feeling that absolute certainty that of all women in the world, this was the one, the only one for me. And since then, night and day, morning and evening . . .

"I ken that my behavior has been unmanly, undignified, especially the one time when . . . when I lost my temper. I was so afraid . . . Still and all, there's no excuse for what I did. I've been battling for my life, though, for should you reject me . . . I'll most surely die."

It was a moment before she came fully alive to what he'd said. In fact, he was already turning away before she responded. "Wait—Cougar, are you saying that you really do love me?"

"What else have I been saying to you these many months?"

Her heart leapt up for an instant, until her reason once again threw water on her hopes. "But even so, it doesn't really change anything, does it? You're the Drummond. You must go back to your clan. They've been waiting for you; they need you."

"But go back *without you!*" he said savagely.

She flinched as if struck; nothing hurt so much as those few words finally spoken aloud. She could barely whisper, "I suppose so."

He turned on her. "Why . . . *why*, lassie? You love me, I'm no' so dense I can no' ken that! Why can you no' be the Drummond's wife? Am I that brutal that you can no' pledge to live with me of your own free will?" His fingers bit into her waist, forcing an exclamation from her, yet he didn't let go. "You'll answer me, woman!"

Perceiving in the sternness of his eyes that the question was not to be evaded, she said, "You never asked me to be the Drummond's wife! The Cougar's wife, yes—a woman he bartered for and bought like a slave—a woman with a name like Flame would do for him. But plain Victorine Wellesley? She evidently wasn't good enough for the powerful, the lordly, the royal Drummond!"

At first he stepped back from this slight but ferocious outburst; then he took her into his arms and crushed her so close that she knew he felt her heart thumping. "You thought I would no' want my mountain wife by me in Scotland? My God! But what then did you think I was meaning when I said I would take you home—"

"You never said as your wife! Pregnant, yes, but . . . you said you would see me 'settled' before the babe arrived. Then—with an illegitimate child, stranded in a foreign country—I suppose you thought I would be so dependent on you that I would have to stay . . . as your—your woman," she finished self-consciously.

"My *woman?* You mean . . . my mistress? Lassie!" He laughed outright, as if the thought were preposterous. "I thought you would no' go home with me unless I did something drastic! I tried to tempt you with descriptions of Castle Drummond, but you were unimpressed. All you ever talked was spring and back to Philadelphia. From the night I discovered you in Savage Goat's camp you've cried incessantly for your freedom and your Philadelphia!"

She stared at him, disbelieving. Gripped by sudden shyness, she put her hands around his neck and hid her face in his shoulder. Then, sure she must have misunderstood something, some key point that would once more dash her foolish hopes with cold water, she looked up into his fierce eyes. They were drilling into hers. In cowardice she quickly pressed her face against his shoulder once more. He couldn't possibly mean . . . She said quietly into the hush that had fallen, "I've no one in Philadelphia anymore. No one anywhere, I guess, but you."

She heard him inhale sharply. "And all that's set us at odds was the question then?" He added suddenly, clearly, and with decision, "Well, I'll be asking it now, and no' a minute too soon 'twould seem: Will you be my wife, lassie—my mountain wife, my Scottish wife, my true wife? 'Tis a home in a castle

392

and a clan to belong to that I'm laying at your feet. I can offer you this and my love. Is it enough?"

A home, a people to call hers, his love . . . so much, a trio of arches through which gleamed an untraveled world whose margins seemed to fall back forever and forevermore even as she gazed in their direction. Her heart told her the answer to his question, quietly and absolutely. She murmured, "I want to be your wife more than anything else in the world."

He still looked a bit stunned, then slowly his mouth broke into a great happy grin. "Aye and you do. You did no' think I'd ask the question if I thought you might say nae to me, did you, heart? I'd have carried you to Scotland in chains if 'twere necessary. Aye, you're that lucky you gave me the answer I wanted."

She felt something then, the full force of the realization that her dreams were coming true; it was like music changing key. "Cougar!" She said his name as though it were an exclamation of joy. She moved forward quickly, fiercely within the band of his arms. Her breasts flattened themselves against his chest and her hands went up to clench the thick hair at the back of his head. She pulled his mouth down and her own opened across his lips. Her back arched and her pelvis thrust against his legs. He keened softly as she kissed him.

Flame sat in the dappled sun before her tepee absorbing health as per Cougar's instructions. Personally, she felt she was fully recovered already; she'd gotten her strength again, walked swiftly, held herself well. There was color in her thin cheeks, and her blue eyes shone with merriment — and with some

393

profounder fire—but Cougar seemed to take such pleasure in pampering her . . . and secretly she took pleasure in letting him, especially when he bossed her with that beguiled affection he was so good at evincing.

He'd left only a few minutes ago to accompany some of the village men on their day's hunt. He'd given her ear a playful pinch. "Do no' be dallying with anybody else while I'm gone." Jauntily he strode away, putting his cougar-skin hat on with a final flourish. He turned back only once, at the verge of the woods, to wink at her with an impertinent schoolboy mischievousness. Then he'd disappeared into the leaf shadows and sundrops and the yellow flowers that were standing up in the returning sun.

She was happy—joyful. She smiled it at every woman who passed by. Cougar loved her. He wanted her to be his true wife. She had everything she needed at last.

Rotten Gut tottered up slowly, an old man with white hair flowing down over his shoulders, breath wheezing with every step. Flame looked up expectantly. She was afraid he might still be angry with her for encouraging Two-Edged Knife to take Lone Goose. (The couple had been gone for two nights now.) He sank down beside her. His wide plain face wasn't smiling. She put her head down and let her hair shield her face rather than look at him again.

Yet he didn't scold. In silence they sat on. Gradually, she relaxed again. The sky floated a few clouds. In the picketed corral the new herd of horses walked warm and spellbound. The earth was flowering in her melted snow. Flame even noted the smell of the wind; it was faintly fragrant with damp leaf-mold.

Eventually, when Rotten Gut did speak, there was

394

a peculiar little grimace on his seamed mouth. He began as if in mid-conversation: "The Waiting Cougar was reared in white-men's ways across the big water. He was taught all the white men's learning; but when he came here he was a bad runner, ignorant of every means of living in the woods, unable to put up with either cold or hunger. He couldn't build a lodge, kill a deer, or kill an enemy. He spoke our language badly; he wasn't fit to be a hunter, let alone a warrior. Good for nothing! The Salish took care of his education; we instructed him in everything we knew. But the Waiting Cougar had high ambitions—so courageous, so daring. Immodest, yes, but he was tough as well, and a man of perception who dreamed big dreams. It was for him to travel in deep solitude and to find bigger trials. He had learned the first lesson he had come here to master—that it was all right to trust his own courage. But he hadn't learned everything yet."

He paused to look at her, his grave eyes as brown as walnuts in rainwater. "It took Flame to teach him the rest. She made him a man."

She was startled, in a pleasant way. "I didn't, really. I don't think I've changed him at all."

"A woman can make a man. Look at Two-Edged Knife. Horses are good for the people, but they weren't what I wanted. I wanted a son-in-law who was a real man—good for something! I knew that the man who could take Lone Goose from me was the one who would deserve her."

Flame found herself wondering what Two-Edged Knife and Lone Goose were up to right now. "She's so young and tender. I hope Two-Edged Knife is being gentle with her," she murmured aloud—and then felt herself blushing at the indecency of her thoughts. She said quickly, "Cougar told me you

395

weren't really unhappy about the way things turned out."

He threw her a roguish sideways glance. "The Cougar knows." His smile was swift and disarming. "You know, too. I heard you tell Two-Edged Knife to take my daughter. 'Take her!' you said."

He rose then, lingering to touch her head almost lovingly.

That very day he was taken ill. It wasn't a sickness exactly. It was more a dwindling away. He lay by his fire listening to Dark Sun telling the old stories. Then late one night he suffered an attack. It left him helpless, able to speak only with difficulty. Flame tended him as she felt Lone Goose would have, Dark Sun and Cougar helping when a man's arm was demanded.

Oddly, Rotten Gut's brown eyes were as radiant as ever. Sitting by his pallet, Flame waited out seven long days with him. When the old man roused, she understood by the touch of his hand what he wanted, and he smiled at her wearily when she responded. Occasionally she sang to him, as softly as the least suggestion of air. Old Christian hymns she'd learned as a child. He seemed to like them.

The following day, in the middle of the afternoon, the watchers around his bedside noticed a turn. He was restless, tense as an arrow in a drawn bow. His lips moved. Dark Sun, leaning over, caught the words his uncle was trying to articulate. The two pairs of sable eyes, so alike, looked at each other, asking for and receiving comfort. There was a great and simple affection in the old man's face.

Dark Sun repeated the old shaman's words aloud, looking at Flame. "He says he will leave his body now, but that he will watch over those who follow, and will always help those who will not turn back."

Flame didn't hesitate, but went to get Cougar.

When Rotten Gut's eyes saw the two lovers at his side, his lips worked in satisfaction. Outside the doorflap an ashleaf maple stirred its greening boughs in the breeze. A hornet, awakened by the day's warmth, was beating itself against the sides of the tepee, trying to get in. Through the smoke-hole the sunlight made a pattern on the rugs. The old man turned his face toward the broken patch of light and went to his stony sleep.

For once Cougar looked more the Scottish nobleman than a mountain man. Flame saw him standing before the makeshift alter under a canvas awning stretched between two trees bursting with verdancy, and the timber-and-stake palisades of Fort Hall. He was wearing a dress kilt, which had been discovered among Rotten Gut's things, saved by the old shaman for him all these years. His tailored ruby jacket still fit him well enough, though now it was a bit tight across the shoulders and in the arms. Nevertheless, its gold buttons had been polished until their hallmarks glowed, bright and untarnished, even in the late afternoon sun, even in the shade of this temporary church.

The youthful clergyman, Mr. Boyte, was a lay missionary visiting at the fort before resuming his Christian-soldier's march northwest to the lands of the "Flathead" Indians. There he evidently intended to preach and sing, teach the "heathens" certain items of gospel, and prescribe for their ailments. His inexpensive frock coat and the double waistcoats he wore beneath it had brought a shine of sweat to his forehead. His hair, slicked back and polished to a killing sheen with pomade, looked as if it had been

397

cut by a tomahawk with a horribly blunted edge.

Cougar had brought Flame south, not with any thought of finding a missionary who would wed them, but because along the upper Missouri River the Blackfeet were everywhere, threatening, swaggering, stealing, killing. Finding Mr. Boyte here simply had been mere good luck.

The man was likable. He seemed to have little of that sanctimoniousness which had afflicted Tobias. If he was as self-deceived about his calling, he seemed also hearty, courageous, and ready. Flame thought he might just get along in the untamed land he was headed for—even if he soon discovered that it was much easier to convert a few defeated Indians at a missionary meeting in Illinois than full tribes here in their wilderness homes.

As Flame crossed the open yard of the fort on Captain Thing's arm, both Cougar and Mr. Boyte seemed a bit rigid in their stance, both staring fixedly at the blowing altar candles. Seeing Flame coming, an Indian child twitched in excited anticipation. The little boy was one of several parented by the fort's interpreter, a half-breed Nez Percé. His Indian wife shushed her offspring and bounced them on her knee, while her husband sat straight as hickory rod. His mouth, wide and horizontal as a frog's, remained firmly shut. Flame wondered if weddings were so intimidating to all men.

She looked at the only other person in the hastily gathered congregation, a French engagé for the Hudson's Bay Company, a man named Eston, and found him smiling pleasantly. Well, then, it wasn't a distinguishing trait: a man could be relaxed at a wedding.

Captain Thing was escorting her under the awning now, and at one side of it, young Mrs. Boyte suddenly began pumping up her tiny organ (which she had stubbornly brought across half the continent for just such occasions). She launched into a wheezy version of Mendelssohn's "Wedding March."

Flame felt immense relief when she saw Cougar smile broadly and say to the missionary, "She comes, an no' a minute too soon, I'm thinking." He turned with parade ground exactness just as Captain Thing brought her up the center of the aisle on his arm. She saw Cougar present his own arm, and she took it, her eyes caught by the smile on his face.

She was glad she had a white gown to wear for her wedding, even if it was borrowed. Cougar had promised her that long before they arrived at Castle Drummond she would have gowns of her own aplenty, "a trousseau such as no bride has ever worn 'afore," yet for now she was grateful to Mrs. Boyte for bringing her own wedding dress from its dusty trail-worn trunk. The two of them had sat with their heads bent together half the day, taking in the waist and letting down the hem so it would fit. Since the Boytes were newlyweds themselves, the lace was only a few months old and still the color of new snow.

Cougar's eyes swept over the dress, then went to her face, her eyes, her smile, her shining flaxen hair that hung to her fingertips and was woven with wildflowers. His expression spoke for him: "Aye, you're that bonny."

And then Mr. Boyte began the ceremony. Soon Cougar was saying, "I, Colin, do take thee, Victorine, to be my wife . . ."

And she responded, "I, Victorine, do take thee, Colin, to be my husband . . ."

It was such a simple thing. Simple and artless and honest. Yet, the words now spoken between them somehow seemed to make all the difference. She supposed that they were no more ritualistic than a Salish chief's exhalation of smoke blown skyward and to the four directions, but they were the words she had needed to hear.

# Chapter Twenty-six

Later, they all filed back across the fort's inner yard. Flame was so unused to regular shoes and dresses that she tottered in her borrowed high heels and tripped on her flounces and had to cling to the arm of her newly confirmed husband. A few Nez Percé showered them with handfuls of wheat, provided beforehand by Captain Thing.

Indeed, the good captain had seen to everything. He'd treated them with the utmost courtesy, in the British tradition, though he must have felt like gaping when they'd arrived at his barred gates yesterday: a mysterious mountain man with a Scottish brogue, accompanied by an unspeakably lovely white woman who seemed to be living as his squaw. The captain had naturally asked some discreet questions, but the pair were hesitant to speak of the intimate ecstasies and sorrows they had experienced. The seasons of their love were as yet so new that they hesitated to disturb the aura of them with a recounting to strangers. As soon as Cougar had discovered the presence of the clergyman, however, he asked for a wedding, and the Captain, though surprised, had complied with all the generosity at his disposal.

The sun had gone down by now, and the spring dusk was soft, the kind one feels might go on for years. The wedding party entered the captain's private quarters where a tea table stood on cabriole legs, sporting a plentiful assortment of food—a plate of cakes, the inevitable steaming pot of Indian tea, even a little jug of fresh milk, but more important, a bottle of the finest French champagne from the captain's private store.

Inside the long cool room Cougar held Flame in one arm and his glass in his free hand as he made his toast: "My wife." The company drank with him, then clapped with pleasure, while Flame looked up at him, her face transparent with happiness.

"Best to no' look at me like that, my heart," he whispered in her ear. "A man can stand only so much temptation, and there are others present. Save your dimples for an hour, though, and 'twill please me greatly to kiss them—and a great many other parts of you."

Her eyes flared wide as she looked about to see if anyone could have possibly heard him. She felt herself blushing, and was quick to take Captain Thing's offer of a seat at the tea table. Mrs. Boyte had taken a seat also, and her husband stood looking down at her. His face was glazed with the unaccustomed effects of the wine. "Will you sing for us, my sweet?"

She beamed and nodded, and lifted her chin to sing, in a surprisingly gentle voice, a song about following love wherever it might lead, even to the highest mountain peak or across the deepest ocean.

Cougar stood with his hand on Flame's shoulder, and she turned her face up to his again. She was still smiling—she couldn't help it, whether it tempted him or not—because she was so happy. His gray-green eyes squinted down at her and he touched her parted lips with the tip of his finger.

The song continued — about frigid arctic nights and fierce noons and lovers cleaving until death. Flame rested her cheek on Cougar's forearm. She was happy, she really was. And so she wondered why a tear escaped her eye and descended down the curve of her cheek.

It had already reached the corner of her mouth when the song ended. All were silent for a moment, and then Captain Thing struck the table with the flat of his hand. "I say! Bravo, Mrs. Boyte! That was superb!" Then they were all applauding, even Flame, and as she sat up the tear broke and fell onto her breast, to leave a mark upon the satin of her bodice. Cougar leaned to murmur, "As soon as we're alone, love, I mean to follow the path of that tear with my lips."

Yet it seemed hours before they could politely take their leave. Flame's heart leapt when at last she heard him say, "Now you must excuse us. We will resume our journey early on the morrow and will be needing our rest this night."

Rest? This night? It was a boldfaced lie, and Flame knew that every one present was aware of it, yet she didn't care. She was too eager to be alone at last with her husband, to fill the night's pockets of wakefulness with love.

" 'Tis the beginning."

Cougar stood with Flame on the level plain. Her heart felt softer, more fragile than a meadowlark's egg. She knew what he meant by what he'd just said; she too was clutched by a happy tension and anticipation, as though here was the beginning of their

403

real love affair.

The last of the mountains were behind them, reaching high and jagged in the clouds but had the blue of distance settled over them. Ahead lay a perfect morning sky. From far off came the bellowing of a herd of buffalo; otherwise silence hung over the country.

She wondered if Rotten Gut could see them standing here, if he observed them from his spirit land with a smile on his mouth and the wrinkles drawn up around his eyes. Rotten Gut, Dark Sun, Lone Goose, Two-Edged Knife . . . faces to be held forever in the chambers of her memory like portraits enclosed in fastened lockets.

"Now we enter the world of words and wheelbarrows," Cougar said.

"I wasn't aware that we hadn't been in the world of words all along," she said impudently. "At least you've never been at a loss for them."

"Be careful, my heart," he said with an occupied air, still looking out over the high plains, "at Castle Drummond there is a room full of relics from my violent ancestral past: pikes, and halbers, gauntlets and dirks, sabers and jeweled stilettos. They were the awkward playthings of my youth; as a man grown I should be able to wield them well."

"Against me?" she protested with mock innocence.

"Against my garden nymph who would like to look down on me from her fountain pedestal." His eyes softened as he turned to her. He let his arms drop onto her shoulders. "On second thought, mayhap I know of a better weapon to tame such as you. And with only one deep thrust I am the certain victor."

She was painfully aware of the color overspreading her face. "Words, words, and more words," she said lightly.

"You know that I have more than words — should it become necessary to employ sterner methods to bring you to heel."

"At Castle Drummond, you mean?" The rose in her young face grew deeper.

She saw the twitch of his mouth, and then the indulgent grin at her attempt to bend the train of his thoughts. "Aye, at Castle Drummond, where there is also a room upholstered in velvets and brocades, and a bed large enough for a mountain man to live in all winter. Mayhap that will be the place to gentle you. I shall lay you down in the milky pools of silk and shut you up in measureless delight . . ." He drew her to him. "Aye," his voice had gained a gruffness, "but for now, prairie grass will have to do — though even here I have so many devastating ways at my disposal to teach you a more comely grace 'tis hard to choose which to use. Lay you down, good wife."

"Is that an order? Just who do you think you are?" she asked playfully.

"Laird of the Drummonds," he answered smoothly, his lips grazing her jaw bone.

"Does the rule of the Drummond extend this far from his home?"

"We'll no' debate that just now. Lay you down . . ." He put up a hand and swept the blown hair out of her face, as if she were a girl. "Flame, do mind what I tell you. I do no' deal out orders often — "

"You most definitely do!"

"Only when I have to, as you should know by now. I'm always ready to enforce them." He swung a leg behind her and pushed her backwards at the same time, causing her to lose her balance. She reached for him involuntarily, and found him pre-

405

pared. Her fall was controlled by his steely arms.

She found herself lying half beneath him in a shallow depression protected from the wind. The grass grew high all around, rippling in the breeze like wheat. His mouth claimed hers.

All was so quiet that when a lark shattered into song overhead, they both started, but by the time they looked, it had gone.

She said, squirming suddenly, "Let me up, Cougar." She even managed to half rise and was lowered none too tenderly this time.

"You do no' escape that lightly. Come, you balk like a maiden—and for God's sake, put away that ladylike smile."

"But it's so open here; you can't . . ."

"Can I no'?" His voice was cheerful with the prospect of impending battle. "Do you wish to play it out yet again? You know full well that the advantage still lies with me as the stronger of us."

"You *take* advantage, you mean." Her hands caught his at the lacing of her dress.

"Aye and I do, and will have you as I desire you 'afore long. Complain as much as you like, aye, rattle your chains, little captive; you'll no' break loose. All this reserve and reticence are only cobwebs in my path."

"You're mad."

"Aye, I think sometimes I *am* gently mad." He kissed her again, then tried a more coaxing voice. "Please, my only light, feel the soft heat of desire and stop pandering to the uncomfortable ruling of your common sense."

One kiss more and Flame's heart was pounding in the prairie spring, demanding to breathe, to taste, to share in love. The horses Dark Sun had given Cougar for their journey moved off, cropping the green

406

turf. Gophers piped at the threat of their hooves and plunged underground, tails whisking. A badger lumbered off to halt on a mound of dirt, watching the two humans with a slow blaze of self-righteousness in its eyes.

Cougar had finished unlacing her dress, and was brushing aside her shining amulet of claws. And then his fingertips encountered warm skin. Her eyes gazed up at him with a distant expression. "Will you really try to tame me in Scotland? Will I have to change, become a countess, and lose all my American manners? Will I acquire a Scottish burr?"

"I hope no', heart. 'Tis such a quaint pleasure to hear you misspeak the King's language. And as for teaching you better manners—'tis no' possible, I've decided."

She blinked as his hand cupped one soft breast beneath the gray doeskin of her dress. "This is dreadful."

"Aye, I know, a dreadful affair is passion . . . sweet, wild, poignant passion." He was rolling her nipples under the supple doeskin. Her body grew warmer.

"You're incorrigible; I laugh to think of you being a lawgiver to your people—their high and mighty laird."

Would he never love her but by an unfamiliar set of rules? Would she always be taken so off-guard?

She made no further attempts to dislodge his caressing hands and his fingers continued to play gently, awakening her. He kissed her face and hair as he stroked her breasts.

Yes, it would always be like this, she decided, she would always be surprised at how easily he could rouse every voluptuous emotion within her.

Kissing her tenderly, he lifted her dress to her

waist, and his hand now probed delicately. Oh, the exquisite touch of his fingertips! He caressed her until her thighs moved apart. She could no more stop herself than she could stop the blood gushing in her veins. She needed him. She accepted everything he said and did. In his arms she felt so released, so lovely. When he smiled, when he looked at her as he was now, she felt safe, willing to try anything, willing to savor her own excitement and sensuality.

"Open yourself for me, wider, Flame, I want to see everything. There, do no' move," he said, surveying her unprotected and extended body, "no' a muscle. Stay exactly like that." His head lowered.

Time stopped for her as she lay in a golden confusion, as if in a warm bath, images unfolding across her mind under the stimulus of first his words and then his mouth.

Slowly, very slowly, she rose to the heights, her little cries growing louder and fiercer. He used his tongue to push her over the border of delight. When her throes commenced, her hands drummed against his shoulders. Still he didn't stop, but held her tightly against his moving lips, until she was in sweet torment. "Please—I can't endure anymore."

He raised up and opened his breeches quickly. His thumbs parted the folds of her to steer his erect part into her. She felt his column of hard flesh filling her. Her eyes were on his face. His arms slipped under her body to grasp the globes of her hips.

He pulled her against him, implanting himself deeper. Her joy climbed on eagle's wings. Her arms circled his shoulders and one leg twined around his thighs. His firm strokes, as stylized as a minuet, impelled her until she again gasped.

He went on, not to be satisfied so quickly or so simply it seemed, his movements becoming more impetuous, until at last he exclaimed as his released zeal surged extravagantly through him into her. He groaned her name in the grip of rapture. Her own body convulsed yet again, joining him in his silver flood of racking pleasure.

It left them washed in love and laughter and stillness and warmth. After she unwound herself from him, he fell onto his back to lay loose limbed, his legs stretched inelegantly. He drew her head to his chest. It was the moment of total male ease that she'd learned to adore.

She propped her chin on the hard bone of his shoulder. "Cougar, please don't call me 'Flame' when we get to Scotland, at least not in public."

He laughed. His gaze moved over her hair lying like a flaxen mantle around her shoulders. "All right . . . Victorine." He made a face. "Satisfied? It does no' fit you half so well, but I'll exert myself to remember. And you shall call me . . ."

"Colin." She nuzzled her cheek against his arm.

"Nae; I think a pretty 'my laird' will do better."

"Oh! I will not!" Her head spun up.

"Are you that sure? When you enter my castle you'll be mine more completely than ever. You'll be mine past reprieve. And mayhap you'll find 'tis best to call me whatever I desire."

She felt a twinge of discomfort. Scotland was such a foreign place, so far from everything she knew, as strange to her as the mountains once were — and he had dominated her there, thoroughly.

His lips were spreading slowly in a grin. He laughed, and she realized he'd only been teasing . . . a little.

"You!" She cuffed at his chest. Then she gave him a smile that dimpled her smooth cheeks. The smile, the dimples, were all he needed it seemed.

"There are things I want to teach you . . ." he began.

"Yes, teach me everything." She moved closer, as if his words drew her. "Show me, please," she whispered, turning her head up to his mouth. But then she drew back again, and gave him a quick, unsure smile. She knew her cheeks were ruby red.

He gave a soft laugh, reaching for her.

She would always remember that day, a pungently sweet one in the middle of April. They had half of a continent and an ocean to cross, and time was waiting for them, but they dallied.

For 'twas only the beginning.

# Epilogue

By the end of June, 1837, reports of a strange phenomenon were drifting down out of the Rocky Mountains into the various western forts that frowned over the plains below. For anyone looking for beginnings—those embryonic moments when something formerly undivined comes into being—it was an example of such to fascinate.

The tales were about a woman. Now, there were thousands of women in the mountains—Arikara, Nes Percé, Shoshone—dusky, mysterious girls, some of them beauties of high rank (and most with extravagant and quicksilver hearts), but what gave the story of this particular woman spice was the hint that she was white. A white woman from east of the Mississippi, virgin and apple sweet.

In truth, no living white man could claim to know first hand of such a woman, and the men of the forts, surly and indifferent to all but profit or soldiery, sensibly doubted her very existence. After all, this was the nineteenth century. Few could be bothered, even in their minds, with drawing dotted lines between the stars. People were concerned with practicalities, with slavery and the abolition of slavery, with wild speculations in land, canals, roads, banks, buildings, cotton planting, with machine-made shoes and horse-drawn grain reapers and trade unions—even with women's rights to an education.

The men of the mountains, however, having lived with the Indians and having grown more used to dealing with edgeless dreams, were wise enough to know that the hush of portent should be welcomed with humble faith. They cared not that question on question arose. And in the supple flux of these open minds a song of legend was born: a white spirit-woman in the mountains, claimed by a renegade with glass-cold lips, a creature called the Waiting Cougar. This feral being, half-cat, half-man, pro-tected his right to the woman's favors with a ferocity fetched up from the vagaries of nightmares. It was said he would kill without second thought—with inattentive violence—to keep her fast.

And keep her he did, in a lost alpine valley through the winters, wrapped close to him in silver wolfskins. In summer he let her swim in the slow carp pools and spilling trout riffles and lakes of the western slopes of the Bitterroot Mountains. One of these was said to be named for her: Lake Flame. For Flame was what he called her, because she had skin as pale as beeswax, hair as flickering as strands of silk, and eyes as brave as lone candles burning against the dark of night.

The campfire stories featured her to be very much alive. And alive meant attainable. Many a forlorn mountain man, as he made the rounds of his traps, half searched and half yearned through the thrash-ing snowflakes for that pale-haired nymph of the high places, that ephemeral dream held imprisoned in reluctant thralldom to her secretive lover.

As the years passed and she was not discovered

opinion among the mountain men began to vary. Yet, even the few who had lost faith could be made to concede that for a brief season she may have actually drawn breath in that wilderness. They wanted to believe she was there yet, but they reminded their fellows that nowhere had any of them found a trace of her, let alone the demigod who was supposed to possess her.

Eventually, whether or not she ever existed in fact became unimportant, for men with yearnings care not whether there are historical records on file to verify the objects of their desires and dreams. It seemed there was a special space chiseled out of that province of allegory into which this cadenza just fit, as if foreordained and perfect.

And there are those who still claim that in the hour before dawn, when the air in the mountains is like wine, you can hear voices echoing off the highest peaks: a deep voice calling, "Come, the sky looms wide and 'tis a distant cry to the world's edge. Come, I know a trail, a fine trail, a braw trail, though 'tis endless. It leads to the moon. Will you follow it with me, heart?"

The answer, heard always on the first shafts of the sunrise, comes as a sigh of light: "I will, my love, yes; I shall be at your side wherever it leads, always and always."

# <u>FREE</u> Preview Each Month and $ave

Zebra has made arrangements for you to preview 4 brand new HEARTFIRE novels each month...FREE for 10 days. You'll get them as soon as they are published. If you are not delighted with any of them, just return them with no questions asked. But if you decide these are everything we said they are, you'll pay just $3.25 each— a total of $13.00 (a $15.00 value). **That's a $2.00 saving each month off the regular price.** Plus there is NO shipping or handling charge. These are delivered right to your door absolutely free! There is no obligation and there is no minimum number of books to buy.

---

## *TO GET YOUR FIRST MONTH'S PREVIEW... Mail the Coupon Below!*